The Devil's Judgment

The Vengeful Prince Saga ~ Book 3

CHRIS PISANO and BRIAN KOSCIENSKI

HELLBENDER BOOKS

an imprint of Sunbury Press, Inc.
Mechanicsburg, PA USA

HELLBENDER BOOKS

an imprint of Sunbury Press, Inc.
Mechanicsburg, PA USA

ISBN: 978-1-62006-219-7 (Trade paperback)

Library of Congress Control Number: 2019940316

FIRST HELLBENDER BOOKS EDITION: May 2019

Product of the United States of America
0 1 1 2 3 5 8 13 21 34 55

Set in Bookman Old Style
Designed by Crystal Devine
Cover by Lawrence Knorr
Cover art by Koa Beam
Edited by Lawrence Knorr

Continue the Enlightenment!

PROLOGUE

FAT DROPLETS OF blood flowed down her forearm in three streams. The cut on her wrist from the shackles was not too bad. It was the imperfection of the wood digging into her back that agonized her the most. Attempting to shift, to change her body placement, to move off the burl in the wood failed. Discomfort was the purpose. She was chained to a rack after all.

Arms spread wide, legs spread even wider, Dearborn Stillheart was naked except for the cold metal around her wrists and ankles. She still had free range of motion for her head though, which she took advantage of. "You don't have to do this."

The guard, a squat knuckle of a man named Methel, was still panting, trying to catch his breath from the ordeal of dragging Dearborn from her cage to this room of cold, cut stone. The other four guards were breathing heavily, one shuffled about with a limp from where her foot bent his knee in the wrong direction, and another paced along the far wall massaging his arm because of the twist she had given it when he first grabbed her in her cell.

When the six guards had come to take her from her cell, they made assumptions. They thought that living on bread and water in the dungeon for a year would have weakened her. At first, it did, but she found a mischief of rats. Her bread went to them, and when they became large enough, they went into her belly. Through careful planning, she managed to help the colony grow, their population burgeoning to the point of feeding herself three times a day as well as setting up trade with the other prisoners close enough to pass their bread to her through the bars. The guards expected a weak sack of meat, not an Elite Troop soldier still capable of putting up a fight. They had discovered their mistake after she killed one of the guards by jamming her fingers into his eye sockets and wriggling them around.

"Shut up," Methel growled, bending over to pick up the rags that were once her clothes. He had made a joke earlier about wanting to get Dearborn naked, even if she were taller and more muscular than most men. A knee to his groin ensured that he regretted it.

"You're going to end up like your friend, the one I killed."

Methel wheeled around, pointing his index finger so close to her face that she could smell the dirt on his glove. "He was no friend of mine, just a shitbag who forgot who you are. I didn't, and now you're chained up. You ain't killin' me. You ain't gonna kill no one."

"If I don't kill you, the king's brother will."

She hit upon a concern, could see it in Methel's eyes. He tried to hide it, but they widened just enough as his stubbled face lost a bit of the anger. He leaned in to whisper into her ear, "King's brother will kill you first, I believe."

Dearborn wondered if he might be right. Shadows played across the hallway walls just outside the door. The king's brother was coming; Prince Daedalus was coming for her.

The five guards dropped to their knees when Daedalus entered the room, even the one with the bad leg, tears streaming down his face as he bit his bottom lip. Daedalus did not acknowledge their action, showed no sign of recognizing that there was anyone else in the room other than Dearborn. When he entered, she forgot there were other people in the room as well.

Daedalus strode in with arms extended as if receiving exultation from a coliseum full of spectators. He wore an outfit befitting such an entrance—snakes. Dozens of snakes of all sizes and colors slithered over his naked body. Pythons wound themselves around his legs, over his waist. Smaller garden snakes draped over his shoulders and languidly traveled along his arms. A few wriggled between the forearm bones of his skeletal arm. There was only one snake that concerned Dearborn—the erect, single-eyed snake with its burgundy head.

Smiling with the glee of a child with wealthy parents on his birthday, Daedalus brought his hands together; flesh fingers intertwined with bone fingers to create an unintentional allegory about the union of life and death. Taut but thin muscle moved beneath the serpents, as well as a belly starting to go soft from too many of life's tastier indulgences. Loose curls of black hair fell about his face and neck, slicked into haphazard locks from sweat. "Oh, Dearborn, look how we find ourselves. I'm so happy to see that you dressed for the occasion."

As he laughed at his own joke, Dearborn felt her nakedness, her weakness. No, not weakness. Just the perception of such a notion. Just because she wore no armor did not mean she was unable to protect herself. A quick mind and well-timed words could protect just as effectively as flawless plate-mail and sharpened sword.

Daedalus continued toward her, his erection guiding him, his smugness a thicker cloak than the snakes. "This is a momentous occasion, Dearborn, one that will crown so many of my accomplishments. Now, I will mark this occasion, celebrate—"

"The first anniversary of usurping the throne," she interrupted.

Daedalus stopped, his face twitching with indignation, not expecting to have his prepared speech interrupted. Dearborn continued before he could gather his wits. "Yes, I know very well that today marks exactly one year since your brother took the throne and you seized control of the kingdom."

The angry prince's nostrils flared as he started walking toward her again. "Very good for you for finding a way to keep track of time in your dungeon cell. It won't change your fate, though."

"I didn't think it would. I've been expecting this all year, preparing myself to make this unenjoyable for you."

Daedalus stood between her legs, close enough for a few of his snakes to leave his body and slither over hers. He tried to sneer, display confidence, but her comment visibly disrupted him "You've been expecting this? Chained to a rack, as I—"

"Of course, I have. You're so predictable."

As if struck by lightning, his body tensed against his will. More snakes slid off him, his rage burning inhospitably hot. Eyes wide, he grabbed her hips, the tips of his fingers digging in. His skeletal right hand drew blood. "Predictable?"

Pushing past the pain, resisting the urge to flinch, she pressed on. "Yes. I knew you would do this, and I knew you would wait for the first anniversary, fabricating some celebration fit for a charlatan to culminate your obsession with me."

"Obsession?" he shrieked, hands squeezing tighter.

She wanted to fight, to squirm. She had the urge to scream and vomit. She went against everything her body wanted to do and just stared at him, fighting to extinguish any form of spark her eyes might hold. "You've been thinking about me ever since I've bested you in the quarterstaff competition during the Summer Festival when we were in our teen years. Every once in a while, when you lay awake at night, you feel a dull throb in your lower back where I hit you with my winning blow. Any time you best an opponent, you put a little extra into your victory because you know there is one victory you could never have. This act now, this moment is all part of some misguided fantasy about revenge against me, but lest you forget, it's your hatred for me that has driven you to this. Your need for revenge against me has made you better yourself, raise yourself to the necessary level to use your brother as a mere figurehead to rule the kingdom. If not for me, you'd never have the country of Albathia. You should be *thanking* me."

With every word she spoke, his eyes became more bloodshot, his breathing more ragged. Saliva dripped from his chin as foam bubbled from the corners of his mouth. "Thanking you? Gave me the kingdom? This. *This* is what you are owed!"

He thrust.

A cold lump of skin slapped against her vagina.

As if watching gold turn into mud, Daedalus looked down and took a step back. Dearborn thought about laughing, but that tactic would yield nothing but pain. Instead, she tried, "You can't. And you know why."

The mask of sanity had been tossed aside, Daedalus looked back to Dearborn with anger, questions, questions about his anger. Without needing him to ask, Dearborn answered, "You can't because I would bear your child, probably a son. It's highly unlikely that your brother will produce an heir, so my child would be rightfully in line for the throne. You wouldn't be able to kill him, to kill your son, because you need to be better than your father. You'd raise him to be the future king, seeing *my face* every time you'd look at him."

Almost naked from lack of snakes, Daedalus retreated a few more steps. He pointed with a bony finger from his skeletal hand, his whole arm shaking. "Kill you! I'll kill you right now!"

"Really? That would be your revenge? Please exact *that* revenge against me!"

Every breath a growl, Daedalus looked around the room for answers. "My men. I have five guards right here. I will order them to tear you apart!"

The guards all kept their heads down, giving no acknowledgment that they were the topic of conversation. "But the hands tearing me apart won't be *your* hands. You would have *no* satisfaction from giving a mere order."

The vengeful prince's eyes darted from side to side. Were his mind a clockwork machine, springs would have snapped from gears grinding so hard. Suddenly, his breathing slowed, his face relaxed. A wide smile slid across his face while his brows remained trapped in a deep furrow. "Your name then. To this day, I still hear how a select few people talk about Dearborn Stillheart. The reverence reserved for gods on the tips of their tongues. I shall make it so everyone will know your name. The *whole kingdom* will know your name. They will *hate it*. They will spit your name from their mouth as if rotted fruit. I will keep you alive and healthy and unsullied so you may have your body strong and your mind crisp when you see my ultimate revenge against the name Dearborn Stillheart. So you may see *my face* every time you hear that name!"

Completely naked, his erection returned, looking more like a malignant growth without the cover of serpents. He made his way to leave but paused to garner the attention of his guards with a finger snap. "Take her back to her cell. We will gild it and keep her food plate from ever going empty. And when I find Perciless, I shall make sure to display her like an exotic animal found at faire and show my brother what is to become of him."

With one final snap of his fingers, he left, leaving the guards to follow his orders.

When I find Perciless. He hadn't found his brother, Prince Perciless, the king of the usurped throne, yet, and there was no mention of her children. Daedalus did not know they existed. As the guards released Dearborn from the shackles, she maintained direct eye contact with Methel, even when the shorter man furtively looked away. Her lips curved into a smile, one that could be mistaken for a manifestation of sinister thoughts. But it was a true smile, one of happiness. If Perciless avoided capture and her children were still alive, then there was hope, and that made her happy.

ONE

IDERIA WAHL PULLED her long blonde hair back and wrapped it firm with a thick leather tie. It was time to work. The ogre she had been watching all morning finally left the leather shoppe with a small pouch in hand.

The ogre was young, about her age, and rather fit for his kind, one of the few who had a chest larger than his waist. From a pocket on his vest, he pulled out a pair of spectacles and donned them as he wandered to the nearby fruit stand. With the meticulous eye of a jeweler, the ogre examined a Tsinel Valley plum, picking it up and holding it mere inches in front of his face. There was not a cloud in the sky and the Day Sun's descent and Evening Sun's rise offered plenty of light to look for imperfections. Satisfied, he nodded to the stand's proprietor and placed the fruit in his pouch. He plucked another plum from the bin and started the examination process over again.

As if she were simply strolling about town enjoying the weather, Ideria crossed the street, careful not to sully her boots in any horse offerings. She was impressed at how well the ogre handled the plums. They were dense, heavy fruits, but with a flimsy skin. All too often people would have to endure a day's worth of purple fingers from mishandling a Tsinel Valley plum, but the thick-fingered ogre finished his purchase of half a dozen with clean hands and placed them in the leather bag. After a quick tie of the pouch to his belt, he pulled out a folded parchment from another pocket. He focused on the paper as he started down the street. Ideria followed him.

After a few blocks, Ideria sensed trouble. The Constable and his wife were chatting as they walked down the street, either oblivious to the ogre walking toward them or expecting him to move out of their path. Either explanation would not have surprised Ideria; the Constable and his wife wore hubris as if it hid their flabby bodies more than the fine clothes that adorned them. The wife's rings and necklace glinted with her every step. It wasn't the expensive clothes or the flashy jewelry—fancy glass if the rumors were to be true—that Ideria worried about. Her concern was for the leather pouch tied to the Constable's belt. Ideria hastened her pace.

As if there could not have been any other possible outcome, the Constable collided with the ogre. His wife whooped and then laughed, each roll of her fat jiggling in time with her cackles. The Constable bumbled and blustered, threats of arrest the first words from his mouth until he noticed that the young ogre was a full head taller than he. The parchment fell from the ogre's hands.

"A thousand apologies, sir," the ogre said adjusting his glasses. "It appears that these spectacles have malfunctioned on me."

The Constable's wife tittered. "Oh, dear boy, you gave me such a delicious start. But I'm okay now, no harm done."

"You are too kind, madam. Forgive me, sir, but I may have wrinkled your jacket. Here let me help," the ogre said and brushed his hands over the Constable's arm. "Oh, my paper."

The Constable glared at his wife as the ogre bent down to pick up what he had dropped, his hands still brushing over the Constable. "Last wrinkle here. Bit of dirt on you as well, sir."

The ogre straightened to his full height and displayed the warmest of smiles. "Good as new, M'Lord, M'Lady."

The Constable's wife hooked her husband's arm as they continued their walk down the street. She waved with her other hand. "It is, dear boy. Well done. But you watch where you're walking from now on."

Just as they had practiced many, many times, Ideria walked behind the ogre as he waved with his right hand, the parchment flapping away as a distraction, while she took the pouch he had waiting in his left hand. No one saw a thing.

Ideria kept walking, eyes straight ahead. People only noticed what was directly in front of them unless someone else brought something to their attention. If she looked back, that might cue others to do so as well. She turned down the first alleyway where a harpy waited.

Long black hair hung low, obscuring the harpy's face. Ideria always wondered why Joy felt the need to hide. Even though her skin had a green hue, she was very pretty. In fact, if not for her legs being covered in black feathers and having talons for feet, she could pass as a human. She would also have to do something about her wings, as they twitched behind her back. Without saying a word to each other, Ideria tossed the leather bag to Joy and she took flight even before it was in her hands.

Ideria had one last thing to do before the meeting, one last part to play. She exited the alley and heard, "Hey! Hey, you there! You, the big girl!"

Predictably, it was the Constable running toward her as best his flab would allow while holding his purple-stained hand away from his body as if infected by a strange disease. Also, predictably, he referred to her size—taller with more muscle covering her broad shoulders than most men. She stopped and forced a tiny smile as she greeted the Constable. "Yes, sir?"

He wheezed from both the sudden exercise and red-faced anger as he waddled to a stop. "The ogre. Where is he?"

"I'm sorry? Ogre?"

"Yes, ogre! The one I was talking to, who ran into me."

"Why would I know where an ogre who ran into you is?"

"You walked right past him!"

"Doesn't mean I know where he is. If anyone should, it'd be you. You say the ogre ran into you and you held a conversation with him. Logic dictates that you would have a better idea of where the ogre is than a random girl on the street who never saw an ogre in the first place."

The Constable's jowls flapped, and his head shook. Eyes like two white islands of anger in the crimson sea of his face, he said through gritted teeth, "You. You lying—"

"Now, Dear," the Constable's wife said as she finally caught up to him. She still attempted to be prim despite the rivers of sweat cascading from her hairline. Using her husband's arm as a guide, yet keeping a mindful eye on his stained hand, she pulled him away. "We've had quite an unfortunate day. Let's leave the poor girl alone and go home. We'll find the ogre later."

Ideria walked away as well as if nothing had happened. No need to bring any further attention to herself. She followed the road out of the town of Bulderswith but took a seldom-used footpath that branched off and led into the forest. The road itself led to Hemmson, but a path was starting to form between Bulderswith and the burgeoning village of Orsrun, at the base of Green Mountain. Half a decade ago, it had been discovered that the sneaky mountain had been hiding gold, a thick vein running from one end to the other. Ideria loved visiting Orsrun; a new block, a new section, a new shoppe seemed to appear every month. No two visits held the same sights. Of course, with a population growth such as that, it called for constant policing by the king's guards. Ideria had been taught from the time she was a child to avoid the king's guards. At all cost.

Deeper in the woods, Ideria strayed from the footpath, past the trees that looked like lovers clutched in a tight embrace, around the three boulders that had many myths about why they were there, and into a small clearing that few knew about—mainly woodland creatures and Ideria's friends. No woodland creatures at the moment, but her friends were there waiting for her.

Rue, the young ogre, clapped and bowed. "Bravo, milady, bravo. Well done as always."

Ideria chuckled and curtsied. "I couldn't have done what I did unless you did what you did. 'It appears these spectacles have malfunctioned on me.' Excellent performance."

Rue pulled the spectacles from his pocket and put them on, keeping them close to the tip of his bulbous nose. He crossed his eyes and wiggled his fingers, jerking his upper body about as if in a bizarre dance. "Oh, deary me! These spectacles of mine are failing me."

Ideria laughed. Rue's antics even elicited a chuckled from his sister, Joy, the harpy. She sat on a massive log in the center of the clearing, next to Nevin, Ideria's brother, while he divvied up the coins from the Constable's pouch. Even though he was the youngest at seventeen, he was the most trusted and usually the leader of their little band of thieves. He often denied his role neither wanting it nor enjoying it, but the other three had agreed that he would be the one to tally the plunders. The best leader was the person who had no desire to be one. However, he did sometimes enjoy planning their capers, such as the one that just yielded fifteen gold coins for each of them.

"Fifteen?" Ideria asked as she sat on the other side of Nevin. He was an extremely handsome boy with sapphire eyes brighter than the blue Evening sun and short, black hair that always seemed to be mussed. There was little question as to why he held Joy's gaze, her eyes peeking out from her curtain of hair. "That's our best haul yet!"

"It is," Nevin confirmed as he handed a small stack of coins to his sister. "It just makes me uncomfortable that it came from the Constable of Bulderswith."

Ideria snorted in contempt. "He's the worst part of a horse's ass. I remember Mother and Father complaining about him all the time."

Regret bittered her tongue as soon as the word left her mouth. They both died ten years ago, but being two years older than Nevin, she recalled more memories of them. Nevin showed no overt reaction to what she had said, but she could tell that she would have to apologize later.

"I don't like the Constable, either," Joy said. Her wings shivered when Nevin placed the coins in her palm.

"Eh, he's never done us wrong, Joy," Rue said as he cascaded his coins from one hand to the other, then repeated the process. One last time and he waved his hands. The coins disappeared. His sleight of hand skills were second to none, even better than her own, Ideria had to admit. Especially for an ogre. "He leaves our family alone."

"That's because he doesn't want to have anything to do with our uncles. Now that he knows you pilfered from him, he might be inclined to visit later."

Rue removed his spectacles and pointed them at his sister. "He doesn't know anything about anything, as he so often proves by bragging about the cheap baubles around his wife's neck as if they were real jewelry. In his mind, I'm just another ogre, tall and green."

"Tall and green, and as fit as a logger, and as well-spoken as an esquire."

Tapping the spectacles against his chin, Rue considered his sister's words. He placed his spectacles in his vest pocket and said, "Let's go home and devise an alibi just in case."

With a quick wave, Rue and Joy left the clearing, the ogre through the trees, the harpy above them. Ideria was alone with her brother. "Ummm . . . Nevin? What I said earlier about mother and father complaining about the Constable, I meant to prove that he's deplorable, not to be hurtful."

Nevin slid down from the log and smiled at his sister. Soft. Warm. Forgiving. He started in the direction of their home and she walked next to him. "I know, but that's not what has me concerned. I remember our parents, more so our mother. You look exactly like her, except for your hair color."

Ideria sighed. "I know, I know. Our 'uncles' and our 'grandparents' have been telling me that for years now. I've heard it a hundred times. That and you look more and more like our father every time the suns rise."

"True, but I don't stand out."

That hurt. It was a simple truth, and impossible to blame Nevin for the pain his words caused, but it hurt, nonetheless. She mumbled, "I know."

Nevin dropped her coins into a satchel. He pulled out a bit of dark material from the satchel as an aid for his next set of words. "You're not wearing your cloak today. The next time the Constable sees a blonde woman bigger than most men, he'll know it's you. Even if he doesn't suspect that you were a partner to the ogre, he'll still recognize you."

"I look like a man in that cloak." Her words were whinier than she had intended.

"Precisely the point."

"But I'm a girl, and a pretty one at that. I want to be fitted for dresses and catch the eye of young men."

"I understand, but—"

"You don't understand, Nevin. As you already stated, you don't stand out."

It was Nevin's turn to sigh. Ideria knew very well the point he was trying to make, she just had no desire to hear it. As Nevin opened his mouth, they exited the woods to the road, but Ideria grabbed her brother and retreated behind a tree. The king's guards.

There were three of them. Two of the guards were off their horses harassing four women with a donkey-drawn cart. The third remained on his horse, trotting it in tight circles around the scene. The guard closest to the women was also the fattest of the three. He sauntered even closer as he said, "Come now, Lasses, we're upstanding members of the king's guard. We're here to help you."

Ideria hated the way the guard talked to the women as they huddled together, two of them shaking. He was a squat man with thinning hair and had gray stubble upon his leathery face. She hated the way the other two guards laughed, sinister and lacking mirth. The oldest of the four women tried to stay between the guards and the girls. "I already told you, we have no money. We're just going to Phenomere to look for work as handmaidens."

The old guard dug his thumbs down the front of his pants and lifted, the material outlining the obnoxious bulge of his crotch. It disappeared when he let go, his pants falling back into place beneath his belly. "Well, as it so happens, my men and I are heading back to the castle as well to receive our new orders from the king. We would be more than happy to escort you."

"That won't be necessary," the matriarch said.

The two guards on the ground started to fiddle with their belts while the one on horseback licked his lips. "Oh, but it's our duty. We all have duties to fulfill. Each and every one of us."

Ideria clenched her fists, but Nevin grabbed her wrist. Leaning close, he whispered, "We can't."

"We have to."

"This could lead to trouble."

"This could lead to nightmares if we do nothing." Ideria yanked her arm from Nevin's grasp and grabbed her cloak from the satchel. With haste, she donned it. The hood covered her face, but her ponytail poked out. She left the confines of the forest and elicited a look of surprise from everyone, even from the scared and crying girls.

"My, my, you're a big girl, ain't ya?" the grizzled man said, finally turning his attention away from the women. Ideria advanced on him. No introduction, no threats, no warning. She reeled back and let loose, her fist connecting with his cheek so hard that his feet left the ground. He bounced, cushioned by his soft girth, and got to his feet quickly. But not fast enough. Ideria got two more punches in, both pulping his nose.

The other guard on the ground drew his short sword to aid his embattled comrade. His feet went out from under him and his face smacked the dirt road. He tried to get up but ended up on the ground again. Nevin. Ideria knew that if she jumped into battle, he would follow her.

The guard on the horse kneed his steed closer, but Ideria paused in her beating to glare at the man. Eyes widening, the guard stopped his charge. The horse brayed, its legs high-stepping to back away. Ideria growled and the guard allowed the horse to gallop away.

"Cowardly bastard," the grizzled man cursed, his swollen nose making his words thick. His whole body heaved with every breath. He clenched his fists, ready to hold his ground until the thump from the other guard falling distracted him. He spat a gob of blood and limped to his horse. As he, too, fled, he yelled over his shoulder, "Bitch!"

Nevin stopped his attack and allowed his opponent to get to his feet. The guard made the wise choice of mounting his horse and racing away.

Two of the girls hugged each other and the third continued to cry. The matriarch of the four rushed to the siblings. "Thank you! Oh, by the gods, thank you. We have no money to give for your kindness and bravery."

Nevin took the woman's hands and filled them with fifteen coins. "You can repay us by forgetting this incident ever happened. Take the road back the way you came. About a mile there will be a footpath on the left. Follow that to Orsrun. This will buy you a room for a month, plenty of time to find work."

The woman's eyes became slick with tears. She tried to speak, but her voice cracked. Nevin smiled and the woman's body relaxed. The magic in his glance could calm a charging bull. He patted her hands and said, "You're welcome. Now, please, hurry along. The faster you go, the sooner you can forget about us."

Ideria gave a polite grin and wave as the women guided their donkey back down the road. Nevin tapped her arm and said, "Come on. Let's go home and devise an alibi. Just in case."

TWO

LANDYR AWOKE WITH a start, shoved into consciousness by an aggressive dream. Not quite a nightmare, but far from soothing. The same dream he had been having for ten years of the same things. Of teeth. Of claws. Of horns. Of long flowing hair the color of gushing blood. Of blackness that moved, a living darkness. Of the arousal caused by fear, and sexual release. Of *her*.

Smacking his pasty lips, he stretched his limbs and quickly realized he was not alone in bed. Something heavy rested on his chest, and he looked down.

A breast.

Green and amorphous, purple veins raced along its paper-thin skin to a nipple so dark it could be considered black. As he had done many times before, he shoved the breast off his chest and sat up to finish stretching. Sitting on the edge of the bed, he took inventory of his clothes scattered upon the floor, slightly amazed he found everything. The nearest wall contained leaves and vines and flowers and stems from all sorts of plants. If not for the window in the middle of it all, he would have sworn there was no wall there, just the growth to hold up the roof.

Bony fingers crawled along his shoulder, looking like the knuckled legs of some green spider. The index finger stroked his cheek. "Care for a morning tug?"

Leelanna, the goblin witch, lay naked behind him like a smear of wrinkled skin upon the bedding. Thinning red hair

like frizzed yarn pulled blindly from a skein framed a grotesque painting, the centerpiece a nose that dangled like a
flaccid penis and jiggled when she spoke. Landyr stood and
grabbed his pants. "This is not the way to entice me back."

"Oh, I'm so sorry, my dear." She got out of bed and as she
walked to him, her body shifted. Wrinkles smoothed. Warts
retreated. Tits and ass firmed with every step. Her face traveled back decades, finishing as a young goblin maiden. Her
nose was still beaklike but had a certain elegance in the
way it flowed from her brow. A goblin could be beautiful,
especially with golden eyes like hers. For Landyr, though,
the reason why he visited her bedroom was her hair. Long
flowing hair, the color of gushing blood. Like in his dreams.
Like *her* hair. "Is this a better way to entice you?"

It was, and he thought about accepting her offer. Not
knowing exactly how much of the morning had elapsed, he
decided against it and put on his shirt. He needed to meet
the others. "Do that again the next time I come through
town. Before I go, I still need what I paid for."

Leelanna laughed. In this form, it was a melodious
sound; in her other form, a horrid cackle. As he sat back
down on the bed to put his boots on, she glided her fingers
over his cheek. They were soft, warm, inviting. Instead of
succumbing to his desires, he put his other boot on.

He waited by the door and she sauntered over, her firm
breasts bouncing in a hypnotic rhythm. As she handed him
three large bags of medicinal herbs, she reached up and
grabbed the back of his head with her other hand. One last
kiss. Soft, warm, inviting. Satisfied that he had enough
memories to last until their next meeting, he pulled away to
see she had slipped back into her natural form. He did not
care. He expected it. Her cackle acted as her farewell behind
him as he walked away.

Leelanna's hut was a footpath and a cart path away from
the main road, one that led to the town of Ironcore. Landyr
had always liked this town. A simple town with a simple
name. The main road went all the way through the town
right to the iron mine at the base of the mountain. Men
worked until their muscles told them to quit. Those with

families went home to them; those without went to the taverns. This town also happened to have a goblin that happily replenished medicinal supplies for a tussle under the sheets with Landyr. He placed the pouches of newly acquired herbs into the proper containers of their supply wagon once he entered the stables.

"There are other ways to pay," Perciless said, placing a hand on Landyr's shoulder. The prince always said that the morning following a transaction with the witch.

"It's no bother at all, your majesty."

Perciless offered a pitying smile. Over the past decade, the utterance of "your majesty" by Landyr meant it was time to change the topic. "Well, then you are in time for the meeting."

"Nothing in this world could make me miss it." Landyr's sarcasm was obvious and he shared a guffaw with the prince.

"I always appreciate your candor, General." Perciless still chuckled as he went to help Thorna and Brokar prep the horses. Landyr hated that the prince referred to him as a general. His Elite Troop was once forty strong; men and women capable of besting any opponent. Unless the opponent was an army of living skeletons and a handful of mystical dragons. His Elite Troop now numbered three. Brokar and Rolin were like brothers—similar in sturdiness and inseparable. The only noticeable difference between the two was their choice of hairstyle: Brokar opted to run a blade over his skin once a week while Rolin reined his flowing locks into a ponytail. Thorna wore her hair in a ponytail as well but did not interact that often with any of the men other than Landyr. Most mornings began with her asking Landyr if he needed her for any special tasks. The answer was usually no, save for the occasional mission to disrupt a supply chain benefitting the king's army. They allowed him to be general out of courtesy. He had no true authority over them at all.

"You smell like flowers," Cezomir, the werewolf forever trapped in bipedal wolf form, said as he approached to help Landyr secure the containers in the cart. His nose twitched and his muzzle rippled as he sniffed the air around Landyr. "And goblin twat."

"Considering your bedmate is a cat, do you really want me to tell you what *you* smell like?"

Cezomir growled as both men paused from their duties to look at Lina as she helped Rolin with the bedrolls and cooking supplies. "My bedmate is far more attractive than yours."

There was no arguing that point. Landyr agreed with him. She was a Yullian, a cat in human form from an enigmatic tribe and land she could never call home again. Gray fur covered her and ran the length of her body, mostly hidden by a thin linen top and trousers. Despite the dense fur cover, Landyr could see the rippling of powerful muscles whenever she moved. He was vaguely aware of Cezomir saying something in his ear, but it was lost amidst his baser thoughts as Lina turned away from him and he stared at the way her ass strained against her pants, a captive entreating release. Landyr envisioned himself grabbing a handful of her powerful hind side, straining to squeeze against the rippling hardness, only to lose control of the dominance of the situation, and have it overtake his hand, instead.

Lina turned as Landyr was lost in thought and, though her movement broke his concentration, it was only a second before he focused on the swaying of her ample breasts, and he was lost again in his fantasies. He was vaguely aware of licking his lips, but then a firm poke in his shoulder roused him as if from his trance.

"Perhaps you should draw a picture," Cezomir growled, "it will last longer."

"I . . . ," Landyr faltered. He was clearly caught being in the wrong and there was little wiggle room even for his well-rehearsed tongue to find an escape.

Lina walked over to the two men, her normal stride was such an easy gait that Landyr caught himself on the precipice of falling into another trance. She stopped before them and said, "Well, you two are certainly acting very friendly towards one another. What common ground did you find to talk about?"

Cezomir laughed as he turned his eye towards Landyr. The look on his muzzled face Landyr interpreted as the equivalent of a raised eyebrow.

Landyr sputtered for the briefest moment before his words found traction. "We were discussing the upcoming meeting, of course," he said, gesturing with his hand between himself and the werewolf. "We both found it odd that our guests hadn't arrived yet and were just wondering how much longer we should wait before we consider something to be amiss."

"I would say that you needn't wait much longer," Perciless said, striding up to the trio.

"My king?" Landyr asked.

Perciless smiled. "Meaning that they are here at last. Escort them to me, please."

Landyr regained his wits, seeking to exit an uncomfortable discussion, and covering the length of the stables to the open door. He was greeted by two individuals: a man and a woman.

The man was slightly beyond middle-aged, with a torso like an ale keg. Tousled hair, reddish in hue like the Morning Sun, sat atop his rounded head. His face was ruddy, and he was clearly winded as breath wheezed its way between parted lips that had seen the unkind effects of either too much wind or too much sun. His clothes were fancy, though clearly worn from use. His voluminous mustache quivered as he scrunched up his face in greeting.

"Mayor," Landyr said, shaking his hand and inviting in the pair of arrivals.

The woman was dusky of complexion, her skin bright about the face, as though vine ripened. Long hair, dark and lustrous as obsidian, was plaited into a single braid that reached to her mid-back. Small, round eyes of green as deep as weathered copper, blinked at Landyr. Tall and thin, she stood like a patch of crane grass untouched by the hand of man or beast. Landyr couldn't guess her age by the wrinkleless skin around her eyes or by the stately mien that seemed to belie the hint of youth about her.

Her clothing was fine and fresh, exotically colored in black and greys with some teal in a crosshatched pattern that was foreign to Landyr's eyes. Her shoulders were bare as was a small diamond shaped patch of her lower back.

Landyr felt strangely at peace in her presence as he bowed and took her long, bony-fingered hand in his, crowning it with a quick kiss as he welcomed her inside.

"Honored guests, this is King Perciless," Landyr stated, leading them farther into the stables.

Perciless parted his hands in an inviting gesture. "Thank you for coming, Mayor Felindrous, Lyyra of Tsinel."

"Thank you for keeping hope alive, your grace," the mayor of Ironcore replied, after peeking over at his companion and acknowledging her nod of consent.

"Please, there is no need for titles. Perciless will do."

"I am in a great hurry if it pleases you, Perciless," Lyyra said. "We, the leadership of my country, that is, wish to see your brother removed from his position as king as quickly as possible. His war with us is a constant threat to our way of life. We are not incapable of protecting ourselves with great ferocity, but I fear that he has resources at his command that would demand great sacrifice if we are to prove victorious. We have lived as neighbors in perfect peace when you sat upon the throne and we wish to see you return to your rightful place."

"I do not wish harm upon my brother, nor do I seek the glory of rulership; however, the danger of allowing him to continue with this war is unacceptable. He must be deposed for the good of my people and yours."

"Yes, this is why we think that you must gather your forces and strike at him with haste," Mayor Felindrous said with a little more eagerness than Perciless thought safe.

"We are preparing our forces, I can assure you," Perciless smiled thinly. "But we have been doing so in secret, from town to town, just as we've done here in Ironcore. We are not ready to unveil ourselves just yet. At the moment, our presence is still unknown to Daedalus and we must use that to continue to grow our numbers for as long as we can."

"But in doing so," Lyyra argued, "you are extending the war at the cost of Tsinel lives. You must take up arms and come to our aid."

"Believe me," Perciless countered, "if we had the strength to do so, we would take up the challenge immediately, but to do so prior to having adequate numbers would be foolish. If we charge in recklessly, then we will be destroyed and all hope of defeating my brothers will be lost."

Lyyra frowned at his words. Perciless imagined that she thought him a coward.

"People will die in even greater numbers if we attack too soon. I promise you that we are working as quickly as we can to bolster our forces."

"But when? When are you going to be ready?" Mayor Felindrous asked, wringing his hands together.

"Yes, when?" Lyyra asked as if pressing an attack of her own. "Do you have a specific number of days in mind, or are you pursuing an elusive feeling of preparedness?"

"I must beg your patience," Perciless said. "Daedalus is wearing himself thin. We are waiting for the proverbial straw to break the camel's back. I can sense that moment will be coming soon."

ThRee

BALE PINKEYE SAVED the world two decades ago. He should have been lauded, exalted everywhere he went and given the rewards often known to accompany celebrity status. At the very minimum, his name should have been added to the list of all the greatest ogres, right at the top of the heroes' list. At times he fancied himself to be an individual who could offer great insight about the way the world worked, finding time to pontificate poetically to anyone within earshot. Afterward, the listener would be sure to tell him that he forever changed their life, right before they disappeared the very next day. Bale's chest always bloomed with pride, and he took their words to heart, assuming he inspired them to cut through the tethers of fate and choose a different path. He believed he could also make the list of all the greatest ogres as philosopher or cleric because of this but felt it more accurate to be placed on the heroes' list.

But he was on no list, ogre or celebrity or otherwise. Only a handful of people knew he saved the world. Those he told not only disbelieved him but laughed. Just as they were laughing now.

Bale was ankle deep in mud and pig slop, surrounded by laughter. A dozen guards sat on the thick fence that formed the pigpen. They laughed each time he fell.

About an hour ago, a boar got loose. The guards exhausted themselves getting the thing back into a pen, one getting wounded in the process taking a tusk to the thigh. But they corralled the beast into the wrong pen.

The boar was a Furonian Valley boar, this one larger than any man sitting on the fence, each tusk thicker than an arm. The pen held domestic sows, too small to survive any form of ardor, but the men were too drained to get the boar out of this pen and into the proper one. They had just enough energy left to release Bale from his dungeon cell to do the task for them and to place wagers among themselves if he would survive the experience or not.

Bale had fallen twice just getting into the pen and two more times getting to the center where the boar snorted and paced in circles. It had been eying the sows until Bale got close enough.

The boar shook its head, flinging mud as it swiped its tusks against the ground. Bale assumed that it did not appreciate being interrupted while trying to gain attention from the sows. He could empathize, but he had a job to do and no desire to face the consequences if he failed. He tried to calculate how bad those consequences might be when the boar charged him.

Even though he was a foot taller than any man on the fence and twice as heavy, he had no desire to get into a head-on collision with a charging Furonian Valley boar, especially one built from nothing but muscle. He dove out of the way to escape a goring but landed perfectly for a face full of muck.

Spitting mud and slop from his mouth, he got to his hands and knees. Right when the laughter got louder was when Bale realized that in this position, he presented his rump as an enticing target for the boar. The sounds of churning hooves sloshing through the mud told him to brace for impact.

A smack of meat against the boar's skull.

An eruption of laughter.

Bale had very little grasp for the physical sciences, so he envisioned that he would fly. He was confused and mildly disappointed when the attack sent him cock over nose, rolling halfway across the pen. After coming to a stop, he thanked the minor deities in the ogre pantheon that the boar had its head down for the collision, keeping its tusks out of the way.

The boar charged again and Bale prayed to the major deities.

Bale squirmed and rolled around, trying to get any form of footing in the mud. Windmilling his arms, he got to his feet, only to fall ass first into a patch of loose slop. Luckily for him, it was the best tactical maneuver he could have executed. The splash was grand, a wave directed right at the boar's face. Temporarily blinded, it squealed and pulled up, slowing just enough for Bale to jump on top of it.

Getting his hands on both of the boar's tusks, he drove its face into the ground. He outweighed the beast, but not by much, and the creature had far superior muscles. Its legs kicked trying to gain any form of purchase on the slippery ground while its stout body squirmed. Bale hoped his bulk was enough to keep the boar pinned. He wanted to make the creature tire itself out, and then he would be able to lead it back to the proper pen.

"Hey, Greenie!" one of the guards yelled. "Just got word from the pen master that this was one of the boars scheduled for slaughter. Go ahead and just kill the damn thing."

As if the creature understood, it unleashed another wave of thrashing. Still unable to get to its feet, it managed to roll, driving Bale into the muck. Tightening his grip on the tusks, Bale thrashed around as well to get back on top of the boar. He shook his head to clear the shit-smelling mud from his face and mouth. "Then give me something to kill it with!"

The men laughed again, but Bale could not see them to know why. "You got it, Greenie."

As the laughter came to a crescendo, a whistle split the air and ended with a sharp pain in Bale's right ass cheek. An arrow. Someone shot Bale with an arrow. "Whoops! Sorry, Greenie. I was aiming for the boar."

Bale had fought against demons from the very depths of Hell, had lost friends and family, had sacrificed his way of life for the betterment of the world, and this was how it repaid him—a face full of pig shit and an arrow in the ass.

Angry beyond words, he howled and yanked the arrow free. Wailing like a mythical creature from a cautionary tale to keep children in line, Bale stabbed the boar in the neck. The beast released an angry squeal, one that Bale matched with pitch and timbre, but surpassed it in volume and duration. Bale howled the whole time he stabbed the boar again and again, rainbow arcs of blood spurting through the air. Crimson sprayed Bale so fast it washed away the brown, painting him red. Bale raged on, stabbing well past the pig's death. There was no more laughing.

Panting, he stood and wondered if the dead creature was luckier than he. Bale turned to the guards on the fence and decided to take payment for his efforts. *A sight I must be*, he thought as he stomped his way toward them—larger than any three of them combined and covered in blood and mud. The guards all jumped from the fence and drew their weapons. One had pulled his short sword and waggled it at Bale. That was the one he wanted. Before the guard could reel his arm back to strike, Bale snatched the sword and turned around. None of the guards attacked, but there was plenty of posturing and yelling. Bale cared not one bit. He was hungry.

In his beefy hands, the short sword was a mere knife, and Bale used it as such to carve a large chunk from the boar's hindquarters. The guards made threats and aimed their weapons at the ogre after he finished and approached them wielding the short sword. He handed it back to the guard he took it from. Bale turned his back on all the confused looks and started to walk back toward the dungeon entrance at the back end of the castle. He was tired and wanted to rest.

Falling into place as if they were the ones to initiate the prisoner return, half of the guards escorted Bale into the castle and left the other half to deal with the boar. Bale trundled along, following a specific path along numerous hall and stairwells, a route he had walked many, many times over the past ten years. The cut stone hallways were quiet. They were always quiet, save for the occasional cry of pain or the gurgle of death coming for one of the other prisoners.

Sometimes at night, silence embraced the dungeon so tightly that he wondered if he had gone deaf, if not for the guttering of flames in the sconces upon the walls. Bale turned one final corner, into a room that had iron bars to the right and to the left. Bale was home.

"By the gods, Bale!"

The only other person who lived in this room.

Dearborn Stillheart.

Bale's cage was on the right side of the room while hers was on the left. These cages were built specifically for them. They were larger than any other cell in the dungeon and offered far more amenities, almost comparable to the hospitality of a public house. They each had a bench and a mattress that was stuffed with new straw twice a year and a new blanket once a year. Dearborn even had a window. High enough on the wall that she could only see out of if she used her incredible strength to pull herself up, but too small to escape from. Her head would get stuck if she were ever fool enough to try to put it through.

The guards snickered as they closed the cell door behind Bale and exited the room.

"Are you hurt?"

"No. But they shot my ass with an arrow."

Dearborn moved from her cell to his and gently took the chunk of meat from his hands. "Come on. I haven't used my bath this week. You take it."

"Okay," Bale mumbled as he trudged from his cell to hers. A metal container had been jammed into the corner of her cell. Another accouterment of unknown origin. It was meant for her alone, the water changed once a week, but she would allow him a soak now and again. Usually after the guards humiliated him in some fashion.

Dearborn had been skinning rats. She collected a half dozen carcasses and a large bowl she had hidden under some straw in the corner. She placed the little skinned bodies in the bowl as well as the chunk of boar that Bale had brought and moved to Bale's cell. Bale got in the tub. The water was not warm, but it felt nice. Soothing. As he washed away the filth from his skin, turning the water reddish brown,

Dearborn sat in his cell cutting up rat and the boar. When she finished, she took the bowl and walked to the edge of the doorway to the hall. After a quick peek in either direction, she slipped out. She had been doing this for nine years now.

When Bale and Dearborn were first brought here, he thought he was going to be executed. After all, they supported King Perciless and fought against his brothers Oremethus and Daedalus when they brought their dragons to Castle Phenomere to take the crown. In an effort to save his people, King Perciless abdicated the throne to Oremethus, the rightful king by birth, not by ability. Prince Daedalus wished to subject Perciless to unimaginable pain, but Bale and Dearborn chose to be instrumental pieces in his escape. Bale mused that he was just a born hero, always willing to step up in such situations. However, this time, it led to his capture and imprisonment.

Ten years ago, these cells locked, and they had no amenities. Cold stone. Dark nights. Every noise from the hallway could have been Death coming to claim them. Hunger their bedfellows. Their meals were nothing more than stale bread, which Bale shoved down his gullet as soon as he got it. Not Dearborn, though. She conveyed it into something better.

A hole in the corner of her wall led to a colony of rats, one she helped feed with her bread. Bale helped by giving half of every meal to her. Within months, she had become a sort of rat farmer. Bale enjoyed his rats raw and whole while she skinned hers.

Something happened exactly one year after their arrival. Dearborn had been taken from her cell. Bale spent the next few hours crying, thinking she had been executed. He almost pissed his britches from excitement when she came back. Things were different from that point on.

She never told him what happened, never once talked about that day. But from that point on, they got bedding and benches, more and better foods. The guards turned a blind eye when she figured out a way to pick the locks, and they never investigated any rumor they surely had heard about her sneaking around. Even though they had better food, she still kept the rat colony thriving, harvesting some whenever they needed a little extra meat in their meals. If their bellies were full and she needed to cull the colony, she would give them to other prisoners.

By the time Bale finished his soak and went back to his cell, she had returned. Shoulders slumped forward, Bale sat on his bench and moaned, "I'm beginning to think they don't respect me."

Dearborn chuckled as she returned to her own cell and closed the door. "Of course, they don't, Bale. They're minions of evil."

Bale liked her voice. It was nice. Comforting even when she said things that he would rather not hear. She rarely used it, so he savored these moments. "I know. But I help them out so much. Today was catching a boar. Last week was cleaning the fire pits. Last month was unclogging the sewage exit. And they ask me to spar with them all the time."

"It's not sparring, it's target practice," Dearborn huffed. Her voice held notes of sympathy and anger.

"Either way, it keeps me active."

"There are much better ways to do that."

To demonstrate, she gripped the bottom of her window and pulled herself up until her chin touched her fingers and then lowered herself. She repeated the process. Bale lost count after ten, mainly because he struggled with numbers larger than that. "I know."

He had hoped she would say something else to keep the conversation going. Instead, after a few minutes, the only noises she made were quick puffs of air as the veins started to protrude from her bulging arms. She dropped and turned toward the doorway. Voices in the hallway.

Crossing her arms, she leaned against the wall just as Methel entered with two other guards in tow. He looked none too happy to be here and stood before Dearborn's cell. "How's the princess today?"

Dearborn simply stared at him, her face devoid of any discernible emotion. Methel stared back, his face a frozen mixture of anger and hatred with a good dose of fear swirled into it. Had anyone ever looked at Bale with respect, he assumed it looked like this.

"Need anything, M'lady?" Bale knew sarcasm, though, and Methel's words dripped with it.

Dearborn remained stolid with her expression, blinking only when necessary. Ever since the mysterious incident from nine years ago, Methel had provided Dearborn and Bale with all the comforts they had now and even asked if she needed anything else. She never accepted the offer. After every silent rejection, Methel did the same thing: snorted, spat on the floor, and growled, "Suit yourself, princess."

"Tired of obstinate women this week, ain't ya?" the one guard whispered to him.

"Trouble with the ladies?" the other guard asked.

"Heard he got his ass kicked by one last week. A blondie thing right outside of Orsrun. Handled him and his two riding companions with ease."

"Yeah? She make off with his balls, then?"

Methel turned and cuffed the one guard's head hard enough to draw blood. In a growl so deep Bale swore he felt it from where he sat, Methel said, "Not that I need to explain myself to the likes of you, but she was massive. Large as a young giantess. Now, if you ever want a test of skills you must simply name the time, the place, and say your farewells to all your loved ones."

Methel punctuated his statement by shouldering past both men to leave the room hard enough to make them stumble. Heads low, neither guard dared to look at each other or the prisoners and simply followed.

After a few loud heartbeats, Dearborn spoke. "Bale."

"Yes, Dearborn?"

"We're going to plan our escape now."

FOUR

IT WAS DEARBORN Day. Methel hated Dearborn Day. He always had to clean up the mess.

He wondered if the girl would be rendered comatose or maddened. He preferred comatose. Much easier to deal with. Sling her over his shoulder and take her to the nurses in the abbey. The maddened ones were so much worse. Violent fits of fear were often taken out upon him. One time a girl scratched him deep enough to warrant a bandage. He did not like that at all.

He rounded one final corner to get to the ceremony room—the "snake pit" as he referred to it in the sanctuary of his own mind—and stopped in his tracks. Speekore, the scientist waited in front of the closed door of the ceremony room.

A hobgoblin, like any, in some respects, Speekore was taller than most and lanky. His limbs were long and seemed to move slowly to the casual observer, but certainly fast enough anytime he needed to be somewhere to perform a torturous experiment. To Methel, he looked like a giant green spider, the way he skittered along the castle hallways. Yet, much creepier. He had no way to gauge how old a hobgoblin was, but Methel assumed the scientist to be old for his species. Misshapen discolorations of darker green looked like islands upon his bald pate. What hair he did have grew in varying lengths from the back of his head and rested like cobwebs upon his shoulders. To add to the monstrous image, his eyes were hidden behind thick glass cups embedded into his skull, and his chin was metal, a forged approximation of a jawbone. It did not move, affixed to his head, and his upper lips rippled in unnatural ways when he spoke, allowing for glimpses of tiny teeth and the flicker of a fetid tongue. No, Methel did not like Speekore the scientist, not one bit.

"Hobgoblin." Methel's standard greeting to the scientist, the most courteous one he could muster.

"Human." Speekore's upper lip peaked just enough to expose rotted little pebbles of teeth.

That was the extent of their conversation as they waited outside the door together in silence. For Speekore, interaction was a way to ferret out weakness. With anyone else, he would talk until he got a reaction, a way to dig into a person's mind and soul, excavating any tidbit that might be useful in the future. Not with Methel, though. Methel had learned that the best way to silence Speekore was to remain silent himself. He was curious as to why the scientist was here, but with patience, all would be explained. Spending a few minutes in awkward silence gazing into the nearest sconce while the scientist stared at him was nothing compared to the experiments that happened in another part of the castle. The door to the ceremony room finally opened and Daedalus strode out.

The prince was naked, every wiry muscle exposed to the world, his taut skin glistening from sweat and ceremonial oils. His black hair was plastered to his head, neck, and shoulders in clumps from the same liquids. Judging from his deflating erection, the ceremony had just ended.

Moist air flowed from the ceremony room in waves. The flames of the massive braziers in the four corners of the room burned thick, heating the buckets of water suspended over them. The room needed to be hot and humid for the snakes.

Hundreds of snakes wriggled around the room, the vast majority squirmed together along the far wall to form the bed of the Dearborn Day ceremony. Atop the bed was the girl Methel had to fetch. Naked and curled into a ball, she shivered and twitched, her unblinking eyes staring at something far, far away. Methel assumed it was hope, something in the distance that would never get closer, a mirage that would never become real.

"Your Highness," Methel nodded to the prince as he started to go into the room but stopped when Daedalus placed his skeletal hand on his shoulder.

"A word, please, General." Methel was at an age where the list of things that concerned him was short and waning. An unscheduled conversation with Daedalus was close to the top of that list.

The prince then addressed Speekore. "Take the girl to the abbey nurses. Do not deviate."

The hobgoblin's upper lip curled into a smile as he gazed longingly into the room. "I will try."

"You will succeed. She will make it there in a timely manner, unmarred. I have other scientists, many of them curious about the inner workings of hobgoblins."

Speekore's enthusiasm deflated like an emptying water-skin. "Yes, Sire."

After a moment to observe that the hobgoblin was following orders, Daedalus walked down the hallway, the dripping fluids adding a bit of a splash to his bare feet slapping against the stone. Methel kept pace. "I'm off to meet with the other generals regarding the war effort and find that I have no other time but now to meet with you."

"I understand."

"Have you checked on my prisoner?"

"I have."

"And?"

"She is well. Healthy. I believe she may have not only forgotten that she is in any form of prison but forgotten that it was you who put her there."

"Perfect. Soon it will be time to finally reveal to her my revenge, what I have been planning all these years."

"Yes, Sire."

"I've been so busy lately I've almost lost sight of that. With the war. Hunting down whatever wizards are left. Finding Perciless. Cleaning up whatever messes my brother makes.

My brother . . . I need to meet with him as well. His ability to govern is certainly lacking. How has he been of late? Any recent . . . incidents?"

"The king has not razed any towns due to paranoid delusions for months now."

"Good, good. This has been the longest stretch. Do you think he's getting better?"

"Do you want me to say yes, or do you want me to speak the truth?"

Daedalus sighed and ran his fleshed hand through his hair, sweeping the clumped locks from his face, and scratched at his head. Methel believed that to be more from frustration than any form of itch. "Speak the truth."

"I believe he might be getting worse. With the wizards in his personal guild, King Oremethus still seeks ways to hunt and kill "demons." He's commanding the wizards to develop new spells or teach him the languages found in arcane and unholy books."

"Demons," Daedalus muttered to himself. "My brother is the real demon with this obsession and wasting the wizards' time and skill like this. They should be on the battlefield, not locked away in laboratories and libraries."

"He is the king after all. They are his wizards to waste."

"Yes, yes, yes. I'm well aware of that. Has your Elite Troop found any more to add to his guild with your latest mission?"

His Elite Troop. It had been his Elite Troop for nine years now and he still wasn't comfortable with his role in it. It had become his the day that Daedalus formed it, and that was only because he was the closest guard when the idea came to fruition. Angered to the point of spitting while he yelled, Daedalus conceived of the Elite Troop hours after Dearborn Stillheart verbally emasculated him. That week, the prince assembled a dozen of the most ghoulish monstrosities for Methel to command. Over the nine years, a few had died, but Methel made more than adequate decisions, a fine General indeed. But he wasn't perfect. "We did. We found four in the remote town of Rothrol. However, one sacrificed himself which allowed the other three to escape to Tsinel."

Daedalus balled his skeletal hand into a fist and back-handed the nearest wall. Small chunks of stone scattered across the floor and the prince looked down at them, almost surprised. His gaze shifted to his own genitals as if he had forgotten that he was naked. A shake of his head to put this information out of his mind, he looked back to Methel. "That is unfortunate. Clearly the doing of my other brother. Ten years of rousing my towns, my villages, my cities, turning them against me and we are no closer to capturing him than we were when he first escaped. I knew I should never have let that lecherous creature live. His connections to the criminal underground have done precious little good. Information leading to the capture of a traitor here and there hardly warrants his current standing with the king. Perciless has been recruiting for a secret army and if my estimates are correct, it must vast in number by now. Large enough to strike any day, so it's time to reallocate resources. You and the Elite Troop will find Perciless and bring him to me. Anything you need will be made available to you, even if you'd like to increase your ranks. Just go tell the lecherous creature and garner from him all of the information he has about the last known sighting of Perciless. Now, I'm off to meet with the generals to see why we haven't won the war with Tsinel yet."

Without so much as a nod, Daedalus turned and went about his business. Methel chuckled to himself while picturing Daedalus naked with his cock swinging about yelling at a room full of generals. His mirth was fleeting, though, replaced by duty. He had to see "the lecherous creature."

Haddaman Crede.

Methel groused inwardly the whole way to Haddaman's room, behind a lonely wooden door at the end of a dead-end hallway. He assumed there were secret passages and fake walls throughout this area because he rarely saw Haddaman move about the castle, yet the lecherous creature continued to run a successful criminal organization under the name of Vogothe. Methel never once looked past the worn bricks and chipped mortar for any kind of switch or lever. He simply did not care. Every time he ventured this far, he just wanted to say his piece and flee.

Knuckles hovered close to the door, yet he could not bring himself to knock. Not just yet. He needed to weigh the options of leaving this life behind first. He had plenty of gold stashed away to give him comfort during his fading years. No more horrors of this castle, no more killing in the name of king and country. As he did every time these thoughts crossed his mind, he dashed them, knowing very well that his life would end at the blade tips of the very Elite Troop he commanded. Fate was but a noose that slipped tighter the more he struggled. But before he could rap on the door, a voice from behind it said, "Enter, Sergeant."

Methel hated the lecherous creature.

The door opened upon a whisper even though all others in the castle creaked and squeaked. Minimal light made its way through the thin gaps between the curtains. Methel's old eyes struggled to adjust to the darkness, too quick to glance from one amorphous shadow to the next, desperate to make out what moved and lurked about. And the heat was intolerable. He refused to step any further into the room than past the threshold, but the torrid air caressed him, coaxing forth a few beads of sweat. The smell of rot, earthen musk, and fungus soon followed.

Methel knew the layout of the room, and what crept around in it, so that helped his eyes adjust. Against the entire right wall, mounds of large capped fungus grew. Bulbs the size of small men grew from the decaying trunks of trees. The slimy film that covered everything glistened in the faint light. Hundreds of slugs half the size of his hand crawled among the folds of the mushrooms and burrowed into the wood of the dead trees. They were the source of the flowing, dripping mucus. Haddaman harvested it, needed it. Deeper inside the room, the slugs fed on other things; things Methel would rather not think about.

A bulk shuffled across the floor from the left side of the room, slowly making its way out of the darkness. The bull head was first, its eyes long since dead, marble white and glossy. A tongue lolled out of its mouth, gray with one of the slugs crawling around on it, its mucus trail flowing to the floor in long strings. The horns looked dry and paper-like, but Methel knew very well that the bones were hard, the tips sharp. The rest of the minotaur stepped into the faint light, an abomination against nature. Deader than anything moving had the right to be, it could stand to well over fifteen feet tall. Necromancy and dark sciences kept it animated for the sole purpose of transporting Haddaman Crede.

When on its hind legs, the minotaur looked as if it were carrying a child swaddled to its belly. It took but a mere heartbeat longer than a glance to realize it was no child and there was no swaddling. It was Haddaman.

The minotaur lumbered closer to Methel, then dropped forward, propping itself sturdy with its knuckles to the floor. Haddaman now dangled from the thing's belly. Limbless, charred and melted nubs protruded from his shoulders and hips, long strips of deep crimson muscles attached Haddaman to the moving corpse of the minotaur, making him look like an aborted fetus refusing to relinquish dominion of the womb. Wide membranes, the viscera of pulling an undercooked steak from the bone, ran from underneath flaps of Haddaman's skin to the various parts of the minotaur's underside. The corpse moved as Haddaman wished it; a puppeteer pulling the strings from under the puppet, as part of the puppet.

Dozens of slugs made their way across the carcass, their secretions needed to keep the corpse from rotting. One slug crept too far along the bull cheek and fell to the floor. The minotaur lifted its right hand and gestured to it. Haddaman asked, "Would you be so kind . . . ?"

Methel picked up the slug and the phlegm colored creature squirmed between his thumb and index finger, ooze dripping over his knuckles. He wanted to crush it, drop it to the floor and stomp on it. The last time he did something like that, though, Haddaman exaggerated the story to Daedalus. Methel's punishment was a month of sewer duty. However, that did not stop him from reaching up and shoving the slug into the left nostril of the bull head.

"Aah, yes. Thank you, dear Methel." As the minotaur put its hand back on the floor and returned to its original stance, Haddaman swayed. A slug crawled across his forehead, the skin wrinkled from deep burn scars. "It is very fortuitous that you came to see me."

"Why do you think that?" Methel was unable to muster more than a flat tone. He hated interacting with Haddaman, and hated conversing with him more so.

"I've been hearing a very interesting rumor this morn, one involving you."

"Is that so?"

"Indeed, it is. This rumor is about a run in between you and a girl near the town of Orsrun."

"I have heard this rumor, too."

The minotaur lifted its right hand and ponderously stroked the bottom of its slacked chin, a simple move for the living made blasphemous by the dead. "I am made to wonder, is there any truth to this rumor?"

"Some rumors are true, others are not. Surely one as wizened as you is aware of this."

"Indeed I am. I am also aware enough to discern truth from tale, and there is certainly truth to this tale."

Methel shrugged. "So say you."

Haddaman chuckled, a tiny and innocent noise reserved for children. "The General of the King's Elite Troop should not be thwarted by a mere woman, don't you agree?"

"Go ahead and make your jokes. I've heard them all."

"Oh, you misunderstand, dear Methel. No jokes about this woman handling you so deftly. To do what she did might be more of a testament to her abilities rather than your advancing age or diminishing prowess."

Methel chuckled. "Ability and *size*. Could be a bastard product of a human and giant."

"Large, you say?"

"Very. Blonde. A young thing, too, from what I could see under her hood."

"I wish to see this young, blonde giantess. Take me to her."

Conversations with Haddaman offered few moments of smugness from Methel, so he savored them whenever they made themselves available. Intertwining his fingers behind his back, he rocked back on his heels and smiled. "No."

The minotaur's fingers curled to knuckles as it lurched forward. The act would have been intimidating had it not caused Haddaman to start swinging. "What did you say? Remember to choose your words wisely, lest you wish me to repeat them to Daedalus."

This had been the moment Methel had been waiting for. He took a step forward to enjoy this, no matter that he was now close enough that slug secretion oozed from the bull's head to his shoulder. "You have my blessing to do so, for all you would be doing is repeating his own words to him."

Haddaman's lips pulled back into a sneer. "How do you mean?"

"The only reason I ventured to this part of the castle was to tell you of the prince's new assignment for the King's Elite Troop. As you have failed repeatedly, he now wishes us to have a more hands-on approach in questing for his brother, Perciless, since you have been so inadequate at it, and instructed me to get whatever pertinent information you might have on the matter."

The dead muscles of the minotaur flexed as Haddaman's words filtered through clenched teeth. "You lying, treacherous—"

"Remember to choose your words wisely, lest you wish me to repeat them to Daedalus."

A look of horror swept across Haddaman's face as the minotaur stood on its hind legs and stumbled backward. "You speak the truth."

"I know no other way to speak, a concept sneaks such as yourself fail to grasp. Now tell me what you know."

Half of Haddaman's face went slack, the other half remained in a rictus grin, the burn scars having sculpted it as such. He licked his lips, his tongue resembling the slug on his forehead. "Very well, General. Perciless and his protectors have been meeting with an ambassador from Tsinel in the town of Ironcore, usually twice a year. My sources tell me that they were just there. I can think of no better place for you to start."

Methel gave a slight bow, scooped the slime from his shoulder, and flicked it to the floor, and then turned on his heel to leave. This was the first Dearborn Day in nine years that he actually enjoyed.

CHAPTER 5

IDERIA GRABBED A fistful of her cloak around her shoulders and pulled, shifting it. "It's tight."

"I doubt that," Nevin replied, tone even and calm.

Ideria gripped the short sword tighter. Because of her size, it looked more like a dagger, like the one Nevin tossed from hand to hand. After their run-in with the king's guards a few days ago, they decided to better prepare themselves.

Today was market day in Orsrun. Their grandparents had given them permission to be here with the sole purpose of examining the tables and stalls set up along both sides of the road and reporting back to them what goods the locals had to offer. The siblings took the opportunity to spend some of the coins they had stolen from the Constable.

"It's too heavy."

"It's lighter than mine."

"Then it itches."

"I doubt that, too."

Ideria huffed. "I just hate wearing a cloak."

"It's the same cloak you've been wearing for the past four years."

"I know. That is why I stopped wearing it."

Ideria waited for Nevin's rejoinder, but he held it while he handed ten coins to the blacksmith's wife. She was surprised and appreciative, happy to move something more expensive than nails, hinges, and horseshoes. Ideria tied her sword to her belt and then moved along with her brother.

They now needed to seek out a leatherworker to see if any sheaths might be available for purchase. Away from any potentially curious ears, Nevin continued with his lecture. "You decided to stop wearing your cloak and then one of the first things we did was pilfer the constable of Bulderswith. You interacted with him, so he will undoubtedly recognize you if he were to see you again."

"He might recognize me, but in his mind, I'm not suspicious."

"In his mind you *are* suspicious. You're a memorable individual at the scene of the crime against him. He may be a deplorable person, but he is still the constable of Bulderswith after all. We must assume that he has some skill necessary to get that title."

All this talk of suspicion was making Ideria paranoid. Someone was watching her, the tiny hairs tingling at the base of her neck told her so. She looked over each shoulder as best she could with her hood being up. In the shadows of an alleyway across the street, a large figure moved about. It held the shape of a minotaur, but it was hunched over and jerked around awkwardly as if it had forgotten how to move. Something in its hand glowed blue, the light exposing its face. It was indeed a minotaur, but one that caused insects to skitter down Ideria's spine. Its face seemed dead, tongue dangling from the side of its mouth. It retreated deeper into the alley, blue light disappearing.

Was that horrific creature truly watching her, or was it some deformed beggar too afraid to come into the light? She thought about telling Nevin, but as her fear subsided, so did her belief that it was something nefarious, so instead, she decided to continue the argument with her brother. "Right. The constable from Bulderswith, not here, not Orsrun."

"They're neighboring towns. You don't think those in charge talk to each other? You don't think the towns have relationships? And don't forget about our grandparents. Even though they don't leave the farm all that often, they still visit these two towns, as well as Hemmson for that matter. What would happen if they heard a rumor about a large blonde girl stealing from those of elite status in the area?"

"They're not our grandparents."

"Captain Wahl and Marrim are our grandparents. Their blood may not flow through us, but neither does the blood of Draymon or Bartholomew, yet we refer to them as our uncles. They all have raised us since the king and his dragons took our parents from us."

"Then maybe you should take something back from the king." The voice came from behind them. It was a man's voice, human from the sound of it. Deep, yet calm, like an attempt to be friendly. "We could always use a couple of men—"

Ideria turned and moved the side of her hood just enough to expose part of her face. She needed to see if she was going to test the strength of her newly purchased sword on whoever snuck up behind her. A human and an orc, both able-bodied with dirt-streaked faces. Miners, no doubt. She was right that the voice came from the human. His face rippled with a vast array of emotions. Confusion, regret, pity. This was not the first time she saw these emotions, not the first time someone mistook her for a man. The human cleared his throat and continued, "—individuals such as yourself. You seem solid enough and smart enough to know the wrong son of the late King Theomann sits on the throne."

Nevin pulled close to Ideria and leaned forward, his voice barely above a whisper. "We're just a couple of nomads."

"Nomads and miners all look the same when cast under the shadow of tyranny."

"What do you expect us to do?"

"No need to whisper, boy. In fact, be louder. Spread the word that Perciless—King Perciless—is still alive and recruiting for his secret army."

"Secret army?"

"Yes. He and his entourage are going from town to town, giving hope to everyone. When the time is right, we will all rise against Oremethus."

"How do you know we're not agents sent by Oremethus?"

The orc and the human laughed. It was the orc's turn to talk. "Because I can smell the goodness on you."

Ideria held up the coin bag she lifted during the conversation. "We're not completely good."

The orc looked down to his belt, then snatched his coin bag from her hand. "Your pretty face won't always be able to get you out of all the trouble your hands get you into."

"When that fails, then that's what this is for." She split her cloak to expose her weapon.

"No need for that, girly. We just wanted to offer you an opportunity."

"I assure you, we appreciate that and will mull it over," Nevin said.

The human and the orc looked at each other and shook their heads. They walked away and the human mumbled. "Children. They just don't understand the importance of politics."

Ideria chuckled to herself, satisfied with the outcome of that exchange until Nevin grabbed her arm and pulled, forcing her to look him in the eye. He was angry, his blue eyes as cold as a frozen lake on a sunny day. "Was any of that necessary?"

"Don't tell me that you found any interest in their conversation."

"Of course I didn't, but we *just* finished discussing how we need to stop drawing attention to ourselves."

"No, you finished lecturing *me* about me drawing attention to us." Ideria punctuated her statement by yanking her arm from his grip.

Nevin sighed and reached out for her again, this time a supportive hand on her shoulder. "What's going on?"

Frustration built up within her. Her desire was to end this conversation and move on, but if she tried to dance around it, then it would just become arduous. Nevin would not let his question go unanswered. "I'm a freak."

"What? Why would you say that?"

Ideria sneered. Either he was patronizing or ignorant, and neither concept sat well with her. "Don't be thick. I'm taller than anyone we've seen today. I may not be the largest person walking around, but I certainly possess the most muscle."

Nevin looked confused. "So you're a little different. Rue is much smarter than any other ogre and Joy is green."

"Rue still *looks* like an ogre, and Joy still *looks* like a harpy. I don't look like a human woman."

"You look like Mother."

No arrow pierced the heart deadlier than the truth. Ideria knew very well that she looked like her mother and had been wondering a lot lately if she faced the same issues, had the same problems. Her mother's father was a blacksmith who ran into some financial troubles, so her mother joined the army when she was Ideria's age. Did she feel that was the only option available to her? Were the only two choices available to Ideria farming or army?

"I wish Mother was still alive. Maybe I wouldn't feel so destined to be alone."

"I wish she were alive, too. And Father. Don't forget, they found each other, so it's doubtful that you're destined to be alone."

Ideria snorted. "They needed to fight armies of demons and save the world to find each other. I'm not entirely sure I'd wish to do that to meet the love of my life."

Nevin held out his arm and flexed his bicep, teasing her about the very thing that upset her. "But you'd be so good at it."

Either he was a genius for finding a funny way to move her past her consternation, or he was a heartless fool for not understanding what bothered her and trivializing her emotions. She laughed, never knowing him to be anything less than a genius and a loving sibling. "Yes, with my new purchase of mighty short sword, I shall slay all the demons."

"There's the spirit! Now let's find a sheath for that mighty short sword of yours."

The tanner had some utilitarian sheaths, but nothing more intricate than what she could make herself with some time and patience. He certainly had a variety of tanned hides for her to choose from should she wish to go that direction, but she wanted something more elaborate. She wanted something with more flair than what a man would carry. Orsrun had one leatherworker, and he displayed his wares for sale today. Ideria was pleased.

She spent almost an hour attaching different ones to her belt and testing how well her short sword worked with them.

Nevin had the patience of moss covering a stone, helping her with each one, even pointing out a few she might like. It was right when she made the decision on the perfect one when she heard the first scream.

"Dragons!"

No one on the crowded market street reacted at first, the proclamation bordering on ludicrous until the shadows appeared, and then all of the people in the market reacted at once. Chaos. Screams. Running. Not knowing where to go, most ran toward the buildings, until a dragon made of metal crashed through a set of two-story buildings. Their construction was sturdy, but wood and shingle were no match for the size and power of an armor scaled beast.

The masses now knew what to flee from but they had yet to find a safe place to flee to. A dragon of shimmering blue and white scale landed at one end of the street. It pulled its wings tight to avoid the buildings. The beast was large enough to damage the surrounding buildings if they were its target of attack, but unlike the metal dragon, it lacked the sheer bulk to do so with ease. Instead, it extended its head, neck parallel to the ground, and released its breath. Lightning. White bolts of electricity hummed and crackled as they arced from its opened mouth. Deep black char marks gouged into whatever the tips of the lightning bolts touched. For those not fortunate enough to find shelter, they were turned to charcoal mid step, a malicious insult to the person they once were, and crumbled upon impact with the ground.

The other side of the street offered no escape either, where a dragon of gemstone landed, carrying King Oreme- thus. The creature's multi-hued scales glittered with every color of jewel and flowed in intricate patterns over its body. This dragon, too, unleashed its breath in the form of dust. Motes, glimmering in the sunlight, sprayed from its mouth and shredded the flesh from all that they touched. The drag- on blasted wherever the king pointed, and the king pointed to anyone crossing his path while yelling, "Demon! There! Another demon!"

Ideria had never seen the king before, but she would most assuredly never forget how he looked now. Nothing about the man seemed regal. Shoulders rolled forward as he leaned in to converse with his dragon, his long hair wild, his eyes maniacal.

"What is happening?" Ideria whispered to herself.

Nevin grabbed her arm and ducked under the stand holding the leather worker's goods. "I believe this is the very thing our grandparents and uncles warned us about concerning our king."

All of the vendors ran to their respective homes, most located right behind their stands and tables. Nevin looked around for the best form of escape. Ideria saw a river of people rushing to the nearby mountain, a jut out containing a mine shaft. "Nevin, this way."

Ideria reached for her brother, but he pulled his arm away. Instead of taking the chance to escape, he tackled her. Her confusion was short lived as something crashed into the leatherworker's stand. Splintered wood and chunks of leather rained down upon Ideria and Nevin.

The metal dragon.

The beast's wings destroyed the stands as it ran down the market street, chasing those fleeing to the mine shaft.

Debris falling from them, the siblings stood. Nevin still looked around for an escape, but Ideria could not stop watching the dragon. Her fists clenched. Her teeth ground together. This was not acceptable. She could not stand around and plot her escape while others cower in a hole waiting for their deaths.

Nevin grabbed her arm. "This way."

It was her turn to yank her arm away. "No. We have to help."

"You can't be serious."

"What would Mother and Father have done?"

Nevin sighed. "I saw a group of children that are huddled together in a dangerous spot. I'll get them to safety, you distract the dragon from the people in the mine. But that's it. Nothing more. We get out of Orsrun. Promise?"

"Promise."

Catching up to the dragon was easy. It would intermittently pause to finish any snack it caught, and it stopped once it reached the mine shaft. If the stories she heard were true, the metal dragon did not possess the gift of breath, relying on its sheer strength and impenetrable skin to impose its will. It roared at the mine entrance and then clawed at the opening. Each swipe tore away a chunk of the mountain. The dragon tossed boulders aside as if mere pebbles. Ideria struggled to maintain her balance after each one hit the ground.

Short sword drawn, she pondered about her options. The thing's head was large enough to swallow three of her without effort. She had been lamenting her abnormal size moments ago, but now found herself to be as useless as a toddler next to this creature. Any sword strike would go unnoticed, any punch or kick would be no more effective than trying to tickle the beast. If she tried to yank it by the tail, she would be blessed with a popped joint or pulled muscle. Its tail, though.

The dragon was scaled with the gray metal of weathered armor, but it was scale, nonetheless. There was overlap and imperfections like any other reptile. Close to the tip of its tail, Ideria found a seam large enough to slide her sword in and pierce flesh. A tiny sword poking the tail of a monster? She hoped that it would be a sensitive spot, unused and unexpected. After all, a minor stub of her little toe always yielded much greater pain than a punch to the shoulder. She hoped this was something similar.

Cave opening now wide enough, the dragon paused in its demolition and tried to jam its head into the hole. It snapped its jaws and children screamed. This was the only motivation Ideria needed to test her theory. She ran to the tail—limp as the beast pressed its chest to the ground—and stabbed the flesh through the seam. It sank deeply enough to draw blood and she yanked it back out. Success!

Throwing about more chunks of rock, the dragon yanked its head from the mine entrance and roared. As soon as it turned its head, Ideria ran back into town. She did not look behind her; she knew very well it was chasing her. Instead, she looked forward and ran toward the area where lighting erupted from the ground. She hoped the streets would have been emptied of people by now, but there were still plenty running around. Panicked. Screaming. Injured. As she ran to where the others ran from, the lightning dragon stepped into the street, its head jerking as it moved its gaze from one running person to the next. There was a constant buzzing in between the cracks of thunder every time the dragon opened its mouth to release jagged bolts of electricity. Her skin tingled, but she pressed on, running even closer. She threw her sword.

Hitting a moving target with a sword while running was as easy as extending an index finger to point. That had been a part of the constant training she had been receiving all of her life from Grandfather Wahl, Uncle Draymon, Uncle Bartholomew, and the dozens of different fighting trainers they had brought to the farm over the years. She never thought she would have a need to use her learned skills, but she was happy to have them now as her sword flew through the air and pierced the lightning dragon's eye.

Roaring loud enough to shake the world around it, the dragon reared up on its hind legs and clawed at the sword stuck in its eye. After digging it out, the dragon dropped back to all fours and released its pain and fury with a blast of lightning upon the closest thing—the metal dragon.

With every blast of lightning, the metal dragon twisted its body in unnatural ways, a dance of agony. A blooming flower of light and death, a ball of electricity swirled around it as tendrils of lightning lashed out and left charred marks on the street and the buildings. The lightning dragon stopped its assault and pawed at its eye as it took flight. The metal dragon continued to screech with noises no living creature had ever made while twisting and folding in on itself. The arcs of electricity finally slowed and stopped. The dragon no longer resembled what it had been mere seconds ago, now a misshapen ball of metal, appendages warped beyond recognition. Thin streams of blood the color of melted pewter trickled along the street, the only evidence the heap of metal was once alive.

Ideria watched the death of the metal dragon play out before her from the shadows of an alleyway. The sweat from her brow turned to ice when she realized that she had just killed one of the king's dragons. The penalty for such an act was beyond her comprehension. She had hoped for a simple zap from the lightning dragon, one strong enough to discourage the metal dragon from continuing. Not this. Now, her life was forfeit and unspeakable tortures await her. "What have I done?"

"You stood up to tyranny." The man who had talked to her about the secret army emerged from deeper within the alley. His orc friend stood behind him but pointed to the street where the twisted remains of the metal dragon lay. "And saved lives."

Ideria looked at the product of her actions. Other towns-folk started to gather, men and women creeping out from their hiding spots to see if the danger had passed. They cringed, some even retreated back into the buildings they had come from when the king and his gem dragon landed next to the metal dragon. The dragon showed no interest in its fallen brethren. The king cried out as if he had lost a child and ran to the hunk of metal. "No! Nooooooo! Who did this? Where is the man who did this? Ten thousand coins for the person who brings him to me!"

Upon hearing the bounty the king just placed on her head, Ideria turned and clenched her fists. "Undoubtedly, you two will be very rich, but I'll make sure you have perma-nent injuries, though."

The orc walked past her to the edge of the alleyway and crouched as if getting ready to run. "Undoubtedly, you have yet to learn there are things more valuable than gold."

The human walked past her as well but paused to point at the other end of the alley. "At the end of the alley make a right. Drop your hood and let that pretty face get you out of this trouble."

The pair then ran from the alley to the right. The human yelled, "This way. I saw him go this way!"

"Get him!" the orc added.

Whether or not the townsfolk believed them or if they were all a part of the secret army reacting to two of their members hardly mattered at the moment. Those on the streets ran in the same direction as the human and the orc, all giving chase to a ghost. Even King Oremethus climbed on his gem dragon and pursued.

Grandfather, grandmother, and her uncles all taught her and Nevin to be wary, to trust no one outside of the family, lest they wished a dagger in their backs. Maybe there were still good people in a world where kings destroy their own villages? Whatever the motivation was to disregard an easy ten thousand gold coins, the two denizens gave Ideria an opportunity not only to flee but remain anonymous as well. Following the human's instructions, she ran the opposite direction down the alley and turned right. Nevin greeted her.

"You killed the metal dragon!"

"Hush! No one knows it was me, and I wish to keep it that way. How did you find me?"

"From where I was, I saw you dive into the alleyway. I was on my way around the back of the buildings."

"We've done all we can do. Let us go."

Despite wishing to forget this moment, for the entire trip back to the farm, Nevin lauded her with praises of killing a dragon.

Six

DAEDALUS LANDED THE dragon with such force that a fissure of pain shot down his back. The landing, the pain, was purposeful, part from the pressing need to be here, part from the anger caused by the need to be here. He was busy; too busy for this. The culmination of his Dearborn Day celebrations would be upon him soon, meaning he could finally reveal his revenge to the holiday's namesake so she could spend her remaining days alive cursing her own name. He needed to schedule time with Oremethus to yet again try to convince him to allow their armies greater use of the wizards and the dragons and that they could be used to hunt demons every day *after* they win the war. Despite their minimal use in a skirmish or battle that found itself too close to Albathian borders, the war should have ended years ago if not for the ineptitude of their generals, whom he had recently met with. The damnable country of Tsinel had but one dragon and one wizard worth anything! But it was a void dragon and a wizard who could summon portals—the only wizard with such power—and they were enough to confound any invasion tactic he and his generals attempted. He started the meeting by stripping his least effective general of title and turning him over Speekore. He promoted the next in line. A promotion always boosted morale before a planning meeting.

After sending Methel and his Elite Troop to hunt down Perciless, Daedalus needed to shift resources to fill the void of hunting down rogue wizards. There were still many rumors about wizards in Albathia which meant there were *too many* free wizards in Albathia. Those who dabbled in the mystical arts were too powerful—they had access to nefarious benefits unavailable to Daedalus. That was unacceptable. Within months of his brother taking his rightful place upon the throne, Prince Daedalus had performed his duty as an adviser and a good citizen of the crown and prepared an argument as to why sorcery should be banned unless they pledged to use their mystical crafts for the good of the crown. Daedalus had seen an opportunity to wield the power disallowed to him. Any captured wizard had a choice—declare fealty to the crown or die a horrible death. The wizards' guilds were raided and burned to the ground. The wizard population had been dwindling over the past decade, but there were still too many. Too many.

Today, he wished to spend time devising a plan, to take inventory of his available resources necessary to finish off the wizards once and for all, but he had no chance. His day had been ruined by Haddaman. Not even an hour after breakfast, his vision crystal glowed blue, and it filled with Haddaman's disgusting visage telling Daedalus that he was needed in this burgeoning mining town because of Oremethus and his obsession with demons.

Twenty years ago, Oremethus gained possession of The Satan Stone, one of the five ensorcelled stones used to shred the fabric between this world and Hell causing the Demon War. Because of the stone, the war, what he witnessed and lived through, Oremethus' mind shattered and reformed into one of singular purpose—find and kill demons. Daedalus learned quickly how to manipulate that obsession for his benefit. Of course, Daedalus could not control all aspects of his brother's degraded mental state. The demons were not real, they did not exist, but that never stopped Oremethus from seeing them and taking a couple of his dragons to destroy a town a few times each year. Why Haddaman was here in Orsrun, Daedalus would have to find out later. Now, he needed to meet with the town leader, if he were still alive. He was also curious if the events that had happened here had anything to do with why he could no longer feel the metal dragon in his mind, a sensation stripped from him earlier today.

Daedalus dismounted from his dragon. The beast stretched and fluttered its wings. Though made of bone, it still acted like any other creature of flesh and muscle.

Had he arrived on horse there would have been a reception party. Town leaders would have demonstrated their prowess at being sycophants, offering Daedalus anything he could want, as many assistants as he needed. That would have been if this were a more diplomatic reason for his visit. Instead of coming by horse and being lauded, he had to arrive by dragon and be feared. There was nothing wrong with being feared, though.

The number of years he had been alive asserted themselves in the form of aches in his joints and stiffness in his muscles. He stretched them away and undid the first few clasps of his riding leathers—black snakeskin with polished white bone sewn into the coat and pants to loosely mimic the skeleton within. Even though his saddle was crafted for comfort, it was still a long ride between Phenomere and Orsrun. Even his hand hurt.

He removed the padded leather gauntlet from his left hand and stretched his fingers. There was no true need to wear one on his right hand, yet he wore one to complete the aesthetic of his riding outfit. From his elbow to his fingertips was bone. He wiggled his skeletal fingers, unable to feel the sensation, but admired the action. The dark arts of wizardry grew these bones from a once severed stump. To this day, it still amazed him.

No town leader had yet come to greet him. Whomever that had been must be dead. No matter. Daedalus would just have to handle the situation, just as he always did. First, he needed to handle his brother.

Oremethus was easy to find; after all, he was standing between two dragons. At the edge of town, the king and his creatures had their backs to it. Shoulders slumped, the king sulked. The gemstone dragon sat straight and perfectly still. The lightning dragon sat as well but used the back of its front claw to fuss with its eye. Daedalus approached. "Oremethus?"

The king sighed. He looked off into the horizon but addressed his brother. "There were demons here, Daedalus."

"I know, brother. I know."

"Dangerous ones. Tricky ones. They tricked my dragons to turn on each other."

Daedalus looked around. "How many did you bring?"

"Three. But these demons were tricky."

"You said. What happened?"

"The metal one is dead."

Dead? Of all the dragons they had, Daedalus had always assumed the metal one would have been the hardest to kill. Maybe this was truly the work of demons? Daedalus pushed that thought aside. It had been twenty years since he last saw a demon. Logic dictated that there must have been other factors in play. "How did the metal one die?"

Oremethus finally moved his attention away from the distance and stroked the shimmering scales of the lightning dragon. "The demons tricked the lightning out of this one. Tricked it into unleashing its fury on the metal one."

Daedalus walked around the dragon and looked at what it was fussing over. A wound. Its eye had been wounded, stabbed as Daedalus surmised. A wounded animal would lash out, especially one not used to being hurt. Although a person clever enough to trick one dragon into killing another was a demon in their own right, Daedalus doubted that a denizen of Hell was the culprit today.

"I saw them, Daedalus. I saw them skirting between the buildings, flitting from shadow to shadow. But I was too slow. I'm always too slow. I destroyed another town and have nothing to show for it."

Daedalus had no care for the town. He barely knew it existed before today. What he did care about were the dragons. They were one of the few things nature got right, one of the few things Daedalus admired. They were also the thrust of his conquest machine. They kept the people afraid and aided his troops in battle whenever his brother deemed it necessary for them to be involved. Daedalus had many plans for the metal dragon and now had to alter them all.

One thing still buzzed around his mind like a gnat—why did his brother attack this town, and why now? Usually, when Oremethus discovered "demons" within a town, it was after some research, after making his own deductions. This attack seemed more impulsive. Either his brother was traipsing further away from sanity, or he, like the lightning dragon, was tricked. "How did you discover this town had demons lurking within it?"

"Haddaman told me. He contacted my vision crystal and told me about the demons in this town. He was here—he's still here—and told me he saw demons."

"Haddaman, you say? I believe I'll have to exchange words with him. Now, you head back to the castle, and we'll discuss this demon hunt in more detail later. I will address the people of Orsrun."

Oremethus mounted the gemstone dragon, and then looked down to his brother. "He was right, Daedalus. Haddaman was right. There were demons in this town. I saw them but couldn't stop them."

As the dragons took flight, Daedalus muttered, "I have no doubt in my mind that you believe that, dear brother. No doubt in my mind."

Haddaman was going to die today. Daedalus did not know if his bone dragon had the sensation of taste. If it did, then Daedalus would feel bad for giving the command to eat the stumped body of Haddaman Crede and the rotting minotaur carcass. First, he needed to address the town.

Daedalus strode along the main road and entered town, but paused when he saw the twisted remains of the metal dragon. Even in death, the thing was magnificent. He would be sure to retain that magnificence in the form of using its scales for new armor and the underlying skin for new riding leathers.

Since Orsrun was a newer mining town it lacked many of the customary buildings. No town hall, no central meeting place, not even a dais to stand upon. No matter. Daedalus walked to the center of town, to the intersection of the two largest roads and called out, "People of Orsrun! Gather before me."

The citizens stopped working on cleaning away the debris and started to assemble before him. Over a hundred weary faces looked upon him, a few tired bodies swayed as they struggled to stay upright. The town was home to more, but this was plenty. What he had to say would disseminate among the populace. "People of Orsrun! Your king did you a great service today."

Murmurs made their way through the crowd, no single voice heard above any other. None would dare. They all knew who Daedalus was, all heard the rumors and stories. He let the rumblings die down before he continued. "We had heard this town hosted traitors to the crown, scoundrels, and cutthroats willing to sacrifice your integrity, your way of life to support my treacherous brother, Perciless. The king deemed that the population of filthy traitors became so great in this town that he needed to personally see them eradicated."

Daedalus paced with his hands folded behind his back, slow, measured steps so he could watch their faces as he spoke. A few had shifted from anger to concern. Had he the time and resources, he could have ferreted out whom within this crowd was truly a part of Perciless' secret cabal. Ever since Oremethus had taken the crown, Daedalus had been fighting against two kings; the king of Tsinel protected within castle walls, and his brother, Perciless, a nomadic king who ruled from the shadows and more of a legend than any religious myth passed down from parent to child. But Daedalus did not visit Orsrun to suss out traitors. He meant to turn his brother's mistake into an opportunity to spread discord.

He paused in his pacing just long enough to pick up a stray brick from the debris with his skeleton hand. "Unfortunately, the king had to use drastic means. If gangrene affects the hand, one must cut off the arm. Sometimes the arm can be replaced with something stronger." To demonstrate, he crushed the brick to pebbles. The crowd winced, the message received.

Daedalus brushed his hands together and went back to pacing. "This whole incident could have been avoided if there were any of you brave enough or smart enough to have let our dear king know of such maleficence. In fact, you would have been rewarded for such loyalty as would anyone who would come forth with information about who killed my dragon."

Knowing how the rest of the events would play out, he stopped pacing to don his riding gloves and let the crowd whisper amongst itself. From somewhere in the center of the crowd a voice called out, "He was wearing a cloak. No one could see who it was."

Daedalus nodded, moderately impressed someone had the courage to speak. "Fair enough. I shall be off. The crown extends its regrets that it had to get involved the way it did."

As the crowd dispersed, he remembered one last thing. "Oh! Deliver the remains of the dragon to Castle Phenomere. There will be coin waiting for you."

Haddaman was easy enough to find. Daedalus needed merely to explore the roads behind the main buildings to find his advisor. A wagon large enough to necessitate eight horses to pull, tented by walls of purple velvet with gold filigree and tassels stood out in a town like this. Despite its ostentatiousness, it was still less noticeable than the abomination it hid. Daedalus yanked the back flap open and was assaulted by the stench carried on the burst of humidity. The minotaur sat in the middle of the wagon, legs crossed with Haddaman looking like a slime-swaddled baby on its lap.

Haddaman welcomed Daedalus, the minotaur's hands spreading with invitation. "Greeting, my liege."

"What are you doing here?"

"Doing what I always do, my lord, making important discoveries while skulking about shadows and alleyways."

"Making discoveries meant summoning my brother to this town?"

"It did."

"Why?"

"Oh, to make some very, very delicious discoveries, indeed."

"Do not assume you will live past this conversation. You have been an adequate enough adviser and information gatherer, but your value to me rests with what you can provide for me in the future, not what you've done for me in the past. You will need to move your tongue faster to supply an adequate explanation as to why you have interjected yourself into my busy schedule, subsequently getting one of the king's dragons killed."

"I assure you, my prince, I have garnered information you will find most valuable. Maybe the most valuable ever, I predict. I know who killed your metal dragon."

"Bold words from a creature whose life is about to end."

"It will not end today." For being so large and dead, the minotaur's hand moved with grace and gently held out a vision stone. The edges of the stone glowed blue while a perfectly clear image of a young woman's face filled the center.

"By the gods," Daedalus whispered. "If not for the blonde hair, I would have mistaken her for Dearborn of yesteryear."

The image flickered and changed to a new one. The vision crystal now showed the young woman in a cloak with a young man. "I would be remiss if I didn't tell you that her traveling companion has an uncanny resemblance to Dearborn's late husband."

Children? Dearborn had children? Daedalus snatched the stone and cupped it with both hands. This. This would be his ultimate revenge against Dearborn. Oh, the horrors he would perform on these two in front of their mother! He laughed a shrill maniacal noise that sounded alien even to his own ear. "Oh, my dear advisor, your bold prediction was correct. This is indeed valuable, valuable information."

Platitudes started to roll from Haddaman's mouth, but Daedalus had no interest in hearing them. He turned a deaf ear and left the tent. He strode back into the center of town with purpose. "People of Orsrun! Gather around once more."

The people assembled, trepidation within their movements, concern upon their faces. While they gathered before him, his bone dragon made its way through the streets, tucking its wings to squeeze between the buildings, and stopped behind him. The people gasped and angled their bodies as if to run.

A few dozen people stood before him. There were more filing in, but this was enough. It had to be. He was losing patience and wanted answers now. He held out the vision crystal and walked close enough to those before him for all to see the image. He did a single pass and then stood next to his dragon. He pointed to the person closest to him, an old man in the early stages of developing a permanent stoop. "You. Who are these two?"

The old man shook his head. "I'm sorry your grace, but I don't kno—"

The dragon breathed on the man, a stream of white dust. The crowd screamed as the old man shriveled like a plum shrinking to a prune. His skin sloughed away, and his organs slipped free. All that remained was a skeleton, the clothes falling to the ground or hanging from the bones.

The old man was no longer alive, but the skeleton still moved, and it grabbed the person closest to it. A woman long past her birthing years, blubbering and falling to the ground. Daedalus asked her, "Who are these two?"

She shook her head and brought her hands together in prayer. "Pl . . . please . . . I don't . . . please . . . ."

The dragon breathed on her. Before her transformation to a skeletal servant was finished, Daedalus moved onto the next person the crowd. The people cried and screamed and held each other, but none of them ran. Daedalus had been a prince all of his life and knew his subjects, knew they were too afraid to move, fearing that there might be some punishment worse than what he was doing to them now. But before he could ask the question a third time, a voice came from the crowd. "I know! I know who they are."

The crowd parted for the two skeletons as they made their way to the lone woman in the center. They each grabbed an arm and marched her closer to Daedalus. "Who are they?"

"I don't . . . I don't know their names, but I over-heard them talking while they were at my stand. I'm . . .

I'm the blacksmith's wife and they were at my stand this morning, talking. They mentioned the Wahl's being their grandparents."

"The Wahl's. Where do they live?"

"A farm. A double farm, actually. Five . . . five miles that way."

A collective sigh of relief rippled through the crowd when the skeletons released the woman. Daedalus mounted his dragon and it took flight, snatching up the two skeletons with its claws once it became air born. Meetings and plans and wizards and war be damned. Even Perciless. Nothing was more important than introducing himself to Dearborn's children.

SEVEN

IDERIA RUBBED HER temples. All the bickering made her eyes cross. As soon as she and Nevin walked through the door after their trip to Orsrun, both of their grandparents sensed something amiss. Even though there was no Wahl blood in her veins, Ideria wondered if they had a direct connection to her mind. There certainly was one to her heart, because hers broke while Grandmother cried during Nevin's recounting of the tale.

Nevin reported all the details as mere facts, a dry reporting as if he had heard the story from a friend of a friend. No sooner than he finished, Grandfather collected Uncle Draymon and Uncle Bartholomew and he had Nevin tell it again, this time even more stoically. Arguing ensued. The first few rounds, Ideria participated, but no one changed their minds, simply restating their opinion in different ways and different volumes. She remained perfectly quiet for over half an hour and her disappearance from the conversation failed to alter it one iota.

"This is fantastic!" Bartholomew added emphasis to his statement by slapping the table they sat around. "Our Ideria single-handedly killed one of the king's dragons. We should be celebrating this, not arguing about it."

"She took unnecessary risks," Draymon countered.

"And potentially exposed herself," Grandfather added.

"We couldn't stand by and do nothing," Nevin said, his calm tone never once wavering.

Grandmother's response to his words never varied either. She put her hands on one of Nevin's and one of Ideria's and said, "You two are so brave and selfless."

"Don't encourage that behavior, Marrim," Grandfather scolded. "Such actions will lead them to an early grave. There is a reason why Bard's sing about the bravery and selflessness of heroes. It's because the heroes can't do it themselves."

Bartholomew huffed and rolled his eyes. "We should be elated that they followed our training so well. The first time fate calls upon them to use their skills, they performed beyond what we could have hoped for. Beyond what any of us who trained them can do. If we didn't want them to stand up to the king, then why did we bother training them?"

Draymon answered, "To make sure they had a fighting chance against the king if he or his brother ever found out they existed. Certainly not to traverse the kingdom as dragon slayers."

Of her two "uncles," Ideria favored Draymon over Bartholomew. They were both over twice her age, and their tired faces and gray hair showed it. However, Draymon possessed an air of a more traditional instructor. The wrinkles on his face came from the consternation of having students. Pulled back into a ponytail, his brown hair was streaked with many strands of white, but his eyes still held the brightness of wonder, still curious and ready to absorb everything the world had to offer. He also had the willingness to share it. Bartholomew had gray around his temples, and a permanent squint hiding his dark eyes. He had learned from the world as well, but rather ways to exploit his skills for the betterment of his coin pouch. He had certainly taught Ideria and Nevin plenty over the years, but she desperately hoped that world beyond the nearby towns wasn't as duplicitous as he always made it out to be.

A wicked smile accompanied the newly sparked glimmer in Bartholomew's eyes. "There is a hefty sum of coin to be made in dragon slaying."

Grandmother huffed. "Rogue!"

Bartholomew shrugged a shoulder, barely acknowledging her comment. It was an accurate one. He and Draymon met over a decade ago, partnering for well-paying jobs. One such job was commissioned by King Perciless himself, back when he sat on the throne. During that mission, they crossed paths with Dearborn and Diminutia, and joined them to fight against the king's invading brothers. They lost—the whole country of Albathia lost—as King Perciless abdicated his throne and barely escaped with his life. Dearborn and Diminutia were not as fortunate. Draymon and Bartholomew had a change of heart and dedicated their lives to keep the children of Diminutia and Dearborn hidden from Perciless's brothers. And to help Captain Wahl train them.

The two mercenaries went about their lessons differently. Draymon aided Wahl in teaching Ideria and Nevin weaponry and fighting styles, Bartholomew's lessons involved sleight of hand and stealth. When Ideria and Nevin mastered what their guardians had to teach, Draymon and Bartholomew sought out masters of various disciplines from all over the country. As with their personalities, they each prioritized their beliefs. Draymon brought warriors, Bartholomew brought scoundrels. Grandmother disapproved of scoundrels spending evenings in her house. Over the years, not a single guest caused any sort of trouble, even the ones too fond of ales and mead but nevertheless, Grandmother disapproved.

"Gaining coin is hardly the goal," Grandfather said.

"Then what is?" Ideria was surprised that it was her voice. "keeping us hidden away from the world?"

"Ideria . . . ," Draymon started. She wanted none of his words. She had heard them all before, again and again, so she stood up from the table and walked to the window. This was how she lived her life — separate from the world, only able to look at it through a window. Behind her, she heard her brother pleading her case for her, explaining her feelings since she was unable to articulate them well, like a cross-eyed simpleton walking down the streets needing the aid of a loved one to translate her blathering to anyone she tried to talk to. She was frustrated and disappointed with her grandmother the most. Men were far simpler, content to be rigid trunks and boughs while women were more flexible and freer, dandelion puffs excited by the strongest breeze to take them from where they were born. Had her grandmother never been a seed upon the wind? Did she not understand Ideria's needs? Alas, these musings were pointless. Her grandmother agreed with Ideria's actions in Orsrun, but she would never defend them, never agree to her leaving the farms and setting out on her own.

Everyone argued. She and Nevin either did the right thing or the wrong thing at Orsrun. No! They had done the right thing. These four raised her and her brother after their parents died, teaching them right from wrong. Saving people was right. It was that simple. No more watching the world from behind a window. Determined to make her thoughts and feelings known, she organized her arguments, but it took too long. The window was supposed to show her a better life, a world for her to explore. Instead, the window showed her doom. Prince Daedalus arrived.

Fear. He was the personification of fear, the kind that oozed through her body and locked her joints. Her eyes widened past the point of pain, and her whole body quaked. She could only stare.

The dragon's presence caused the livestock to fuss. All the animals ran to the corners of their respective pens and stalls to cower, too terrified to make even the slightest sound. Daedalus dismounted and removed his riding gloves to expose that dreadful skeletal arm of his.

"Ideria?"

She heard her name, even recognized that it was her grandmother's voice, but she had no faculties to respond to it. She could only watch Daedalus walk toward the house.

"Ideria, are you . . . ? Oh . . . ! Oh, by the gods! Ideria, please, we must hide you. We must hide you and your brother now."

"What? What is it, Marrim?" Grandfather called out as everyone stood, bodies tensing in alarm.

"Prince Daedalus is here. He came on that damnable bone dragon, and he brought skeletons."

Skeletons? How did she not notice the moving, walking skeletons? The cold emptiness of the dark holes of bare skulls. Staring at her. Through her. Did they see her? Were they capable of seeing? Such conjectures mattered little at the moment—the prince drew closer.

Hands grabbed at Ideria, pulled at her. Bartholomew and Draymon guided her and Nevin to the backroom and closed the door. They each raised their index finger to their lips. Even if Ideria had the propensity to speak, she was smart enough not to do so even though she disliked the idea of leaving her grandparents at the mercy of a madman while two of the men who trained her how to fight were looking for a means of escape. She wanted to be out there, and so should they.

The back room was used as a bedroom for Ideria and Nevin. Bartholomew and Nevin found rucksacks and filled them with clothes as quietly as possible. Draymon wrapped his hand with a shirt and stood next to the window. Ideria inched closer to the door, knowing there was a gap between the door itself and the frame just wide enough to see through.

Daedalus burst through the front door.

Grandmother screamed in surprise and Grandfather yelled, "Hey!"

"Where are they?" the prince screamed, eyes bulging, face beet red.

Grandmother dropped to one knee and bowed her head. "Your Highness! I assure you that we do not know what you mean."

"You do, you lying bitch! Where are they?"

"Your Highness!" Grandfather barked. He held his hands out while backing away. It seemed like an act of fearfulness, but he was making his way toward the wall with a sword on display. "Please. I once served in the army of your father. My wife and I now farm. We pay our taxes in full and on time. We do our part to support the kingdom as your citizens. All we ask this very moment is that you explain what you are looking for so we may help you find it."

"*What* I'm looking for?" The Prince walked toward Grandfather while the skeletons clattered their way to Grandmother. The old woman raised her head. Her eyes went wide and then she went back to looking at the floor. Grandfather continued to back away from the approaching prince. "Don't play coy with me, old man. You know very well I seek no 'what,' but instead 'who.' If I must play your silly game for no other reason than to speed up this process, then so be it. Where are the children of Dearborn Stillheart?"

"No!" Grandmother shouted.

Daedalus snapped his fingers and his skeletons tore into the old woman. Her clothing, her skin, shredded. The skeletons tossed aside bloodied chunks of meat, borrowing deeper to the bones. Her screams were brief.

Grandfather roared as he grabbed the sword from the wall and slashed at the prince. The younger man parried the attack with ease, using his skeletal hand to slap the sword away. Keeping his bone fingers tight together, Daedalus thrust his hand upward from underneath Grandfather's jaw, shoving it into his skull as if stuffing a game bird for dinner.

Ideria screamed and burst from the backroom. She had no plan, no rational thought. Her grandparents were gone and those who took them were still here. As soon as she entered the main room, she grabbed the dining table and lifted it over her head. She slammed it down on the skeletons, the impact rattling the windows. Wasting no time to celebrate or regain her wits, she grabbed Grandfather's sword and hacked at the prince. Her attack was as ineffective as her grandfather's.

Daedalus caught the blade with his skeletal hand and pulled her close. His smile grew like an infected lesion, wider and wider, almost consuming his entire face. Using both hands, she attempted to wrest the sword from his grip, but her attempt was futile. He pulled her close enough for his breath to burn her cheeks. "You look exactly like her. I'm going to enjoy killing you in front of her."

Ideria froze. The mention of her mother stopped her assault. She could see pure bliss in his eyes as thought about killing as if he were a poet expounding about his sadistic love of her death. A thin trail of saliva ran from the corner of his disgusting smile. Grandfather's sword crumbled like cheap tin in the prince's skeletal hand. For the first time in her life, Ideria knew true fear, the feeling that weakened her bones and shattered her joints.

"Ideria!" A figure blurred past her and slammed into Daedalus hard enough to knock him to the ground. "Run!"

She knew the word, knew the concept, but her legs refused to comply until Draymon grabbed her arm and pulled. Bartholomew pushed her along as they ran to the back room, to the opened window. "Nevin's already in the shed."

The shed. She and her brother had been trained for this moment. She knew they were living within the shadow of danger, but never fathomed that it was the king's brother who cast it. Out the window was escape.

Bartholomew pushed her through the window while Draymon pulled. She flopped onto the ground, but Draymon grabbed her arm and pulled her to her feet. To the shed. Nevin was already inside waiting for her, reaching for her. She stumbled through the door, her shoulder burning from being pulled, and tumbled into the hole. The entrance to the tunnel was sloped and she slid on her hip the whole way down. Nevin landed next to her, but with much more grace and control, and immediately grabbed her to help her to her feet.

The bone dragon roared. It was close enough to shake the ground. Dirt fell from the ceiling. Shouting from Draymon and Bartholomew. Their voices growing louder. Nevin pulled at Ideria, guiding her deeper into the tunnel.

Another roar. More yelling. Ideria hated not being able to help. She so desperately wanted to run back up the slope and finish the fight. But that was not to be. Two bodies fell down the slope. Bartholomew and Draymon. They were both alive and as soon as they hit the ground, they each kicked at a support beam. With little impact, the beams cracked and, by design, gave way to the ground immediately above the sloped entrance. If the shed did what it was constructed to do, it would collapse on top of the controlled cave-in, making it even more difficult for them to be followed. Even if Daedalus and his dragon cleared away the detritus, all they would be greeted with was a large divot in the ground.

The tunnels. As part of their exercise routines growing up, Ideria and Nevin worked on digging these tunnels, at least once a day. She hated it, every single second of hacking at the earth with a dull pick and scooping it away with a flimsy spade. Now, she thanked every god whose name she could remember that she had a route to flee.

There was no light, no sound but the ragged panting of four people who had their lives destroyed in a matter of minutes. Keeping her fingers gliding along the wall, Ideria moved deeper into the tunnel. Almost to the precise number of paces, she found what she knew to be there. A box containing torches and flint.

Ideria lit four small torches and distributed them. No one spoke, the looks of anger and loss on dirt-stained and bloodied faces said more than words could articulate. It was enough that they had lived through the ordeal, they did not need to discuss it and were not in a position to mourn their losses yet. They were still too close to the prince, muffled noises of dragon clawing at the ground came from above. She was content to follow while Draymon and Bartholomew led the way. She wanted to quiet her mind, push away the horrors she had just witnessed, allow her heart to grieve the people who had been her grandparents for the past decade, but one question loomed so large it allowed no room for any other thought: *Did Prince Daedalus imply that my mother was still alive?*

EIGHT

LANDYR WAS HAVING a pretty good morning until Rolin's head exploded.

A simple day of shopping in the market. It was easy to forget that he was on a perpetual mission to protect the king and save the world. It was easy to forget that he was a general to the man next to him and not his friend. They should have been sparring, not attempting to find the ripest melon in the bushel. Due to his forgotten priorities, Rolin's headless body fell to the ground and the other patrons close enough to have witnessed it began to panic.

Landyr ducked behind the produce stand just as more blood splashed on him. The chest of a man next to him blew apart. Two notched sticks of gleaming metal were lodged deeply into the building behind him. How could two feather-less arrows have caused so much damage? A streak of blue punching a fiery hole into a nearby cart answered his question.

An archer on the rooftop of the building across the street. As he drew back the bowstring, crackling blue energy swirled around the arrow. It glowed brilliantly as it flew through the air. Landyr dove from behind the fruit stand just as it exploded.

The barrel he now hid behind offered little in the way of protection. It was not large enough to obscure his entire body and he doubted it would serve well as any form of shield against iron arrows carrying blue explosive magic.

He absolutely hated magic, so unpredictable and extremely difficult to fight against. The one saving grace about magic was the wielder was still a being of flesh and blood. Flesh and blood were still no match for tooth and claw.

Cezomir, the werewolf never able to turn human again, scaled the outside of the building across the street and reached the roof with such speed that the archer had no time to react. The beast set his teeth into the archer's neck while dismembering his fresh kill. Unfortunately, after tossing the body parts over the side, Cezomir snapped the bow in half. Landyr hated magic, but he would have loved to have gotten his hands on that weapon.

Doubting that this was a random act of a lone zealot bereft of motivation, Landyr peered around the barrel to assess the situation. The market patron with the hole in his chest the only civilian fatality and the last of the screaming market goers were fleeing the streets. Except for one—a hobgoblin down the street aiming a glowing blue arrow at him. Landyr was slammed to the ground just as a streak of crackling blue zipped by his face.

Thorna. Despite almost dying, or perhaps because of it and the accompanying rush of newly heightened senses, Landyr was acutely aware of Thorna straddling his body. Her thighs pressing against him, the smell of mint within her long, brown hair tickling his face, her ass against his crotch. "Let me up."

They were behind another produce cart. Thorna never looked away from where the attack came and gripped the cart edge for support, but she did as commanded. As she moved along the length of the cart in a crouch, the thick leather of her pants pulled tight, accentuating her hips. She was too distracting. If he lived through this, he would need to find some form of release. He was in the mood for a centaur lass. It had been quite some time since he had been with one, so he would have to check the local brothels to see if there were any available. That was *if* he got out of this alive.

Another bolt of blue light flashed over their heads and hit something behind them close enough for Landyr to feel the heat of the explosion. Glancing over the cart, he wondered how quickly the hobgoblin could reload such an extraordinary device. No time at all apparently, as the hobgoblin had the bow drawn all the way back, the new projectile swirling with blue light.

Returning the favor of saving his life, Landyr pushed Thorna away and then jumped in the opposite direction. Curled on the ground with his arms covering his head, Landyr braced for the explosion, readying himself for a flash of fire, or at the very least the flaming remains of the cart to rain down upon him.

Nothing.

Still protecting his head with his arms, he opened one eye. No fire. No destroyed cart. He opened his other eye. As still as a statue, Thorna stared straight ahead with her mouth agape.

Landyr thought she might be ensorcelled, coerced by dark magic to stand perfectly still while the archer took aim. But with the weapon like that, there was no need to aim to hit the target. He hurried to Thorna, and reached for her to rouse her from her stupor, but stopped short when he saw what captured her attention. Cezomir.

The werewolf had taken care of this assailant as well. As with the one on the rooftop, Cezomir had broken the enchanted bow and separated the hobgoblin's torso from his waist. The hobgoblin's lower half dangled from the beast's left hand, all but forgotten. The arms jiggled every time Cezomir shoved his snout into the hobgoblin's ribcage, the torso in the beast's right hand.

Getting his fill of the organs found within the shell, Cezomir dropped both halves. Sticky green hobgoblin blood stained his muzzle while small chunks of meat slopped to the ground from his claws. Even though Cezomir insisted that there was still a human element within him, Landyr often wondered how much. Looking at this beast now, he assumed the percentage to be quite small. Any thoughts of scolding the werewolf for destroying the mysterious weapons of the enemy evaporated from his head like spilled water in the desert.

Uncertain as to how close to the surface the animal within came, Landyr addressed his travel companion with a simple, "Thank you for saving us."

Cezomir used both hands to wipe the goblin slop from his face and tongue to lap it away. "Thank you for setting up the delicacy for me. Hobgoblins are such unique creatures—disgusting and foul on the outside, but so delectable on the inside."

Thorna's face turned a shade of green that almost mimicked the hobgoblin's skin. Bringing her hand to her mouth, she looked toward the rooftops. "We must be wary. They were clearly together, so there may be more."

"I agree. We need to protect King Perciless, first and then try to figure out who . . . ?" Landyr's question faded away as the answer came to him. The hobgoblin wore loose black clothing with leather strips to bind it to his body. It was a uniform. Even before Cezomir's influence, the clothing was dirty and torn, but it was a uniform nonetheless, with a sigil emblazoned on the metal of his accessories. The Elite Troop of the King's army. Landyr wore a similar emblem.

When Perciless sat on the throne in Castle Phenomere, only the best and bravest of the best and bravest wore the mark of the Elite Troop. Now that Oremethus was king, he altered the emblem and gave an Elite Troop position to those who were the deadliest, most lecherous. Not a single member now had any form of honor, only happy to hunt and kill whoever the king told them to. As of late, Landyr had heard tales that the Elite Troop spent their days hunting and killing wizards. Obviously, they had a new objective. "He's a member of Oremethus' Elite Troop. Get everyone together. We're leaving now."

Thorna started to walk toward the headless body of their comrade. "What about Rolin? We can't just—"

Landyr grabbed her arm. "We have to. We will mourn him, and we will recount stories of him over drinks, but we cannot take him with us. The townsfolk will either burn him or bury him. That's the best we can hope for."

"But—"

"If Perciless dies then Rolin's sacrifice will become mean-ingless as would the past ten years."

Without so much as a glance toward Landyr, she turned on her heel and led Cezomir away. Landyr's guts twisted from the loss. Having spent every single day with a person for a decade while traveling half a continent, shifted labels from "subordinate" to "friend" even "family." Rolin would be missed. Later. Now, Landyr had to do some reconnaissance. Were these archers with the mystical bows the only repre-sentatives of the Elite Force? Were they scouts? Assassins?

A threat still remained. He could feel it. The townsfolk felt it, too, none coming out of the surrounding buildings, their sense of survival outweighing their curiosity. Landyr drew his sword, his muscles tensed. Stepping in slow circles, he eyed the tops of the buildings as he moved down the street, the same direction his colleagues had run. Any alleyway he passed, he paused to see if there was anything suspicious, then moved on. It would take some time to meet up with the others, but he had to make sure no one followed them.

He had been involved with the military in some capac-ity for two-thirds of his life, his thirtieth year alive having been celebrated a few months ago within the sheets of a satyr prostitute. These past ten years on the run without any formal discipline or ways to train had made him dull. He needed the help of a few hidden citizens screaming for him to duck to avoid the battle ax.

Dropping to his knees, Landyr felt the rush of air over his head. Tuck. Roll. At least a few innate reflexes still lived within him. Back on his feet, he readied his sword and got a better look at his assailant. Another hobgoblin. But this one didn't look like the other two and possessed no ensor-celled weapons, just a half-rusted battle ax and a slightly bent dagger.

The hobgoblin's plate mail looked as if it had been forged by a blind smith. Dents and pockmarks infested the metal in between the random folds. The armor was not fitted over his arms and chest, rather his torso shoved into it. Patches of calloused green skin grew over, through, and around the armor, even along his hands. The armor did not extend below his chest, his thick leather pants seemed to cover only flesh. But the armor extended upward, strips of metal creeping along his neck and face. A dull, silver band wrapped around his head, embedded in his gnarled skin, with only two holes available for his bulging eyes. It hissed as it raised its ax and charged.

Too used to sparring with his comrades or raiding a poorly guarded army supply chain now and again, Landyr was ill prepared for the ferocity of his attacker. He took one step back for every three the hobgoblin took forward. He still had a bit of intuition, though, ducking the battle-ax again. It struck the stone wall of the nearby building hard enough to make the hobgoblin yelp in pain, but he did not drop the ax as Landyr had hoped, and it still had the wherewithal to stab with his dagger. The jab came from an awkward angle and Landyr dodged it with ease, but he was too close to use his own sword, so he lowered his shoulder into the creature's chest and shoved as hard as he could. He pushed his attacker backward and tried to take advantage of his offensive press. He slashed three times, each strike blocked by the ax.

Landyr ran.

Cursing his lackadaisical attitude toward training these past few years, Landyr thought his legs were faster, remembered his cuts and turns to be quicker. He ran between buildings and down alleyways, timing his spins to swing his blade at his pursuer. The ax was large, and it slowed the hobgoblin, the price of wielding such a piece. Landyr found a road that led out of town, through a field to a nearby forest. He hoped to outrace the hobgoblin to the nearby forest and find a tactical advantage there. He was wrong.

The hobgoblin was losing speed but still had enough strength to throw his ax, the handle striking Landyr between the shoulders. Fighting through the pain and the following momentum, he tucked his head and rolled. Back on his feet, he faced his adversary. Like in town, the hobgoblin's attacks were furious and unrelenting. Basic jabs and slices with his dagger, Landyr blocked or dodged them with ease, but had no opening to make any true offensive of his own. The only times the hobgoblin stopped attacking was to reach for the battle-ax on the ground, but Landyr kicked it away each time. The fight went on for too long and his energy waned. He could not keep the hobgoblin at a far enough distance and a well-placed punch knocked him to the ground.

Landyr was dazed. No, he was tired. His body might not have moved as fast as it once did, but it was his soul that had given up. He had been a nomad for so long, traveling with a secret king who went from town to town preaching dead ideas like a counterfeit messiah. A soldier fought for his country, something tangible, something real. Fighting for a possibility, for a dream that dissipated every time he reached for it, was not for him. He had nothing to fight for. The hobgoblin sensed it and ran his pulpy tongue over the slivers of steel fused to his lips as his eyes grew even wider.

Landyr debated about closing his eyes as the hobgoblin retrieved his ax but with his last strip of soldier's dignity, he would meet his end, greet his release, with his eyes open. That decision changed his life.

The air rippled behind the hobgoblin. So briefly Landyr assumed it to be some thick vapors caused by an unknown source of heat. Then it split open as if the sky itself opened its maw to yawn. Or a window letting salvation through in the form of a dragon.

Blacker than the void of nothingness, it flew through, wings spread wide. Within one flap, the dragon tucked them against its body, scales so dark the delineation between wing and body disappeared. Like a lightning strike, the dragon attacked, clamping its jaws shut so fast that the hobgoblin had no idea he died. The dragon could have swallowed the hobgoblin whole but decided to chew on him while it settled on the ground.

It was her.

It was his love.

It was Chenessa.

She was as beautiful as the last time he had seen her ten years ago when she first became the dragon. Not so much became the dragon, he reminded himself, but rather possessed the void dragon. Chenessa was a shadow demon born in the pits of Hell after all. However, she was unable to free herself from the dragon. Even if she wanted to, it made no sense in light of the current state of the world. She was one of the reasons why the country of Tsinel had been fighting King Oremethus to a stalemate these many years instead of falling to his army of skeletons. Of course, never far behind was the other reason—Silver.

Hovering in the air, close to the still opened portal, was the wizard Silver. He, too, no longer inhabited his own body. Instead, his essence was forever trapped in the wretched body of an ancient wizard, one of shimmering green skin and glowing red eyes. The body had only a torso, head and arms; organs and lengths of entrails hung freely as if in an abattoir's display case from tattered black robes.

Landyr hated wizards. After all, the mad wizard Wyren brought the Demon War upon the world twenty years ago, and the equally mad wizard Qual fused the twelve World Builders with dragon eggs ten years ago, which led to the ascension to power by Oremethus and Daedalus, possibly the maddest of the bunch. Sure, Silver aided in bringing an end to the Demon War and possibly saved the world by inhabiting Qual's body, but Landyr hated him because he got to be with Chenessa.

"Chenessa," Landyr whispered.

The dragon swallowed what she had been chewing and shook her head, neck and shoulders rippling as well. The ridge of spines running from the base of her head to the center of her back turned crimson red, the color of fresh blood. The scales running parallel to the ridge shifted to red as well, giving the illusion of long, flowing hair. Like she had when she was a dark elf.

Landyr had met her ten years ago while he was a member of King Perciless' Elite Troop, on a mission to find missing children. Chenessa had been a dark elf with long, blood red hair, the hair that had haunted his dreams these past many years.

"Beautiful."

Chenessa bowed her head and looked away. Her voice vibrated the ground he lay upon, yet remained feminine, enticing. "Thank you."

"How did you know I needed you?"

She swung her head back around. Her black eyes were one shade different than the blackness of her scales. "I felt it."

"Take me with you."

"That would be no life for you."

"*This* is no life for me." Landyr sniffled and realized he was crying.

Chenessa brought her head close enough for Landyr to lean his forehead against her snout between her nostrils. Her forked tongue snaked from her mouth and ran along his chest, his neck, his cheek. As it glided along, Landyr cupped it with both hands and licked it as it passed over his face. The taste of charcoal and death sent his eyes rolling back into his head with ecstasy.

Chenessa took flight and left him with, "After Daedalus has been defeated and Perciless returned to his throne."

Before Landyr could shout any farewells, Chenessa and Silver disappeared into the closing portal.

Panting, he took a moment to collect himself. He needed to rejoin the group and make plans to leave this place quickly. However, when he rolled over, his erection swelled to the point of pain and he decided to find a nearby tree to hide behind so he could relieve the pressure.

NINE

DRAYMON WORRIED ABOUT the kids. It had been over half an hour since they left the tunnels behind and the siblings showed no sign of grief. Plenty of anger, but no grief. In the tunnels, he and Bartholomew mentioned where they were heading, and as soon as they got out, Ideria charged ahead, a step slower than running. Nevin caught up with her and they exchanged whispers, ending with the young man turning to cast silent aspersions.

Five minutes into the trip, Draymon attempted to offer comfort and break the silence by catching up to them and placing a hand on Ideria's shoulder. Without hesitation, she slapped it away and said the only word of the journey: "No."

Had her grief manifested itself into this anger? Was she so mad at Prince Daedalus that she lashed out at all around her? No, that did not sit right within him. She certainly allowed Nevin within her sphere of influence. Bartholomew made no efforts to open his mouth, simply offering exaggerated shoulder shrugs any time Draymon turned to him. Whatever the cause, he deduced it best to remain silent until they arrived at their destination.

He was proud of them, though, how they handled themselves. There was no creature in any fairy tale or campfire story a greater monster than Prince Daedalus. The children were ready for him even if they had no idea until today he was why they had to remain all but hidden away from the world. They had been well trained up until this point and had displayed an eagerness to continue learning. And now, it seemed, an aptitude with their skills. In a way, Draymon almost felt sorry for anyone who stepped into their path. At the moment, however, that someone appeared to be him.

He frowned. Maybe this was not such a good idea, for their current destination held allies, but now that there was an obvious divide between the siblings and him, how would their allies align? Perhaps a different destination would prove to be a wiser choice. Though the struggle for him was real, one consideration rose above all others, crowning his thought process, trumping any misgivings: it was time. If Fate had decided that it was time for Ideria and Nevin to know the truth about Daedalus, then it was time for the siblings to make their own decisions about how to handle the truth. He had done his best to protect them, now he was sure that it was time to help them, instead.

The kids continued to run ahead of the adults. They knew the way well enough. It was a quiet and emotionally uneasy journey for Draymon, but before he knew it, the sounds of people engaged in daily chores reached his ears. He closed his eyes, not sure if he was prepared for this, but knew that it was going to happen regardless of his readiness.

Draymon and Bartholomew hastened their pace for the last few steps, exiting the forest right behind the siblings, on to the property of those the children viewed as friends. Sweeping the stone pavers that led to the front of the house was Rue, the only family member of House Pinkeye that Draymon liked. The young ogre was very intelligent and quite charming, very unbefitting his race.

Rue glanced up as Ideria and Nevin approached. Even a simpleton could deduce from one look that the foursome had suffered an ordeal, one ending in loss. He dropped his broom and jogged to the siblings, but not before yelling toward the house, "Uncle Phyl! Uncle Lapin!"

Once close enough, Rue placed his hands on the shoulders of Ideria and Nevin. "What happened?"

Ideria opened her mouth to talk, but her chin trembled too much, calling forth tears and stopping her from forming words.

Tears streamed down Nevin's face as well, but he was still able to explain what occurred. As he told the story, more of Rue's brothers and sisters filed out of the house. A dozen in total by the time Nevin finished.

Draymon stayed a few paces away, letting the kids have their space, and listened for clues as to why they might be deflecting their anger at him. He heard nothing more than just the facts and was joined by the patriarchs of the house, Phyl and Lapin.

A satyr and a rabbit.

A talking rabbit.

Viewing it as a process of give and take, Draymon had never been one to worry over the way that life treated him. By and large, he was always willing to give a little more in the hopes that a little less would be taken, all with minimal complaint. But each time he met Lapin he couldn't help but consider the possibility that his life simply sucked. Lapin greeted the children, his charges, giving little rabbit hugs and forming human words with his little rabbit lips. Draymon realized that "give and take" were not in balance for everyone. After Phyl and Lapin greeted the children, they made their way to Draymon and Bartholomew.

"Lapin, it's good to see you, as always. Phyl . . ." Draymon always struggled for things to say to the satyr. He was sure that somewhere there was a line not meant to be crossed with the satyr, but he was never quite sure where that line lay . . . or which side of it he truly wanted to be on. It was with great relief that he watched Phyl wave to him in response to his acknowledgment of the satyr's presence before turning away to greet Bartholomew.

Draymon, not wanting to be rude, made his way down the seemingly endless line of half-ogre children, clapping each one on the shoulder giving a half-hearted hug and smile in salutations. He saved Rue for last, knowing that he would be able to share a few carefree words with the boy, but he had been preoccupied with Ideria and Nevin this entire time.

"Please, come inside," Phyl said, gesturing to the opened door. "You've all been through a lot and could use the comforts of some hospitality."

Everyone filed into the house. Phyl and two of the younger girls immediately went into the kitchen to start some tea. The rest of the ogre/harpy family guided Ideria and Nevin to the couch. Bartholomew stood on one side of the couch, Draymon on the other, uncomfortable by everyone staring in his general direction with pity in their eyes. Lapin hopped into the middle of the room and sat up on his haunches. "It saddens me to hear about your grandparents. I didn't know them well, but they were good people. They treated my nieces and nephews fairly. Much better than most anyone else in any of the neighboring towns. For this, I am at your service."

"Thank you, sir," Nevin said with a courteous nod.

Ideria remained silent. Nevin gently elbowed her and she swatted at him. Even though the room was silent, he whispered, "Don't be rude."

"I'm too angry to be polite."

"Angry?" Lapin asked. "At Prince Daedalus, I assume?"

"Yes, and—" she cut herself short, but not before glancing toward Draymon.

Draymon's mind raced again. It was he who she was mad at. But why? What could he have possibly done while aiding in her and her brother's escape to warrant such anger that she struggled to control her own words?

"And . . . ? Draymon?" Lapin asked.

Ideria closed her eyes, her nostrils flaring with every breath she took. A whisper barely loud enough to be heard, she said, "Yes."

Lapin looked to Draymon. It was now his turn to shrug his shoulders in ignorance. The rabbit turned back to Ideria. "Why?"

Opening her bloodshot eyes, she growled, "He's been lying to me. He's been lying to Nevin and me for all of these years. My mother is still alive."

A cacophony of metal clanging and ceramic shattering from hitting the floor sounded from the kitchen. Phyl poked his head out from the kitchen. "She knows?"

"If we weren't certain before, we are now," Nevin said.

"Phyl!" Lapin shouted. "You idiot!"

"Sorry, Lapin," Nevin said looking around to Draymon and Bartholomew. "But the looks on my uncle's faces gave it away before Phyl said anything. As well as the look on your face."

Lapin's mien softened as he cast his gaze to the floor.

Phyl made his way from the kitchen, head hanging low, his hooves softly scuffing the floor. "Take it easy on your uncle. Or at least spread your anger towards him amongst all of us. Draymon is a good man. He only wanted to protect you."

"Protect us from the truth?"

"Protect you from yourselves," Bartholomew interrupted. "It wasn't a perfect childhood. We couldn't give you that. We constantly trained you and we wouldn't let you past the nearest towns. We feared that if we told you the truth then the knowledge would have consumed you with directionless anger and grief."

"Instead you gave me directed anger. Thanks," Ideria growled, throwing a look of disgust in Draymon's direction.

Draymon's heart broke. He had been dreading this day, fearing the look in her eyes would leave an indelible mark upon his soul. He wanted to hug her, to hold her. Yet, instead, he blurted, "Be mad. Be mad at me all you want. It was never an easy decision."

"No, it was a cowardly one. Spare yourself the pain of breaking of our little hearts and all of that. You took my name from me. Nevin and I have been the Wahls for so long that I forgot we were Stillhearts. I don't even know who I am."

"But you know that you are someone. You have no idea what that means to me. You were never alone, nor forgotten. We have no idea what has transpired in the years since . . . since—"

"Since you watched my mother get captured by Prince Daedalus?"

"You have no idea what happened. All of us would have taken her place. She made me swear to protect you two. We didn't lock you up in a cage. We taught you that the world is a dangerous place and how to survive, how to fight, how to stand up so that one day—"

"So that one day what? So that one day you could tell me the punchline to a joke I was never included in?"

"So that one day you could make your own decisions, Ideria," Bartholomew answered. "It was never up to us to determine which day that would be. But Draymon made sure that you would be ready whenever that day came. I don't think you realize how difficult it is to dedicate your life to preparing someone to leave you behind."

"Like you left my mother behind?"

"Ideria!" Nevin snapped. "We weren't there. Before today the greatest cause we ever fought for was to rough up a drunk hooligan who was creating trouble for the locals while passing through town. Our uncles and our grandparents sacrificed a great deal on our behalf, more than I'm sure they've told us."

"But they *lied* to us, Nevin. They told us our mother was dead."

"What would you have done had they told us the truth?"

"I would have looked for her, of course!"

"Exactly. Please tell me how far do you think you would have gotten at ten years old? Armed with only a heart full of anger and a head full of revenge, and your eyes not yet far enough from the ground to properly see over a bar top?"

Ideria snorted and shook her head as if trying to blow away an unpleasant smell. "I would have waited until I was better prepared. I wasn't stupid back then."

"Then why are you being stupid now? How long would you have prepared? Another year? Three years or four years when adolescence first greeted you?"

"No, obviously!"

"When, then? When during the last ten years would have been the *perfect* time for you to enact your plot of vengeance?"

"Certainly not ten years!"

"And what of me? You're just going to leave me behind because somehow you claimed dominion over our mother? She's no longer my mother now, is that it? It's your sole duty to find her?"

"No! I . . . I . . . I'm so sorry, Nevin." The tears flowed once more as she leaned over to hug her brother. She sobbed within his embrace, the only noise in the room.

Until Rue stepped forward. "Excuse me? I hate to bring this up now, but if what you're saying about their mother is true, then wouldn't it be reasonable to think that the same could be said about my father? He was involved in the same battle to save King Perciless, correct?"

"Rue!" Ideria looked up from her brother, tears still streaming down her face. "You're absolutely right! I've heard this story a few times and I've always heard it the same way."

"Oh, my," Phyl exclaimed. "I think the tea is burning!" With that, he scrambled for the cover of the kitchen.

Lapin muttered a colorful expression before heading to the medicine cabinet under the excuse of not feeling well. Everyone in the household, family member and guest alike, knew full well that the medicine cabinet held only treacle of an alcoholic variety.

"Draymon?" Ideria glowered at her uncle.

"No," Rue said. "I think Draymon deserves a break. Despite Nevin's eloquent defense, I cannot fully condone his logic, but I think I can at least appreciate that in his heart he thought he was doing the right thing. No, I think one of my uncle's needs to answer me. Uncle Phyl? Uncle Lapin?"

Phyl came back into the sitting room from the kitchen, dabbing his eyes with the corners of his apron.

"Steam got in my eyes," he said.

"It'th true," Lapin hiccupped, three empty bottles rolling across the floor in front of him. Despite everyone's emotions rising to the surface of their skin, Draymon had to take pause and allow himself to be amazed at how quickly the rabbit consumed that much alcohol.

Lapin hopped to the feet of his eldest nephew. "Rue, you are a thuch a beautiful child. Your uncle Phyl and I couldn't bear to watch you thuffer with knowledge that you couldn't use to make you any better. We concocted the lie. Phyl and I. We took it to Draymon and . . . and . . . and that other guy standing right there," Lapin waved at Bartholomew, almost toppling over as he did so. "It was uth. No. It was me. Your uncle Phyl wanted to tell the truth, but I convinthed him. I had less to lose than him."

"How did you have less to lose, uncle Lapin?" Rue asked.

"I couldn't allow you hating Phyl. It would have deth-troyed him. He'th your uncle, your *real* uncle, once married to your father's sithter. So, I figured, who cares if someone hates a rabbit?"

Rue looked to his eleven siblings, exchanging facial expressions and slight gestures. He looked back down to Lapin. "Uncle . . . I mean that with the reverence in which it was intended. We all love you as such. Yes, we feel betrayed. But we forgive you."

Lapin used a front paw to wipe away a tear. "You are thuch an amazing ogre, my boy. All you kidth are amazing."

"Excellent. I'm glad you feel that way since you and Uncle Phyl will be aiding me in my quest to find our father."

"*What?*" Phyl screeched.

Hands behind his back, Rue bent over to get closer to the rabbit. "Correct me if I'm wrong, but as our guests began to settle in, you mentioned that you would do anything for them due to the Whals being nice to us. I can only assume that Ideria and Nevin will be joining us, because we can only assume that their mother is being kept with our father, and they have expressed interest in finding their mother."

For the first time in the past hour, Ideria smiled. She grabbed her brother's hand and shouted, "Yes! We will be joining you."

Rue continued, "It would be foolhardy for the three of us to venture on this quest alone."

Lapin's beady black eyes became cross. "You know what? Okay. You're right. Your Uncle Phyl and I will help you."

Draymon stepped forward and nodded toward Bar-tholomew. "As will we."

"I'm joining you, too," Joy said.

The largest of the brood stood up, the nut-brown tuft of hair atop his pointed head mere inches from the ceil-ing. Woe, a boy who resembled his father in every way from what Draymon remembered of Bale Pinkeye, with one exception—the hump on his back. His voice could be felt when he spoke. "I'm coming, too."

Bartholomew rubbed his chin while walking in a small circle around Woe. "I like this one. We'll need him."

"I just don't know that I can do this," Phyl sobbed. "These kids are everything to me. And I'm retired. Did I mention that yet? I'm retired from adventuring!" Phyl exclaimed, his finger wagging back and forth between his chest and each of the various youths assembled in front of him.

"We are doing this, Uncle Phyl, with or without you. But if it's without you, then I'm not sure I can forgive you," Rue said.

Phyl sighed. "What about the other nine children?"

Faith, an ogress with a beak and harpy legs, the second oldest of the bunch, stepped into the middle of the room. "I will stay with the rest of the kids while you are gone. Try to hurry. Bring back our dad."

Phyl sighed on top of a sigh. "Where's my ankle bracelet? The one with the crossed morningstars? I gave it to one of you. I'm going to need it. Oh, and my cooking pans, too. We're going to need to eat while we're gone and who is going to cook for us if it isn't me?"

Draymon cringed at the thought of consuming Phyl's cooking, but solidarity was necessary. He decided to say something, to give everyone else the same sense of solidarity. As he opened his mouth, Lapin took one final swallow from the bottle between his paws, and then tossed the empty vessel into the corner. "Tholidarity!" the rabbit yelled and passed out.

ᴄᴇɴ

DAEDALUS LANDED HIS dragon in the middle of Castle Phenomere's courtyard. It caused quite a fuss among the people focused on their daily duties. Women covered their mouths to stifle their screams. Children and the elderly froze where they stood, nary a stray breath given or taken. The men cast their gazes downward while trying to slide into the nearest shadow as quietly as possible, attempting to usher the closest woman, child, or elder with them out of sight. No one wanted to attract the attention of the dragon, or worse, the prince.

Dropping the reins, Daedalus dismounted his dragon by jumping from its shoulder. Whatever pain he felt in his knees from absorbing the shock was gone within a dozen steps, his anger a unique salve that burned away all other pains and ailments and there was no better fuel for his inner fires than failure. They were in his grasp, the girl close enough to taste her breath. Using a preplanned escape route, they slipped away through an elaborate tunnel system. Deep underground, his dragon clawed through the ground in random spots until Daedalus found a tunnel. Hours of digging, following the tunnel only led to a double-back. He spent even more time rampaging through the nearby forest only to find a household of children seemingly conceived by a harpy and an ogre. Children never possessed useful information so he returned to the farm to let his dragon have its fill of livestock. He killed what the dragon left alive. Now back at the castle, even though the people were all quiet in attempts to go unnoticed, he knew word would get back to the dragon handlers soon enough. He had no desire to wait for them; they knew how to return his dragon to its pen. He had more pressing matters.

Storming through the hallways of the castle, Prince Daedalus thought of different ways to torture Dearborn Stillheart. Not with racks or spikes or cuts or creatures, but with words and ideas. He planned on letting her know that he knew she had children and that he would find them. He would let her imagination take care of the torture for him. Nothing would stop him from finding her children. But there was one person who could make him put it on hold: General Perrator.

The general was a self-proclaimed half-giant. At eight feet tall, Daedalus assumed the boast was true. However, that claim was not enough to explain the tusks growing upward from his bottom jaw, nor the clawed fingers. There was more going on with the general's genealogical history than he was willing to share, and the different possible combinations of horrific creatures needed to make a beast such as the general even made Daedalus shudder with unease.

"We need to talk," the general said, striding toward Daedalus.

"Not now," the prince replied.

"The king is pulling troops from the Kallistah Pass."

Daedalus stopped walking and gave the general his attention. The truth of the matter was that the general was so wide in the shoulder that Daedalus would have been unable to walk past him in the hallway without turning sideways, ceding some form of control. Having a half-giant for a general was a double-edged sword. There was no member of the army he could not instill fear into with anything more than a simple look; however, he felt no fear of anyone, including the sadistic brother of the king. Daedalus' ire bounced off General Perrator as it were nothing more than a handful of pebbles being thrown at his plate mail. Instead, the prince would have to sacrifice a moment of time to deal with the general's issue first. "My brother wishes to what?"

"I believe my words did not lack clarity."

"How many troops?"

"All of them."

"For what purpose?"

"None was given, but I can make assumptions."

Daedalus made the same assumptions. Demons. This was not a unique occurrence. Many times before, the king had pulled troops from an active battle site to have them quest for the demons that lurked only in his imagination. Daedalus had neither the time nor the desire to deal with this predicament. Pain started to throb between his eyes because deal with it he must. "Very well, I'll find the king and convince him to reverse the command."

"Thank you, sir." The general gave a deep bow and then turned on his heel to walk away.

The pain in Daedalus' head grew with each successive throb to the point he was starting to lose his vision. He knew what was happening and fought against it until he was finally alone in the hallway. Panting as sweat rolled down his face and neck, he leaned against the wall waiting to be transported to . . .

. . . he was in a bed. He remembered this bed, one that would never leave his memory. It was a makeshift infirmary, a lone room deep in the middle of the castle with no windows and a damnable drip that echoed away in some unseen corner. The room smelled of mildew. A faint scent of feces still lingered. It would be years before that smell truly disappeared.

This was two weeks since the horse-riding accident of his early teen years. Two weeks since his older brother, Perciless, betrayed him by letting him fall from a horse onto a fence and face first into pig shit. He had broken ribs as well as contracted any number of filth-borne diseases causing nonstop vomiting for a week and a half. He hadn't overturned anything for the last three days and developed a semblance of an appetite. The castle physicians still insisted that he consume nothing more agitating than water and bread crusts. After bile flowing over his tongue for a week and a half, he desperately wanted something sweet. Finally, after the drip and the smells and the stomach pains drove him to silent tears, his prayers were answered.

The lone door to the infirmary opened. A screeching noise that radiated all the way from his ears down to his neck. He hoped it was one of the physicians coming to tell him that he no longer needed to be sequestered in this room and was now free to go. No such luck. It was just Oremethus.

Normally Oremethus resided alone atop Daedalus' list of those he hated the most. But it was Perciless' fault that Daedalus was in imprisoned in this bed, so he sequestered the anger for his eldest brother. That and he so desperately wished for some form of distraction that even the sight of someone so despised was now a welcome image. "I'd ask how you're feeling, but I can only imagine the level of pain you're in. I wanted to come and check on you."

"I . . . I appreciate that."

"I assume Perciless has yet to visit you."

Too angry to form words at the mere mention of his brother's name, Daedalus frowned and looked away.

Hands behind his back, Oremethus strolled over to the bed and uncomfortably close to Daedalus. "He does feel bad. As the idiot should."

Confused by his oldest brother's statement, Daedalus looked back to him. "What?"

Oremethus shrugged a shoulder. "It's his fault that you're in here. So, you didn't secure your saddle properly. I hardly think that *this* is a just punishment for such a small infraction. Instead of helping his brother, his flesh and blood, he chose to follow father's rules and remain quiet, content to watch you fall to harm. His compliance led to your injury and subsequent discomfort."

It felt good to hear Oremethus say those words, even though he, too, often marched merrily along with father's procession. "Father and his damnable rules."

"Father may have made the rule, but he wasn't there to stop his son from getting hurt. Perciless was. He was right beside you and could have stopped this calamity by simply lending you a hand." To punctuate his statement, he brought his right hand out from behind his back. On his palm rested a piece of cake, topped with frosting the castle baker made from buttercream and strawberries.

Despite the fact that he wanted to hide his enthusiasm, Daedalus smiled and snatched the cake. He used his index finger to capture the icing and guide it all into his mouth. Happiness exploded on his tongue. The cake was sweet and delicious as well, but without the icing became drier with every bite. As if Oremethus could sense the dilemma, he brought his left hand from behind his back. A large cup of milk, spiced with cinnamon, nutmeg, and vanilla. Daedalus' favorite.

"Father said to follow the physicians' orders," Daedalus said, wiping away the milk remains from his upper lip.

"No matter how father pits us against one another, you're my youngest brother and I will always love you, more than anyone else. Don't ever forget that."

The world went to black . . .

. . . and Daedalus woke up on the floor, leaning against a wall. The coolness of the stone felt good against his burning skin. It had been a long while since he last had a spell like that, a memory of the past so intense it was as if he left the present to go visit it.

Getting to his feet, he dusted himself off as his brother's words echoed in his head, "Don't ever forget that." He did. He had forgotten that Oremethus visited him when he was sick and that he broke the rules to sneak him a treat that offered a moment of bliss within a maelstrom of pain. Immediately after Daedalus had been able to leave the bed, his father was praising Oremethus and patronizing Daedalus while Perciless just existed, a happy dog patiently waiting for a scrap of food. King Theomann was a terrible father and an even worse king, the reason for all of Daedalus' problems. Now that Oremethus was king, and Daedalus held his ear, things for the kingdom of Albathia would be different, starting with the conquest of Tsinel. Of course, Daedalus still had to convince Oremethus to stop withdrawing troops from critical war fronts for foolhardy reasons.

Oremethus was in his "hunting room" as he referred to it, an old banquet hall now dedicated to his obsession with hunting demons. A detailed map of Albathia was painted on the walls, ceiling, and floor. Every town, road, stream, and farm represented. Lengths of twine spanned from wall to wall to floor to ceiling. Sometimes a quarterstaff planted in a pot was needed to support a run of twine too long to keep from losing its shape. The twine had been dyed different colors, the shades each representing something different. What, Daedalus could hardly remember. Thousands upon thousands of individual twine strings ran taut throughout the entire room. "Brother?"

"Here, Daedalus!" came from somewhere toward the middle of the room. The twine web so thick, Daedalus could see but a quarter of the way in. He so hated entering this room. There were windows along the one wall, normally enough to light the entire room from the rise of the Day Sun to the fall of the Evening Sun, but they had been painted over and the density of the twine prohibited the light from either sun from venturing too far into the room. Flame of any sort had been prohibited, even that behind the protective glass of a lantern. The one and only time Oremethus had been more extreme in his issuance of punishment than Daedalus was when he executed a servant trying to clean the room after she accidentally broke one of the twine strings. Everyone in the castle now passed by this room only when they had to, and they did so with hastened pace.

Careful not to pluck a single string, Daedalus moved through the web, the dark fear of being watched by a room-sized spider tickling the hairs on the back of his neck. There was a stretch along the corner of the wall and floor where the twine created a tunnel, one that Daedalus used to shimmy the rest of the way to his brother.

Getting to his feet and a little winded from having to use his arms to propel his whole body, Daedalus approached his brother. Because no flames were aloud, Oremethus had a wizard work a spell to place upon the vest he was wearing now, to make it glow a soft yellow, mimicking candlelight. His face was stern but showed no emotion. Daedalus knew this look. He was deep in thought, his mind asking a thousand different questions at once. "How goes the hunt?"

"Not well," he mumbled. "Haddaman warned me of the demons, but I was ill-prepared to face them."

Daedalus looked at the map. Orsrun. Twelve strings of four different colors wrapped around a thick nail protruding from the center of the town. The strings went in all different directions, some even to the ceiling or floor. Oremethus pinched one of the strings and whispered to himself about the location attached to the other end of the string. His mutterings only made sense to himself.

"Orsrun?" Daedalus asked.

"A demon killed the metal dragon there. I knew there were demons there, but I was sloppy, and it cost us one of our dragons."

"Is that why you pulled the troops from Kallistah Pass?"

Oremethus stopped whispering to himself and gave Daedalus a look that made him feel stupid for asking. "No."

After taking a breath to compose himself, Daedalus asked, "Then why?"

"Our supply lines to the troops there have been getting disrupted. Tsinel is more knowledgeable about that valley than we are. Every skirmish there, we have lost. Even if somehow we won, what do we really gain? Tsinel's city of Kallistah is known for its wealth, its gold, the reason why we attacked it in the first place. Since our initial attempt failed, they undoubtedly have evacuated the people and moved the gold. Conquering an empty city, especially one with a location of no strategic value, is a moral victory at best, depending on how many men we lose."

Daedalus couldn't help but smile, a pleasant surprise that the king still had enough of his faculties to know what was happening around him and make good decisions with the data he had. "Yes, brother, you are absolutely correct. If the opportunity arises, I'll create more skeleton soldiers and send them to Kallistah Pass. However, you have yet to tell me where you are sending them."

"I'm going to break them into smaller units and have them scour the lands to find our brother."

"Find Perciless?"

"Yes. I have heard a lot of mention about him lately. He keeps avoiding capture and he is winning over town after town with the hopes of him returning to the throne. All of this talk about our brother has made me realize that he has yet to pay for his crimes."

"His crimes?"

"Yes. Against you. He has been the biggest source of your pain ever since we were children. He was father's favorite and was able to get anything he wanted by simply doing whatever he was told. I grew up insulated from his inanities because of my training to take the throne. But you not only had to live in his shadow, you had to suffer for it. I couldn't be there to shield you from such a life, but I want to be there for you now."

A sting formed behind Daedalus' eyes. For the first time in decades, a tear rolled down his cheek. "Oremethus . . . ? That is very thoughtful of you. Yes, call the troops back to the castle and we will equip them with the means to find our brother."

"No matter how father pitted us against one another, you're my youngest brother and I will always love you, more than anyone else. Don't ever forget that."

Daedalus opened his mouth to reply, but Oremethus' eyes glossed over and became unfocused. Attention back to the map, he plucked the strings while speaking soft sounds full of gibberish. Going back the exact way he came, Daedalus left without any form of farewell, knowing his words would go unheard.

Back in the hallway, thoughts of telling Dearborn about her children occupied his mind, although now without quite the same fervor as before the interruptions. When he turned the corner from one hallway to the next, he found yet another interruption standing before him in the form of Speekore.

"Ah, Prince Daedalus!" the hobgoblin said, torchlight glimmering off a fresh patch of viscous liquid on his leather apron. "I was hoping to find you. Haddaman mentioned that you had just arrived."

"Haddaman's back in the castle? Already?"

"Nothing but the best steeds for him, I presume."

Daedalus shook his head and waved his hand to dismiss his scientist while he started back down the hallway. "Be that as it may, I hardly have time for you."

"I need only the scant seconds to say the following: the hundredth has arrived."

Those words held Daedalus stronger than any tether or chains. "Did . . . did you say that we now have one hundred?"

"I did indeed."

The torture of Dearborn Stillheart was just about to become sweeter.

ELEVEN

"WE NEED HIM, please," Perciless said. Brokar saluted and then went off to find Landyr.

When Cezomir and Thorna gave him word of the morning attack, Perciless ordered everyone into the small hideaway. They needed to relocate, he reasoned, but only after the danger had passed. The group grabbed up what few items of importance there were in the room and stowed them away for travel. Minimal words were needed at this point . . . moving had become second nature to them. It took less than an hour from when Perciless made his request to the sounds of Landyr and Brokar bringing horses the house. Under the baleful stare of the Morning Sun, they mounted up and moved out. The evacuation was quiet and somber, each member of the party mourning Rolin.

The destination had been predetermined and an out of the way little place called Manafor's Glen became their new temporary haven. The safe house was paid for already and keys turned over months ago, during the last time they visited.

Perciless and his small group of companions entered the little dwelling, while Thorna waited outside with the horses. Cezomir and Lina entered first, having been farther ahead of the rest of the party, lest the newly procured horses catch the scent of the predators. It took only moments to declare the ground floor and attic free of interlopers. Cezomir found the concealed door to the cellar where they would spend most of their time while they were here and lifted it free to inspect the lower levels. When his lupine senses were satisfied the area was secure, Perciless asked Thorna to stable the horses while he asked Landyr to join him for a trip around the town for supplies.

They were quick about their business, garnering some food and minor items of use. Perciless was careful to keep his face shadowed by the cowl of his cloak and displayed only a handful of low-value coins. He couldn't keep himself from asking a few questions about the conditions of life in Manafor's Glen and exchanging a few pleasantries with some of the simple townsfolk. The common folk truly were his people after all, and he enjoyed no company more than their own, for without them, nothing worthwhile could ever exist. It was a far cry from what he had heard his brothers say while growing up. Oremethus believed that the simple folk were numbers of the economy, while Daedalus saw them only as a stepping stone to achieve his own selfish ends.

When they returned to the safe house, everyone was already inside. Perciless paced around the few rooms of the ground floor. "It helps me think," he often exclaimed to anyone who pointed out the habit to him.

As he walked the length of the room and back, he allowed everyone to get as comfortable as possible in the chairs around a simple wooden table. Landyr, Brokar, and Thorna ripped chunks from the loaves of bread in the center of the table and pulled their share of jerked meat from a sack before giving the rest to Cezomir and Lina. They each had a bloated water skin to wash down their meals. Finally growing tired of the floorboard squeak that accompanied his third and seventeenth step, Perciless stopped pacing. "I apologize for picking a wound before it can heal, but we need to review the events of this morning."

"I had a delicious breakfast of hobgoblin," Cezomir said while slipping a sliver of dried meat into his mouth. "I just wish I could have eaten it before it killed Rolin."

"As do we all, my friend. As do we all." Perciless started his pacing again, this time along a different path. "Did you find any clues about them or their motivations before you ate them?"

Landyr placed his heels on the table and leaned back in his chair, stretching his arms back as far as they could go. "The hobgoblins that attacked us were soldiers, definitely Elite Troop judging from the insignias all over their uniforms."

"Do you think we stumbled upon them out of bad luck? There were only three of them."

"It doesn't seem likely. Two of them had ensorcelled weapons and one of those two had been sitting in a position to snipe at us. I believe it was reconnaissance."

Perciless completed another circuit around the room. "For years we've been hearing that my brother's Elite Troop has been hunting wizards."

"It seems like they have new targets now," Thorna said.

"It's clear we're being hunted," Landyr said. "How did they find us? How do we know that this place is safe? For how long?"

"The new Elite Troop used magic," Cezomir said. "Their arrows were ensorcelled. Is it possible that some mage could have tracked us?"

"My brother has long since started his own wizard's guild. It's safe to assume that the Elite Troop has one," Perciless said.

Landyr returned his feet to the floor and sat up straight. He closed his eyes tightly and scrubbed his fingers through his hair, from frustration, Perciless had learned over the years. "The gods only know what kinds of disgusting magics the king's wizards are dabbling in."

"What about Vogothe?" Lina asked.

"The crime lord? The king of the societal underbelly? Now you think he's somehow involved?"

Cezomir shrugged his massive shoulders. "Makes sense to me. Rumor has it he has more knowledge about the kingdom than historians."

"Rumor has it that he works with Oremethus and Daedalus," Thorna said.

"Rumor has it that we are the only criminals he doesn't own," Lina added.

"Bah!" Landyr jumped from his chair with enough force to knock it over. "Rumors, rumors, rumors may as well be goat shit for all the good they're doing us. We need facts."

Perciless broke from his pacing to stand behind Landyr. "Rolin was a friend to all of us."

"But it was my fault that he's dead."

"You did not shoot the arrow."

"I'm his general."

"You never refer to yourself as that title, so do not do so now to shoulder guilt you shouldn't have. And I'm his king, so by your logic, I shot the arrow."

Landyr clenched his fists and then released. With a slight slump in posture, he turned the chair upright and returned to sitting on it. "Point taken. But we need more information."

As if on cue, a knocking came from the main door. Perciless gestured to it and said, "Then let us find out if our guest can provide some."

Cezomir and Lina growled while the other three at the table went wide-eyed and tense, readying themselves to kill whoever might be on the other side of the door. Landyr stood and moved close enough to Perciless so his whisper could be heard. "Am I correct to infer that you *invited* someone to our secret safe house during a time when we should be using extreme caution?"

"Yes. This is an individual I personally know. We can trust him."

"We lost Rolin because we trusted our environment."

"We lost Rolin because we got sloppy by not deferring to our contacts enough. I will not make the same mistake."

Another round of knocking came from the door. Landyr drew his sword and positioned himself so when he opened the door he could stay behind it. A young man entered. "King Perciless."

Landyr grabbed the back of the man's shirt with one hand and placed the tip of his blade to the man's back. He slammed the door closed with his foot. "What is your name?"

"Wells! Wells Penderson!"

"This is unnecessary, Landyr," Perciless said.

Ignoring the king's words, Landyr continued, "State the nature of your business."

"I was invited by the king."

Perciless sighed. "Landyr, stop. Wells, how old were you when we first met?"

"Five. I was five years old, Your Highness."

"Can you briefly explain the circumstances of our meeting?"

"It was . . . it was right after the Demon War, right when you became rightful king. You found me. You found me hiding in the rubble of my home. My parents had been eaten by the demons, so you rescued me and you personally found me a new family, one who preached love."

Landyr released Wells and sheathed his sword. He mumbled, "Compelling story."

"I think so, too," Perciless said. He turned to the young man and shook his hand. "Thank you for coming, Wells."

"Of course, Your Highness! How may I serve you?"

"I was wondering if you would be able to provide information."

"I will provide all that I have."

"We were ambushed earlier today by the king's Elite Troop and unfortunately lost one of our friends."

The young man lowered his eyes, his tone reverent. "I am quite sorry to hear this, M'Lord. I heard the Elite Troop was hunting wizards, not kings."

"We have heard the same. In the morning we will be starting our long trek to Murveen. Is the mayor still loyal to my name?"

A large smile crept along Wells' face as if he had no ability to stop it. "I have a lot of friends in Murveen. I visit quite often. Yes, the mayor is very much loyal to your name, as are many, many of the citizens."

"Excellent. Thank your time, Wells. I apologize for being so brief."

Wells tilted his head as if he were waiting for one more question. "Have . . . ? Have you not heard?"

"Heard about what, my friend?"

"In Orsrun. The king brought his gem dragon, metal dragon, and lightning dragon. Daedalus said he was looking for traitors, but we all know why he was there. He would have destroyed the whole town if not for a girl."

"A girl? Who is she and what did she do?"

"A farmer girl named Ideria Wahl. She killed the metal dragon all by herself."

Everyone in the room reacted with a gasp or grunt. Landyr whispered, "Impossible."

"Not impossible, good sir. Very true. I went to Orsun as I heard and saw the remains of the metal dragon. Dead and twisted into a ball."

Perciless looked to his traveling companions and smiled. "We need her, please."

⊂WELVE

ONE END OF the quarterstaff caught Bale's cheek with a meaty slap. Everything was going according to plan. Bale was not fond of the plan, because of all the pain, but he reconciled to himself that the pain was going to happen anyway, so there might as well be a plan attached to it. It still hurt, though, to be beaten with quarterstaffs.

As a part of troop training, the king's army would come by the dungeon of Castle Phenomere for a little live action practice. Bale always made such a great target for the most novice of recruits. A living, moving target that was not allowed to hit back. This practice session, though, Bale had a plan.

Two more hits, in rapid succession to his chest and he backed away. "Please stop."

Emboldened by the encouragement by his commanding officer and the cheers of his fellow recruits, the young soldier with the staff continued his attack. He advanced faster than the ogre retreated and landed three more solid blows. Bale stumbled this time. "I . . . I beg you. No more."

His words were fuel to the recruit's fire. A strike from the right end of the staff, another from the left. So confident in his moves, the recruit spun and hit Bale squarely in the shoulder. The beaten ogre went flying into the weapons rack.

This was the hardest part of the plan. Bale knew he had the acting skill necessary to make it seem like the recruit with flimsy arms was hitting harder than a fussy wench with a pillow. He even angled himself well, getting closer to the weapons rack with each hit. The tricky part was to launch himself into the weapons rack without getting skewered or sliced. A halberd fell onto his shoulder with enough force to draw blood. Not a lot, just enough to lend credibility to his performance. The pain caused by the cascade of other weapons falling on top of him certainly helped as well. "Ow."

"Dolt!" one recruit called out.

"Buffoon," another soldier mumbled.

"Damnation. He's bleeding."

"Clearly he's had enough," the commanding officer reported. "You and you, escort him back."

The two closest recruits looked to each other with the crinkled noses and curled upper lips of freshly formed sneers. Neither of them tried to help Bale up and just stood watching as he brushed away the many spilled weapons, while the rest of the soldiers broke away into different training groups.

"C'mon, you sack of festered meat. Move along now." The recruit connected his boot to Bale's rump as a form of encouragement.

Bale rolled his neck to stretch away the knots and then massaged it to keep his hands busy, so he did not ruin the plan by getting himself executed for strangling two twit recruits. They walked behind him as he entered the castle through the corner entrance at the rear, the one designated for supply deliveries. Just as Dearborn said, today the staff was unloading a full wagon of packaged spices. The cooks and servants and even a few guards carried the goods, each tightly packed sack about the size of a brick. Time for more acting.

Bale slowed his pace and increased his wobble. He listed to the left, his feet shuffling as if he had forgotten what they were used for. He successfully timed his stumble and landed on a neatly stacked pile of flour, bursting a few bags. The servants backed away, while the staff berated the soldiers for bringing an unstable ogre through their loading area. The one recruit made obscene gestures to the staff, while the other repeatedly kicked Bale until he stood up and began walking in the correct direction. Once past the loading area, both recruits took turns slapping Bale and hurling verbal abuses at him for the remainder of the trip back to his cell.

Dearborn was where Bale had last seen her; in her cell sitting on her bench. She was leaning forward, resting her forearms on her lap, her black hair creating a curtain over her face. She remained still as the soldiers shoved Bale back in his cell, giving him one last kick for good measure.

The recruits left the cells exchanging boasts about what they would do to Bale during their next practice session. As soon as they left, Dearborn flipped her hair back and rushed over to Bale's cell. "You're bleeding again. How badly did they hurt you?"

Bale grabbed a fistful of straw from the one corner of his cell and used it to wipe away his blood. No need to dirty his shirt. "This? This was me. I couldn't dodge my own attack."

"I'm so sorry, Bale. I hated to ask you to do what you did."

"It's okay. It had to be done." He knew she truly felt bad and that she would have done it herself if she had the same leeway he had in regards to leaving the cell area. She had no issues sneaking from this cell area to the other ones on this floor to help the other prisoners as best she could. If she got caught on any other floor, then that would undoubtedly get the attention of Daedalus. It had been nine years since either Bale or Dearborn had seen the vengeful prince, and if neither of them saw him again before the end of their days, it would be deemed a victory. However, now that they were planning an escape, they might very well catch his attention. But to escape, they needed to execute their plan. "And it worked."

Dearborn smiled. "Truly? You got what we need?"

Bale returned her smile and reached into his pants pockets. He pulled out two burlap bags, each packed tightly. He then reached into his left pocket and showed her the dagger that he pilfered from the weapons rack after he fell onto it. It was a very nice-looking weapon, too. It might be missed, but there was no way anyone in the army would suspect their ogre pet could have been the one who absconded with it.

Dearborn took the pilfered items and went back to her cell. She hid them in the corner under some straw.

Bale placed his hands on his hips, thumbs on his lower back, and arched backward. That did nothing for the pain in his side. He walked into Dearborn's cell and asked, "Would you be able to help me with my side, please?"

Dearborn went to her bench and laid down. "Sure. I could use the exercise."

Once she was ready, Bale lumbered over to her and leaned onto her outstretched hands until his feet were off the ground. One hand on his hip, the other on his ribs just below his armpit, Dearborn held Bale sideways. He went limp, the muscles by her hand releasing. She lowered him and then pressed him into the air again. The rhythmic movement was relaxing, and the odd angle helped him stretch out. She must be really excited by this plan. She usually stopped at fifteen and her best ever was nineteen. She made it all the way to twenty-three before returning him to his feet. She asked, "Did that help?"

Keeping his arm stiff and rotating it at his shoulder, he replied, "It did. Thank you very—"

"Hurry!" came from the main doorway. A pageboy ran into the room and said, "Get back in your cell. Hurry."

Bale had a difficult time remembering names and this boy was no different. He remembered that his thirteenth birthday was recent and that he had a fondness for Dearborn, because she would teach him basic fighting moves and offer him words to say to girls he was fond of. His eyes were wide with panic, so Bale did he was told.

"Why?" Dearborn asked, closing her cell door after Bale ambled into his own cell.

"Lock your doors, too. He's on his way."

The pageboy was gone before either Dearborn or Bale could ask, but they both locked their cell doors. That was more for show, since each of them had the means to pick the locks.

Fingers wrapped around the bars of his cell, Bale pressed his head against the cage and pressed his lips together. "Psst! Psssst!"

His efforts yielded a spray of saliva that ultimately cascaded from his chin and along the bars. His attempted whisper was no quieter than his regular speaking voice. "Dearborn? Who do you think it is?"

Dearborn stood by the bars as well. "I don't know, Bale."

"The pageboy seemed really scared."

"He did. It's as if he was talking about . . . Oh . . . oh, by the gods, Bale. There is only one person he could be talking about." Dearborn's voice quaked as she moved away from the bars. "He hasn't forgotten about me."

"No. No, I haven't," Daedalus said before he entered the main room. It had been nine years since Bale had last seen him and he looked just the same, save for a few more wrinkles under his stubbled face and more gray streaks in his wild black hair. He still had the eyes of a madman and his smile made Bale feel like he had snail slime oozing over his spine. "I've been looking forward to this day for a long time, my dear Dearborn."

Bale had never seen Dearborn anything less than confident, let alone afraid. She stood in the center of her cell with her fists clenched, eyes wide. Bale had not expected to see Daedalus today, and it was clear neither did Dearborn. The prince had taken her by surprise. She could snap his neck with one hand, Bale was confident of this. She had single-handedly killed one of the twelve dragons! It was an adolescent, not full grown, but she broke its neck by herself, nonetheless. If she could break a dragon's neck, she could break this man's neck. Bale wanted to help, so he asked, "Why?"

Daedalus turned to Bale and frowned. The prince was still smiling, though, and the new expression made the ooze flowing over Bale's spine drip faster. "Why? Did . . . did you just ask me why?"

Bale was three times his size, yet he shrunk away from the bars of his cell as Daedalus approached. There were no keys in the prince's hands, nor any dangling from his belt, so Bale felt a sense of security due to the cell's bars. "Yes. Why do you hate her so?"

"Well, my ogre friend, let me tell you. First, you need to understand my life has not been easy. I've spent half my life with an almost debilitating detestation of filth and when I finally got over that, I was penniless and powerless. As I started to experience life, I lost my arm and was thrown into a dungeon." As he spoke, Daedalus removed his riding gloves to expose his skeletal hand. He gripped one of the bars to Bale's cell and squeezed. "All of these problems can be attributable to three people: my father, whom I killed; my brother, Perciless, whom I'm hunting; and Dearborn Stillheart. My father made me, my brother shaped me, and Dearborn added the finishing touches. But to add specificity to your question, dear ogre, she publicly humiliated me. When we were adolescents, during a quarterstaff exhibition, she beat me in front of all the Spring Festival goers. She stripped me of confidence, made me the butt of many jokes. No one saw me as a prince after that. Barely anyone acknowledged I was a human, let alone royalty. Dearborn Stillheart broke my dignity."

"So, I hurt your feelings decades ago?" Dearborn asked. "And for this paltry infraction upon your ego, you still seek revenge against me?"

Daedalus let go of the bar to turn and address Dearborn. Bale ran his index finger over the indents left in the metal.

Facing Dearborn's cell, Daedalus continued, "Oh, I will exact my revenge. I will break you. I will shatter you from the inside and I will do it without so much as laying a finger on you. You see, I've been planning this for nine years, the very moment after . . . after our last encounter. From that moment on, this country has been celebrating Dearborn Day, a monthly holiday when my Elite Troop finds the most magnificent maiden of the lands and brings her to me so she can pay tribute to your name nine months later."

Daedalus backed away from the two cells, closer to the lone door to the room. Dearborn ran to the bars and gripped them tightly. "Monster! Those girls did nothing to deserve what you did to them."

"I think you mean what *you* did to them. Had you simply lost the tournament those decades ago, had you not tried to stop Oremethus from rightfully ascending the throne, had you simply died, then I wouldn't see *your* face on so many women!" His sneer turned to a smile when he turned to the doorway and his voice held a hint of song as he called out, "Dearborn! Come in here."

A boy walked in carrying a swaddled baby. Wearing the smile of a snake ready to eat a nest full of unguarded eggs, Daedalus took the baby into his arms. "Beautiful, isn't she? Her name is Dearborn. She is my newest child." He then gestured to the boy. "This is my first born. His name is Dearborn. And here are all of my other children, all named after you, Dearborn."

More children filed in, the older ones carrying the babies, the toddlers holding hands of those with more years of experience walking. Some looked around, a few of the babies cried. More and more came in, and Bale had a hard time counting that high. They continued to squeeze into the aisle between the two jail cells, bodies pressed together, faces against the bars. The children were all different heights, yet each was only a fraction different from many others. Their hair color varied slightly as did their noses, chins, mouths. But they all had the exact same set of eyes, the eyes of their father. "One hundred, Dearborn. Or, should I say one hundred Dearborns. All named after you. There will be a hundred more and a hundred after them, and when they're ready to take from the world what's theirs, then everyone will know their names. Everyone will know *your* name."

Silent tears flowed from Dearborn's eyes as her knuckles turned white from the pressure of her squeeze. Daedalus laughed. "Come, children, it's time for your schooling."

Daedalus started to exit along with the one hundred children but stopped at the doorway. As the children flowed around him, he turned to the Dearborn in the cell and smiled, one of disarming warmth. While petting the newborn nestled in the crook of his arm, he said, "Oh, I almost forgot. I found out about your children. Don't worry, I won't kill them. But I will cut off your son's eyelids, so he won't miss a single second of the time I spend with your daughter."

The last of the children left and then he followed.

Dearborn roared a noise that sent lightning strikes of fear through Bale's entire body. It was a sound he had never heard before. It was undistilled hatred. He trembled even after she stopped screaming and made her way to her bench. Bale realized what she was doing when she reached underneath and procured two halves of a dinner knife and a fork with one tine. Her lock picking kit.

Bale fell to his knees and lunged for his bench, grabbing his kit as well. Using the same three implements, he raced to pick his cell door before she could. The logic of his actions had yet to catch up to him. He just knew that she was going to attack the prince and he had to stop her.

The only sounds in the room were the two prisoners racing to unlock their door first. Bale looked up to assess her progress but saw that there was no benefit to peeking. Picking a lock was an all or nothing scenario, any gradient between "opened" and "closed" was insignificant.

Bale had no talent for picking locks, nor any form of a proclivity toward why he felt the need to get his cell door open before she did. He struggled to keep his thick fingers steady as sweat threatened to blur his vision. He had never beaten her at anything before. Until today.

Bale opened his door a split second before she could open hers. It was just enough time for Bale to lunge across and slam it shut on her. So angry, no words came from her mouth, just the wide-eyed glare of bloodshot eyes.

"Dearborn, wait. We have a plan."

Dearborn pushed on her door. It budged. Bale's feet slid across the floor as she pushed harder, prompting him to talk faster. "You can't kill him now. Think about it. If you kill him now, in front of a hundred children—a hundred of his children—they would seek revenge on you, and that's even if you live that long. Don't you think you would die shortly after you killed him?"

Bale's feet continued to slide. The door continued to open. "And that's even if you could kill him. His skeleton hand is strong, Dearborn. He bent the one bar of my cell door. His hand bent metal."

Bale's statement made her push harder, the opening almost wide enough for her to slip through. "And his brother! The king! If you kill Daedalus, you won't be protecting your children. King Oremethus will hunt them down and kill them."

With one final push, Dearborn opened the door enough to exit her cell. Bale let go of the door and backed down the aisle, hands out in front of him. She could get past him, by out-maneuvering him or out-muscling him. Either way, it was going to hurt. Bale started his day with pain, so he figured he might as well end with it. "Dearborn, please. We have a plan to escape. We have a plan."

Fists clenched, she was on him faster than he anticipated. Her arms were around him and he expected her to pick him up and slam him to the ground. Or to squeeze so hard that his lungs could take in no air and he would pass out. He did not expect her next move.

She buried her face in his chest and cried. In between sobs, she whispered, "My babies, Bale. He's going after my babies."

"We have a plan. It's a good plan. We have a good plan and it will work." Bale kept repeating his words as Dearborn cried.

THIRTEEN

THE VOID DRAGON engulfed the hobgoblin with one bite, then chewed, and swallowed as it landed in front of Perciless' general. The dragon and human communicated with each other. There were no sounds accompanying the images Methel watched, just silent defeat.

"Have you seen enough?" Juruk asked.

Methel regarded his sergeant, an albino satyr, and a nasty looking one at that. Much larger than his brethren, long alabaster scars ran the length of the milk-white skin of his bare chest. His leg fur was becoming yellow tinged from time, patches on his left thigh permanently lost to long-forgotten battles. Thin black chain wrapped around his right leg, one end embedded in his hoof, the other end anchored to his hip. Eight more black chains formed a dangling ladder up the right side of his torso, waist to shoulder. Each chain's anchors were six inches apart, a knotted scar where metal dug into skin. There were only three chains on his face: a short length under his right eye, one from his nostril to his ear lobe, the final one from the center of his chin to the back of his jaw. Any time Juruk spoke, Methel wanted to grab all the chains and yank them from his pale skin. "I have. You can cease your spell, Lazzim."

The wizard with the cloak of fire grunted and closed the mystical window that allowed everyone to see the failure of the Elite Troop's three-man assassination team. The wizard's voice was that of a hissing campfire. "Anything else, General?"

"Nothing for now."

The wizard left them to join the rest of the Elite Troop camped out at the bottom of the hill. The wizard was a powerful one and had no qualms demonstrating his abilities, such as with his cloak. Cowl and cape of dancing flame, yet it did not burn anything it touched unless Lazzim wished it to. Methel was no friend of the wizard, nor with any member of his Elite Troop for that matter, but he trusted the wizard more than the others. Lazzim was quick to do heinous work in the name of the king when first approached so many years ago. Methel had Lazzam's allegiance as long as he gave the wizard the opportunities to use his magic to inflict pain every once in a while. Juruk had no allegiance to anyone, just to his sword, a lover's promise to keep it bathed in blood.

Standing next to each other atop a hill overlooking the town where they had sent their assassins to find and kill the once King Perciless, Methel and Juruk watched in silence. From this distance, the town looked peaceful enough, as they were unable to see the happenings on the street, but Methel knew there was a commotion, townspeople running amok and looking for answers. Perciless and his crew were packing their things and planning their next move, Methel was sure of this. Juruk broke the silence first. "We should move in now."

"That would be very imprudent."

Juruk inhaled deeply through his nose. "Is that fear I smell?"

"If the word 'imprudent' is too big for you, all you need to do is ask for the definition instead of exemplifying your ignorance through boorish insults. It would do us no good to go charging into a town that is dealing with the chaos that happened in one of their markets."

"Chaos is always good. Less chance of deception coming from a person who is confused and scared."

"Chaos has a time and a place. It is true the citizens might be more willing to give us information now, but they have none to give. Those we're seeking are faceless strangers to the people down below."

"They certainly would know Perciless."

"There is no indication that he was even there."

Juruk laughed and shook his head. "I have yet to understand why Prince Daedalus has chosen you to be general of the king's Elite Troop. Either you're arguing for the sake of arguing or you're too short-sighted to realize that if Perciless' men are there, then so must he be."

Methel frowned and crossed his arms over his chest. They were not quite as thick as Juruk's, but he knew how to use them, and he could best Juruk if he had to. This, he was certain of. "His men could either be running reconnaissance or lagging behind to verify that they aren't being followed. As to why I'm the general, I'm better than any other candidate offered to Prince Daedalus. I could demonstrate that now by either shoving your horns up your ass or by coming up with a plan for what we do next. If you wish the first choice, I'll make it quick because I'm starting to get hungry and want nothing to stand in the way between me and a quick bite to eat. If you wish the latter, then fetch Lazzim and Samillia."

Right hoof kicking at the dirt like a bull ready to charge, Juruk snorted and shook his head. "You can't truly mean that you'd be willing to—"

Impassive, Methel looked nowhere else other than the town below, almost bored. "You're choice, *Sergeant*."

Juruk gave the impression that he contemplated the options before him, but Methel knew that was merely posturing. Even if Juruk opted for combat and somehow won, Daedalus would never accept that and there would be a steep price to pay for the satyr. No one wanted that. Juruk did as ordered; he left and returned with the two Elite Troops members Methel had requested.

"You wish to see us?" Samillia asked, her forked tongue quivering with every "s."

Turning his back to the town below, Methel kept his arms crossed, tone even, as he regarded the snake woman. She was one of his best warriors and took great pride in being a member of the Elite Troop. Her leather armor was always clean and well maintained, segmented to accommodate her serpent tail. Green snake scale covered her body, even her human torso. "I have a mission for you, Samillia."

She smiled, an event so rare that Methel had forgotten that she could be quite alluring. Even her vertical-slit yellow eyes went from menacing to enticing. "I will carry it out to success or die trying."

"I have every confidence in your abilities." Methel nodded at Lazzim. The wizard held out his hand, and the air rippled above it. Two streams of fire arced from his palm to form a frame, the image of Landyr's face in the center. Methel pointed to the image. "Find and seduce the prince's general. In case you've forgotten, his name is Landyr."

Samillia's smile disappeared. "My mission is to fuck a human? Is that all I am? The Elite Troop whore?"

"I couldn't give a rat's dick if you lay with him or not. Just seduce him enough to make him give you information. What is their path? How many soldiers in their secret army? When do they plan on unleashing it?"

"Seduce a human. Normally humans do not find me seductive."

"Obviously, he's no normal human." The image within the flame changed to Landyr embracing the dragon's tongue and licking it. "It seems to me he wishes to share intimacies with a dragon. Meaning, if he wants to fuck a dragon, then he'll want to fuck you."

Juruk snorted in amusement. "I'd have a better chance of seducing him than Samillia does."

The snake woman slithered closer to Juruk and drew her sword, just as curved as her twitching tail. Before any of this bravado turned into murder, Methel snapped, "Samillia! Despite Juruk having zero control of the words that leave his mouth, he is still your sergeant. And I am still your general giving you an order."

She sheathed her sword, her tongue poking from between her lips in short, tight flicks. Methel opened the small sack tied to his belt and pulled out three coins. He tossed them to Samillia, and she caught them with ease. "Go into town and buy civilian clothes. I'm asking you to do something we never trained you for in the barracks, but it is something I'm certain you can do."

She offered him one last glare before slithering down the hill.

Samillia made her way through the grasses on the way to town and Methel dismissed Lazzim back to camp. Juruk moved close to Methel, his breath stale and hot as he said, "I believe you still retain allegiance to ex-king Perciless."

The albino satyr was wrong. The ex-king did the same for Methel as he did for all of his other citizens. Nothing. The only true favor from Perciless came as an opportunity for Methel to swing a sword rather than forge one.

Before the Demon War, Methel was a blacksmith doing his best to raise two daughters after his wife died around their youngest's fifth birthday from consumption. His work was not the highest quality, but none could compete with his prices or turnaround time. He wanted coin in hand as quickly as possible for his girls and wanted to make sure his community had what it needed to hinge doors, nail boards, and shoe their horses. For two years after his wife's death, he pounded out a good life for his daughters. Until the Horde came.

Praeker Trieste and his horde of villains raided Methel's town looking for cursed gemstones. As Methel defended his shop against three orcs, a griffin devoured his daughters. To this day he could still see his youngest daughter's severed arm dangling from the corner of the creature's beak.

The retribution was swift and bloody. Methel mourned, sitting in the center of his blacksmith shop with what remains of his daughters he cut from the griffin's belly and crying until he passed out. The following day, the fraction of the town's populace that survived gathered to decide their fate. The entire town has been either burned to ash or broken into splinters and pebbles. They decided to make a pilgrimage to Phenomere, capital and castle of Albathia. They arrived at what they had just left.

While the mad wizard Wyren ripped open the membrane to Hell and released its demons, Praeker and his Horde attacked Phenomere, decimating the city.

The new king Perciless was quick to devise plans for rebuilding after the war. Methel thought about offering his skills as a blacksmith but decided against it. He smithed for his daughters and his community. His daughters were dead, and the people of this city were strangers. He joined the army instead.

So depleted, the king's army had little concern about his advanced age, just his willingness to learn. And he did. Others were faster, smarter, more talented, but Methel was dead inside and executed every order without question or complaint. Six years of unwavering service got him promoted to castle guard. He volunteered for the night rounds because it gave him the least contact with anyone else and whatever might be lurking in the shadows of the hallways was far less terrifying than what lurked around in the shadows of his heart. Until Oremethus came back.

The transfer of crown from Perciless to Oremethus was swift but sloppy. Perciless escaped. The new king was obsessed with demons. The youngest brother was a sadistic nightmare. And dragons were involved, damnable filthy beasts. But Methel kept his mouth shut other than to say, "Yes, sir," and ended up being the main prison guard for the ex-soldier woman and the ogre.

Over the years, Methel turned many a blind eye to Dearborn's antics. She skulked the halls to supply the bounty of her rat farm to the other prisoners and he pretended not to notice. He even opted to stay as a prison guard when he accepted the opportunity to hunt wizards.

As with every operation under the Oremethus regime, opportunity came in the form of orders from those higher in authority, and Methel was ordered to become a wizard hunter. He knew little about the motivations of those behind the Demon War, but he knew a wizard had started it. During his tenure as a wizard hunter, he captured and killed the most, garnering the attention of Daedalus. The twisted prince wished to besmirch the name of Dearborn Stillheart and all that it stood for, so he turned his eye toward the career that she loved—The Elite Troop.

Daedalus wanted a group of bloodthirsty miscreants ready to die for an opportunity to kill, and willing to kill to complete any mission given to them. Methel was his first choice for general. However, Daedalus also picked the other forty members as well, much to Methel's chagrin.

"No, Juruk, I owe Perciless nothing. My every opportunity and advancement came during Oremethus's rule. You, however, were pardoned by Perciless for all the war crimes that you committed during your time as one of Praeker Trieste's Horde members yet faced a life of nothing but following orders ever since Oremethus ascended the throne. Of the two of us, who do you think Prince Daedalus would suspect to be the most treasonous?"

A growl rumbled from deep within the satyr's throat, but he did nothing else other than turn and walk away.

Methel knew his time was short, but he wanted to see what Perciless had planned before he brought the prince to the king.

FOURTEEN

NEVIN WATCHED. IDERIA was his sister, but observation was his best friend. His mother taught him the benefits, but noticing the machinations of the world came easily to him. When a person opened their mouth, their other senses closed, so being a naturally quiet individual allowed Nevin access to the world's input.

With a sister like Ideria, it was easy to go unnoticed. If asked, she would deny being infatuated with social interaction, using the excuse of needing to hide in shadows or behind cloaks. Those instances were not as often as she made them out to be. The need for a common guise within a crowd was only necessary if there was potential danger. In reality, she was quick to accept conversation anytime it was offered. Laughter was easy to elicit from her. She never quested for attention, but she always received it, making it easy for Nevin to hide in her shadow. Even while wearing a cloak, she could not go unnoticed when walking into a room. Nevin would watch those watching her. Especially when entering a crowded tavern such as this one.

The Giant's Den was huge, the biggest tavern Nevin had ever seen. No surprise, though, since it was the most popular tavern in the bustling city of Bernum, large and ever expanding. Trees with thick trunks grew throughout the tavern, supporting the opened second floor, where the rooms for rent were located. Even here, though the crowd was thick when Nevin and Ideria entered, they were greeted with sideways glances and more than a few stares.

Still angry with their uncles, Ideria offered no form of communication with them other than answers to direct questions. It made for the six-day trek to Bernum one of whispers among two separate groups, the "uncles" and the "children." Even though they did not react quite as negatively as Ideria did, the children of Bale Pinkeye were upset that they had been lied to for a decade about their father's demise. Ideria's stance was simple—no forgiveness until Dearborn and Bale were found. Her contemporaries rallied around her in solidarity. As soon as they secured rooms in Bernum, Ideria went off to ferret out information of Dearborn's possible whereabouts. Bartholomew believed that she and Bale were being held at either the Hellweb dungeon system or in Castle Phenomere itself. Bernum was positioned between the two; Hellweb one day to the north, Phenomere two days to the south. Taverns held information and Ideria went right for the largest one. Nevin did as he had done his entire life, followed her.

A couple of coins and a question slid across the bar's top. The bartender answered with a head nod to a table in the corner. There a man sat alone, even though the round table could support four. Uninvited, Ideria sat in one of the three empty chairs and said, "I heard you know something about someone I'm looking for."

The man stayed perfectly still, except for his watchful eyes, until Nevin sat down, then a smile played across his stubbled face. Nevin had observed a smile like this before and made assumptions. Scum. Liar. Cheat. But Nevin did as he always did when Ideria became so singularly focused, he kept his mouth shut.

The man's tongue swiped across the dead skin of his dried lips. "I know a lot of things and a lot of people. I'll need more details and we'll see if I can help you."

"We're looking for a couple of prisoners held by the king. A large woman. Tall and muscular like . . . like me. And an ogre, like . . . like . . .,"

"Like them?" the man asked turning to the side. Rue and Woe sat a few tables away with Hope.

Ideria scowled. "Like any other ogre. Have you heard of these two prisoners?"

Placing his elbows on the table, the man turned his attention back to Ideria and leaned in, his smile even wider this time. Nevin went from simply distrusting him to downright hating him because of that smile. "Of the ogre and the woman who looks like you? I have indeed."

"Do you know which dungeon they're being held in?"

"Indeed, I do." Like the drawbridge of a castle devoted to lechery, the man lowered his hand to the table, empty palm face up.

Nevin was worried about the phrase "who looks like you." Was the man just playing off what she had said, or did he know Ideria was the daughter of Dearborn? He wanted to extricate himself and his sister from this situation. Ideria had other plans, as evidenced by the coins in her hand.

Below table level, Nevin grabbed her wrist. Reasoning with her would be out of the question, but he did want her to think about what she was going to do. The fire behind her eyes burned brighter than any candle or oil lamp in the tavern and he released her arm from fear of being engulfed by the inferno raging within. She was determined to make a bad decision and he could do nothing to stop her. Fortunately, Bartholomew could.

As if manifested by a wish, the mercenary turned knight appeared between the siblings, his knife slashing downward. The table shook upon impact and Nevin's first thought was the wretched man's hand would be affixed to it. Instead, the knife struck between the man's middle and ring fingers.

No longer smiling, the man withdrew his hand, a small bead of blood rolled between his knuckles from a wound no larger than a cut received from handling counterfeit papers. With no hint of worry or fear, the man stood, and still spoke directly to Ideria. "There are all kinds of rumors swirling around a place like this. There are quite a few about a girl . . . a girl I'd guess to be your age . . . who killed one of the king's dragons. Have you heard this rumor? I bet you have, maybe you've even been mistaken for her since these rumors state that she was a girl larger than most men. Within all of those rumors, though, there is one thing that is an absolute fact—the king has a bounty on this girl's head."

The man disappeared into the crowd.

Staying next to Ideria, Bartholomew bent down and spoke softly to her. "We have received information from much more reputable sources that they're being held in the castle's dungeon. Try to get a good night's sleep, because we'll head out at first light."

Ideria stood and walked away, aiming for the table with her friends.

Bartholomew sighed. "Well, we all know how she feels. How about you, son?"

"I understand that you and Draymon and the Wahls did what you had to do. I can't say it doesn't hurt, but it had to be done. I share my sister's zeal and anxiety in finding our mother, but not her tactics."

"Good. We uncles were counting on you to be the intermediary between the angry and the guilty. I know she won't listen, but if you could at least suggest to Ideria that she should wear her cloak, then you've done everything you can to help allay suspicions."

"Understood." Nevin was not certain Bartholomew heard him as his uncle disappeared into the crowd.

Nevin knew his role to play. He had been playing it is whole life. Sometimes he was the only one who could talk to Ideria, get her to listen whenever she refused to hear what the rest of the world had to say.

The table the others sat at was long with two benches. Woe was the largest by far, even larger than Ideria, even though he garnered his extra height through the point of his head and a significant amount of his girth came from the numerous sweet cakes he had consumed over the years. He and Ideria took up one entire bench. Nevin sat next to Hope, her wings fluttering as he took his seat. Rue was beside his sister. "Has Ideria told you our destination for tomorrow?"

"Yep," Rue replied.

Normally Rue spoke for the siblings, but he sat in silence, fidgeting with his spectacles to the point of removing them, scrutinizing them, and then returning them to their perch upon his nose. This became routine whenever he was upset. Everyone at this table had a lot to process, a lot to prepare for. What if the stories of their parents still being alive were false? A clever trap set by the king and his brother? The stories being true were no easier to bear—how could nine enemies of the king breakout two prisoners from the castle's dungeon, possibly the most fortified location in the country?

Everyone stared at the table, projecting their hopelessness to the twisting labyrinth of the uneven flow of the wood grain. For no reason, Hope said, "Maybe we need to focus on the one good thing that came from this."

All eyes were on Hope. Ideria, confused, bordering on incensed; her brothers weary. Nevin found himself confused as well, never once knowing Hope to make an attempt at optimism. He wondered if an ailment afflicted her. The faintest of smiles accompanied a slight twinkle in her eye as she looked around the table. "Us. I hate to think of it, but if events didn't happen the way they happened, then we would have never met."

Ten years ago, Draymon showed up to the Wahls' house. The stranger said a few words to them and Marrim Wahl broke down in tears. Even Hander, a retired army officer, hardened by the horrible forge of war, shed many tears. Draymon was introduced as "Uncle," but neither Nevin nor Ideria believed he was blood. His propensity to care for them knew no limits, so they took to him as if he were a legitimate uncle. He taught them how to fight, and often became a focal point of frustration when it came time to dig the tunnels, but he also taught them meditation techniques, which Nevin enjoyed immensely, and reminded them that the ways of combat were to protect the people they loved.

A few months later, their other uncle, Bartholomew, showed up. He had rakish good looks for a man with streaks of gray in his hair, and his sinister smile bedeviled those who beheld it. Danger was a shadow to him, never disconnected from him, no matter how seemingly insignificant. Nevin knew he and his sister should have been afraid of him, but he, too, quickly endeared himself through the humor found in his quick tongue and the wonder of sleight of hand magic.

His lessons were far less tiring than Uncle Draymon's, yet more complex. His mastery was of social situations and how to manipulate those within them to get what he wanted. And if that failed, then he would use swift, nimble fingers to pilfer. He, too, soon felt like an uncle.

Half a year later came another knock on the door. On the other end stood a satyr and a talking rabbit claiming that they fought beside Draymon and Dearborn. Children at the time, both Nevin and Ideria found the whole idea intriguing and funny—a drunk rabbit spouting naughty words! The Wahls' helped Phyl and Lapin purchase a tract of land with a house on it large enough to hold the twelve children of Bale Pinkeye. Nevin and Ideria enjoyed their uncles but were more than excited to finally get the one thing that had been lacking for all of their lives—friends!

A two-hour walk, or a one-hour run, and they could visit. They enjoyed the company of all twelve, even the ones too young to join them on adventures. The loss of parents created an unbreakable bond, an immediate understanding from all when an unexpected bout of melancholy struck for no reason or something random triggered a strong memory. All twelve were the product of Bale and Cherish, an ogre and a harpy. However, their mother did not die but instead left them with the pseudo-uncles. The loss of her husband had been too great in her heart, so she ran off with his sister, Uncle Phyl's wife at the time because she reminded Cherish of Bale in mind, body, and spirit. But the loss of a parent was the loss of a parent, no matter the circumstance.

Very soon after meeting, Nevin and Ideria learned that the older children of the ogre-harpies had similar skills when it came to pilfering. Tavern owners refused to serve Lapin after a round of inebriated tirades and the children were too young to purchase from distillers, so he taught them the finer points of teamwork when it came to thieving a crate of booze now and again. Plus, the cost of feeding twelve per-petually hungry children was astronomical, especially when the only set of hands old enough to make a wage belonged to a foppish satyr.

"She's right," Nevin said.

Hope smiled at him. Again, an act that he had seen her perform infrequently. "Thank you."

"As tragic as the reason why fate had put us together, we would most certainly have never met otherwise. I can't fathom how hellish Ideria's and my lives would be had we no contemporaries to befriend, no others who could understand our situation. Now, we have potentially found something that we thought lost to us. We have the rare opportunity to fulfill a wish that we've all made secretly in our beds at night while awaiting slumber. Tomorrow starts our journey."

"He's right," Hope said to her brothers. "I don't know about you two, but I . . . I can't remember what Father looks like."

Rue pointed to Woe with his spectacles and said, "He looks like him."

"You know what I mean."

Rue sighed and returned his spectacles to his face. He put a meaty hand on his sister's shoulder. "I do. I miss father and am willing to travel across the lands and into the keep of Castle Phenomere to unshackle him. If. If he's still there and still alive. Now, I'm off to get some sleep, so I may begin this journey with fresh legs and a clear mind."

He stood and walked to the nearest set of stairs leading to the second floor. Woe stood as well. "What he said."

Hope lost her smile and turned back to Nevin. "Is . . . is it okay that I believe he is still alive?"

"If it weren't, then you wouldn't be named Hope."

The green skinned harpy's eyes slicked over from the promise of tears. Her smile was smaller this time as her bottom lip quivered. She stood from the table as well and whispered, "Thank you," before she left.

"Nice speech," Ideria mumbled. "Put them in a better mood."

"It was meant for you, too."

"Only one thing can put me in a better mood."

"Obviously that's us getting captured, tortured, and killed."

Ideria frowned. "How could you say something like that?"

Nevin offered a nonchalant shrug of his right shoulder. "I'm simply making deductions based on the information you've given. For the past six days, you've been moping around like a princess unable to wear her favorite dress to the ball. You've shown zero interest in planning anything. And you know very well that you should be wearing your cloak everywhere we go. Without it, you're begging to be recognized. There is quite a bounty out on the girl who killed a dragon, from what I hear."

"Our grandparents died right before we learned that—"

"That they and our uncles have been lying to us for the past decade. You've said that already, repeatedly. I've stated my rebuttal and if you didn't appreciate it the first time, stating it again would do no good. Everyone knows how you feel, except maybe that potted plant in the corner of the room. If you wish to take a moment and go whine to that as well, I can wait."

Her eyes were as cold as the blue ice they resembled. Muscles under her ears flexed as she clenched her jaw. Nevin knew exactly what to say to make her scorn dissipate. "Never once did you ask me how I feel."

Ideria's anger crumbled away like a poorly constructed statue. Her face softened, and Nevin timed his next statement perfectly, right before she gave way to tears. "I do feel the same way, trust me, but we need to move our emotions past where they are now because stagnation is far too dangerous. Over the next couple of days, we need to plan, with our uncles, with Rue, Woe, and Hope, and with their uncles, a way to sneak into Castle Phenomere itself and break our mother out of prison."

FIFTEEN

"ARE WE SURE we want to do this now?" Bale asked.

Dearborn pulled the ends of cloth to tighten the knot. She pulled again to ensure its sturdiness. The makeshift sling needed to support fifteen pounds and it could jeopardize their plan should it give. She slung it over her shoulder, the ends crossing over her chest and back. "The longer we wait, the more time Daedalus has to hunt down my children."

"I know, but it will be dawn soon. We need darkness for this plan to work. You said so yourself."

"I said it's better with darkness. And we still have darkness, so we'll need to quit bickering and act quickly. Are you ready?"

"Yes. Are you?"

"Almost." Dearborn placed the three packages Bale had pilfered from the kitchen, one of them just today, into the sling. She tucked her two knives into the rope garters she had tied around her thighs.

Bale had also somehow brought back a great length of rope. He told her that during the training exercises he had seen it coiled up by a pile of chopped wood. After a quarterstaff blow to the gut, he needed to void his bowels and ran behind the pile of wood. None of the soldiers wished to see the ogre perform such a bodily function, so they had all turned away, leaving Bale plenty of opportunity to lift his thick tunic and wrap the rope around his chest and waist. Now, he stood at his opened cell door with the rope looped over his shoulder and across his chest. "Okay. Lead the way."

Having fought demons without help from any form of divine assistance, Dearborn no longer believed in the gods, yet as she and Bale scurried down the hallways away from their prison, she recited every prayer she could remember.

Dearborn had never been to this part of the castle, but she knew where she was going if her powers of deduction did not betray her. For the past nine years, she listened to stray conversations between guards, asked subtle questions of the messenger boys and pushed the limits of where she could sneak off to at night. She knew where she and Bale needed to go by where others had gone. More accurately, they sought one hallway that everyone left out of their stories. It was on the ground floor, and close to the stairwell leading up to the prisoner cells. Dearborn and Bale had little issue getting there, the most difficult part of the trip being the effort of summoning the courage to make the journey to the lone door in the middle of the short hallway.

Using her foot, Dearborn opened the door with ease. As she suspected, there was no lock, not even a latch, just a chunk of roughly carved wood on hinges. She made no acknowledgment of Bale's audible gulp and stepped inside the room.

The darkness was oppressive, had a weight to it, like a wall that stopped the hallway light abruptly. Dearborn felt the need to shoulder her way into the darkness, deeper into the humid room. The darkness created blindness, but she could tell that it moved, every inch of the room. The sound of a million moist sponges being released after being squeezed to its limit filled the room, broken up by Bale shuffling his feet across the stone floor behind her.

He was here. She knew it. "Light a torch."

The squishing noises stopped as did the moving darkness. The only sound in the room was her heartbeat.

A spark of flint and the tip of a torch was lit. Wavy shadows made the features of the dead minotaur's face seem even more ghoulish, the somber appearance of death. The sickening voice of Haddaman Crede slid through the thick air, "My dear Dearborn. I've been waiting for this day."

"Dearborn? The floor is moving." Bale spun in slow circles, shuffling his feet to move away from the undulation.

"Just slugs, Bale. We talked about this."

The minotaur lumbered to one of the walls and lit a sconce. Close to the sconce was a holder for the torch. The flames provided enough light to reveal a cow carcass, a horse carcass, and two human bodies among a pile of bones. All four bodies moved as if reacting to dreams while asleep, but Dearborn knew there was no dreaming. Slugs fed upon the bodies, the rout so large that they caused the movements.

"They may be slugs, but I assure you, they are not the kind that gardeners tut about while fussing to keep them from their plants." The pride in Haddaman's voice induced nausea within Dearborn more than any slug could. She hid that feeling with a smirk as she leaned down to pluck one of the dozen making their way up her leg. Like a showman, she held it in front of her, between her thumb and finger. "I'm very well aware of how special they are."

A quick pinch, followed by a burst of blood, and the slug went limp. A snarl twisted Haddaman's lips. Dearborn dropped the dead thing and said, "They are your eyes. They are how you are able to see all the workings within the castle."

Bale backed closer to Dearborn and mumbled, "So that's why you always killed any slug you saw and fed them to your rats."

"Yes, Bale. I wanted to make sure Haddaman didn't know what we were doing in our cells over the years. He should be thanking me for keeping his little secret. I can't imagine either King Oremethus or Prince Daedalus would appreciate being spied on."

The minotaur stood, its imposing form almost scraping its horns on the ceiling. Haddaman dangled from the veiny cords between the beast's legs like genitalia, his own manhood growing as he talked. "My dearest Dearborn, even though I couldn't see inside your cells, I knew very well what you were doing. Raising your rats, feeding your fellow prisoners, making friends of the pageboys. Planning an escape. It is *you* who should be thanking *me* for keeping your secrets. A gratitude that I intend to collect now. Daedalus's cock may wither at the thought of possessing you, but I assure you, *mine* won't!"

The minotaur took an awkward step forward, its fingers curled and ready to grab Dearborn. She procured one of her knives and Haddaman laughed. "That tiny little thing against my minotaur? You expect to stop me with that?"

The corpse's arm swiped at Dearborn, but she ducked it with ease.

Bale danced about. "Dearborn! There are more slugs than I can step on."

Now was her time to strike. She took one of the packages from her sling, sliced it with her knife, and tossed it to Bale. She did the exact same thing with the second package. The third she kept for herself after slicing it open.

Bale held a package in each hand, the granular contents spilling from the slits.

Salt.

The ogre had the wherewithal not to panic, not to dump the contents all at once. In controlled motions, Bale made sweeping arcs with his hands, spreading sheets of salt on the slugs around him, starting with the mounds by his feet and extending outward. The blanket of flesh on the ground rippled and squirmed away from Bale. Wasting no time, Dearborn reached into her package and threw handfuls of salt onto the minotaur. Should she live through this, Dearborn knew she would never forget the screams from the dead bull's throat. Haddaman screamed too, from anger rather than pain.

The minotaur retreated and Dearborn advanced, splash after splash of salt. Scraping and clawing at its bull head, its bovine legs quivered with each step. Dozens of slugs fell away, meaty raindrops slopping against the floor. Haddaman bounced against his carrier, spinning around. Two decades of Dearborn's pain and anger could be summed up within this stump of a man, an evil beyond comprehension.

Savoring one last second of her revenge, Dearborn threw the last of the salt directly at his face. She ended the human filth by jamming her knife into his temple. To make sure this part of his life was over, she grabbed his neck and held him steady, while she watched his eyes fade to gray, his twisting lips twitch to a stop.

"They're dead," Bale whispered kicking through the piles of slug carcasses. "All of them."

That statement was music to Dearborn's ears. "His connection with them was far greater than I imagined. But we still have to hurry."

Resting on its haunches the minotaur no longer moved. Dearborn moved behind it and ran her blade down its spine. Dozens of dead slugs spilled out from the newly sliced skin. Bale joined her in her efforts, snapping and removing bones, scooping out gelatinous globs of what was once muscle. "This smells awful, Dearborn."

"Push past it for our children."

Grimacing, Bale shoved his left leg into the cut minotaur, then his right as if donning pants. His feet stopped at the top of the minotaur's tibias and Dearborn used some of the rope to secure them. Bale's hands went in next, turning the minotaur's arms into sleeves. He stood straight to get accustomed to balancing on bones and walked about the room to get acclimated to the bulk. Dearborn helped pull the rest of the carcass over Bale's head and shoulders, fighting with the contents of her stomach as the ogre made retching noises. To help him see and breathe better, she made a few slices along the base of the minotaur's neck. To complete the disguise, Dearborn climbed atop Haddaman.

If she were to cut him free, she would have nothing to support herself on the minotaur carcass, so she fought down the bile rising from within and placed one knee on the clammy skin of the man she just killed. The membranes and veins connecting Haddaman to the minotaur were slimy and difficult to hold on to and she had a small area to rest upon, but Dearborn grabbed enough to wriggle herself onto Haddaman's back. The web-work was much more unyielding than she expected, but she tucked her legs under herself and settled in among the rubbery tubes. The slugs were dead, but their mucus remained, oozing along the membranes and over Dearborn. She took a moment to close her eyes and recall a memory of her children. "Bale? Are you ready?"

"Yes." His voice was muffled, but she could still hear him.

He stood and she bounced against the minotaur's thighs. After a few seconds, Bale took his first unsteady step. Then the next. The fear of Bale's muscles giving way rolled around in Dearborn's thoughts, but for now, he was able to maneuver the minotaur, while she dangled from it.

So far, the plan was working. The smell and the thick secretions of dead slugs oozing over her body were almost unbearable, but so was the notion of staying within these walls, while Prince Daedalus hunted for her children. The halls were still mostly empty, a servant here and there and as she had hoped, they lowered their heads and hurried along as soon as they sensed that the lumbering form of the minotaur was near. It was easy to be in a disguise when no one wanted to look at it. Even the guards walking their patrol or stationed outside bolted doors opted to look everywhere the minotaur was not.

Bale's movements were slow and jerky, every other step twisted the fleshy cords around her more with the occasional slug body falling onto her hair. She had a difficult time seeing the entire world around her, but she had a good idea about their location. They turned down one last hallway, the one that led to a seldom-used side door at the back of the castle.

Bale stopped.

Dearborn tried to push the filmy cords away and adjust her position without disrupting Bale's balance. She wiped away a curtain of slime as a dead slug slid down her arm to see what blocked their escape.

Speekore.

The wretched hobgoblin was at the end of the hall talking to a guard. They were too far away to hear, but Dearborn deduced what they were talking about when the guard pointed to the other end of the hallway, to her and Bale.

Bale turned and lumbered back down the hall they had just come from. Each step came faster than before. Dearborn's world bounced and spun, disorienting her. Bale turned down another hallway, but she had no idea which one. In the distance, Speekore called out, "Haddaman!"

The running took a toll on Bale as he ran down another hallway, panting turned into grunting. Dearborn tried to right herself again, figure out where they were in the castle, but she had never been to the ground floor before and had no idea what landmarks to look for. The hallway was poorly lit gray stone and had three massive doors. Sobbing, Bale limped to the first door and tried to grab the metal latch, but it was impossible to do so with dead fingers, so he slammed his shoulder against it to no avail. Sliding along the wall for support, he made his way to the next door. This one opened with ease. Dearborn oriented herself just in time to wish that the door had been locked.

Wall mounted torches and burning oil lamps numbered in the dozens and lit the room as if there were no walls to block the twin suns. Not a single shadow was to be found. This was Speekore's laboratory.

A man meticulously tacked to the wall like a prized butterfly, collected and immortalized for its beauty, had been flayed. Every inch of skin pulled away in flaps, pinned against the wall. Liquids dripped from the openings of dozens of copper tubes keeping his muscles and organs shimmering, his heart beating. Only his face remained untouched, his quivering lips repeating the words, "Kill me."

Other men dangled by wires from the ceiling, their bodies disassembled. A webwork of viscera connected the segmented pieces of arms and legs to and among the half dozen torsos. Each man was alive and awake, their hands and feet moving in a perpetual attempt to flee their fate. Pained faces also begged, "Kill me."

A dozen women strained against tight shackles along the other wall, all in various stages of pregnancy. The smallest belly swelled well beyond full term, while the largest drooped to the future mothers' knees as if their children would be born fully grown . . . if their progeny were even human. The life contained within pressed against their skin; the unmistakable outline of a hoof, the swirling imprints of tentacles, multiple hands. Every woman looked to the lone figure not tethered to the laboratory itself and moaned, "Kill me."

Dearborn wished she could grant their collective wish, to end their misery as humanely as possible. Now was not the time. Later, after she and Bale escaped this wretched place and found her children. Then she will come back and destroy this castle brick by brick.

Bale stopped in the middle of the room as if the repeated whispers of, "Kill me," had lulled him into a macabre trance. This gave Dearborn the chance to examine the room, find a way out. "There! Bale, there's a door at the back of the room."

No sooner than Bale started to step toward the exit, Speekore entered his laboratory. "Haddaman! Why did you run? What are you doing here? I came looking for you, because all your slugs have suddenly died, and I wanted to . . . Wait. You're not Haddaman!"

Bale ran to a cage by the exit, one that held half a dozen people, naked, dirty, fear stretching their faces into grotesque parodies of life. The closer he got, the more feverishly they reached for him through the bars as they yelled at him for help. Bale extended the left hand of the minotaur and the caged people took it. They pulled and yanked, their desperate fingers tearing at the arm with the effectiveness of butcher knives. Each grasp pulled away a strip of dead flesh, a chunk of rotted muscle.

"Guards!" Speekore called out. "Guards! To my laboratory!"

Dearborn tried to jump from Haddaman's back but found herself too knotted up in the pulpy strands. Handle slimy, her knife was difficult to wield but she used it to hack at the veins. There was too much give for her blade to find purchase. She finally sawed through one, but it was hardly enough. But Bale found success with his impromptu idea; the people in the cage tore away the minotaur's left arm.

His own arm now liberated, Bale grabbed the door handle and pulled. "I know where we are!"

Dearborn was happy to hear that until she realized that meant they were close to the sleeping quarters of the army trainees. Bale bounded down the hallway, bouncing off the walls, running from the shrill cries of Speekore, "Guards!"

Doors opened as confused young men peered out. A few stepped into the hallway, but Bale had worked up enough momentum to plow them over. The hallway led to the kitchen and the kitchen led to the world beyond the castle. The new soldiers chased them, their shouts louder than the din of Bale crashing through cooking equipment and utensils.

The horizon hinted at the first rays of the Morning Sun and for one fleeting moment, Dearborn felt free. In the span of one heartbeat, there were no soldiers, no dead slugs, no rotting minotaur carcass, no laboratory of horrors, no evil in the world. Just the hope of a new day. In the next heartbeat, Dearborn was back to reality.

The trainees caught up with the escapees outside, a wave of living bodies crashing into one dead one. Faceless hands ripped through the minotaur corpse and tore away the visceral webbing to get to Bale and Dearborn. Bale roared and lunged at the group; Dearborn swung blindly with her knife. Too many bodies proved that quantity trumped quality. Arms and legs pinned, Dearborn looked to the horizon again. Vision blurred by tears, she saw the first sliver of sunrise. As she heard Speekore issue commands to the soldiers, it might as well have been sunset.

SIXTEEN

THE CASTLE OF Phenomere was a monstrous structure. It was so large and sprawling that it needed to adjust to the surrounding terrain and so the royal architects had lost all hope of symmetry. Ideria had learned from her time spent with traveling scholars at her grandparents' table, that due to the unparalleled growth of Albathia, each new king felt the pressure to add to the castle. Prosperous people were happy people, and happy people had families, and prosperous, happy families grew. More families meant more resources expected from the king and his court. More governance, more law enforcement, more schools, more soldiers to protect it all. Every half-decade, the king needed to decree that more space was necessary for the castle. Up went more turrets and barracks while castle walls grew onto all adjacent piece of land.

The back corner of the castle was one of the more forgotten spots. If more expansion were needed, then it would have to flow around the healthy lake that was already too close to the one wall as well as deal with the forest. Hundreds of trees from the encroaching forest would have to come down first. It was from these trees that Ideria studied the back corner of the castle in the burgeoning light of a new dawn.

The corner turret was like none other, a round tower so large it could house everyone from a goodly sized village with ease. Walls extended from two parts of the tower to form a corner and a connection to the main structure. This turret held a barracks for newest recruits of the king's army, a kitchen, and the dungeon.

"I know what you're thinking," Nevin whispered from behind Ideria.

She had hoped waking up before everyone else would have yielded a moment's worth of peace and quiet, an opportunity to study the structure and situation. Younger brothers always seemed to ruin plans of older sisters. "I doubt that you do."

"You're thinking about how many kicks it would take to get through the tower door. You're thinking about storming through the hallways swinging your sword wildly about and killing every soldier in your path. You're thinking that you would kill any dragon that may be on premises. You're thinking of tearing off the bars of mother's cage. But worst of all your thoughts, you're thinking that your stupid plan would actually work."

Younger brothers *often* ruined plans of older sisters. Sometimes friends could be just as bad.

Rue ambled up to the siblings and looked over Ideria's shoulder. "So, what are looking at?"

"My sister is thinking of ways to kill herself," Nevin answered.

The ogre squinted and adjusted his spectacles. "Oh. So, she's thinking about how many kicks it would take to get through the tower door, storming through the hallways swinging her sword wildly to kill every soldier and dragon in her path, and then ripping off the bars of her mother's cage?"

"Yes."

"Does she think that nonsense will actually work?"

"Knowing my sister, she does."

"Damn fool plan if you ask me."

Ideria huffed. "Well, I didn't ask you, and I wasn't thinking that. Even if I was thinking that, it's not such a bad plan."

"What plan?" came from above. Joy dropped to the ground, flapping her wings once to soften her landing. "If it's Ideria's then it probably involves kicking down the tower door, storming through the hallways, swinging—"

Ideria slapped both palms against her forehead and closed her eyes. "For the love of . . . I was not thinking of that."

"So, you were just exploring your feelings, while gazing upon the tower?" Rue asked.

"Of course not. I was certainly trying to come up with a plan, just not the one you fools keep insisting on."

"No? What do you have so far as a plan?"

Kick the tower door down.

Use sword to kill all soldiers and any dragons.

Rip the bars from Mother's cage.

Ideria rubbed her eyes with the base of her hands. "I don't have one yet."

Leaves rustled as Woe shuffled his feet along the forest floor. He stopped in between his brother and sister. "Should we go help Dad?"

Ideria removed her hands from her face to see a commotion by the tower, but not what Woe was talking about. Soldiers chased a minotaur. Few details could be seen from this distance, but it looked sickly and she was surprised that it moved so well. "It's a minotaur, Woe, not your father."

"But . . . but it is Father. Inside the minotaur."

Everyone watched. No one took a breath. Two dozen soldiers brought down the minotaur. Barking commands from behind them was Speekore, the mad hobgoblin who practiced in dark sciences and experiments. A chill ran down Ideria's spine from all the horror stories she had heard about him and to see him with his glass encapsulated eyes and metal jaw.

Something was off with this minotaur. It was moving as if it were a puppet. When the soldiers brought it down, it fought back, but by twisting in unnatural ways. Then a figure burst from the thing's back. Large. Green. An ogre. A hitch caught in the throats of Bale Pinkeye's children as their father attacked the closest guards. The minotaur carcass still moved, though. A human hand reached out and flailed about as soldiers tried to grab it. They finally succeeded and pulled a woman from the belly of the beast. A large woman with long hair as black as a starless night, as black as Nevin's hair.

Dearborn Stillheart.

"Mother?" Ideria whispered as her legs started to move her out of the forest. Her feet moved faster toward her mother, the woman she thought was dead, the missing piece in her heart. Faster she ran. She heard voices shout after her from behind, but could not make out what they were saying, nor did she care. Faster still. The wind stung her cheeks and she had no concept of how fast she was sprinting until she contacted a soldier. He wore only pants, no armor to protect him. She caught him under the shoulder, popping it out of the socket and cracking his clavicle, and launched him through the air. She took a breath, allowing her mind to catch up with what her body was doing. It was difficult as the last cognition she could muster was standing within the bordering forest. Now she faced a dozen men and one screeching hobgoblin. More men flowed from the opened turret doorway as Speekore raced toward it, yelling at them to fetch weapons. Some of the men stopped and ran back through the door, while others sprinted toward the skirmish in progress.

Ideria became aware of her surroundings as a fist connected with her jaw. The blow was glancing and not solid, but enough for her wits to gather. The castle was twenty paces in front of her, a large pond next to it she had not noticed it from the forest, now a hundred paces behind her. The grass beneath her feet was short, obviously munched on by domesticated sheep. Light from the Day Sun danced of the placid waters of the pond. Her mother was alive; the only obstacles keeping her a reunion were the newest recruits of the King's army.

Soldiers wrestled with her mother, struggling to contain her limbs. Ideria rushed to her aid, but the soldier who punched her swung at her again. A decade of having been trained by Draymon, Bartholomew, and the best instructors they could find developed certain instincts within Ideria. She let that training take over, dodging the punch with ease and grabbing the man by the scruff of his shirt and the top of his pants. Little effort was needed to lift him and a scant more so to throw him into a pair of oncoming soldiers.

Ideria only made it two steps before three more men converged on her. Their lack of armor gave her the advantage. Fist to nose. Elbow to cheek. Foot to sternum. But sheer numbers stripped away that advantage.

She felled two, but three more appeared. Then another. And another. She backed away, but they all advanced on her. Surrounded her. They were trained in tactics and this one was simple: quantity over quality. She wanted to keep them at optimum striking distance, but they closed the circle they had formed around her. She went hard at one soldier and broke his arm in multiple places, but the other men took advantage of the calculated sacrifice and crashed in on her.

Their strikes were weak, too close to put any force behind their hits, but they were coming from everywhere. Front, back, sides. She had no strategy for this situation, becoming direr by the second. Until a streak of blood splashed across her face.

The struggle stopped. Every soldier looked suddenly confused, none more so than the one in front of her with the blood gushing from his sliced open throat. He fell, his face disappearing and making way for another face: her brother's. Nevin's dagger was warm with blood, yet his face held no expression, just his piercing blue eyes. Cold as a painted statue, a simulacrum of a human with all the outside pieces and none of the inside ones.

Two of the other soldiers suddenly disappeared from the mass of bodies, yanked away by Rue. Holding one in each arm, the ogre slammed the soldiers together and dropped their limp bodies. Another soldier vanished, this one hoisted into the sky by Hope. The harpy strained her arms and wings to lift the squirming soldier and when she achieved the height of the turret's roof, she let go. The man hit the ground with a thud. He no longer squirmed.

Bartholomew and Draymon joined the fighting, tearing through the soldiers with precision knife cuts. Their efforts thinned the number of soldiers descending upon Bale. Thanks to the help from her brother and her friends, Ideria was free and charged toward her mother. As easy as picking ticks from a dog, Ideria tossed the soldiers away. Behind her played the sounds of men dying; in front of her, Mother. Down to the last three, her mother had been freed enough to help. She wasted little time in ending the lives of her captors as she broke their necks.

Ideria cried, her bottom lip twitching so hard that she had difficulty forming the word, "Mother?"

Tears ran rivers from Dearborn's eyes, the same blue eyes that Ideria saw every time she looked in a mirror. A similar face, too. If not for the hardness and weathered skin, it might have been the same.

Dearborn placed her right hand on Ideria's cheek, her left on Nevin's as he joined them, standing next to Ideria. She opened her mouth, but no words came out, only a howl of pain from being struck by an arrow.

Ideria's world went red. She had no idea what caused the phenomena, blood in her eyes or something shifting inside of her, but everything changed to different shades of red. Her mother's face twisting in pain. Her brother's face in open-mouthed shock. The grass of the field. The stone of the castle. Every weapon-wielding soldier rushing from the open doorway.

She heard no noise, just the slow, steady thump of her heart. Not even her own screaming, an act she only assumed she was doing from the rawness burning hot in her throat. She saw no true motion either, just an image frozen in time with every beat of her heart.

Thump. A sword in her hand.

Thump. Gape-mouthed faces of anguish from dying soldiers.

Thump. Multiple geysers of blood captured mid-spray.

Thump. Severed heads just above the ground like over ripened fruit falling from a tree.

Thump. Blood.

Thump. Blood.

Thump. Blood.

"Ideria!"

Her mother's voice.

The world's colors came back to Ideria as did sound. Life moved at a regular pace now, her mother and brother and friends running to her. It hurt to breathe, and she was not sure if she was inhaling too fast or too slow. Her arms and legs shook, her joints all throbbing in unison. She had a sword in each hand and dropped them; they were too heavy to hold any longer. When she spoke, her words weighed more than the swords. "The rest . . . of the . . . soldiers, Mamma."

Ideria reached out for her mother but froze when red liquid flowed from her arms as if she pulled them from a pool of ink. Reality started to push through her dream state. She had killed people. She killed the soldiers who shot her mother with an arrow. How many, though? She started to look down. How many had she killed to have this much blood on her? Her mother stopped her. Both hands on her face, Dearborn kept her daughter from looking down. "They're gone, Ideria. There are no more soldiers."

Ideria could not feel her mother's skin through the wash of blood on her face. Her body shivered. Was this a chill? Or fear? Dearborn embraced her and whispered in her ear, "It's okay, Ideria. It's okay. You did what you had to do. It's okay."

"Mamma? The arrow?"

"Hit my leg. I've had worse injuries."

Still in her mother's arms, Ideria looked up to see her friends gathering around, all wearing the same mask of wide-eyed shock, except for Bartholomew. He wandered from one body to the next, kicking them to make sure they were dead. "Someone give her a cloth and let's get out of here."

Bartholomew could be bluntly honest without the need to coat his words with sugar. A tiny smile tugged at the corner of Ideria's mouth until she noticed a ripple in the nearby lake. Small waves rolled outward from a central point, but nothing had dropped into the water to create such a disturbance. More waves formed from nowhere. *Not from nowhere*, Ideria realized, but from under the water.

A geyser erupted as if the lake held something so offensive and vile the water needed to vomit it out as quickly as possible. The column of water returned to the lake in a gushing splash and what remained was a dragon. The water dragon.

It fell gracelessly from the sky, scales shimmering the dark blue of an ocean. It was smaller than the other dragons, one wing stiff and brittle, the front half of its right side wrinkled and folded from burn scars. Its leg there was shriveled and less agile than the others. A decade ago, the inferno dragon had belched a splash of magma on the water dragon during the insurrection battle of Oremethus, taking the throne from Perciless. A bit of pride pulsed through Ideria knowing that her mother was there and fought bravely for the side of righteousness. Her mother's effort left lasting effects on the scarred dragon. Despite its deformities and smaller size, it was still fearsome.

Claws digging into the ground, it landed and immediately opened its mouth to release a torrent of water. The column slammed into Bartholomew. He disappeared within the deluge, and when it stopped, his broken mass was hundreds of feet away.

"Uncle!" Ideria cried out. She tried to run to him, but her mother still held her, tighter now that they were under attack. Ideria wanted to run to the broken remains of the man who added levity to her training, who taught her tricks and told her secrets that she would have never learned from anyone else. But her mother refused to let her go and angled herself between Ideria and the dragon. Her mother used her body as a shield.

Her friends scattered trying to surround the dragon, each of them screaming for its attention. The beast's tail twitched as it hissed at each of its attackers. Anytime it prepared to release its hurricane breath, someone threw a knife or sword. It was usually Draymon, but the others helped as well. Hope even dropped a few heavy shields on the dragon's head.

The dragon lashed out. It snapped its jaws at Hope, swung its tail at Rue and Bale, swiped its claw at Draymon and Nevin. It became very focused on whoever it was attacking, not turning toward the various shouts and screams. It only paused when a shadow on the ground glided by. Everyone stopped and looked up.

The rising Day Sun acted as a backdrop to a terrifying silhouette—a winged creature approached. Another dragon? No. As the shape drew closer, it mutated from a winged animal to something more. Arms and legs of a human became visible but much larger. At the last second, Ideria recognized the shape, and she smiled. It was Woe.

The winged ogre dropped from the sky, using both hands to swing a mace with a head as large as her torso. He brought it down on the dragon's skull, just behind its right eye. The dragon roared in pain and turned toward its attacker to release another torrent of water.

Woe touched the ground long enough to bend his knees and launch himself into the air again. Within three flaps of his wings, he was face to face with the dragon. The beast opened its mouth to strike, but the ogre closed it, bringing the mace upward this time, slamming it against the underside of its jaw.

"Mother," Ideria said as she gently pushed Dearborn away. "Woe is attacking the dragon. We have to help."

Dearborn acquiesced, releasing her daughter and allowing her to pick up the swords she had dropped. Dearborn found one on the ground as well and followed Ideria into the skirmish.

Woe continued to club the dragon's head, while everyone else on the ground sliced at its body. Dearborn and her children focused their attacks on its chest by its mangled leg. It snapped its jaws at them but missed as they dove out of the way. The dragon whipped its head to the side to ready another strike, but Woe timed his attack perfectly, striking the monster's chin. The dragon's head drooped and everyone on the ground took advantage of its stunned state. A flurry of knives and swords cut through the scales of the dragon's neck releasing rivers of blood.

The dragon backed away, its bad leg giving out. It released one enfeebled attempt of a roar and collapsed. The only celebration came in the form of short-winded hugs.

Draymon started to walk toward the forest. "We need to leave. We'll celebrate our victory and mourn our loss later, but now we have to leave before any more soldiers arrive."

Upon hearing the word "soldier" Ideria looked back to the castle, to where she had attacked the throng of soldiers. She saw what she had done and fell unconscious from shock.

SEVENTEEN

"NOT OFTEN I get human clients," the satyress said, open palm in front of Landyr's face.

"That's because most humans aren't as enlightened as I."

"Or as flush with coin." She wiggled her fingers.

Landyr laughed as he rolled to his side and grabbed his coin pouch from under the bed. She had asked for three when she first crossed the threshold, but her skills were far beyond satisfactory, so he grabbed four coins from his pouch.

As he rolled back over, he sat up and cupped her hand, while placing the coins in it. Then he ran both hands up her arm, their paths deviating upon reaching her shoulder. His left hand slid down her side and stopped at the middle of her back, while his right slid over her bare breasts one more time and nestled in her leg fur. He kissed her and when he finished, she cooed and said, "You wish to go a third time?"

"Not tonight. I just wanted to keep one more memory of you."

The satyress giggled as she stood from the bed and ran her fingers through her hair to tame the wild curls bounding from her head to her shoulders. She donned a vest to hide her bosom and slid hoops of gold jewelry over her right horn. As she exited the room, she blew him one last kiss and said, "You have been one of my favorite clients. Ask for me if you ever lay your head down in this town again."

Landyr laid back on the bed and enjoyed the tingle of sweat evaporating from his skin. It had been too long since he had been with a satyress. Even longer since he had been with a dark elf. "Damnation."

His mind flooded with images of Chenessa as a dark elf, as a demon, as the void dragon. The satyress calmed the burning he had in his loins, but not the fire in his head. For that, he would need mead

Pants, boots, shirt, and he was on his way down from the second-floor rooms to the tavern below. A stool at the bar and coin on the bar top, and he was on his way to washing away the images in his mind.

"Hello." A woman's voice from the seat next to him. As soon as he looked over all he could see was green skin and cleavage; the cinched corset made sure of that. She wore a tricorn hat with one willowy blue feather stuck in the side. The way it was placed on her head and how she held herself, Landyr could see nothing more of her face than her chin and full lips. "Would you like some company tonight?"

Her voice sounded familiar, but he could not place it. At first, he thought it might be Leelanna, the goblin witch, but her hair was blood red, while the locks flowing from under this woman's hat were fawn brown. "Always, but I usually insist that I know who my company is."

The mysterious woman lifted her head.

Thorna.

Landyr almost jumped off his stool. He grabbed her arm and discovered the green of her skin was nothing more than a powder that left no stain and could easily be removed. "What . . . ? What is the meaning of this?"

Wearing a predator's smile, she purred, "I wanted to get your attention. Did it work?"

"Get my attention? Why?"

"Maybe I'm lonely. Maybe I'm tired of summoning up a stranger to satisfy a need. Maybe I no longer want inexperienced young men or the stench of stale ale that accompanies older men. Maybe it's time you and I explore."

"That is not a good idea."

"Why not?"

"Because I'm your general."

"That notion is more repugnant to you than alleyway horse shit. Never once in the past decade have you ever tried to refer to yourself as a general let alone made any attempt to live the title."

"Be that as it may, I—"

Thorna yanked her arm from Landyr's grasp as if he no longer deserved the privilege of touching it. "It's because I'm human, isn't it? Everyone knows you spend your days pining for a dragon, while you spend your nights with a woman from any species other than human. Tonight was the first time you looked at me like a woman, and that was only because I powdered my skin green."

This was the first time anyone was so blunt to him. Cezomir would chide him now and again, but he never blatantly stated that Landyr no longer preferred the company of his own kind. He felt like a child being accused of fearing darkness. "That's preposterous. Whether you're human or not, it just wouldn't be a good idea. Do you really think now this is the best time to attempt this? We were attacked by Daedalus' Elite Troop just two weeks ago."

"*Because* we were attacked two weeks ago is the very reason to attempt this now. Other than helping a local militia break up an army supply chain or aiding a Tsinel spy across hostile lands—that was the closest we have come to the king's men in the last ten years. The winds are starting to swirl, Landyr. A hurricane is coming soon and who knows if we're going to survive it."

She was right. Things had been out of sorts of late in every town they visited these past few weeks. Rumors were scurrying like rats about the happenings in Phenomere. But were these rats running from a sinking ship, or toward a bountiful meal? "I understand your feelings of uncertainty, especially with the loss of Rolin. I miss him greatly. You're right about my title of general. The only one who sees me as one is King Perciless. Rolin was much more than a mere subordinate. He was a friend. He was family. You all are, even the deplorable Cezomir."

"Let's not forget, Cezomir and Lina tried the same thing I'm proposing and have made it work ever since."

"If you're looking to explore the potential with someone that you've known for so long, then what about Brokar?"

"He and Rolin tried the same thing I'm proposing years ago and had made it work."

"Wait . . . what? Really? I never knew."

"Clearly. You've been too busy pining over a dragon."

"That's not—"

"Fair? Nothing about this journey has been fair."

"I know that. We've all sacrificed way too much. I was going to say accurate."

Thorna snorted and stood. As she did Landyr turned and noticed the satyress across the tavern sitting with two other satyrs. She smiled and waved to him. Thorna noticed the gesture and shook her head. "Right. Not accurate in the least. I've made a fool of myself, so I'm just going to go to my room and remove this ridiculous powder."

Landyr wanted to call out but had no idea why or what he would even say. Letting her leave, no matter how misguided her anger might be, was the best strategy for all involved. He kept repeating that to himself as he went back to his ale, hoping he would believe it soon enough.

"Trouble with your woman?"

The voice had smooth femininity and an enticing throatiness, but the last thing he needed tonight was anything to do with another woman. She was sitting to his right and he turned just enough to see red hair from his periphery. That was also far enough to show that he acknowledged her. "She's not my woman."

But she could have been. Landyr thought about that as he turned back to his left to look for Thorna, but she was gone. Maybe he should go to her room?

"Well, that's good," the woman continued, "Because I'm tired of all the men in this tavern telling me that they're married."

Landyr shook his head and chuckled. It was immediately obvious that men told her that because she missed the subtlety of politeness. As much as he hated to be hurtful, he was in no mood for the company of a stranger and needed to express that as plainly as possible. "I'm sorry, but I'm not—" he started, but when he saw the green scale of her skin and the slits in her yellow eyes his intentions spun half circle and he finished with, "—from around here."

"Interestingly enough, neither am I."

A snake woman. A beautiful one at that. Landyr originally thought that the satyr had satisfied his needs, but his burgeoning erection proved him wrong. "Pity. I was hoping to meet a local to show me around this city."

"Oh, really?" A smirk tugged at the corner of her lips, while her left eyebrow arched. "That truly is a pity, then, since it doesn't appear that I'm able to assist you."

"I never said that."

"But you clearly stated your wishes."

"Just one wish and it wasn't even really a wish. More like hope."

"The difference between the two concepts is . . . ?"

"Hope can turn into a wish. Here, I'll demonstrate. I wish to know your name and I hope you'll tell it to me."

"My name?" She glanced away, and then quickly looked back into Landyr's eyes. If she had been fending off her smile, she lost the battle. Her lips parted to expose a forked tongue that flickered a little with every "s" and two rows of evenly jagged teeth. "Samillia. My name is Samillia."

"You paused to debate about giving me your true name or not. I'm flattered that I received it."

"Why do you believe that I gave you my true name?"

"The way you look at me. The way you smile."

"So, I'm that easy to read? Well, let's see how well you do. Your name is?"

"Landyr. Am I lying?"

Landyr liked the way the tips of her forked tonged slid over her bottom lip as she contemplated her answer. "No. You are not."

"No?" He kept his eyes locked onto hers as he took a long pull from his mug. She was so mesmerizing that his mead tasted differently from the last time he sipped it. The sound of her voice raised the temperature in the entire bar, his skin warming with her every word.

"I can tell by the way you look at me. The way you smile."

"That's my line."

"It is, and I'm sure you've used it on many women."

"Only the beautiful ones." Landyr surprised himself with those words. They were true, but not his first choice.

"So, therefore you're a stranger in this town? Because you ran out of beautiful women to seduce in your home town?"

The world along Landyr's periphery began to blur as her eyes became all that he could focus on. A soothing warmth flowed through him. The truth with her was so easy, felt so right. "No. I'm here because I'm aiding King Perciless in the building of his secret army."

"Now that you've told me this, I fear it's no longer a secret."

Landyr took another swig of his mead, unable to pull his gaze away from her comforting eyes. "Very few people don't know about our secret army. Even Prince Daedalus, the pile of human manure, knows about it. He just can't find us."

"How do you know I'm not working for Prince Daedalus?"

"Because you're a woman."

"What does that have to do with my allegiance for or against the prince?"

"You've undoubtedly heard what he does to women. Rapes them. Keeps them captive in his castle. Has his twisted master of the sciences do sick experiments on them. How could any woman hold allegiance with filth like that?"

Her eyes disappeared. No. They did not disappear, but rather Samillia looked away and the rest of the world reappeared. Landyr's own eyes burned, watering as if he had not blinked in weeks. The warmth disappeared; the hairs on the back of his neck standing on end from the chill of his cooling sweat.

The past few moments were muddled in his mind, leaving him uncertain as to why Samillia now looked so rueful. Was it something he said?

As Landyr turned to reach for his drink, he caught sight of something from the corner of his eye. Thorna. Green powder long gone, she had traded her corset for a loose tunic and no longer wore the hat. Whatever flirtations her face had once known were forgotten, now replaced by an anger that would make the devil cringe. Landyr cursed his luck, demonstrating to himself that her accusations were accurate, having denied them just moments earlier. As he stood to go to her, she stormed away to the tavern exit.

"Landyr?" He so enjoyed how Samillia said his name and it hurt to ignore her. Instead, he followed Thorna, trying to determine the proper set of words that would better this situation.

"Thorna?" Outside, the cool night air rejuvenated him, sweeping away the stuffiness of the too warm tavern. He still had no idea how to manipulate the conversation to his favor, but he felt more prepared for it. "Thorna, wait."

She made it to the other side of the road before she stopped and spun around. "No. Whatever you're about to say, don't. I'm not some bar trollop to seduce with sugary words, nor am I your betrothed to whom you need to explain your actions. You have made it abundantly clear that our relationship is to be professional only, with no chance whatsoever to explore anything more."

"I just wanted to explain myself."

"You don't have to."

"I feel like I must. What you saw was not at all what you might think."

"No? Is that why you brought her along, to corroborate whatever pathetic excuse you attempt to muster?"

"Bring her . . . ?" Landyr turned to find Samillia had followed him. "Samillia? Why—?"

She flicked her tail and a glint of steel caught his eye. A knife.

"Why do you have—?" Landyr started to ask but stopped short when she threw the blade at him.

Too surprised to dodge, Landyr could only watch the knife fly between Thorna and him and sink to the hilt in a stranger's throat.

The man dropped the dagger he was holding and brought both hands to his neck as he fell to his knees. Two more men with daggers rushed toward Landyr and Thorna. He had no idea what was happening, but his training and reflexes kept him alive more than his conscious mind. The dagger slices were wild and uncontrolled, easy to block or dodge. These were the attacks of a brigand whose knowledge of a blade failed to move beyond cutting food or threatening innocents. Taking the dagger proved little challenge for Landyr, and even less so to use it to end this cretin's life.

Thorna also disarmed her attacker, however, her killing blow was more than a simple throat slice like Landyr's. Instead, she stabbed the man. Repeatedly. Well past his death. Landyr wanted to say something to make her stop, but as the sprays of blood splashed her face and tunic, he thought better of interrupting her. He assumed some other external catalyst would make her stop, much to his chagrin the external catalyst came in the form of screams erupting from the tavern.

"What is happening?" Landyr asked the attacker that Samillia saved him from. However, the knife had gone too deep and the man lay dead in a puddle of blood pooling from his neck. "Damnation! Thorna, the tavern!"

Questions about Samillia buzzed around Landyr's mind like agitated hornets, but he swatted them away, no time for them now. The men they had disposed of were not an isolated trio of bandits. Up and down the streets other men with weapons laughed and whooped as they chased women or bludgeoned the elderly. The town was under siege, but not from some army or militia. A consortium of the wicked. Was Samillia a part of this? Was she setting him up? If so, then why save his life by killing the lout who tried to sneak up behind him? A part of it or not, she followed him and Thorna as they ran across the street to the tavern.

Thorna aimed for the door, brandishing the blood-slicked dagger she recently procured, but Landyr grabbed her arm. Using prudence as a divining rod, Landyr dragged her to the closest window to see what they were about to rush into.

There was too much commotion within the tavern to get an accurate count of those within, but Landyr estimated more than two dozen. That number stunned him. How was it possible to have a band of miscreants so large? Every plan Landyr concocted was dashed to shreds as the skirmish in the tavern intensified. The patrons attempted to fight back, but they were outnumbered. Then everything stopped, all eyes looking up to the second-floor landing. King Perciless.

The window's glass was too thick to hear distinct words, just muffled voices. Perciless walked down the stairs, Cezomir, Lina, and Brokar in tow, and allowed themselves to be taken into the custody of the attackers. Landyr shook his head in awe—his king was willingly giving himself up to stop the invaders from hurting anyone else. Undoubtedly, he was telling the brigands the truth, letting them know who he was. Whatever he was saying seemed to be working. The fighting stopped. Any citizen in the clutches of an attacker was freed. The group of miscreants escorted the king and his protectors out the door and down the street.

Hiding in the nearby alleyway, Landyr pointed his dagger at Samillia. "Were you a part of this? Did you help set us up?"

Her hair flowed like water as she shook her head. "No. I swear. I just wanted a nighttime tussle between the sheets."

Landyr believed she was not a part of this sudden invasion, but as he thought about the weightless feelings of being ensnared by her eyes, he knew she was up to something more sinister than a simple cure for loneliness. "No? You are quite skilled with a blade."

She shrugged her shoulders and pointed to Thorna. "So is she. A girl can't be too careful."

Thorna snarled at Samillia and walked out of the alleyway. "Come on. We need to follow them."

Landyr slid the dagger between his belt and his pants. "Do you know who those men kidnapped?"

Samillia shook her head. "No. Should I?"

"That was King Perciless and thanks to your skills, you're going to help us rescue him."

EIGHTEEN

DAEDALUS STOOD IN the hallway, arms crossed over his chest to keep his anger from exploding from it. The stench was the only thing that distracted him from his rage. The smell of the festering meat, the sourness of death made sticky by the moist air. How did Haddaman keep his room so humid?

Four barrels. Two castle guards poured four full barrels of oil on everything in this room. The hundreds of dead slugs, the piles and piles of bones from whatever animals Haddaman had been feeding to the slugs, the rotted hay used for bedding, and the remains of the room's master in the center of it. Both guards had already vomited from the sights and smells, and Daedalus considered adding them to the list of things to be burned. Such weakness should not be tolerated. Alas, he had more pressing matters on his mind, as General Perrator kept reminding him. "Your Highness, we must devise a plan to deal with the ramifications of this."

"I wish to enjoy this moment, general, and I wish to enjoy it in silence," Daedalus hissed.

The guards demonstrated that they did not share the same wishes as the prince. As soon as the liquids had been emptied from the last barrel, both guards scurried from the room with their heads down, the one burying his face in the crook of his arm to stifle retching noises. Daedalus let them leave.

Ten days ago, he had received word of Haddaman's death, the notion bringing a smile to his face. But the cost of such good news was too high. Dearborn had escaped. Not only did Daedalus lose his prized possession, but she had help from her children, the very things he sought. It took only two days of sleepless flight to return from his hunt, and then he began to scour the surrounding towns and cities looking for that bitch and her whelps. His efforts were fruitless, and he was fatigued. He needed rest, a fresh mind to solve this puzzle. But first, he needed a bit of merriment.

Holding a stick of wood to the flame of the nearest wall sconce, he savored the time it took for the end of the wood to catch fire. Almost ceremonially, he took three steps to the side, away from the doorway. Perrator moved away from the door opening as well, except in the opposite direction. Daedalus smiled and tossed the burning stick into the doorway.

The flame caught with ease, yellows and oranges danced with each other in the room, flaring into the hallway any time they hit a larger pool of oil. Once the heat dissipated enough, Daedalus moved to the doorway and watched the contents of the room burn. Satisfied that Haddaman had not somehow possessed the foresight to procure the services of a necromancer to raise himself from death should he meet it, Daedalus walked away. General Perrator followed. "Has your catharsis been satisfied?"

"Until you opened your mouth."

"I feel I would be doing a great disservice to you and the king if I did not bring up that you just completed a funeral pyre for your advisor."

The prince's chuckle came unannounced and in the form of a snort. Advisor, indeed! Daedalus allowed the sick creature to live because of his ability to pull information from the shadows. Any suggestions made by Haddaman benefited Haddaman. If any part of his advice benefited the king our country, then it was merely a scrap of food left over from someone else's feast. "Am I to assume that you wish to take his role?"

"I do not wish to, but I see that you are lacking any other feasible option."

"Baah! I have plenty of better options than you."

"Am I to assume you wish Speekore to fill Haddaman's role?"

"Don't be so daft, even in jest. That slimy hobgoblin is a dozen hells worse than the foul wretch whose remains I just burned."

"Very well. Who else will ascend the ranks to become your new advisor?"

"General Yulunda Griff. That fellow is both cunning and far more affable than you."

"Clearly not, or you wouldn't have damned him to Speekore's laboratory last month."

Daedalus stopped in his tracks and regarded General Perrator. Everything about this man exuded war, from the battle scars to the muscles forged from fighting. Were the general a sculpture, then the artist used a battle ax to carve him from a rogue mountain boulder. There was nothing Daedalus could do to threaten this creature. He assumed Perrator drank poison for breakfast and used knives to scrub his skin clean while bathing in acid. How many soldiers would it take to subdue Perrator? Would it be worth the cost?

Daedalus knew to give that order would be to waste one of his greatest resources. Since he had no means at his disposal to threaten the general, then the notion of garnering the truth through the liberal use of fear was nothing more than a whimsical fairy tale. Yet when Daedalus looked into the half-giant's eyes, he saw no hint of a duplicitous nature. The general would tell him the truth simply because he was a good soldier. "Very well, advise me."

"The troops the king has removed from Kallistah Pass—"

Daedalus slammed his skeletal fist against the wall, leaving a crater as bits of stone shot in all directions. "Damnation! I knew I would regret the decision to make you advisor, but I never imagined it would be mere seconds afterward. I have heard enough about that damn pass. I demand silence from you regarding the topic."

"You may command everything within the castle, sire, including my silence, but outside these walls, you have no influence over Tsinel moving troops into Albathia."

This brute could fold the average man like a single sheet of paper, yet somehow had the wherewithal to know exactly which words to choose to manipulate Daedalus with similar ease. But was that not the job of an advisor, to make those he advised think? To give as much information as possible to make the best decisions? Had he come up with the idea first, Daedalus would shower himself with congratulatory platitudes for picking such a skilled advisor. "You're telling me that Tsinel will invade us through a tiny road cut through the Timeless Mountains?"

"The pass is too small, and the terrain is too unwieldy for entire garrisons with heavy artillery, but foot soldiers and healthy enough steeds can make it through. And the weather has been leaning toward unseasonably warm. Our troops may not have been engaging the enemy, but they were fending off the enemy just the same."

The Timeless Mountains. The northern border between Albathia and Tsinel was a natural one—an ancient mountain range. There were a few other mountains scattered about Albathia, most notably the ring around The Scorched Sea, the desert where Oremethus had found the demon stone that scrambled his sanity. The Timeless Mountains range between the two countries made all other mountains look like foothills. The northern part of the mountain range terminated at the ocean, massive crags of snow and ice leading into frozen waters. The mountains traveled southward for a majority of the continent, keeping Albathia to the west, Tsinel to the east. Halfway down the range was Kallistah Pass. The road was not always flat, but the twenty-mile stretch was the shortest, fastest, and safest way to travel from one side of the Timeless Mountains to the other.

The Horizon River flowed south from the mountains, named for being so wide at the start that an individual standing on one side could not see the other side, just the horizon. The river formed a second natural barrier between Albathia and Tsinel, draining into the Southern Sea. Forests and fields were the final borders as they extended from the sea to the ocean. Most of the war took place there and that was where Daedalus spent his focus. The southern part of

Horizon River did taper in width to create more manageable crossing points, but Daedalus made sure to destroy every bridge that had connected the two countries. He wanted to keep the war contained to one area. Alas, he would have no such luck. "I assume you're going to suggest that I send the troops back to Kallistah Pass."

"No. I'm going to suggest that we disperse the troops to the nearest towns around Phenomere."

Daedalus brushed the dust and stone flecks from his skeletal hand. "Dare I ask why?"

"To help with the local constabulary."

Daedalus wondered if he could drive his bone hand through Perrator's chest but thought better of it. The general eschewed death as if it were nothing more than a fly buzzing too close to his face. Daedalus had yet to encounter anything that could do damage to his arm, yet he feared the general might be able to. He took a deep breath to remind himself that the half-giant was a warrior, not a bureaucrat. "If you are to be my advisor, you need to give me reasons for your suggestions as well as the suggestion itself. Brevity of statement leads to excessive conversation."

Perrator shifted his posture and snarled his upper lip. Daedalus wondered if the general was weighing the options of trying to kill him, frustrated by his demands to act a part he had little training for. "Very well. Vogothe is dead. Even if the criminals who live in the underworld didn't know Haddaman was Vogothe, they have quickly learned that the head crime lord is dead. Many who have any form of power are making a play to be the new crime lord."

Daedalus shook his head, dismayed. "How is that possible? He's only been dead for ten days."

"I have seen firsthand in every army I have ever commanded—rumors fly faster than arrows. Local constables have been sending messengers to the castle this past week requesting out help in the form of troops."

"Are you telling me that crime has increased throughout the surrounding towns so much that the locals can't handle it? How many messengers have visited the castle?"

"Thirteen so far with more every day. The news of this has undoubtedly reached the ears of other local crime lords, each emboldened by the lack of consequence of asserting their influence. The locals do make attempts, but most times they're outmatched. The town of Wrenfeld has been burned to the ground."

"Bah. Wrenfeld. I wouldn't even call it a town. Five public buildings at most surrounded by farms. If these so-called crime lords are focusing on places like Wrenfeld, then we've nothing to worry about."

"A voice unheard by Oremethus will vilify Daedalus and glorify Perciless. Surely you've heard of the secret army that Perciless has been building?"

Daedalus smashed his fist against the wall again, creating a bigger dent than the first one. "Yes! I am very aware of Perciless building his secret army. I have been aware of it for years! I have been hunting him. I paid others to find him. I hired mercenaries and bounty hunters. I captured and tortured wizards into helping me find him. I gave the task to Haddaman and when he provided no results, I've given the order to my Elite Troop to find him. Yes, good sir Advisor, I have heard a tale of Perciless building his secret army."

"Then why add to it? If you can't protect the people, then they will turn to someone who can. We can send a hundred troops to meet up with the hundred that are on their way back from Kallistah Pass with instructions. Five to ten soldiers will be more than enough to help bring any town back to order."

"If I do as you suggest, Advisor, then how do we deal with the situation at Kallistah Pass?"

"Not we—you. Take your dragon to the Pass. You will find either the solders of Tsinel coming into our country, or you will find deserters attempting to leave our country, or both. Whatever you find, your dragon's breath will add them to your army. You will have a firsthand account of the situation and devise the best plan possible on how to handle it. If nothing else, send the new skeletons through the Pass to confound whatever soldiers Tsinel has on the other side."

Daedalus worked his jaw muscles, chewing on the possibility of following Perrator's suggestion. "That is a rather well thought out plan indeed. However, I have a burning in my gut that can only be quenched by the blood of Dearborn and her children."

"Now that she has escaped from the dungeon, what do you think she'll do?"

"Attempt to flee, of course. I've been personally searching the nearby towns."

"If the rumors of the king ordering the troops away from Kallistah Pass, making an unfettered path to Tsinel, reach her ears, then where do you think she'll go?"

Perrator tried Daedalus' patience, but his advisory results had been satisfactory so far. "It seems I shall be making a personal visit to Kallistah Pass."

"Very good. In case Dearborn does not choose that path, I will instruct the soldiers to pass on to the local constables that the crown is willing to pay for the capture of the escaped prisoner and her children, their weight in gold."

Daedalus nodded. "You have some good ideas, Perrator."

The half-giant bowed, an awkward attempt to show fealty. "Thank you."

"Haddaman had good ideas, too. Sometimes, they didn't work according to plan. It'd be wise for you to contemplate that. In fact, to help you remember that, his old room is your new room. Call upon as many servants as necessary to help you clean it to your liking. After the fires die down, of course."

Finally, Perrator's expression shifted to something other than anger, one of discomfort, as he looked at the guttering flames in his new room. It was far from the look of fear that Daedalus strove for, but it was a start. The half-giant sighed. "Of course."

Daedalus stifled a laugh as he left his new advisor alone with his thoughts. He had to get himself and his dragon ready for a trip to Kallistah Pass.

NINETEEN

DEARBORN BRUSHED IDERIA'S hair as her daughter brushed the horse's mane. The flaxen stands flowed through Dearborn's fingers like newly spun silk, a form of Heaven and she would have been content to do this all day. This was Diminutia's hair, her husband, Ideria's father. Although his hair had been twisted by a natural curl, it was impossibly soft. One of Dearborn's favorite things to do was to play with it, just close her eyes to allow her sense of touch to be her only experience as her fingers traipsed through his hair.

"Keep petting me like this and you'll make me go bald," he would say.

"Well, then I guess I need to get all my petting time in before that happens," she would reply and sink her fingers deeper into the curls.

The last time she was able to do that was over ten years ago before he got eaten by one of the king's dragons. He died with valor while rescuing children, freeing them from the same fate. That did nothing to quell the desire to run her hands through his hair again. However, her daughter's hair held the same place within her heart. This would have been a perfect substitute if not for the staining.

The blonde was a perfect match, gilded rays of sunshine, but the glow was muted by persistent streaks and patches of brown. Blood dyed Ideria's hair like an indelible memory that must be cut away. Cut away, she ruminated. Surely the hair would need to be shorn, for she had seen with her own eyes that water would never again remove the stains from her children. This was truly innocence lost. Never again could they open their eyes and look at her with that childlike purity of heart, nor could she look at them as if they could ever toddle to wherever their fleeting curiosity led them. Bathing could only purify the outside appearance, not the mind—nor the heart.

Dearborn wanted to scream, to rail at the injustice of the world that had taken her children away from her and given them back as adults. Adults that had witnessed already too much horror in their short lives. Never again could they close their eyes against the nightmare and reopen them prepared to dream again without the threat of falling back into a chasm darkened by the shadow of death.

"Mother," Ideria started, only to be hushed by Dearborn as she drew her daughter close in a one-armed embrace.

"No words," Dearborn requested. "Not yet." She hummed a quiet tune as her daughter, continued to brush the horse.

When she became aware of Nevin's proximity, she held out her free hand, cajoling him to come closer to her until she could embrace him in the other arm, her hand on his shoulder, her forearm across his chest. Her frame was still large enough that she could cause all three of them to rock to and fro without requiring much effort on her part. She wanted to stay like this forever, for this reunion to last until her eyes closed for the last time.

"We missed you, too, Mother," Nevin whispered, placing both of his hands on her forearm, tightening the embrace.

She kissed the top of his head. These were the curls of her husband, despite the shade being the exact same black that she saw flow from her head anytime she looked into a mirror. Burying her face in his curls, she savored how they felt against her cheeks. This boy had been a child when she last saw him, now almost fully grown, a man by all rights. She had no idea how hard she was squeezing until he moaned, "There's no love like a mother's; always sweet, sometimes painful."

Laughing, she released her children and wiped away the tears, unrealized until now. Her son and daughter were both so beautiful, works of art demanding catharsis. There was no mistaking who sired Nevin, his face the perfect replica of Diminutia's. Maybe not quite as tall and his lean body was framed with the type of muscles only a farm could build. When he smiled, her heart simultaneously broke and melted. It was a magic spell cast upon all who beheld it.

Ideria was a living reflection of her mother. Just as tall with muscles that belonged on a thoroughbred, not a person, yet the curves from shoulder to waist to hip to thigh were undeniably feminine. Just like herself, her daughter lacked any discernible bosom, the sacrifice necessary for the striations of a muscled chest.

How they had both grown, Dearborn mused, and how much she had missed. Her mind was awash with questions and she had to fight her own urges to keep from overwhelming them with a torrent of words, lest she deteriorate into a babbling, blubbering mess. Start with the most important details first, she exhorted herself, as she gathered up her courage and wits into something useful.

"Children, where are Captain and Mrs. Wahl? They were to watch over you. And what of Draymon? He should have helped them until I was able to return to you. Please tell me that you snuck out on them . . . and that you had some good reason to do so." Dearborn steeled herself to wait for their answers.

Nevin and Ideria looked at each other for a few seconds before either of them made any attempt to answer. Nevin lowered his eyes first, an indication to his sister that she should start the story. Without taking her eyes off her brother, Ideria took a deep breath and spoke.

"Grandmother and Grandfather are dead. They were killed by Prince Daedalus, trying to protect the secret of our existence from him. We don't know how he found out about us, but he was most insistent on finding us. We escaped with the help of Uncle Draymon and Uncle Bartholomew. They led us through a series of underground tunnels that we had dug in preparation for such an event. We then went to Phyl's and Lapin's. From there we discovered that they had lied to all of us kids for all these years and unraveled the mystery of your whereabouts. We then set out to find you."

A stinging sensation formed behind her eyes. She had forgotten how to cry over the last ten years until hours ago when she first saw and held her children outside the castle. Now she willed herself not to, the notion of her children coming to rescue her plucked at her heart like the strings of a harp. A parent should always do the rescuing, never the children. "I am sorry that you had to escape like that, but I'm happy to hear you refer to them as your grandparents. They were exemplary people, two that I looked up to and admired. However, you mentioned an 'Uncle' Bartholomew? I assume he was the fellow killed by the water dragon?"

Ideria's eyes became glassy as she returned to brushing the horse's mane and Dearborn instantly regretted her less than reverent tone when asking about the man. This time, Nevin answered her question. "Yes. Uncle Draymon showed up one day to let us know that you and father had died trying to save King Perciless. Grandmother and Grandfather had a long talk and then decided that they would purchase your property and have Uncle Draymon live there so he could train us. Grandmother never liked the idea, but acquiesced, saying that it was better for us to know how to defend ourselves than not. After a while, Uncle Draymon was running out of techniques to show us, so he invited Uncle Bartholomew to live with us and help. He taught us less sophisticated, yet equally useful methods of combat."

"And how to swear and deliver jokes that would call forth blushes from those who heard them. Especially grandmother. She never liked Uncle Bartholomew much."

Dearborn smiled at the images of Mrs. Wahl fussing about coarse language. A smirk touched Nevin's lips as his tone lightened. "That as well as other life skills."

Crossing her arms over her chest, Dearborn displayed a frown that could not be misconstrued any other way than mocking. "Let me guess. Skills I would disapprove of, but your father would encourage."

Both children looked away as pink touched their cheeks. Dearborn chuckled and said, "Obviously those skills were necessary or else you would have never been able to come to my rescue. I am extremely sorry for your loss. Even though he may have seemed like a scoundrel, it's clear to me that he was a good man."

The world around them infringed upon their collectively shared moment as the horse in the stall with them neighed for more food. When their group had come upon this farm, Dearborn suggested that they check out the stables as the farmer was not likely to be present and so that they could inspect the horses and offer fair value for them. Accustomed as she was to farm living, the group decided that she should go investigate the equines as she was less likely to get them riled up as an ogre or someone with wings might.

Immediately evident to Dearborn was the lean and slightly haggard appearance of the horses. She found a small pile of food with ease and even though she was slightly leery about the freshness of the grains, she decided that the horses were probably used to a slight staleness and could still gain nourishment from unseasonable victuals until more choice materials could be obtained. The animals had been mistreated in her opinion, but they seemed to be in decent health, considering. They were serviceable and could be brought back to full vitality at the same time if they didn't push them too hard. It wasn't an ideal situation, but how many times might they encounter the same scenario before better circumstances presented themselves, she wondered. She weighed the situation in her mind and decided that they could travel more quickly with these horses than by risking spending several days, potentially, looking for a better option.

"Nevin, let's bring in the rest of the group. We'll talk more later. I love you both so much, and I'm so proud of who you have both become. I want to hear all about it, but we must stay focused. Remember everything that you have been taught up until now. Daedalus sets the stakes high and he will do anything to cause me pain."

Nevin regarded her with the same blue eyes she had, but there was so much more to them. Entire conversations played out behind them as he calculated what to say next. Dearborn could almost hear every question he wanted to ask:

"Why does the king's brother hate you so much?"

"Is he really spending so many resources hunting us?"

"How did you survive the dungeon and still be healthy?"

"What do we do now?"

"Where do we go?"

Wisdom accompanied his curiosity and he knew to leave those questions for a later time as he led the way out of the stall.

The stables were impressive. Stalls enough for eight horses, though only six were occupied, and a spacious loft over both sets of stalls. There was more than enough room to rent a peaceful night's sleep from the farmer, should he be willing to accept their coin. Before they had fled the killing fields of the castle, Draymon inspected Bartholomew's body and found small pouches of coin within his boots as well as sewn into his shirt and pants. No matter what she might hear about this Bartholomew fellow, she had to admire his forethought.

As they made their way to the exit, she hoped that the farmer was merely poor and struggling. There was no other acceptable excuse for not taking care of these horses. If that was the case, he might be more willing to sell them.

The rest of the group had camped out on the ground, resting as they found a few minutes to do so, except for Rue, who leaned against the barn wall. As Dearborn considered this, she decided that his clothing was too refined to sit upon the dirt. Hardly the kind of ogre with which she was familiar. Bale wasn't above eating dirt, let alone sitting on it.

Bale was attempting to regal Rue and Draymon with stories of his adventures, though neither of the listeners seemed particularly interested in listening and none of them seemed to take notice of Dearborn and her children as the emerged from the barn. Hope, Dearborn noticed, was watching for them, her green cheeks flushing with a soft burgundy color at Nevin's reappearance. Nevin seemed to Dearborn to be almost absent to the world around him, not disinterested in it. So, Dearborn mused, of all the things that my son has learned, he is totally unaware of this girl's interest in him. Perhaps there was time yet to have a motherly effect on her son. That thought made her smile despite present circumstances.

"The horses seem okay to me," Dearborn said, announcing her presence to the group. "They need some consistent meals and no small amount of attention, but otherwise seem to be in good general health. I think we should find the farmer and offer fair coin for them. Haggling for them might be a dalliance that we can ill afford."

Lapin, who was in a field by himself further away than the rest, hiccoughed a response. "So, should I <hic> try to <hic> go reason with him?" A small glass bottle slipped out of the rabbit's paw and thudded against the ground, spraying the rodent with a liquid that further matted his fur. Phyl, who was closest to Lapin, tutted at his friend's indiscretion and attempted to wipe him down, which drew the Lapin's ire in the form of little rabbit paws rapidly swatting in Phyl's general direction.

"I missed you so much," Bale said as he scooped up the rabbit and started petting him.

The children of Bale all smiled at the scene of Lapin swearing and kicking his feet at Bale's rough hand. Their birth father interacting with one of their fathers from the past decade. It was good to see now, but Dearborn wondered how would their relationship change over the years? How could she reform a relationship with Ideria and Nevin? Unfortunately, there was one question that still needed to be answered before Dearborn could ruminate about the evolution of anyone's relationships. "Whether we are able to purchase the horses or not, we should figure out where we go from here."

"Shouldn't we figure that out first?" Bale asked.

"Why?" Draymon asked. He rubbed his thumbs against his temples, trying to shoo away the obvious headache Bale had given to him.

"Well, if we purchase the horses now, then off we go, but if we can't purchase the horses now, then the first place we need to go is to the horse market to buy some horses."

Draymon rubbed harder.

Rue stepped away from the stable wall he had been leaning on and walked closer to his father. There were plenty of similarities Dearborn could see, but the bulbous belly that Bale somehow still had after ten years of less than abundant food from the dungeon was absent from Rue, and he had sharpness in his eyes that Bale simply lacked. "I believe what master Draymon is asking is where to go if we are able to purchase the horses now or after we purchase them from the horse market."

There was a calmness, a patience in Rue's voice that Dearborn had to admire. She was able to deal with Bale only because she killed whatever part of her soul that felt annoyance for Bale's scatological thinking.

"As I understand it, the king has pulled his troops from Kallistah Pass. If we go through that pass, then we are inside Tsinel," Phyl said.

"But why did the king pull his troops? It seems like a setup to me. If Albathia is in open war with Tsinel, then why would he pull his troops from the path to the border, unless he has some sort of a trap in mind?" Draymon reasoned. "It's a direct path, but it reeks like a bad idea to me, almost too good to be true."

"Who did you hear this from, Uncle Phyl?" Hope asked.

"A family heading to it. When Draymon and I snuck into the town over to purchase a few supplies, I couldn't help overhearing about the Pass and asked them about it. They were meeting up with some other families to make a run for it, to escape Albathia."

"They're running into a trap," Draymon mumbled.

"What would you propose, Draymon?" Dearborn asked. "Where would you have us go?"

"A bar?" Bale and Lapin asked in unison.

Ignoring the words as if they had never been spoken, Draymon answered, "Anywhere except the obvious trap. I have no qualms about trying to find a way to Tsinel. In fact, they may be my grand suggestion, but we need to be smart about it."

"Why shouldn't we kill the king?"

Ideria.

Dearborn turned to her daughter and found herself mildly surprised that she stood with the other four children. They comprised a tight pack, close enough for each of them to hear the other should they need to confer in whispers, which, Dearborn suspected, they did often.

Ideria continued, "We all know that Perciless is building a quiet army found in the shadows of every city, town, and village. We find one of them and convince the soldiers it's time to strike."

Ideria's words pulled images of the rescue to the forefront of Dearborn's mind. The feral cries her daughter, her baby, shrieked while decapitating the army recruits would forever haunt her nightmares. The expression Ideria wore while shoving her swords so deeply into the men she only stopped when her elbow was inside of them, sometimes bringing out viscera upon withdrawal, was one of such raw hatred that Dearborn doubted she knew what she was doing. She'd possessed a berserker rage that no parent should ever have to witness their child contend with. Dearborn never wanted her daughter to experience that again. "I've heard those rumors as well. I believe we would sooner find a greedy and desperate soul willing to sell us to the king long before we found a member of Perciless' army."

"More people hate the king and his brother than you're imagining, Mother. Not so many weeks ago, Nevin and I had members of that army attempt to recruit us."

"For supposition's sake, let's say we find a contingent as quickly as stepping foot into in the first town we come to. What then? We raid the castle with a dozen troops? Two dozen people? Pitchforks and shovels and against swords and crossbows. There will be a time for that, but now isn't it. We should make our way into Tsinel to see what we can do from there."

Dearborn implied that she wanted to help with the war effort but had to admit to herself she just wanted to get her children away from it.

"Still a bad idea," Draymon said.

"No," Ideria rebutted. "It is not. Walking into an ambush expecting one is more prudent than looking for a path trying to avoid it. Either we'll waste energy looking for something that doesn't exist, or we'll expose ourselves to enemies. Uncle Bartholomew taught us that."

"Bartholomew's lessons notwithstanding, we should—"

"Then what about your lessons, the ones concerning altruism and bravery. We know that innocent people who are not capable of defending themselves are going to be making that trek. If this is truly an ambush set by the king and his brother, then they are walking right into their graves. We want to fight. My mother has a point about helping the armies of Tsinel, and Kallistah Pass is the fastest way. One week's ride there, one week to go through the Pass."

Draymon looked around to the other adults for any form of help. Bale shrugged his shoulders, while Phyl looked skyward. Lapin hiccupped and lay down on his side. Dearborn smirked and said, "Well, it looks like we're heading north."

TWENTY

THE PUBLIC HOUSE was in the center of town. Larger than most, the town's main road formed a circle around it with offshoots perpendicular to each other, a wagon wheel with four spokes. The denizens had even paved the circled road with cobblestone to reduce the amount of mud created from the road's constant use. What impressed Landyr the most about it was the expansive mead hall where the drinks overflowed, and the food satisfied.

"You're familiar with this building?" Samillia whispered.

"We should be," Landyr answered. "Thorna and I were here just earlier this evening."

As with most public houses, this one served as a town hall for a town too small to have one as a separate building, yet large enough to need a place for the mayor to conduct official business. Meeting with the once and future king was such business the mayor attended to earlier today.

Landyr had been more aware of his surroundings, the meeting was the first between Perciless and a town official of any sort since the devastating ambush from the Elite Troop. The gathering went smoothly enough, the mayor offering fealty and any resources he could when the time came for insurrection. After the meeting was over, Brokar and Thorna escorted the king back to the inn, while Cezomir and Lina went off on their own. Landyr passed a few coins around for some mead and information about the types of local woman he could rent love from. He had enjoyed the hall and made a mental note to return to it as soon as time permitted. Standing across the street from it now with Thorna and Samillia, he wished the circumstance for his return was different.

Samillia brandished three knives; one in each hand and one with her tail. "If you know the layout inside, then this should be a fairly easy—"

Thorna clamped her hand over the snake woman's mouth and pointed to the streets. Landyr held his breath. The shadows of the alleyway kept them hidden from the pair of marauders walking by, but only if everyone remained silent. Samillia frowned and backhanded Thorna's hands away from her mouth. "Touch me again and I'll gut you."

"Keep talking and the cutthroats you attract will do it for you," Thorna hissed.

"Them? Bah. We've wasted too much energy trying to avoid them already." Samillia slithered from the alleyway to the main street. By the time Landyr angled himself to see her silhouette move over the cobblestones, she slit the throats of the two men and then darted to a shadowy corner of the public house, the only noise being the new corpses falling to the ground.

"Still planning on putting your dick in her? I'd be wary if I were you," Thorna whispered as she dashed from the alley to the public house.

He wanted to say, "No," but answering her question would do no good, plus a tiny voice in his mind had yet to eschew the idea. Her use of stealth was frightening, yet tantalizing. Her skills surpassed the need to defend one's self from thieves. She had been trained to do what she just did, to kill and move on, making less noise than a shadow. That concerned him.

Landyr joined the two women at the one corner of the building and they crept along the wall until they came upon a window to the main room. Twenty captors surrounded their hostages, including the patrons of the public house during the time of the invasion. Perciless stood face to face with a bald man whose face and arms were covered in tattoos, jagged lines like black lightning bolts. He wore a leather chest plate, arms exposed, pants made from thick animal hide, and mud-caked boots. The walls and windows were too thick, so Landyr could hear only the muffled voice of the group's leader, no specific words, as he paced in a circle around Perciless, his gestures aggressive. After the end of each statement, each member of the group raised their fists in the air and cheered.

Samillia and Thorna wasted no time with anything more than a cursory glance through the windows and continued to move along the side of the building. Once they got to the back, Samillia used one of her knives and a pin she procured from her belt to pick the lock of the back door. The efficiency she demonstrated once again excited and concerned Landyr.

They slipped through the kitchen and into the main room with ease. There were no guards, but few would be foolish enough to walk into a room with twenty armed men fueled by criminal intent. As with everything else she did tonight, Samillia displayed cunning and training as she glided through the rooms to a hiding spot behind a half wall built off a massive support beam. She relied on timing and speed, but since neither Thorna nor Landyr possessed any serpentine skills, they slowly crawled to the half wall.

The leader's name was Obeed, the name that his charges chanted after he said statements like, "Who led you to wine and women?" and "Who kept your bellies full while other peoples' went empty?"

Landyr wondered if Obeed was leading his troops somewhere with this line of questions that all had the same answer. Was he trying to intensify their mood? Or placate his own ego? Finally, there was a question that caused a reaction from someone other than his men.

"Who is the new lord of the underworld now that Vogothe is dead?"

"Obeed!"

"Wait," Perciless yelled. "What did you say?"

The rowdy cheers settled to dull murmurs as Obeed sneered at Perciless, walking circles around him. "Did you just interrupt me?"

"I'm just seeking clarification about one of your state-ments. Did you say Vogothe is dead?"

"I did indeed."

"When?"

"A couple of weeks ago."

"How?"

"Depends who you ask. Some say his throat was cut in his sleep. Some say he got caught up in a dungeon escape that went to hell. Some say he's resting in the belly of one of the king's dragons."

"What has King Oremethus done about this?"

The circle Obeed walked got smaller, a wide-eyed smile of disbelief on his face. "You want to know what your brother did? Fucked you, he did. Fucked every town and village in this kingdom. Vogothe did more to keep the crime levels low than any constable or sheriff. He who holds either of those positions is the true criminal. That is why I am the new king of criminals."

"Obeed!" his men cheered once more.

"You?" Perciless chuckled. "I've heard more intelligence come from the tail end of a horse."

Obeed backhanded Perciless.

Landyr winced and readied himself to charge toward Obeed. Thorna grabbed his arm to keep him from doing something both foolish and deadly. He acquiesced when he noticed that the king suffered nothing more than a bruised cheek.

"My brother has many qualities, some could be described as unsavory, but stupidity isn't one of them," Perciless said. "What you said is true about Vogothe. Despite him being a deplorable cretin, he did have quite the stranglehold on those who chose to live in the dark underbelly of this coun-try, but I assure you that King Oremethus was just as eager to end Vogothe's reign as he is to end mine. Now that Vogo-the is dead the king will stop at nothing to crush anyone trying to take up the mantle."

"The king is too focused on the war to worry about his people. He cares more about conquering Tsinel than catering to Albathia. Other Lieutenants in Vogothe's army are running around like wild beasts in a ballroom. Messy and shortsighted. Only I have the same vision as Vogothe. I care more about this country than your brother does. I'm eliminating threats by organization. The king? The only help he's offering the locals is giving them a few troops here and there from the regiment he pulled from Kallistah Pass."

"The king pulled the troops from Kallistah Pass? When?"

"This isn't some fucking tea room where we chat about the events of yesterday. I could give a goat's testicle about when the troops left."

Perciless dropped his gaze to the floor and stroked his chin, the action either calming or focusing. He muttered to himself, but Landyr was not able to hear the single person debate.

Obeed slowed his step but still walked around his hostage, his face caught between curiosity and anger. After being ignored for two full revolutions, Obeed hit Perciless' shoulder. "Ey! Did you forget where you are? And the king moving troops away from some mountain pass up north ain't gonna stop me from turning you over to him."

Landyr tightened the grip on his dagger and looked to Thorna. She kept glancing between him and the scene in the middle of the room, awaiting his signal. He knew she wanted to rush in and kill Obeed and his marauders but mistiming that attack could be deadly for Perciless or the other civilians. As much as it pained him to do so, he needed to wait.

Obeed cuffed Perciless again. "How were you once our king?"

"Would you like to learn something interesting today, Obeed?" Perciless asked.

The men who followed Obeed laughed. He did as well, but after a few seconds, he gestured to them to return to silence. Once they did, he stopped circling the king and stood within half a stride of him. He used his thumb to pantomime wiping a tear caused by laughing too hard. "I'm always up for a good bit of education. What might you have to teach me, *sire*?"

"It's coincidental that you called me that because when I was king, I heard what my critics had to say about me. Of course, they were wrong, but do you want to know the number one criticism about me that they got wrong?"

Obeed crossed his arms over his chest and squinted. "I'm listening."

"That I'm not observant. But I am. I'm very observant. For example, the knife in the sheath hanging from your belt is untethered and perfectly positioned for me to take it." Just as Obeed looked down at the knife, Perciless yanked it from its sheath and plunged it into the new crime lord's ribs.

Obeed backed away and placed both hands over his new wound. He looked at the blood dripping from his fingers as if he had never seen it before. Perciless advanced and stabbed Obeed again. "They also say I'm a fop."

A gurgle escaped Obeed's mouth as he grabbed for Perciless' shoulders. The king pulled the knife out only to stab again. "They say I don't like to get my hands dirty."

Perciless twisted the blade and Obeed's eyes rolled up into his head. He pulled the knife out one last time and sliced it across Obeed's throat. The crime lord fell to the ground without further ado. Perciless bent over the corpse he had made and as calmly as explaining a lesson to a child said, "What do you think of those criticisms, Obeed? Would you like one last observation of note? I think this would be the perfect time for Landyr, Thorna, and their new snake-like friend to ambush Obeed's dumbfounded followers."

The marauders might have been organized with Obeed as their leader, but without him, they lacked any cohesion. As soon as Perciless mentioned the others, each criminal looked over his shoulder, training their weapons on whatever possibility might be behind them. None of the civilians they ignored made a direct move against them, but they wasted no time in helping remove the ropes binding Brokar, Lina, and Cezomir.

As with the rogues outside, Samillia sliced through those closest to her with noiseless ease. In a wicked dance with three other partners, she had one knife for each, gracefully escorting them through the ballroom of the damned. Landyr fought with one of the criminals, but took so much longer to finish him it became a struggle filled with parrying two knives and descended into fisticuffs. After the thug dropped lifeless to the ground, he looked to help Thorna, but she was slicing through the King's captors as quickly as the snake woman.

The civilians ran to the closest exit, holding each other and attempting to shield their eyes from the horrors they had experienced. A few screamed as streaks of blood splashed them while they fled. Cezomir and Lina tore through half of the marauders, even the ones trying to escape with those they had held hostage. Landyr had to admire their precision. Despite the guttural noises they made as they bloodied their claws and slicked their muzzles, they were able to pick from the fleeing crowd only those who pledged allegiance to the crime lord. Landyr fought hard to ignore the fistfuls of meat they scooped from the men and shoved into their mouths.

Too caught up with the actions of his feral companions, Landyr failed to notice the marauder behind him. At first, he thought Perciless had gone mad when his king suddenly threw his knife at him. It shot past Landyr's face and sunk deeply into the eye socket of the man behind him. His pitiful moan was the last sound any of the marauders made.

Landyr expected Perciless to give him a tongue lashing for one of his many possible short-comings this evening, from abandoning his post to taking so long to intervene. Instead, Perciless approached with a smile and clapped both of Landyr's shoulders. "It's wonderful to see you! I was worried when you weren't with our group and feared you and Thorna might have been on the wrong side of their ambush."

Landyr returned the king's smile. "I was busy meeting her."

Both men looked at Samillia as she used a dead man's shirt to wipe the blood from her blade. When finished, she noticed the two men staring at her and the hue of her cheeks changed ever so slightly. Landyr assumed that to be a blush. Perciless nodded for her to join him.

"Please, Landyr," the king said, almost singing with joy, "introduce me to this magnificent individual who aided in my rescue."

"Her name is Samillia. We had met at the inn's tavern earlier this evening."

"It's an honor to meet you, your Highness," Samillia replied. Her muscles were toned and taut but did little good in making her attempt at a curtsy look anything other than awkward. Landyr had trained with soldiers more demure than she was.

"He tried to put his dick in her earlier this evening," Thorna mumbled as she walked by on her way to Brokar.

Perciless neither flinched nor wavered as he continued, "The success or failure of that specific endeavor held no bearing on how spectacularly you handled yourself in this situation."

Her green skin almost glowed. Landyr wondered if it was from anger at Thorna's rude comment or the embarrassing amount of praise King Perciless heaped upon her. "Thank you, your Highness."

"I'm assuming you two heard what Obeed said about my brother pulling troops from Kallistah Pass? I believe we should investigate. Rumor is the only thing that spreads faster than fire in this kingdom and I feel that we were the last people to hear about this one. We need to investigate why. If this is a tactical error, then I wish to exploit it. If this move gains them a tactical advantage, then I want to know why. The time is nigh to call upon my secret army, but I need to understand this sudden maneuver by my brother. So, Samillia, would you be willing to join us?"

"Yes," Samillia answered. Her face held a hard beauty to it, silk draped over an angular statue. When she smiled as she answered the pride was obvious, but Landyr swore that he saw elements of guilt as well.

TWENTY-ONE

CEZOMIR THRUST FASTER. Lina matched his rhythm with her hips. His panting came in ragged huffs. She expressed her pleasure with one constant deep, throaty moan. From behind, Cezomir reached around and grabbed her breasts, too big for him to contain with his hands. Her tail curled around the small of his back and pulled with each thrust, encouraging him to go faster, harder. He bit the back of her neck. She ran her claws down the tree she was using for support. It had been too long since they had an opportunity to fuck and they were making the most of it.

When they were finished, her feet were hidden by curved strips of gray bark that she had shredded from the tree. Cezomir laughed as she made exaggerated movements to step from the pile. He cinched his britches and found his tunic. Just for fun he grabbed Lina's clothes as well and held them above her just out of reach. As always, she convinced him to give them back by running her rough tongue over his, while running her hand over his freshly spent manhood. She always made such a compelling argument to give her clothes back he felt he had little recourse other than to hand them over to her.

Waiting for her to put her clothes on, Cezomir closed his eyes and inhaled deeply. The Looping Forest was such a strange area. The tiny leaves rotted differently than other leaves, the smell far more bitter than any other forest. No animals lived in this forest. No pheromones. No decaying carcasses. No piss or shit. Just himself and those he traveled with. Lina's sense of smell was better than his—a fact that he had yet to admit anywhere other than within the private confines of his mind. If he could pinpoint exactly where everyone was, then she must be overwhelmed with the pungency. A sudden odor offended his nostrils and he snorted to expel it. "He watched us again."

Lina sauntered over to Cezomir and gently ran a claw under his chin, sending tingles all along his face. "I can smell him, too. And, just so you know, he's watching me."

"Doesn't matter who he watches. It's disturbing that he wrestles his own snake while watching us."

Lina shrugged a shoulder. "It's his 'thing'."

"His 'thing,' you say?"

"Yes. We all have one. He's a human that will put his dick into any nonhuman female."

"And me? Do I have a 'thing'?"

"You used to fuck fat human women if that's what you mean."

Cezomir grabbed Lina and pulled her to him, her chest against his. As he spoke his canine lips almost touched her feline mouth. "Very amusing. How about you? What is your 'thing?'"

She threw her arms around his neck and kissed him again. "Apparently I like dogs who get shy when they know people are watching him fuck."

Cezomir laughed again, releasing Lina from his grip. "Yet Landyr's 'thing' is still the most puzzling. I've known men who cast broader nets to catch any prey they could find. But to refuse such an obvious morsel . . . ?"

"You mean Thorna?"

"I do. Anytime he gets too close to her, I can smell her loins burst into flame."

"Alas, he doesn't like humans."

"I, for one, find that hysterical, adding to the comedy the fact that he lusts for the newest member of our cabal and she has no interest in him."

"I wouldn't say she's completely uninterested."

"No? I barely smell her when she's right next to me let alone any changes in her moods."

"I can barely sense her either, her moods are very controlled."

"Huh," Cezomir grunted. He started to walk toward where the rest of the group set up camp, undoubtedly breaking it down now that the Morning Sun had climbed over the horizon and pretending not to know that Landyr was hiding behind a tree twenty paces away. "Well, she is mostly snake after all."

Lina walked beside him. "I think it's more than that. Her movements are very precise. She's always watching everything. She never speaks unless spoken to."

"Are you talking about Samillia or yourself?"

Lina frowned. "After ten years, I still can't tell when you attempt to make a joke."

Cezomir laughed and Lina frowned even more.

Thorna approached them as soon as they returned to camp. "Have either of you seen Landyr?"

"I thought I saw him behind a tree wrestling with a snake," Cezomir said.

Upon hearing his words, Thorna glanced over her shoulder to Samillia, helping Brokar and Perciless fasten a bedroll to one of the horses. Lina moved her hand over her mouth to stifle a laugh. Cezomir followed up with, "A different kind of snake."

Thorna looked behind Cezomir into the forest. "Snake, huh? It's been a while since I had fresh snake. I was beginning to wonder if we'd find anything to eat in this damnable forest."

Tears forming in her eyes, Lina turned away, but when Landyr emerged while adjusting his pants, she hid behind Cezomir. Thorna asked him, "So, where's the snake?"

Landyr froze mid-step as if his foot was close to a viper's pit. "The . . . snake . . . ?"

"Yes, snake. Cezomir said he saw you wrestling with one behind a tree."

A hue of pink touched his cheeks as he replied, "Oh . . . yes . . . a snake . . . unfortunately, I was mistaken. It was merely a branch. Sorry to get anyone's hopes up."

"How can one mistake a branch for a snake?"

Landyr chuckled. "Have you not looked around? Everything is gray. A maddening amount of gray. I swore the flames of last night's campfire had gone gray."

"Pity," Thorna mumbled. "I was hoping to eat some snake."

Both Cezomir and Lina burst out laughing.

"What is going on with those two?" Landyr asked.

"That's beyond my knowledge," Thorna answered. "They've been a touch daffy ever since returning to camp."

Cezomir shook his head and went to help the others pack up camp. He made his way to Perciless' horse.

The horse exploded.

In a burst of blood and bones, Perciless, Samillia, and Brokar flew backward. Samillia remained still on the ground, dead or unconscious, Cezomir did not know. Perciless rolled to prop himself up on his elbows and shook his head, strips of bloodied horse hide clinging to his body. Brokar leaped on top of the king as two dozen arrows formed a line down his back.

What caused the horse to explode reeked of magic, but what launched the flurry of arrows was mechanical. Three men worked a mounted automatic firing crossbow; one to aim, one to work the wheel crank, one to feed the machine a continuous strand of arrows tied together by threads.

Cezomir knew little of modern weaponry, but this mechanism of death looked complicated to operate and he hypothesized that if it was complicated to operate, then it must be easy to disrupt.

Running toward Perciless, Cezomir snatched a fallen branch from the ground. Short, but thick, he snapped it into two pieces and threw them at the crossbow operators. His distraction gave him enough time to grab Perciless by the back of his shirt, snatch Thorna's short sword from her pack and Landyr's from his, and then meet the rest of his companions behind the curved roots of a nearby tree.

"Sorry for dragging you by the shirt, your Highness," Cezomir said as he tossed the swords to Thorna and Landyr.

Perciless used both hands to wipe the gore from his face. "Nothing to apologize for. The perception of dignity disappears during life or death situations. Have we any idea what happened?"

"None yet. Brokar's dead, maybe Samillia as well."

Thorna gasped and turned to Landyr. "Brokar . . . ?"

Landyr said nothing in reply as the muscles of his clenched jaw rolled.

"He died saving the king," Cezomir continued. "And there's a wizard about."

"Do you think the king's Elite Troop found us again?" Perciless asked. He pulled a small dagger from his boot as he cautiously glanced out from behind the tree.

"It's possible. Lina and I shall conduct a full and detailed investigation."

Before Perciless could object, Cezomir and Lina sprinted toward the point of attack.

A steady stream of projectiles flew between them. She was far more agile than he, but they had been in situations like this before and weaved their way toward the crew operating the rapid-firing crossbow without a single scratch.

Lina jumped on the man who had been aiming the weapon, all four sets of claws digging into his torso as she sunk her teeth into his neck. Cezomir swiped at the man spinning the crank, removing his face as his claws left gouges in the bone. The remaining man stood in gape-mouth horror, holding an armful of arrows now useless. Without hesitation, Cezomir jammed both sets of claws into the man's chest and snapped his rib cage in two while ripping him open. The dead man's face froze in his last expression, dumbfounded that a werewolf was burying his face in his torso, eating his entrails.

After a few quick swallows, Cezomir dropped the carcass and turned to Lina. She, too, had taken a moment to feed on her kill, chunks of meat sliding from her blood-soaked chin. They rushed to each other and indulged in a kiss. They separated when a branch wrapped itself around Lina's neck.

Cezomir's powerful claws snapped the branch before it could do any harm. This was the wizard's doing. He used his magic to ensorcell three trees, wooden puppets commanded to kill. Again, Lina was too fast.

She lacked Cezomir's strength, but she could still slice through branches as thick as her arm. Cezomir could break those as thick as thigh with one swipe, larger with more strikes. Branches webbed together to ensnare Lina, but Cezomir shredded them with ease. She climbed to the top of a tree, snapped away the smaller limbs, and then jumped to the next one. Cezomir climbed as well, but not very high. Climbing trees was not a skill he had mastered, but he only needed to climb high enough to remove the branches Lina could not. As if merely plucking petals from a daisy, they worked together quickly to remove the branches from all three trees. The roots were too thick for the wizard to make the trees mobile, now just wishbones stuck in the ground.

Cezomir crouched, snarling with his claws ready to rend, excited for the next fight. The trees did little more than waste time and he wanted a challenge more suitable for his blood lust. But there was nothing around him other than Lina, shredded meat, and empty forest. "It was a distraction. The king!"

They ran back, under and around the archways made by tree roots, through the camp with the other horses still braying about one of their own disappearing in such a violent manner, toward the noises of metal clashing with metal. Cezomir noticed that Samillia was no longer on the ground and saw her dancing around the spear strikes between two centaurs.

Landyr and Thorna did their best to keep others of the Elite Troop away from Perciless. Cezomir had seen the prince fight before now and knew that he was not some bureaucratic fop coddled into existence by privilege. He wondered how much protection the prince truly needed as Perciless stood over the body of a felled orc and pulled his dagger from its neck.

Two more bodies lay on the ground wearing the king's insignia, a human and a winged monstrosity. Despite the valiance of his companions, they were still outnumbered three to one. And there was still the wizard. The stench of magic twisted Cezomir's guts and out of reflex, he pushed Lina away just as the fireball engulfed him.

His thick fur protected him from any true harm and smoldered as he dropped to the ground to roll away the flames. The conflagration inside of him raged hotter than any fireball and as soon as he saw the wizard, he launched himself through the air at him. Cezomir had little care that the wizard wore a cloak of flame, he just wanted to kill the bastard. It was not to be.

With a roar, Cezomir slashed both sets of claws as he came down on the wizard, striking nothing but an illusion. The image disappeared and he slammed to the ground, getting a face full of dirt. And a new opponent.

The illusion hid one of the Elite Troop members, one so horrid it gave Cezomir a moment of pause. It had the shape of a human male, but its height and muscle size were both impossibly large. Its head looked as if it had once been a human, but now it appeared as if its features had melted off, leaving nothing more than exposed teeth and globs of folded skin. Its legs were long and thick but bent the opposite way a human's did. Its fingers were long, each one tipped to a hardened point, but scaled as if its hands were ripped away and replaced by dragon claws. The thing had thick plate mail, but not a suit of armor, rather chunks of metal nailed directly into its skin. Cezomir was too stunned to block its kick.

He flew through the air and landed hard again. How did that thing possess such power? The time to be amazed was over, lest Cezomir wished to discover exactly how sharp those claws were. Back on his feet, he growled and charged the clawed beast. It was fast, the claw swipe faster than the werewolf expected. He dropped just in time, slid between his opponent's legs and jumped to his feet with his arm back, ready to use his own claws. Too late. The monster twisted and connected with a backhand to Cezomir's jaw.

Stars burst all throughout Cezomir's vision as he stumbled backward. He jumped out of the way to avoid snapping jaws right in front of another human-shaped creature attacked. This one had two heads on long independent necks and extended snouts holding an impossible number of teeth. Attack strategies ran through Cezomir's mind as the two creatures converged. He backed away and any attempt he made to sprint around them was quickly thwarted by the swinging claws or gnashing teeth. He could only move backward. They were herding him.

The other members of the Elite Troop did the same to Cezomir's companions, some with swords and spears, the others with weapons grown from their bodies. Cezomir looked for a weakness in the encroaching circle of warriors, and one did not exist. Both centaurs were armored from head to hoof, their metal shaft spears unbreakable. The minotaur was twice his size. And the chimeras . . . these creatures were the best parts of claws and teeth and talons from every kind of deadly beast sutured and soldered together. Their wizard walked with fire, his cloaks perpetually burned, while his hands were engulfed in flames. There was no doubt in Cezomir's mind that if he made it out of this alive it would not be without injury. He decided that when the time came, he would charge at a centaur, staying low in an attempt to hobble it.

"Hold," came from behind the line of soldiers. A man's voice, laden with weariness. "Let me through."

Two of the soldiers moved apart to let a human and a satyr through. Judging from their medals—the human wore his on his uniform, while the satyr had his medals affixed to his skin—they were the leaders, general and sergeant Cezomir assumed. Gray streaks decorated the stocky human's hair and the satyr was an albino and the largest Cezomir had ever seen. Black chains and other piercings adorned the satyr's white skin.

"Prince Perciless," the human said in a familiar tone as if greeting him at a dinner party.

"Methel," Perciless replied, just as casually.

Methel ran a hand through his hair as if the act would take away his frustration. "You know what I want, correct?"

"For me to come with you, back to my brothers."

"Correct. Let's just do that. We will need to kill one of your protectors, of course, but the rest we will let live. They call you the king of the people, renowned for your love of them, your willingness to sacrifice for them. Well, you now get a chance to save four out of five of your subjects. All you need to do is pick one—"

"Samillia."

Looks of confusion swept across everyone's faces, none more so than Samillia's. A few members of the Elite Troop laughed. Landyr turned to Perciless and snapped, "You can't be serious."

Perciless looked at the dagger in his hands, as if in contemplation and then suddenly brought it to his own throat. "I am. No matter what happens, they won't kill me. If I don't go with them, then you all die, and I'll still live. If I go with them, they won't kill you, or I will slice my own throat. I could only imagine the horrors Daedalus would perform on them should he find out that they had me in their clutches and then failed to deliver me alive."

Perciless' logic intrigued Cezomir. How far with his threat was the prince willing to go? Everyone in the Elite Troop shifted nervously, none smiled or laughed at the thought of disappointing Daedalus.

"Be that as it may, how could you make a decision like that so rashly?"

"As I said back in Murveen, people underestimate me, often mistaking benevolence for weakness. Lest you forget, I quested for one of the accursed gemstones needed to summon the demons of the Demon War. I assure you during that adventure I . . . I . . ."

Perciless' words trailed off as his eyes went vacant. Something playing about in his mind demanded his attention. The temptation to smack him out of this stupor passed through Cezomir's mind. Alas, he had to do no such thing as Perciless jerked as if awakening from a dream and continued his thought, ". . . I had to make impossible choices and do unspeakable things. So, this decision is an easy one compared to those. I sacrifice the one I know the least, who also happens to be a member of the Elite Troop."

This time it was Cezomir and his companions who were confused, while the mood of the Elite Troop soured.

Samillia looked back and forth between Perciless and Methel. Perciless gave her the same soft smile he gave to anyone he came across, but this time he gestured with his free hand for her to join her true companions, shooing her away.

Back rigidly straight, she slithered to take her place next to Methel. Before any words could be exchanged between the two, the albino satyr punched the back of Methel's head, dropping the human to the ground, and then sliced Samillia's throat. As soon as the blade cut free from her neck the satyr threw it at Perciless. The knife pierced the prince's hand, forcing him to drop his dagger.

Everyone tensed, weapons ready to kill, as the satyr strode closer to the captives. "My name is Juruk. I'm the new general of the Elite Troop now. I do not play foolish games like Methel. We will be taking Perciless back to Phenomere and the rest of you will die."

Cezomir believed Juruk's words to be true.

TWENTY-TWO

IDERIA EYED THE miners. She doubted that they were who they said they were. But she had been the most vocal about trying to help refugees and other people in need during their trek to Kallistah Pass, and just because these five burly men—four humans, one orc—had perpetual scowls carved into the crags of their stone-hard faces did not mean they were in any less need than a houseful of orphans. Although, Ideria would have chosen to travel with orphans even though she never liked the concept of children. They were helpless, noisy, needy, and ungrateful, but very few could be described as killers. None of these men confessed to such an act, but Ideria could sense it from them. Maybe now that she, too, fell into that category she could recognize a kindred spirit. Of course, her friends' Uncle Phyl was now the newest member to carry that exclusive title, and he had not been dealing with it very well. Not well at all.

It had been two weeks since the incident and he still sat upon his saddle with drooped shoulders and watery eyes. Lapin sat next to him on the saddle, half on his lap, and stroked the satyr's leg fur in attempts to comfort him. Neither Bale nor any of his children rode the horses. Other than Hope, they were simply too large. The young half-harpy chose to stretch her wings and spend most of the journey in the air. She said it was for reconnaissance purposes, but Ideria suspected she just wanted to fly above the malaise. They all, however, took turns walking next to Phyl in attempts to liven his spirits. Bale proved to be the worst at it, his meandering words and circular logic often left Phyl frowning rather than pouting. Woe did markedly better by keeping silent, only breaking it with short statements like, "It had to be done," or, "You did the right thing." Rue had success as well, reciting the flowery words of poets. Phyl closed his eyes and looked relaxed as if slumbering in a field of roses when Rue spoke. Hope was the only one to elicit a smile, though, simply by gliding low enough. Feet off the ground, she would kiss his cheek and fly back to the treetops.

Ideria knew little about Phyl, other than this satyr was a true uncle to the ogre-harpy half breeds. He was married to Bale's sister. After Bale had been captured by King Oremethus, she ran off with Bale's wife. Bale had learned about this only two weeks ago, so he was not quite as jovial as the ogre from tales she had heard from her friends.

Phyl had always been nice to her and Nevin, treating them kindly and feeding them if they happened to be around for supper. As a child, she had found the bickering between Lapin and him to be quite amusing. Who could resist the comedic endeavors of a satyr arguing with a rabbit? Even though her interactions with Phyl had been relatively superficial or as a bystander to life affecting him, she felt bad for him right now. It was downright heartbreaking.

* * *

The night following the breakout, she dealt with her feelings about killing people for the first time the same way she had always dealt with anything else—by turning to her brother. She could not consciously recall the actual battle. It was merely a concept that eluded her. She knew how much pressure was needed to puncture skin with a sword and how hard she had to swing to separate a man's head from his body, but not the experience of learning that. She remembered seeing the aftermath, though. So many bodies.

Nevin helped in the escape as well, taking the lives of those soldiers who stood between him and his mother. Unlike Ideria, he remembered each kill. The morning was a bizarre mixture of running and tear-filled "I love yous" from almost everyone in their party. The remainder of the day was spent with the two families congregating while walking without a predetermined destination. Dearborn offered condolences to Nevin and Ideria about finding themselves in a situation to take lives, especially to Ideria. *There were so many bodies.*

Night was spent in the forest, far enough from civilization that no one would notice a campfire, but close enough to purchase a few supplies the following morning. They then stumbled upon the farm with the stable of horses and came up with a plan. Ideria had felt good about the idea until the farmer discovered them.

"Who are you?" the older man yelled, pitchfork primed for stabbing.

Being the least intimidating, Draymon stepped forward, open palms visible. "Good sir, we mean you no harm. We are travelers just passing through. We have fed and brushed your horses and have taken nothing."

The farmer relaxed and lowered his pitchfork. Staying wary he ambled a few paces to peer into the stable. "Brushed and fed the horses, you say?"

"Yes, good sir. In fact, we were wondering if you would be willing to sell two or three of them? We can compensate well?"

"Well, I think I could certainly be persuaded to—" The mention of gold lightened the farmer's mood, but his smile faded as he looked around at everyone in the group. He tightened his grip on his pitchfork. "I heard talk this morning of an escape from the castle's dungeons. A large woman and a larger ogre. I see those two right here."

"They were wrongly imprisoned by a mad king."

"It means sheep shit to me if they deserved it or not, I just know there has to be a reward for their capture. Now stay still and no one gets hurt. My sons should be here soon enough, and we'll all get what we deserve."

"We really want no trouble, and like I said, we can pay handsomely for a few of the horses." Draymon started to approach the farmer as he spoke. Everyone else shifted where they stood and looked nervously to one another. Ideria looked to her mother for guidance.

"You stay right where you are. My sons are right around the corner. Boys! Boys, come along now!" the farmer called out over his shoulder as he waved his pitchfork around.

"Good sir, there's no need—"

"Boys!"

"Stop!"

"Hurry your—"

The farmer stopped screaming. From her angle, Ideria could only see him cough and sputter, blood splashing from his mouth and over his chin. Only once he fell dead to the ground did she see who stabbed him in the back.

Phyl.

He let go of the dagger, still in the farmer's back, and brought his shaking hands to his mouth. Tears streamed over his cheeks as he blubbered, "I'm sorry. I'm sorry. I'm sorry."

★ ★ ★

He had been inconsolable ever since. Bale and Lapin reminded him that he fought in the Demon War two decades ago, but he countered that what he sent to Hell with his blade came from Hell in the first place. The farmer was a living creature, a human. He had misplaced ideals, but he had to summon those because he had trespassers.

Before the sons, if there were truly any coming, could arrive, they took the horses and fled, Draymon leaving two coins in each stall. They rode for days, staying within the confines of the forest. Guiding horses through such terrain limited their speed, but paranoia kept them away from roads and worn paths.

They happened upon the town of Murveen after a week and decided to see if they were far enough away from Phenomere that sight of Dearborn and Bale would only garner sideways glances rather than hope of a king's ransom. Just in case any woman larger than average or any ogre would be met with scrutiny, it was decided that Draymon, Nevin, and

Lapin went into town for supplies and information, while everyone else remained in the forest. The next morning, they returned with refugees.

The news of the dungeon escape did travel, but who escaped concerned no one. It was the death of Vogothe that dominated everyone's interest. That piece of news had more impact on the lives of the townsfolk. The lands were now full of roving bands of brigands and miscreants fearing no consequence for their actions no matter how reprehensible. According to the locals, Perciless and his caravan fought and killed a large group of criminals threatening to take over the town just two days prior. The prince himself had dispatched the gang's leader. There were plenty of sources that said the prince and company were making their way to Kallistah Pass, The miners shared the same story with the group.

"Why didn't you travel with him?" Dearborn asked.

The orc spoke, his thick lips, scarred by deep cuts, moved over teeth that looked more at home as stalactites and stalagmites in a cave than in a mouth, "The prince said flowery words to us in the town, shit about light coming to scare away the darkness and patience and rebuilding and other things less meaningful than a steaming pile of horse shit. But after he left, we thought about his words. We were going to find work at other mines and then thought about what the king did to Orsrun. Ain't no place for us now, ain't no place for us then, ain't no place for us whoever's king. We'd rather drink from the Devil's pisspot than spend another moment in Albathia. We're not following Perciless, we just want to get to Tsinel."

The other four miners nodded in unison.

Draymon pointed to Bale and Dearborn. "You know who those two are?"

The five men shook their heads and frowned even harder. The orc answered. "No. With a face that pretty, we'd remember."

"Thank you," Bale said. "I get that a lot."

Everyone laughed, except for Bale, the experience forming a bond with the newest members of the group.

Even though their motivations differed, the miners offered no encumbrances as the rest of the group decided to push hard along the fastest path to catch prince Perciless. The human miners took turns riding two of the horses, the orc sharing the same size limitations as the ogres. During the abbreviated downtime, they pulled their weight, each gathering wood for a fire or hunting for food. One of the humans even risked the potential of getting bitten by a Hellion Tree Adder, poisonous yet delicious when cooked over a flame. Yet, Ideria still could not bring herself to trust them.

The path led them to the Looping Forest. Ideria had heard of this place but never had any desire to visit it. There was an undeniable beauty to it, but as it was often the way with nature, beauty was delivered in very dangerous ways.

There was only one type of tree in the Looping Forest, ones with light gray bark and slivers of leaves that gleamed silver on sunny days. Even the moss that sometimes grew upon the tree bark was gray and velvety to the touch. Adding to the mystique and the danger were the roots of trees. Starting ten feet above ground, the roots of a mature tree curved outward before disappearing into the earth. The entire forest was nothing more than monochrome archways, set to deceive and confuse the senses. Even wildlife found this area confounding, choosing other environments to eke out a life, so the noises of nature were reduced as well. No birds flew through the branches, no animals on the ground rustled the brush. Uneasy worms turned deep within Ideria's stomach.

"You're veering away from the group," Dearborn said to Ideria as she guided her steed closer.

Ideria shook her head to escape from the traps of monotony and her own thoughts. She tugged the reins to get her horse to follow pace with the rest of the caravan. "Apologies, Mother."

Dearborn chuckled as she reached over to put her hand on Ideria's. "No need to apologize. I just want to make sure you are well. You seem unsettled."

"It's this forest. All so . . . gray. And the trees are all the same. And the roots are all the same. Round doorways to madness."

"I couldn't agree more. Yet, somehow this has pulled Phyl out from his own personal well of pity."

Ideria leaned forward to get a better view. Bale held Lapin in his palm while walking next to the satyr and said, "I spy with my all-seeing eye an object that begins with the letter 'j.'"

A smile played along Phyl's face. "Is it a tree?"

"It is."

Lapin ran his front paws over his face. "Bale, the word 'tree' does not start with the letter 'j.'"

"Try again, Bale," Phyl said.

"Oh. Okay. I spy with my all-seeing eye an object beginning with the letter 'g.'"

"Is it a tree?"

Lapin sat up on his britches. "It can't be a tree, Bale, because the word 'tree' doesn't begin with the letter 'g.'"

A sense of pride could be heard in Bale's voice as he said, "It is a tree, but which one is my all-seeing eye looking at?"

Phyl gave a noncommittal nod to the right. "That one."

Bale frowned. "Damnation. How'd you know, Phyl? Don't matter none. I'll get you this time. I spy with my all-seeing eye and object beginning with the letter 'd.'"

"No!" Lapin yelled. "No, you don't."

Ideria smiled. "I see I'm not the only one being driven mad by this forest."

Dearborn squeezed her hand. "You seemed unsettled even before we entered the forest."

Ideria looked around and over each shoulder to make sure she knew the whereabouts of all five of the tag-a-longs. "It's the miners. I don't trust them."

"No? Any particular reason?"

"They just don't seem like refugees."

"Not the scared women and helpless children you were hoping for?"

"Not hoping for. Expecting."

"So burly men can't be refugees?"

"I never said that."

Dearborn chuckled again. "I know. I don't trust them either. Over the years, Bale has become family, but there are certain limitations to being trapped in the same room with him for an extended period. It just feels so good to actually debate something other than colors or smells."

The argument between Bale and Lapin about whether or not the word "tree" started with the letter "p" or not was now impossible to ignore. It was Ideria's turn to squeeze her mother's hand. "I can only imagine. Actually . . . I can't. I can't imagine the horrors you must have to endure being in a dungeon for ten years."

Dearborn took the reins with both hands and sat straighter. Her eyes focused forward as if watching a stage performance. "It was long, but Daedalus' hatred of me was two sides of a coin. He gave me, and by extension Bale, far more comforts than any other prisoner. Some could argue that we ate better than many of King Oremethus' citizens. He wanted to torture me, but thanks to my training with the army and Elite Troop, physical torture would have been rather meaningless. So, he created Dearborn Day."

"Dearborn Day?" Ideria asked. She swallowed the lump in her throat as her mother took a shaky breath to compose herself.

"Yes, he made his own personal holiday dedicated to besmirching my name. Every month he would find . . . an unwilling sacrifice and impregnate her. Every month for nine years."

"By the gods."

"They have nothing to do with this monster. Just recently, Daedalus introduced me to his children, one hundred strong, *all of them* named Dearborn."

"I'm . . . I'm . . . so sorry."

"Don't be sorry, at least not for me. For those children."

"The children?"

"Yes, I'm sure Daedalus has been twisting their minds, but I believe they can still be saved. Even the oldest is still innocent enough to feel pity for being raised however they're being raised. With no mother for any of them."

"I at least understand that."

Dearborn sighed. "I've spent the last decade in a cage, away from the world. I would go to sleep not knowing if I would wake up the following morning, or what might be waiting for me. I've heard the death knell of many men as their last breath gurgled from them. But there was no greater horror than wondering if you and your brother were still alive."

"Don't forget, you put Uncle Draymon in charge."

"He volunteered."

"He did?"

"I have still yet to fathom why, though."

Ideria giggled. "No?"

"No. Draymon and I met at the same time Daedalus claimed that I ruined his life when we were in our teen years."

"I know this one. Uncle Draymon told us once. It was during a festival and a quarterstaff tournament was set up to be an exhibition for Daedalus. In his mind, it was a chance to prove his superiority over his subjects. He delivered brutal and scarring beatings, including the crippling of Uncle Draymon's hands. Then you came along and beat Daedalus. When he told the story, it was as if you were angel and warrior."

Dearborn chuckled. "I was neither, I'm afraid. Just a girl in her teens trying to find her place in the world. I know he and the other boys who Daedalus beat were certainly grateful to me for winning. But that would have hardly been enough for him to dedicate his life to raising my children."

Ideria was almost laughing now. "Really, Mother? Now I realize that Nevin's cluelessness about how others feel about him is an inherited trait."

Ideria's face was identical to her mother's so she learned how she must look when she became confused, surprised, and embarrassed. "You must be mistaken."

No words were necessary when all Ideria had to do to back her hypothesis was angle herself on her steed to look at Draymon. Dearborn turned to look at him as well. His doe-eyed stare was a portrait of yearning. When he noticed the two women looking at him, he sat at attention and snapped his reins to command his horse to trot farther ahead, toward the front of the group.

"I . . . but . . . how . . . ?" Dearborn stammered.

"I think I shall leave you to your thoughts," Ideria said as she guided her steed back toward the small caravan. The moment of levity was a welcomed one, but the journey was long, and she noticed that the miners were now traveling together in a very tight grouping. She went back to keeping an eye on them.

TWENTY-THREE

"SAMILLIA."

His choice garnered the response he had hoped for. He unbalanced everyone. No matter how small of a reaction they showed, it was enough for Perciless. If they had not reacted, then they were expecting him to answer the way he did. Being predictable could lead to an early grave.

Perciless thought he might need to educate Landyr about the dangers of predictability because his general reacted just as he suspected. That was an issue to address should there be a later time to do so. "You can't be serious."

It was just another decision. Perciless had been king once. But he had to make difficult choices as a prince before that. None more difficult than twenty years ago when he quested for the Self Stone.

Perciless' peripheral vision rippled as his memory ushered his mind into the past. He wished he could stop himself for now was not the time. During these unintended journeys, Perciless felt an unusual closeness to his brother Daedalus . . .

. . . The cave. Perciless was standing before the final chamber within that damnable cavern. The last challenge awaited him after surviving the last trap, another sacrifice. This time it was Taben, a man Perciless had known as far back as he could remember, a knight of impeccable pedigree, and a friend always available to help without question or compensation. Now he was a mangled pile of flesh after setting off a trap. Taben had stumbled on the uneven ground and reached for the cave wall. Perciless never fathomed that a simple touch would lead to thorn roots bursting forth and snaking around Taben. The roots pulled Taben's extremities toward the wall while pressing against the center of his form. His spine burst through his chest, while the only recognizable parts of his crushed face were his eyes dangling from a bundle of thorns.

Perciless blamed himself. This was a fool's errand. At the beginning of this quest, he thought this would be a simple journey, a future topic of a bard's tale. After all, he led a venerable collection of knights and adventurers, handpicked by himself, having personally known them all and understood what they could contribute. At the time, it made no sense to hire mercenaries or bring along unknown soldiers. He needed to trust each and every one of the fifty men who traveled with him. What never occurred to him until it was too late—he would have to watch each and every one of them die.

He stood before the chamber, wondering what horrors awaited him, and why he was even here. This was all for Daedalus. Perciless wanted to connect with him on some level, to save him from himself. The youngest of the trio of princes had always been off center of what most people would consider normal, and Perciless felt responsible for that, for the hardships that Daedalus faced in his young life. He wanted to do something as a form of apology; he wanted to show Daedalus that he cared. He wanted to find the Self Stone and bring it back to his brother. The journey to do so had led him here, to the very item he sought within the dark chamber.

Then a baby cried.

So surprised, Perciless fell down as he backed away from the chamber entrance and almost dropped the torch he was holding. A baby? Impossible. It was impossible that a baby would be in a random cave. But this was no random cave. This was a cave within a cursed mountain hidden from most of the world by a hellish forest. This was the cave with the Self Stone. Any nightmare was possible.

Perciless was mindful not to touch the walls as he got to his feet. The baby's cries intensified and Perciless started toward the cavern entrance, determined to save an infant clearly in distress.

Then he stopped.

Why would there be a baby in this cavern? Demons guarded the Self Stone. Demons haunted all five of the stones needed to open the gates of Hell. This was another test, another riddle to solve, put in place by these very demons, the protectors of the stone. As with every test on this journey, there were dire consequences should the one being tested fail.

Perciless had lost many of his traveling companions to these tests, wrong choices leading to their deaths. No matter how many times he commanded them not to participate, they went against his wishes, stating that the crown came before their lives. Each time a choice had to be made, the first option failed. One particular puzzle took four of his friends. After each one tried and failed, their bones dissolved leaving them as living piles of skin. Every part of their bodies still worked as they slid about the ground like snakes wearing the flesh of men, moaning incoherent words. Perciless had hoped that once the puzzle was solved that they would go back to their original states, bones returned to give them support. No such convenience. The party had been given their pass; the four who failed were doomed to live among the creatures of the ground. They had been given mercy by the tip of Taben's blade, an act Perciless was unable to perform himself.

The crying baby was a test. But a test of what? He had been walking along the path of horrific outcomes from impossible choices. The infant in the other room was just one more puzzle to solve. Perciless straightened his posture while reminding himself of what he had learned from the teachings of great scholars and the tales of heroic warriors. Whatever test he must face to rescue this infant, he found the resolve to do so. He took one step forward.

Then he took one step back.

These were demons protecting an ancient item of immense power. This test was not one about finding the resolve to do something he would have willingly done under any circumstance, rather finding the will to do what he could not do. The demons wished him to kill the baby crying within the chamber.

No. He could do no such thing. He would do no such act. The journey was over now, and he would turn on his heel and head back to the safe confines of his castle. And reduce the valiant deaths of his friends, of fifty good men, to meaningless acts. He could not bear to send a messenger to fifty families letting them know that their son, father, husband had died, because this spoiled whelp lost his nerve while pretending to be important. But the only other alternative was to kill a baby?

Perciless debated, so paralyzed by indecision he sat on the ground to weigh his options. Maybe it was an illusion? Maybe he was mistaken about his assumption of the task at hand? Maybe there was no baby? Every rationalization he concocted a feeling deep within his heart told him that he was wrong. After sitting for so long that he had to shake the feeling back into his legs when he stood, he decided to do it. If he had to slay an infant to give meaning to this mission, to acquire what he sought, then so be it. It had to be done.

Then the crying stopped.

Perciless paused, his breathing and the sputtering flame of his torch now the only noises in the cavern. No. He would not be denied his reward. Perciless ran into the chamber.

A room cut into the stone, small enough for his torchlight to touch all of the walls. In the center was a simple cradle, rocking from side to side, the wood rockers scratching against the stone floor echoed throughout the chamber.

Perciless clutched the torch with both hands, ready to swing it like a club should he need to, and crept closer to the cradle, heart throbbing at the base of his throat, faster with every step. Close enough to touch the cradle, he stopped and looked inside. It was empty. The cloths lining the bottom were warm to the touch. There had been a baby in the cradle mere second ago.

Suddenly he was no longer reliving the past, but rather completely in the present, his friends surrounded by his brother's Elite Troop. He blinked away the last images of that journey of decisions. He had learned that a bad decision was better than no decision. Since then he had lived with the guilty knowledge he was capable of ending the life of an infant to fulfill his quest, even though he did not commit the act. The subsequent knowledge that the Self Stone had never been in that chamber when he arrived—rather it was found decades earlier and kept by the warlord known as Praeker Trieste—did not make him feel any form of relief. He knew that a journey could not conclude unless the first step was taken and decided never to be indecisive again. Thus, his decision to choose Samillia as the sacrifice, and then to reveal that he had deduced her to be a member of the Elite Troop. He came to the conclusion after watching her fight. His brother had kept not only the name of the Elite Troop but the same training techniques as well.

It did not help the situation as he had hoped. The information he revealed certainly caused surprise and confusion, however, it was the Juruk who took advantage of it.

Perciless fought the urge to scream from the immense pain of the dagger blade protruding from the palm of his right hand. His friends snapped to attention and formed a barrier between him and the Elite Troop. Judging from Juruk's words, it was a futile act. Perciless prepared himself to lose the last four friends that he had.

Until an ogre fell from the sky.

The green beast landed feet first on one of the centaurs, the breaking bones sounding like the snapping of branches wrapped in wet cloth. The centaur died before it could release a scream, its front hooves twitching, death stealing the last reflexive moments.

Perciless was mesmerized by the horror and beauty of what he just witnessed. The ogre had not fallen from the sky, he landed. He had wings. Big, glorious wings. And he was not alone.

A harpy with skin the same shade of green as the ogre swooped down from the sky and then back up again, raking her claws up the torso of the other centaur and ripping away curled ribbons of flesh. Blood gushed from the gaping ravines of butchered meat. The centaur screamed and convulsed, dropping to his knees then his side.

The ogre spread his wings and then leaped into the air, taking flight right behind the harpy. All eyes were on the flying creatures, following them as they arced through the air and landed among a motley assortment of individuals, most armed with drawn swords.

Perciless recognized five of them, those who aided with his escape from Phenomere when his brothers laid siege to it a decade ago, including, if memory served him correctly, a talking rabbit. There were three that had the same green skin as the ogre and two with the same bright blue eyes as the huge woman. Five more men, four human and one orc, stood ready with picks and knives.

"My name is Dearborn Stillheart. I suggest you take this bastardization of what you call the Elite Troop and return to Phenomere. Whatever your mission was, it failed. Leave now or we will slaughter you like livestock."

Juruk laughed. He still had over two dozen troops

Perciless assessed his troops as well. He knew nothing about the newcomers other than they were loyal to him in the past and that they certainly seemed proficient in battle, should it come to that. He assumed Cezomir would go after the wizard, while Lina would start with the weakest of the enemies, which in this situation were the three soldiers next to Juruk. Landyr and Thorna would let the battle flow and then react to the biggest perceived threat. However, this was war and situations were always in a constant state of flux.

"So, you're the great Dearborn Stillheart, slayer of the demon war general Ar'drzz'ur," Juruk said.

"I am. I sent him to Hell twice, actually, and I've recently escaped from the Phenomere dungeon to do the same to you."

"You have, have you? Did you fail to notice that you're outnumbered?"

"Only by a few."

"Oh, I think it's more than a few." Juruk snapped his fingers and the five miners grabbed the blue-eyed young adults.

"Ideria! Nevin!" Dearborn yelled, reaching for them. She stopped when one of the men grabbed Nevin from behind and held a knife to his throat. The other four pointed their picks and blades at Ideria.

Juruk smiled and ran his hand over his torso, starting at his hip. His fingers wiggled over each length of black chain, stopping at a short length dangling from two piercings on the other side of his nipple. "Such pretty blue eyes they have. I believe I shall display them from this chain. It's up to you if I pluck them out while they're still alive or after I kill them."

Dearborn cried out and started to lunge toward the Elite Troop soldiers who had been impersonating miners. It took all three ogres to hold her back. The rest of the Elite Troop started to encircle the two different groups. This was something Perciless refused to allow happen.

Gritting his teeth to keep from screaming, he extracted the blade from his hand. The knife was designed for throwing and Perciless had impeccable aim. The blade whistled through the air, true and straight, and the point slid with ease through the left temple of the man holding Nevin hostage. This act was the match that lit the powder keg.

The ogres released Dearborn and joined Ideria in finishing the other three human miners. Dearborn raced to the orc and ripped the tusks from his bottom jaw. His screams only stopped when she jammed them both into his neck.

Cezomir ran toward the wizard but was greeted by a wall of fire. By the time the flames died down, the sorcerer was gone. Cezomir growled and barked, and then joined Lina in attacking one of the chimeras, the beast with two heads. They leaped on the creature at the same time, one on either side. Their jaws clamped down on the beast's necks as they used their legs to shred away chunks of skin and gobs of meat from everywhere below the thing's waist. Satisfied with the kill, they celebrated with a howl and yowl and then bounded on all fours to another one of the chimeras.

Landyr and Thorna converged on the closest adversary— Juruk. He stopped fondling his chains and reached for his sword belt, drawing two. Larger than his adversaries combined, his size belied his deftness with the blades. Neither warrior did any harm, but their constant attack started to take a toll on Juruk. The satyr grunted louder with every strike, every block, until finally, he yelled "Retreat!"

Before Juruk finished the retreat call, the Elite Troop disengaged and fled with such alacrity no one attempted to follow.

Perciless allowed Thorna and Landyr to fuss over his wounded hand, but he was not going to let it stop him from greeting those who saved his life. Landyr tore strips of cloth from his tunic and handed them to Thorna. She wrapped them around Perciless' hand and struggled to keep pace as he walked toward the newcomers. "Greetings and many thanks for your timely arrival. I am Prince Perciless and I am indebted to you. I owe you my life."

Everyone from the other party bowed and Dearborn said, "We know who you are, your Highness."

Introductions were made and pleasantries were exchanged. The mood shifted from that of primal danger to an air of victory. A moment was needed to bury and mourn Brokar. They exchanged information, tended to wounds, and consolidated supplies. Kallistah Pass was their ultimate destination for both parties, so it was an easy decision to travel together. They wanted to keep moving and leave the enemy dead where they lay. There was still one question that needed to be answered.

Perciless crouched down in front of Methel. The recently ousted Elite Troop General was propped against a tree with his hands tied behind his hands behind his back. Perciless slapped Methel's cheeks a few times to wake him up. "So, Methel, what are we going to do with you?"

TWENTY-FOUR

THE JUICES FROM the boar's leg flowed warm and oily over Daedalus' chin. It was hardly a traditional breakfast and he had to resurrect his campfire to cook it, but he was hungry. It was a quick meal and he did not wish to dally for the remainder of the journey to Kallistah Pass. He wanted to make it there by the end of the day so he had his dragon catch a magnificent specimen that had been living well. There were thick chunks of meat on the shank surrounded by nice slabs of fat.

Near the end of filling his belly, Daedalus pulled out the communications crystal. He hated to do this, but his absence from the castle for three full days meant he needed to know what transpired. He activated it by gliding his palm over it. A blue glow emanated from within and seconds later General Perrator's face appeared inside the facets of the crystal. "Prince Daedalus?"

Daedalus tore another piece of meat from the bone and mumbled in between chewing, "Report."

"Your initiative to reduce the amount of criminal activity caused by the absence of Vogothe has been successful."

"Why would I care about that?"

"Because of what happened in Murveen."

Daedalus appreciated short answers, but his general's were aggravatingly brief. "What happ—?"

Perrator hurried to cover up his mistake by continuing, "Murveen was overrun by a band of criminals set on taking the vacant throne of king of the criminal underworld."

"Have our soldiers dispatched the band of miscreants?"

"No. By all accounts, the numbers of our soldiers would not have been enough. Murveen would have been taken over by the criminals, if not for your brother, Perciless."

Daedalus had the shank to his lips, but upon hearing his brother's name he threw it across the field. "Perciless?"

"Yes. Reports said he slit the throat of the criminal's leader."

"How long ago was he there?"

"It doesn't matter. He and his traveling companions are long gone. Rumor has it they were heading north, possibly to Kallistah Pass."

Daedalus looked in the direction of Murveen. He could make it there in half a day. But what good what that do? Perrator had no reason to lie. The Fates would never be so kind to Daedalus as to send both his brother and Dearborn to the same location, to where he was headed. Would they? Maybe the Fates owed him. Maybe this was some form of divine gift. Daedalus turned his attention north, back to the direction of Kallistah Pass. "Very well. The town was saved. I'm sure all the peasants rejoiced."

"Murveen, yes. But there are similar, yet less fortunate, stories coming in from other towns. I'd like to send more soldiers. We would need between 400 and 600 to get the desired results."

A knot formed in the pit of Daedalus' stomach. So many soldiers to fix the problems of the people. Wasteful. "What does Oremethus think of this idea?"

"He is not in the castle. He took the fire dragon and the air dragon to Greengate to hunt for demons."

"*What*? Why in all of the burning Hells did you not tell me sooner?"

"I don't know how to work this crystal. When I went to Speekore and asked for him to show me how this crystal works, he told me not to disturb you with such matters and that you view the king's tantrums as a nuisance."

Daedalus grabbed a stone from the ground and crushed it with his skeletal hand. After three more he was finally able to form words through gritted teeth, although the world around him started to ripple. "Send the 600 troops you had set aside for criminal management to Greengate."

"Sire, I do believe—"

An attack was coming on. A strong one, too. Daedalus despised them but hated to have one in front of anyone else even more so. This conversation needed to end. "I didn't ask for you to share your beliefs! Send the troops. Send them now. Tell them to clean up whatever mess my brother makes. That is all!"

Daedalus dropped to the ground and threw the crystal aside before he was transported back to the past . . .

. . . Back to a few months after his thirteenth birthday. His broken ribs from the horse-riding accident had finally healed to a full recovery. The vomit and diarrhea-inducing diseases from landing in the pig filth had left his body long before, and that was the last time Daedalus felt any predilection toward prayer.

Rain had stripped away any chances of outside activity for the princes, so they decided to play a game of chess siege. Each brother had one thousand cubes of smoothed wood, about the size of a throwing die, and a full set of sixteen chess pieces. They spent hours crafting a castle with walls and towers and blockades and turrets from the wooden cubes, trying to create the best design to protect their chess pieces. Once finished the princes each took a turn, one attack on each of the other two castles. An attack consisted of rolling a marble into the walls to knock over the opponent's chess pieces. A point was gained for each of his brothers' pieces he knocked over; a point was lost for each of his that faced the same fate.

Both Oremethus and Perciless built solid structures with curved walls and a little extra reinforcing block for every one of their chess pieces. Daedalus barely used ten blocks for each of his fifteen other pieces, just enough to raise them off the floor onto a sturdy base. His remaining blocks went into creating a magnificent fortress around the king. Sturdy and impenetrable.

As the game went along, Daedalus lost piece after piece, sometimes even two with one roll. But his king remained standing, nary a wobble from marble after marble slamming into his castle of wooden blocks. The game ended when neither Oremethus nor Perciless had any chess pieces left standing. However, Daedalus lost. He finished in last place despite having the last remaining piece, having his king still standing.

They left the pieces and blocks for the servants to put away and Daedalus complained about the rules of the game. The other chess pieces were meant to be sacrificed, meant to be fodder to protect the king. Why should he be punished for using them as such?

"Those are the rules of the game," Perciless said.

"Of course, you would say that," Daedalus snapped. "The only things that matter to you are rules. Father's rules. Game rules. Instructors' rules. You follow every rule everyone gives you because you want everyone to love you."

"You play the game of life the way you play chess siege. You build strong, strong walls around you and only you. If you continue to play that way, then you will be all you have through the entire game until the very end."

Perciless ended the conversation the same way he had always done, by showing Daedalus his back and making a hasty retreat.

"Don't listen to him," Oremethus said, walking next to Daedalus. "I may have won, but you played a better game. It is never wrong to protect the king, no matter the cost . . ."

. . . No matter the cost. That was why he sent all the troops he could spare, all the troops Perrator could muster. Greengate was a southern town close to the border of Tsinel. More than one battle during the war had occurred near the town limits. What if the king of Albathia were to be caught up in the middle of the war? He had three dragons with him, but if Tsinel happened to be advancing a battalion then they might be able to win by attrition. A loss of a mere 600 troops to save the king was no sacrifice at all.

Daedalus stood up and shook his head, dispelling the last bit of fog created by the attack. He wanted to go back to the castle. He wanted to go to Greengate to help his brother. He wanted to go to Murveen to investigate the last place

Perciless was seen. He wanted to find Dearborn Stillheart. Mounting his dragon, he knew very well he needed to stay true to the plan, needed to get to Kallistah Pass.

Too much. There was too much to do, and Daedalus was the only one who could complete any of these tasks. Incompetence reigned supreme in the castle, the one true ruler. He lost count of how many generals he had to execute for poor performance. The war should have been over by now. What did Tsinel have? A void dragon and the only wizard in the lands who could open portals. What did Albathia have? Dragons. Wizards. Monsters created by Speekore. An Elite Troop. Only he and Oremethus could control the dragons and it was rare when his brother was lucid enough to use them in legitimate battle rather than razing towns searching for imaginary demons. Daedalus hunted and captured wizards, killing those whose egos refused to bend the knee or they failed to add any value to the king's vision. Speekore would rather commit atrocities on any living creature than put his sciences to good use, and all the glorious creatures he had created for war purposes ended up as members of the Elite Troop, made possible by listening to the advice of inept generals.

It was too soon to pass judgment on Perrator as an advisor. He did suggest that Daedalus continue to the Kallistah Pass. If nothing else, it removed a bitter food from the proverbial plate. But now that Daedalus lost himself in thought, it was Perrator that served up that distasteful meal. Then again, if Perrator was right and with this trip, Daedalus was to discover Tsinel exploiting the pathway through the mountains to move troops into Albathia, then he might have to reward that half-giant. And were Daedalus to cross paths with Dearborn Stillheart, then he might have to bathe that half-giant in enough gold to drown him.

Fantasies of rape and blood filled his head, everything from slicing her neck after defiling her in a pit of snakes to his one hundred children flogging her body tied to the rack. So vivid were his daydreams he felt a pleasurable discomfort growing within his britches. It had been too long since he last celebrated Dearborn Day.

The notion of straying from the plan was a distasteful one, but the idea of waiting for his erection to dispel on its own left him with a pain in his lower abdomen. There had to be a town nearby with at least one damsel worthy of Dearborn Day sacrifice. At this very moment, he would even settle for a comely whore.

Guiding his dragon lower, he tried to orient himself. He pictured a map and tried to guess where he was upon it. No luck. Below was nothing but forest with patches of fields. He resigned himself to the notion that he would have to land his dragon and look at an actual map. He aimed for the closest field until he noticed thin wisps of smoke flirting with the sky from behind a group of trees.

Maybe it was a caravan? One escorting a group of virginal women to a convent so they might serve whatever antiquated lord they believed in? Or a family, one with a daughter or two? As he flew over the last canopy and dropped down into the open space, his mind was spinning with possibilities, a game of chance wheel at a carnal festival. What he did not expect to find was one-third of his Elite Troop.

"What is the meaning of this?" he yelled while dismounting. "Where's Methel?"

A dozen troops all jumped to attention, many of which were the nightmarish creatures that could single-handedly slay the dragon Daedalus rode without the need of a weapon. All of them were afraid of Daedalus as he stormed closer, even Speekore's chimeras with no discernible facial features turned away or dipped their heads. They all shifted about listlessly, turning to Juruk for an explanation. The albino satyr stepped forward. "There has been a development in our search for Prince Perciless. It appears that Methel has turned traitor and pledged his allegiance to your brother."

This was the bucket of cold water that allowed Daedalus to clear his mind. Methel turned traitor? Methel was a walking monument to apathy. Daedalus trusted Methel more than any other individual because the man simply did not care enough about betrayal to put forth the effort. Juruk, however, had always made his intentions of being the Elite Troop general known as if he yelled them from mountaintops. Ambition mixing with his duplicitous nature, Juruk undoubtedly killed Methel. But what of the rest of the troop? "Did . . . did you just imply that you *found* my brother?"

Juruk cleared his throat before answering. "We did, your Highness. We even had him captured. It was then when Methel made his intentions known."

Daedalus was dubious of this story, almost certainly a fiction. "And what of the rest of troops? Did they defect, swayed by Methel's sudden change in allegiance?"

"No. They were lost to us in the ambush. Perciless had spent time in Murveen—"

"This news I've heard. He liberated the town from a criminal usurper."

"He did, with help from his traveling party and one of our troop members."

"Wait . . . a member of the Elite Troop was helping my brother and you didn't execute them? You simply watched them aid my brother?"

"Yes, per the orders of Methel. We had located your brother even before Murveen, but Methel wished to gather more information, so he ordered a soldier named Samillia to infiltrate their ranks and learn more about their motivations. I was against this and I now believe that he used her to pass information along to Perciless."

Daedalus knew little about Juruk, just that he appointed him to the Elite Troop under advisement from Haddaman. Juruk was a soldier, though, a warrior, not a politician who could play a character more deftly than an actor upon a stage. There was no doubt in his mind that Juruk was lying, but there had to be some element of truth to draw from because the satyr lacked the ability to spin such a detailed yarn. "You mentioned an ambush?"

"Yes. We had also heard the rumors of . . . the escape from Castle Phenomere dungeon. Those same rumors mentioned that the escapees were near, so we left five of our men behind in Murveen to investigate further. As the fates would have it, they actually found and traveled with the fugitives."

All color seeped away. The world around the white satyr with black piercings changed to variant shades of gray.
The trees turned to charcoal, while the grasses faded to
ash. Daedalus's heartbeat rang between his ears in a piercing rhythm like a blacksmith's hammer forging a sword.
"You . . . you . . . had contact . . . with Dearborn Stillheart
and my brother?"

Juruk spoke quickly to douse the flames building within
Daedalus. "Yes, but if not for Methel's betrayal, we would
have had all of the prizes which you seek. Dearborn traveled with dozens of other travelers, all warriors in their own
rights, and attacked us right when we captured Perciless,
an ambush set up by Methel."

Daedalus stomped over to the closest tree. His eyelids
hurt from the force needed to squeeze them shut and keep
his bulging eyes in their sockets. With his skeletal hand, he
punched and slashed at the tree, chipped wood spraying
through the air. The tree toppled, a cacophony of wood splitting and breaking as it fell into the dense forest. Daedalus
felt the force of it hitting the ground within his chest, where
he finally calmed his raging heart enough to look back to
Juruk and form the words, "Where? Where did these events
take place?"

What remained of the Elite Troop now stood behind
Juruk. Nothing overtly cowardly, just subtle steps to hide
behind their de facto leader as he said, "The Looping Forest.
Two days ago. They were heading to Kallistah Pass."

The Looping Forest was to the west and Kallistah Pass
was north. The temptation to command Juruk to retrace his
steps back to the specific area of interest was great within
Daedalus, but ultimately futile. They were long gone from
that spot and aiming for the same destination as he. He
so desperately wanted to go to where the Elite Troop had
engaged with his enemies, to see where they last were. To be
where they last were in hopes to find any scrap of evidence,
maybe even get a whiff of the faintest of smells. No. That
would be foolishness. He always despised his memory attacks for taking him back to the past, so it made no sense

to consciously do the same. He had to keep moving forward, keep flying to Kallistah Pass and finally get ahead of his adversaries for once. And he would be even more of a fool for not taking advantage of what remained of his Elite Troop. "Juruk, step forward close to me."

The satyr did as instructed without hesitation or question, only pausing when the dragon opened his mouth to breathe its mist upon the other soldiers behind him. Under its miasma, they writhed and clawed away their own skins to reveal the skeletons beneath. In this state the chimeras looked even more terrifying, their frames completely unnatural. Juruk stopped within two steps of Daedalus. "I pledge my life to you, your Highness."

"I know. That's why I'm allowing you to prove yourself to me. I'm taking you with me to Kallistah Pass."

Juruk winced, confused. "You . . . you are going to let me ride upon your dragon with you?"

Daedalus laughed. No, Juruk was not a smart individual at all and Daedalus could not find enough breath to dignify such a stupid statement with a worded response. Instead, he enjoyed watching the look of regret soften Juruk's hard face as the eleven skeletons shambled to him. They encircled the satyr and linked themselves together, creating a cage of bones.

Satisfied that Juruk understood that there was no circumstance where he would ever ride upon a dragon, Daedalus mounted his and they took flight, commanding his ride to grab the cage before aiming for the clouds.

TWENTY-FIVE

DRAYMON SIPPED FROM his cup, the flavor of spiced apple flowing over his tongue, while the sting of acid burned all the way down his throat. He coughed and looked inside his cup, wondering how much liquid was left and why it had yet to burn a hole through the bottom. His reward for enduring the pain was a nice warmth blooming in his belly and flowering up his chest and into his head. He took another drink. This round of coughing was much more subdued, but the burn was no less harsh. The taste of spiced apple was delicious, though. And he chuckled to himself. Somehow in the middle of nowhere, Lapin had found spirits.

The Looping forest bled into a more traditional forest of greens and browns and after a half-day's walk, they decided to rest and find food. Immediately after stopping to set up camp, the talking rabbit insisted that there were spirits to be found around a copse of trees and down a hill. Landyr and Phyl went to investigate and, sure enough, they had run into a traveling merchant and purchased all that he had to offer, four jugs worth. Lapin laid claim to one entire jug for himself, as well as lapping from Bale's cup when the ogre's attention was elsewhere. The rest of the group enjoyed the other three, enough to help everyone relax.

Night had fallen and Draymon opted to stand watch even though the only party member asleep was Phyl, tipsy after one cup of drink, unconscious after another half cup. Lapin was quick to finish what remained. Everyone else was still awake, sitting around the campfire. Stories were exchanged, the two main tellers of tales being King Perciless and Dearborn. Bale made efforts to enhance Dearborn's words, but his attempts were awkward at best. Draymon was too far away now to pick out specific words, but he could hear voices and the sound of laughter reached his ears perfectly. It was wonderful in a way, but he just did not wish to be a part of it.

Ideria still had not forgiven him, barely even acknowledged that he was even a member of their traveling party. Neither had any of the other kids, really. They participated in conversations regarding strategy and planning with him, but that was the extent of things. No pleasantries. To some extent, Draymon could not fault them. They were young, their emotions lived close to their skin and were easily touched. Parents they thought were dead had come back into their lives, healthier than anyone could have imagined. When not fighting for their lives, Ideria looked at nothing else other than her mother with the same wide-eyed wonder of staring directly at a goddess. She heard her mother's every word with a smile upon her face. Even Nevin showed a significant change as well. A young man who kept to himself and analyzed every situation before becoming a part of it, he sat next to the light of the fire instead of the shadows it cast with the hood of his cloak down instead of up. He, too, watched his mother with rapt fascination.

The children of Bale acted the same way. Hope looked as if she could burst into happy tears at any moment. Rue was the intellectual superior to anyone in this group, yet he absorbed his father's words as if every syllable were a nugget of wisdom. Woe shared the same dull look as Bale with a few less wrinkles. Draymon knew enough about the young ogre to see the subtle shifts in his expression every time Bale addressed him. Draymon had spent time with Bale's progeny over the past decade to know them, but not enough to consider them family. He never knew Woe's back hump was actually a way to hide his wings until recently. He taught them a few fighting techniques and showed them how to use tools to build what they needed or fix what they had. Now that they had been reunited with their father, they acted as if Draymon were but a stranger. The way the children treated him would not stick in his craw so badly if they would have treated the other set of ersatz parents with the same level of apathy. Instead, they allowed Phyl to nuzzle close to them as he slept and laughed along with Lapin as he drunkenly joked.

Draymon took another sip and silently berated himself, a fool for having such juvenile feelings. He loved Ideria and Nevin. Their happiness was his happiness. He had never seen them smile so brightly before. No matter the pain he felt, those smiles were worth it.

"They grow up so fast, don't they?" came from the other side of the tree he leaned against. He jolted straight so quickly that a splash of alcohol had sloshed from his cup. He had mixed feelings about that. But he felt comfortable enough to weigh the good against the bad of losing a sip or two of the liquid once he saw that the voice was attached to Landyr. The Elite Troop general leaned against the tree with his left shoulder.

Draymon chuckled and went back to rest against the tree with his right shoulder. "A very true statement. How many do you have?"

"None, to the best of my knowledge. I just know it's something to say when a parent figure is looking maudlin while observing children."

Draymon chuckled again and wondered if he should slow his consumption of the liquid in the cup. He took another sip anyway. "Well, you may not have been a parent figure these past ten years, but you certainly had your hands full keeping the prince alive."

It was Landyr's turn to be maudlin with a long, slow sigh. "I did. But I would be remiss if I didn't mention that I had plenty of help."

Another truth. Draymon wondered how much easier life would have been if he could have added "Elite Troop members" and "psychotic were-creatures" to the list of guardians for Ideria and Nevin. Bartholomew and the Wahl's might still be alive. Nice thought indeed. However, he noted that the Elite Troop now consisted of two members, half the size since the last time he saw them a decade ago. Landyr was next to him, propped up by a tree, while Thorna sat by the campfire, but away from the main group as she whetted her sword. The psychotic were-creatures were nowhere to be found. "So, where are the wolf and the cat?"

"Cezomir and Lina? Either fucking or hunting. Or both. Sometimes they'll hunt something, kill it, and then fuck on its corpse. They're bizarre like that."

Draymon thought about laughing, but there was nothing in Landyr's tone that encouraged him to do so. Was he serious? Or were the spirits lubricating his mouth and allowing the words to slide out faster than they should? "Truly?"

"Truly."

"If so, then how would you trust that whatever they bring back won't have been violated?"

Landyr shrugged his free shoulder. "You can't."

Something shifted within Draymon's stomach. He turned his cup upside down, its contents no longer welcome within him. "Well, that's unsettling."

Landyr pushed himself away from the tree and needed a quick sidestep to keep from planting his face on the ground. "Apologizes. That was not my intent. I merely wanted to extend my greetings and let you know that it's good to see you again."

Draymon moved from the tree as well, the alcohol shifting his world just enough to create a need to touch the bark for balance. Once steadied, he wanted to say something to Landyr, but the other had disappeared.

Hand still on the tree, Draymon walked around the whole thing looking for any hint of where Landyr had gone. No such luck.

"He drank almost as much as Lapin did, so I'm a little surprised that he's still standing," came from behind him. It was a woman's voice, one he had been dreaming about hearing for quite a long time.

Dearborn.

"Draymon?" she asked as she approached, almost as if seeking permission to speak with him.

The uneasiness in his stomach changed from that of apprehension to the flutters of excitement. "Yes."

"We've fought beside each other three times now and we have yet to be officially introduced. I am Dearborn Stillheart."

A smile so broad that it hurt formed along Draymon's face. "Believe me, I know who you are."

"I also wanted to meet the man who raised my children."

"I assure you, Mr. and Mrs. Wahl were the ones who raised them."

"Don't be so humble. They refer to you as Uncle in a very reverent tone."

The strings of Draymon's heart were plucked. He had feared that the damage he had done with his lie would be irreparable. Now he had hope that someday they would forgive him. "After lying to them about your death, I fear that I'm their uncle no longer."

"Nonsense. You did the right thing. They know it as well. Just give a few more days for everyone's emotions to settle. They're smart children."

"They have a smart mother."

Dearborn tilted her head and smiled as if she were surprised that he knew more about her than just her name. "Be that as it may, they've told me that you were their educator."

"They have become exceptional scholars."

"And exceptional warriors."

"And exceptional thieves."

She squinted and drew her lips tight against her teeth. "I don't know how I feel about that news."

"Lapin taught them, drawing upon his many years of experience of being a thief before getting turned into a rabbit."

"Lapin?"

"Yes. He has always had quite a difficult time in the market place. More than a few times he was caught and meant to be made into a meal, but thanks to the dragon magic that turned him into a rabbit, he has an impenetrable hide. After a gutting knife ran harmlessly over him, he would run away, but not before shitting all over the house of whoever caught him."

Dearborn fought to keep from laughing but lost. "Oh, I can only imagine that sight."

Draymon's smile was wide, a true expression of joy. "I have and it usually leads to laughter such as yours every time he tells one of those stories, which just angers him more. But that is one of the drawbacks of being a bunny. And his capture only happens if he's even noticed. Sure, he can talk, but it's difficult for him to make a simple transaction in a bustling market place. So, he taught all the children to steal."

"All the children? Even those belonging to Bale?"

"Yes. In fact, the three that have joined this adventure make quite an impressive team when combined with your two."

"You don't say?"

"I do. Very skilled. Very smooth. Masters of misdirection. Never once have they had the need to run because never once were they caught or even suspected of any form of malfeasance."

Dearborn sighed. "My husband was a thief and I rarely approved when he committed any form of larceny. How could you allow them to be this way?"

Draymon looked over to the children, all five laying in a group, settling in to sleep. "Despite the wrongdoing, they would always do it for right reasons. They took just enough to help the households. If they took too much, they would give the remainder to those in need. They *never* stole from those who would truly miss it. Every dignitary that passed through a town close enough for them to walk to always left lighter. Though their favorite target is the Constable from Bulderswith."

Dearborn's eyes widened. "The one with the wife always in jewels? You jest."

"I do not. They bedevil that fat bastard every chance they get, and his wife often loses said jewels."

Dearborn laughed again. "Oh, praise all the gods, real and unreal. He, too, was Diminutia's favorite target."

Draymon laughed along with Dearborn. "He's still a deserving one, I'm afraid."

Dearborn's laughter faded, but her bright eyes held a bit of mirth even though her voice took a more earnest tone. "I need to thank you."

"You do not. Those children are an absolute joy."

"When I asked you to do right by them, I didn't expect that you would live with them and serve as steward, teacher, and guardian."

Draymon wrinkled his brow, confused by her words. "I could think of no other option for your children."

"I imagined you would check their wellbeing once or twice a year from the shadows, making sure they were still alive."

"For *your* children, I would consider that level of commitment grossly lacking."

Dearborn squinted as she scrutinized his face, searching her memory for why she knew him. Whether she did so with purpose or not, he could not say, but she moved closer to him by one full step. The slightest of smiles tugged at the corners of her lips. "Instead, your level of commitment involved teaching them the finer skills of thieving."

It was his turn to offer a playful smirk. "I need to remind you that it was not under my tutelage where they learned those skills, rather the rabbit's."

"Ah, yes. The rabbit's tutelage. How could I possibly forget that they've acquired their larcenous ways from a creature one rung higher than a rodent on the ladder of intelligence."

"Clearly you haven't seen him drunk as often as I have or else you wouldn't have given him such credit. He's easily two rungs beneath even the slowest of rats."

"I fear I may believe you. So, the rabbit taught my children how to steal, and you taught them weaponry and fighting?"

Draymon held out his hands, most of his fingers permanently curled, a few in rather unnatural ways. "I taught them how to find answers where there are none to be found. How to improvise and think beyond any problem they face."

Dearborn's smile fell away, replaced by amazement as she grabbed his hands. He suppressed a gasp, the sudden sensation of her touch sent warm lightning up his arms. Her hands were as calloused as a farmer's, but her fingers were still soft and warm. However, she regarded his hands as unusual tools, instruments unique in style and function. She whispered, "I've seen you wield a quarterstaff with such deftness that you almost bested Bale and Praeker Trieste in the fighting pits."

Ten years ago, their paths crossed for the second time within the pit of an illegal fighting arena. They each had a different mission, but they had to work together to best the possibly immortal monster, Praeker Trieste. Their time together then was brief, only to see each other once more in the throne room attempting to thwart an insurrection. Ultimately, they failed, Dearborn sacrificing herself to help everyone else save Perciless from his brothers. Now, ten years later, his hands were in hers. "Magnetics."

Dearborn looked up. Even in the darkness her eyes somehow still managed to sparkle. "Magnetics?"

"Yes. I've sewn magnets of differing strengths in various pairs of gloves. My quarterstaff had an iron core and the gloves I use to wield it have very powerful magnets."

"That's brilliant."

"I got the suggestion from a brilliant woman."

Dearborn winced, confused by his statement, then her expression relaxed when she understood what he was saying. She looked down at his hands again, this time seeing the situation in a different light. She let go and then put hers behind her back. Her smile returned, but this time one masking embarrassment. "I assume you mean me, but I must confess I don't remember a particular conversation with you involving magnets, because I . . . I do not . . . remember you."

"Why did you ask me to do right by your children?"

"Because there was . . . is . . . something undoubtedly familiar about you. How far back into the past must I travel?"

"To when we were teens."

"As entertaining as this game of guessing has been, I must insist . . . that . . . you. . . ? Arten?"

"Yes."

Eyes slicked from the start of tears, Dearborn reached to embrace him, then quickly pulled her hands back and brought them to her face. "By all the gods real and unreal. Arten?"

Draymon chuckled. "No matter how many times you ask, the answer is still yes."

A variety of emotions played over Dearborn's face, more obvious to Draymon than if she announced each one. Surprise. Glee. Concern. Pity. "You sacrificed so much. Ten years, for me, for a woman you barely knew when we were both struggling with adolescence."

Draymon had been in life or death battles more times than he could count, but his heart had never raced as it did now. Emboldened, he took a step closer to her, ready to blame the spirits should she object to his forwardness. So close to her he now needed a slight tilt to his head to look up into her eyes. "That woman I barely knew saved my life during that struggle."

A gasp disrupted her breathing. She opened her mouth, but no words were released. Draymon assumed she wanted to ask how, so he told her. "During the festival when Daedalus disfigured my hands, I saw into his eyes. Even at a young age, I knew evil lurked within his mind. A sense of whimsy tickled him because he had the ability to ruin my life. I wasn't the only one who saw that evil as I wasn't the only one left permanently injured. Then you came along."

Dearborn scowled and shook her head. "That was day one of his quest for vengeance against me. His hatred of the world was unfocused and by defeating him I gave a name to his hatred. My name."

"But you also gave your name to hope. You showed us that evil could be defeated. You showed us that charity and compassion still existed. You spent time with each one of us who lost to that bastard."

"The time I spent all those years ago was worth ten years of being a surrogate parent to children you had never met?"

"It was a blessing, every minute of it."

A tear slipped free from its well, leaving a shimmering streak along her cheek. She smiled. It was not wide and beaming, but it brimmed with emotion. She inhaled deeply.

"I must thank you for many things, including being a blessed mirror, showing a reflection of me that I had always wished to see. Now, if you'll excuse me, Kallistah Pass is four days away, three if we push ourselves, and I feel sleep beckoning me."

Dearborn walked away.

The fire from the spirits had long departed Draymon's body, but he hardly noticed as a new warmth grew from within his heart.

TWENTY-SIX

DEARBORN WATCHED DRAYMON. The way he moved in the saddle, his muscles compensating for the gait of the horse in a pleasant rhythm. It had been three days since their discussion. This was the first time she looked at him as a man, not a trainer or surrogate guardian for her children.

He was certainly a handsome enough man, although after having no one else other than Bale to look at for ten years, even Phyl had become "handsome enough." He was almost as tall as she and very fit, not a single roll along his waist from excess ale or spirits. She could still lift him with one arm, but she could overlook that if he could, and it certainly seemed like he was willing to do so. Or was he?

Dearborn replayed the "thank you" conversation they had three nights ago. He made no pledges of undying love, nor made any form of amorous intentions. But he pledged loyalty, and to a man, that was akin to love. And he did have a look of yearning upon his face. Even the best of gamblers could nary hide that special look of fondness for the heart of another.

If he did indeed wish more from Dearborn than to repay her for something she had done a lifetime ago, should she be interested? He did an amazing job with her kids—both healthy and capable adults whom she was exceedingly proud of. They were none too happy with him now, but that would pass. She might even have to intervene and accelerate the forgiveness process should she deem it prudent to do so. But what of her feelings for their father?

Ten years separated her from the time she had lost him, but those ten years left her no opportunities other than to pine over her lost love, to replay his death in her mind. It made matters worse that her son was a spitting image of her deceased husband, his hair color the only difference. Nevin stripped away all chance of her ever forgetting what Diminutia looked like. How could she fall for another man when the ghost of her husband would forever haunt her? Then again, due to her size she had never dreamt of finding love once, let alone a possibly for twice. Her daughter was equal in height and build, her younger muscles always rippling when she moved. Did her daughter share her same anxieties as she at that age? Dearborn had been in the army for three years by the time she was her daughter's age, having given up the idea of ever having a husband or family. Maybe it would give Ideria hope that she could find a man if her mother acted as an example.

Dearborn almost slapped herself to bring her attention back to the reality of the moment. Daydreaming flights of fancy were for school girls infatuated with farm boys and stable hands, not an army trained enemy of the current regime. If she wanted a man, she would get one. So would her daughter if she wanted to pursue that path, as she was far stronger, smarter, and more confident than Dearborn had been at that age. Dearborn felt foolish and almost neglectful focusing on a single person this whole time instead of everyone else in the caravan.

Over the past day and a half, they had crossed paths with and joined three other groups of people. They were getting closer to Kallistah Pass and more people were braving the landscape of snow to trust the rumors about a way to escape from Albathia. This new caravan numbered over two dozen. Considering what happened the last time they allowed a stranger to join them, she needed to be more vigilant, less trusting. These people, however, were nothing like grizzled miners. Mostly women and elderly, a few men, four wagons total and another dozen horses. The travelers from

Bulderswith even brought three goats and two chickens. And they were generous in sharing milk and eggs.

The temperature dropped as thick forests gave way to rolling hills covered by a thin blanket of snow. Dearborn's children and Draymon had a few extra furs and blankets as did Perciless and his small cohort. It was enough to keep from freezing, but not enough for comfort. The group from Orsrun had over-prepared with plenty of supplies to combat cold weather in one of their two wagons, but they had no protection against the bandits or the wild. They had been fortunate for the first part of their journey, having no run-ins with any thieves, but a pack of wolves had begun to harry them and the beasts started to grow in number. The refugees from another town burned by the king and his dragons feared an attack until they crossed paths with the other caravan from Orsrun. All of the travelers were so happy to find a party of benevolent warriors to accompany them for the rest of the journey. The refugees shared what they had, especially since the werewolf and cat woman were able to provide enough deer and boar for everyone, every night.

Just because none of them seemed nefarious did not grant them innocence. Yes, among the travelers there were nothing but faces full of hope and promise. That did not mean there were no cutthroats, no assassins, nor mercenaries with pockets stuffed full of the king's gold. Dearborn's tingling nerves sang to her songs of doom and betrayal. She wanted to confer with her children and guided her horse among and around the other refugees, greeting them with smiles and waving hands as she passed. She found Ideria and Nevin with a small group of others who seemed to be their contemporaries in age, all laughing while exchanging stories.

Dearborn sighed. The worst part about chasing ghosts was no one else could see them. Were there even ghosts to chase? It had been so long since she had been around others in any form of social situation that she no longer knew how to act, what to look for in how people acted. Ten years of dealing with guards had made her paranoid. The only one who never treated her, or Bale, too badly was Methel.

Methel. She should have savored the twist in fate the brought him to her as a captive. There were no bars around him, but his hands were bound together and tied to the horse's saddle. A blanket was draped over his lap to keep the bindings hidden from curious eyes, while the hooded figure of Perciless rode next to him, away from the main group, discouraging interaction. Landyr and Thorna remained near them and vigilant. Methel had remained silent this entire journey, not answering a single question, nor making any requests. He ate when food was brought to his mouth, drank from water skins and uttered not a single syllable. Dearborn had tired of his silence and was determined to end it.

Sitting up straight in his saddle with a bored look in his eyes, Methel seemed as if he were on an uninteresting trail ride. Perciless still rode next to him, but his hood was up, casting shadows over his face, just a rider wishing for solitude. Dearborn's horse matched the gait of Methel's as she guided it closer. "Why?"

Methel grunted a form of chuckle as Perciless turned his head to face the conversation. Words heavy, thickened by the pasty tongue of a dry, unused mouth, Methel answered with his own question, "Why what?"

These were the first words he had spoken since capture. Possibly they had simply been asking him the wrong questions. "Why were you kind to me?"

Methel snorted. "If you considered my actions nice, then I worry about the life you had before you wound up in the dungeon."

"Everything is comparable. Compared to the life I had before, your actions were those of diseased vermin. Compared to the insults and taunts from the other guards and the way the army recruits treated Bale, then your actions could be considered nice."

"Verily?" Perciless asked from the other side of Methel.

"The lock of my cage door was easy enough to pick open and Methel always turned a blind eye anytime I slipped free to garner meager supplies or help the other prisoners. He never spat on me or in my food. Never disciplined me when I eschewed the advances of a spirited recruit following the urges of his cock. I just wish to know why."

Methel went back to answer with silence.

Dearborn leaned closer. "Perhaps your cock suggested a different way to find your way into my bed?"

Methel laughed, a scratchy cough of a dry throat. "Cunt always has a price to it, no matter if it belongs to a wife or a whore. You 'eschewed' handsome and healthy recruits by giving them bruises and broken bones. I don't believe an old man like me could have survived your rejection. I never felt the need to act beyond that of a guard, because I found you . . . interesting."

"Interesting?"

"Indeed. My wife was a dull woman. Sweet and kind, for sure, but a dull woman, nonetheless. After she died, I started pounding metal before the Morning Sun came up and didn't stop until well after the Evening Sun disappeared. I needed to feed my daughters. I needed to slip as many coins as I could to any educator I could find to help my daughters move beyond dullness. They, too, died. Not only did I lose the ability to recall their faces, but I lost who they could have become as well. To see you, a strong, proud, smart woman . . . well, because of you, my daughters have faces in my memories once again."

"My father was a blacksmith."

Methel chuckled again, this time hiding a sadness within it. "See? Interesting."

"It sounds as if there's a heart of a good man behind that chest of yours, Methel," Perciless said. "How did you end up being *general* of the Elite Troop?"

"Being a good man gives you a dead family. Your brother gave me opportunities. I would not be alive now had I turned down any of those opportunities."

"You receive your orders from him, don't you?"

"Directly from him."

"How . . . how is he?"

Methel laughed. "Daedalus? Mad, of course. His mind is that of a stepped-on hornets' nest. And getting worse."

"Worse?"

"Yes. Your efforts have been a constant source of agitation as well as the war effort. Everything's now compounded by Dearborn's escape. Oremethus is making matters worse by either chasing demons or mismanaging troops." Methel looked at Dearborn as he completed his thought. "And then what *your* daughter did has him shitting razor blades sideways."

Perciless tilted his head, the hood falling just enough to expose one quizzical eye. "Dearborn? What did Ideria do?"

Dearborn was proud of what her daughter accomplished, wanted to sing her praises from the tops of mountains. Ideria, on the other hand, was uncomfortable with her actions and requested that her mother share the story with no one. The gears of Dearborn's mind slipped as she tried to think of a believable lie or a way to steer the conversation away from this topic, but she was too late.

A smile grew along Methel's stubbled face, one Dearborn assumed to be sadistic, yet a sparkle in his eye made her think he, too, was proud of Ideria. "Well, your Highness, judging from the commotion over there, I think we're all about to find out."

Next to one of the slowly moving wagons, her children walked with a few other humans roughly their age. Dearborn was too far away to hear specific words but judging from her daughter's frantic gestures begging silence from her audience, she was upset by whatever they had learned. Dearborn snapped the reins and her horse sped to a trot. Sure enough, as she got closer, she could hear that Ideria's secret was out.

"Shhh! I beg you," Ideria said, her index finger bouncing off her lips. "Please don't tell anyone."

"But we must!" one of the girls said. "It's because of you that we're still alive to make this journey. Papa! Papa! Come quick."

"No, please. Please, don't."

Too late. The girl's father rushed around the corner of the wagon, eyes wide with fear, just as Dearborn arrived. Ideria looked up to her mother, and repeatedly whispered, "I'm sorry."

Grabbing his daughter with both hands, the older man asked, "What is it? Is something amiss? Are you hurt?"

The girl's smile was so bright and warm it could have melted the snow around her. She put her hands on her father's. "Quite the opposite, Papa. We've just learned that Ideria was the cloaked figure that saved us from the king's dragons."

The man's eyes shimmered from the pools of forming tears as he released his daughter and slowly walked to Ideria, looking her up and down in scrutiny. "Blessed be. Is this true?"

Ideria stood in silence, her cheeks turning pink from more than just the chill in the air as those within earshot began to gather. The girl ran up to Ideria and grabbed her arm. "It's true, Papa. It's her. She was the one who pulled the metal dragon away from the mine shaft."

"And then killed it," a voice called out from the gathering crowd.

"Blessed be!" another voice said.

"Is this true?" came from behind Dearborn.

Perciless.

The people around Ideria separated enough to accommodate the horse. They exchanged pensive looks and whispered among themselves questioning who this cloaked rider was, but they let him through. Perciless dismounted the horse and stood before Ideria. "Is this true, Ideria? Were you the one who killed the metal dragon?"

"Yes, but I didn't mean to. It was an accident."

Perciless reached up and lowered his hood. All of the refugees gasped, his name passed around the group as if whispering it imbued the speaker with magic. "Oh, Ideria, do not hide behind the walls of modesty. From what I've heard you lured the metal beast away from children hiding in a mine and then tricked the lightning dragon into destroying it."

Head bowed down, Ideria reiterated, but with less conviction this time, "It was an accident."

Nevin stepped beside his sister and put his arm around her in a conciliatory manner. "It's true that you had no idea the lightning dragon had the power to reduce the metal dragon to a pile of molten slag, but it was your hand that sent the knife on a perfect trajectory into the lighting dragon's eye."

Ideria's blush deepened in color as a gleeful murmur spread through the crowd.

Perciless stepped even closer to her. "Ideria, you are a hero. What you did was nothing short of miraculous. You alone did something that entire battalions haven't been able to do. It's because of you that Albathia still has hope."

Random locks of her blonde hair shielded parts of her face, but Ideria lifted her head and looked to her mother for guidance. Dearborn understood her daughter's apprehension, unaccustomed to so many eyes upon her. Despite her confidence, ability, and desire to fight, she was would rather not have the attention and accolades that came with being a storybook hero.

Perciless must have read the same story Dearborn did because he waved his hand with a flourish, his voice deepened by bravado. "Good people of Albathia, please join me in my journey to Tsinel, our neighbor and greatest ally against the scourge known as Oremethus and Daedalus. My brothers are not good for this kingdom, nor are they good for you fine people. You deserve more. You deserve better."

The people applauded as he mounted his horse and turned to face the last few miles to Kallistah Pass. "Within the borders of Tsinel, I will make plans to end this misery. I will to return this country to you, the people, after all, we have a dragon-slayer with us!"

Everyone cheered, even Dearborn, swept up in the charisma of Perciless and the hope emanating from the people. Emotions flowed like a full barrel of ale after tapping as the caravan continued onward. Perciless informed everyone that he intended to make his way to Tsinel to confer with their king. He felt that the time to strike against his brother was nigh and wanted to garner council from his allies. He promised a bright future.

The last few miles passed by within minutes. Smiles and laughter, plan making and dream sharing allowed everyone to move forward through the snow with no complaint of sore legs or cold feet. Dearborn could not help but get caught up in shared enthusiasm. Deep within her still stirred the instincts of a soldier, telling her to place king and country before herself. She reminded those stirrings that doing so had led her to nothing but heartbreak and time in a dungeon. Had she no other priorities she would have given aid to Perciless, but now she had children to think about. The dirt in Tsinel was just the same as the dirt in Albathia. She might have to learn different crops, but she had existed as a farmer before. Not just existed, thrived.

The downside to inspiring speeches and hope for a bright future was that her children were getting swept up into the current. She was proud of them for wanting to fight for the betterment of tomorrow, but she hoped they would never have to. Duplicity was never in her nature, but she feared that she must become a quick study. Once in Tsinel she needed to find ways to pull them away from this situation, show them that they could have long, healthy, productive lives if they stepped back and let someone else fight. The mood of the group intensified as they ascended one final ridge to Kallistah Pass.

The flat plain of land did not quite level out, rather the incline was far less steep. The mountains had grown in size as they had trekked closer every day, but Dearborn still felt a sense of awe course through her as they approached the base of the range. Gray and angry jagged chunks of stone pierced the ground as if the discontented underworld wished to escape its confines. Shades of white tipped the mountains, while the browns and greens of lichen and moss ran along the base. The pass itself, with its opening wide enough to house a small town, looked almost inviting. So inviting, that another ten-person caravan was setting up camp.

At first, the others were apprehensive of a large group of strangers holding swords and having ogres in their party but relaxed in their stances as they were greeted with smiles and outstretched arms. Leading the way was the father of the girl who exposed Ideria as the dragon slayer.

Hair whiter than the snow, his head poking through the opening in the center of a simple diamond shaped animal skin, he led the way with extended arms. "Greetings fellow travelers! We, too, are going to start our journey to Tsinel in the morning. And we come bearing something greater than food and clothing—hope. With us, we have the great King Perciless, and we accompany him to a better way of life!"

Those were his last words.

A clump of bones fell from the sky and crushed the man. As red seeped along the snow, the bones disentangled themselves to expose a large, white satyr concealed in the center. As the skeletons separated from each other, Daedalus landed his dragon in a blast of snow and wind. Dearborn knew that she would never see Tsinel.

TWENTY~SEVEN

NORMALLY A DRAGON made of bone ridden by a mad prince would have been the tactical priority for Landyr, if not for the massive satyr and a dozen armed skeletons in front of him. The dragon paid no mind to him or Thorna, turning its attention to those refugees that were setting up camp by the Pass entrance. One blast of dragon's breath and the prince suddenly had another dozen skeletons. The dozen in front of Landyr was a more pressing matter.

"I'll take the six on the right, you take the six on the left. We can share the satyr," Thorna said.

Landyr appreciated her confidence, despite it being misplaced. They each had a sword, but so did all the ambulating skeletons, and the satyr had two. Landyr and Thorna drew closer together as their bony adversaries surrounded them. He stole brief glances to see if any of his companions were in any position to help. Too many people were running around in circles with no place to hide. Dearborn's children ran to the newly formed skeletons, the passion of youth guiding their hearts. Dearborn chased after them.

The circle tightened. A few of the skeletons were missing parts, a couple of leg bones, a few arm bones scattered around where the dragon had dropped them. He whispered to Thorna, "We should focus on the weaker ones."

"I agree," she replied.

A shadow slid across the ground, followed closely by a second. Something was flying overhead. Rather, someone.

Two streaks of green flashed before Landyr and raced upward. Three of the skeletons disappeared, leaving behind eddies of snow. Landyr wanted to call out his gratitude but Hope and Woe dashed away too quickly. They used the skeletons they picked up as projectile weapons, hurling them at Daedalus and then swooping out of harm's way. The prince cursed as the dragon impotently snapped its jaws and coughed out its pernicious mist.

The ogre children's attack left a sizable gap in the perimeter of skeletons. One big enough for Landyr and Thorna to exploit. Instead of a shrinking circle, it was now a curved line. The skeleton at the front of the line had no chance to swing its sword before Landyr disarmed it at the shoulder allowing Thorna to decapitate it.

They were able to destroy two more before the rest were able to regroup. The skeletons moved slower than humans, magic an inferior substitute for muscle, so Landyr and Thorna dodged their attacks with ease. The chimera skeletons were more troublesome.

The secrets of how Speekore created these monstrosities were revealed, chunks of metal held bone to bone, extending limbs past the lengths that nature intended or combining parts of two creatures that never belonged together. Three of these chimeras remained and each stood half again as tall as Landyr. They were slow, but their sword swings were strong and constant, their longer arms reduced their chances of decapitation.

The skeletons moved around, surrounding the two remaining Elite Troop members. A fire ignited within Landyr's wrists and rapidly spread up his arm. The sword strikes were coming from everywhere and all he could do was block them, his sword singing from the repeated beating. Thorna grunted after every clang. The hits were getting harder and harder, shaking the ground with every blow. No. Not the swords. They were not what caused the ground to shake.

Bale.

The ogre rumbled his way through the fight, crashing into the bone combatants.

Landyr and Thorna exchanged glances, each savoring the all too brief moment of respite. In a tangled web made of bone, Bale did a masterful job of avoiding the swords, but that meant exposing himself to the raking claws of free hands and bites from sharpened teeth. Unable to stomach the notion of allowing another to absorb pain meant for him, Landyr took one more deep breath, raised his sword to jump into action, only to be met with a backhand to his nose.

A hundred exploding stars burst into his vision as he stumbled backward. Juruk had now joined the fray, making his presence known with a sword through Thorna's gut. Doubling over left her exposed to take a knee to her face and she dropped to the ground, lying motionless in the snow. Both swords at the ready, Juruk strode toward the skeletons.

"Bale!" Landyr called out as he stumbled his way closer, the lower half of his face throbbing.

The ogre heeded Landyr's call and threw a smaller skeleton at Juruk. The mess of bones slowed the satyr, just enough. Focusing on one of the chimera skeletons, Bale kicked at its misshapen legs, breaking them both at the knees. With a roar of determination, the ogre yanked the sword-wielding arm from its socket. The bone hand still gripping the sword, Bale wielded the arm as best he could. Even though it was flopping around by the hinge of its elbow, Bale used it well enough to clash steel with Juruk. With his other hand, he worked his fingers into the rib cage of a smaller skeleton and used it as a shield against the other skeletons.

Landyr rushed to Thorna and placed his hand on her cheek, his thumb under her nose. Her skin was still warm, and he felt her breath. He carried her to the closest wagon and placed her on it. There was enough clothing strewn about to make ersatz bandages. It was far from ideal, but it would have to do; Landyr needed to help Bale.

Take the easier opponents first, this was his plan. Using his sword like an ax, he swung at the exposed joints of his enemies any time an opportunity presented itself. Even the larger chimera frames had a difficult time defending against

Landyr, while Bale repeatedly bashed at them with a skeleton torso, its arms and legs long gone.

Stabbing yielded no results. A blade skidding along bone was as good as a miss. Landyr could only chop, but these actions were effective. If he missed a joint, he still cleaved away at bone, weakening it with cracks. Limbs fell away as if he were hacking at moving trees, damaging it to a point where he could easily lop off its head until he felled them all.

Juruk took a step back and tightened his grip on the swords. Landyr knew of him, heard the stories and saw the aftermath of Daedalus' bastardization of the Elite Troop. Calling himself the general of a troop that consisted of four members felt foolish to Landyr, almost patronizing. But he would be damned if he would let this monster tarnish its name and live. "Bale, we need to—"

The ogre roared and lunged at Juruk. The satyr dodged the attack with ease and slashed at Bale. Green blood streaked the snow and Bale dropped to his knees.

There was only a subtle difference separating bravery and foolishness, and Bale crossed that line. But it gave Landyr an opportunity to draw blood from Juruk's arm, the spray as black as the chains decorating his body. The satyr struck back. Landyr blocked the blow and it felt like stopping a rolling boulder.

Juruk moved faster than he should for a creature his size, each strike that Landyr blocked a punishment. The attacks came so quickly that Landyr had no other recourse than to block until his arm went numb. He faltered and Juruk's knuckles connected with his cheek.

The snow felt good against his face. Landyr had no memory of hitting the ground, just a dull recollection of being in a fight. And danger. *Move* came to him suddenly. He rolled over to his back, unable to do more. Juruk stood over him, inky blood sliding down his arm, cascading over his sword, the implement promising Landyr's demise. Juruk snarled, his ugly face twisting horrifically, as he raised his sword over his head. A quick prayer to whichever gods listened to the thoughts of washed up soldiers raced through Landyr's mind. He wanted his final thoughts to be pleasant ones, of

Chanessa, the dark elf, the demon, the dragon. He wondered if, by some miracle, she would appear out of nowhere and rescue him once again. Instead of a dragon, however, he got an ogre.

Bale grabbed Juruk from behind and hoisted him over his head. With the force of a collapsing mountain, Bale slammed Juruk's back against his knee. The resulting snap shook the snow from nearby tree branches. The satyr roared and twisted, with his dying blows trying to reach Bale with one of his swords. Bale put an end to his flailing with a final twist of the satyr's neck.

Landyr tried to stand, but vertigo pushed him back to the ground. His world spun, but he could still see the ogre. "Bale? I thought Juruk finished you."

"Ha! It's a small cut on a big belly."

Landyr chuckled, but the very act made his view of the world ripple.

"Come on. The others need our help." Bale gestured for Landyr to follow, as he ran toward the dragon.

Landyr got to his knees, the best he could do, as he fought with his blurring vision. He concentrated and the world around him came slowly back into focus just in time to witness the horrors of Daedalus. The dragon breathed out once again and more lives of good people were ruined. The refugees tore away their own skin, desiccated insides spilling to the ground like an overturned bushel of long rotted fruit. More skeletons now ready for battle. These poor people would never garner the freedom they sought.

Cezomir and Lina fought with the newest skeletons. Lapin aided them as well, but his actions accounted for very little, except skeletons wobbling where he had gnawed at their ankles. Woe and Hope continued to pester the dragon, dropping rocks and branches on it. Phyl, Rue, and Dearborn did what they could to usher as many refugees into Kallistah Pass, fending off as many skeletons as possible.

Dearborn fought with two skeletons, alternating her attack from one to the other. She jammed her sword through the skull of one, but it became stuck. Instead of attacking Dearborn, the other skeleton grabbed a nearby refugee, a woman trying to sneak by. By the time Dearborn freed her sword, the skeleton dragged the screaming woman away from the pass.

Such an odd tactic, Landyr thought since the only drive the other skeletons had was to kill. Dearborn rushed to the woman's aid and Landyr wanted to yell out a warning, but the only noises coming from his mouth were raspy grunts with every exhale. His faculties were returning, but not fast enough.

Dearborn lopped away the limbs of the skeleton as if trimming an unruly bush and then cleaved its skull in half. A few pieces of shattered bone twirled through the air as the rest of the skeleton fell into a clump. Then the trap was set.

The skeleton had used the woman as bait, separating Dearborn from everyone else. With the mountain to her back, her escape options were limited. Daedalus and the dragon appeared preoccupied with the greater battle, but it was only an act. Landyr's heart turned to ash when the dragon whipped around in a half circle and ran for Dearborn.

Trapped, Dearborn looked left and then started to run to the right, but the dragon shifted too quickly, forcing her to retreat to her original position. Without wasting time with theatrics or speeches, Daedalus tugged on the reins. The dragon's head reeled back as it opened its mouth. Snapping forward, the beast released its bone-white breath. Before any could touch Dearborn, Methel launched himself into her and knocked her clear.

Within the mist, the woman Dearborn had just saved wailed as her muscles shriveled and fell away, her innards turning to dust and dispersing as miasma on the wind. Methel's skin sloughed from his bone as he remained still, looking at Dearborn. Before his face gave way to the skull beneath, he used his final breath to say, "Interesting."

"Baaah!" Daedalus yelled in disgust. "You fool! Your sacrifice only added mere seconds to her life as I command you to kill her!"

The woman's skeleton stood and shambled next to Methel, angled toward Dearborn as she got to her feet, defenseless. Methel had hit her so hard she dropped her sword. The skeleton that was once Methel bent down and picked up the weapon.

And promptly decapitated the skeleton next to him.

Landyr rubbed his eyes with his palms and shook his head. The hit he took must have left him daft because he just saw one of Daedalus' skeletons kill another. Sure enough, the remains of Methel turned to the dragon and advanced.

The beast sprayed its mist again, with no result. Daedalus snapped and tugged on the reins, but the dragon was too confused to obey. It growled and backed away, releasing yet another bone white cloud.

The cold of the snow seeped through Landyr's clothes as he took a few wobbly steps forward. He wondered if Daedalus regained control of the dragon or if the creature knew the proper course of action. It flapped its wings in quick, strong bursts, just enough to leave the ground and bank around the corner of the mountain's edge, into the Pass. Finding future soldiers, it landed, pinning many of the living against one of the walls.

Landyr entertained the novelty of prayer once more, hoping for divinity to help again. The rescue came in a way he could not have possibly fathomed and he seriously wondered if he might truly have direct access to the gods.

The dragon stretched its neck parallel to the ground and spread its wings upward, ready to strip the life away from everyone in front of it. Then a howl pierced the air. Not of a dog or wolf, but of a great cat that had been backed into a corner, warning of impending danger. A second yowl echoed through the pass, joined by others.

Everyone looked around. Landyr limped his way closer to the entrance of the pass, fighting through his intermittently blurred vision to scan the nooks and cracks of the mountainside for the source of the noise. A lion jumped from above the dragon.

Not a true lion, rather one shaped like a human and wearing clothing. As soon as the cat creature dug its claws into the dragon's neck, more of its kind flowed down from the walls. Twenty. Thirty. Landyr was unable to count, just surprised that they were swarming the beast.

Daedalus slashed at the cat creatures with his skeletal hand, drawing blood with each swipe. The dragon clawed and bit as it backed against the mountain wall. It blew another breath of mist, covering half a dozen cat creatures.

Nothing happened.

Another roar of frustration this time from Daedalus. His command to everything around him was a scream of, "Die! Die!"

The dragon spun and pushed his wings down, taking a brief flight out of the pass and back onto the snow-covered field, clear of the cat creatures. Crouching with its wings drawn tight to its body, the beast was poised to attack, its rider screaming, "Kill them! Kill them all!!"

Landyr was thankful that his friends and companions were no longer trapped and for these mysterious cat people, but he had hoped for more time for them to retreat farther into the pass, or at least find places to hide. Some might survive the impending attack, but there would be deaths.

Then they disappeared.

All of them.

Perciless. Dearborn and Bale, and all their respective children. The others he traveled with. The remaining refugees. All the cat people. Vanished in a blink.

The dragon's head reeled back, and Daedalus screamed again. No words, just one long scream of anger. The dragon spun a few times and then finally took to the air.

"Landyr," a pained whisper came from behind him. Thorna. Alive and on her side, she pointed. The Elite Troop wizard.

Hands aglow, the wizard waved them toward the pass opening. He had made everyone disappear and Landyr wanted to know where and why. He could think of no better way to ask than tackling him and driving him into the ground.

CWENCY~EIGHC

SWORDS AND CLAWS encircled the wizard. Ideria wondered what good any of that would do against an entity that wore fire as clothing and just made everyone disappear.

As with most magic, the act of vanishing was an illusion, a deception. The wizard turned everyone invisible, making Daedalus think they had all slipped from the confines of this realm. It was an impressive trick, but a trick nonetheless, and it did not diminish Ideria's thankfulness for it.

She and her brother fought against the skeletons to give the refugees a chance to enter Kallistah Pass, only to fight against the refugees as Daedalus' dragon turned them into more skeletons. A battle she thought they were going to win after Methel in skeleton form rebelled against his master.

But Daedalus was determined, and he still commanded a dragon. As Ideria and the others tried to sneak the refugees and themselves deeper into the pass, the dragon landed in front of them, cornering them against the mountain wall. Ideria hated the thought of dying by Daedalus' hand. She just found her mother. She knew nothing of the Yullians, where they came from or why they helped, but she was thankful for them attacking the dragon. But even they did not seem to be enough. The dragon's breath had no effect on them, but the beast had other ways of defending itself. Then everyone disappeared.

"It's obvious that you made us all invisible to my brother and his pet," Perciless said. "But you are a member of his Elite Troop, so I question your motives in assisting us."

The wizard did one full rotation, studying the faces of everyone in the circle around him. The flames of his robes and hair faded. Long white hair flowed over dull brown robes. Then his hair fell out, a few locks at first, then in waves to reveal short dark hair on a weathered and weary face. "I was with your brother's Elite Troop for one reason only—to infiltrate."

Landyr lowered his sword and stepped closer to the wizard. "You look familiar."

"We traveled together in an effort to discover the nefarious plan behind the disappearance of the twelve World Builders used to create Oremethus' dragons."

"Hemmer?"

The swords and claws lowered, the circle loosened as Landyr stepped to the wizard and embraced him.

Ideria knew the stories. Every child remembered the tale of how their parents met if they had been fortunate enough to hear it. The Horde razing towns, the Demon War, the madness of Oremethus were all just subplots to the bigger tale. Twenty years ago, her parents had met. Ten years ago, they were taken from her. Oremethus called upon an ancient wizard to fuse the powers of ancient items imbued with arcane magic into a dozen dragons. At that time, Uncles Draymon and Bartholomew had been tasked by Perciless to find Oremethus. They crossed paths with a group of wizards accompanied by the Elite Troop to find who had been stealing the artifacts. Landyr was the last member of that Elite Troop and Hemmer was one of the wizards. Silver, a lifelong friend of her father's, sacrificed his body and moved his mind and soul into the disgusting body of the ancient wizard who had helped Oremethus. Now Silver traveled with the void dragon—rumor stated that Landyr was in love with this creature—using his unique skill of creating doorways to help Tsinel with their war effort against Albathia.

After a brief exchange of pleasantries between Landyr and Hemmer, the ex-soldier stepped to the side and allowed Perciless to interject himself into the conversation. Bale, Dearborn, and Landyr joined in as well. Phyl kept fussing, convinced that the Yullians wanted to eat him, while Lapin kept him calm by yelling, "Shut up! You're being stupid!" Cezomir and Lina kept to themselves far away from the group. A trio of Yullians watched their every move and growled at them. The rest of the Yullians surrounded Methel, the skeleton content to stand in one spot.

Ideria thought about heading over to the cluster of people to voice her opinion. She might not have the same training or a number of battle years associated with her name, but she had experience. She had escaped Prince Daedalus twice now and killed one of his dragons. She deserved to be heard.

"Where's Woe?"

Rue's question distracted Ideria. A cursory glance was all that was needed to see that he was no longer with them. "We're certain that Daedalus' dragon did not get him, correct?"

"Very," Nevin said. "He was right here with us after Daedalus flew away."

Nevin was right. Ideria remembered him being with them as well. Hope looked skyward and fluttered her wings. "Maybe he's flying. He likes to do that when he gets upset."

"He's upset?" Ideria asked. "How can you tell?"

Rue shielded his eyes from the dual suns as he examined the cloud-streaked sky. "He's not one for adventure and ever since we found father, all he talked about was wanting to go home."

"*Talked* about?"

Rue gave a slight shoulder shrug. "Talked. Mumbled under his breath. Kind of the same thing with Woe."

"This is true." Ideria joined in looking skyward, but her attention slowly made its way back to the group talking with Hemmer. She made up her mind; she was going to join them. Before she could take her first step, a hole ripped open in the sky right above Hemmer's head.

* * *

A strip of fur ran full and thick from the top of Lina's head down to her tail, twitching and puffed. Cezomir had rarely seen her this upset. A low rumble emanated deep from within her chest, one warning of danger, as she paced in the snow. Across from them were three Yullian, two male and one female, doing the same thing. Bristled fur. Puffed tails. Deep, rumbling growls. Cezomir would have felt bad if he needed to kill them after they contributed to driving away Daedalus. He grabbed Lina's arm and said, "Come here."

Lina gave him a dry hiss at first but allowed him to lead her away. They walked toward the horses and carts. During the attack, everyone who had control of a horse had enough wherewithal to loop the reins around any available handle or knob on the carts. The horses fussed as the two predators walked among them. Cezomir released Lina to grab a satchel from one of the horses.

Whiskers twitching, Lina looked over her shoulder and mumbled, "They're discussing the fate of the wizard."

"You don't care about that and they'll make whatever decision they're going to make with or without us. Now, tell me why you're no longer a Yullian."

Lina snapped her attention back to Cezomir and snarled. "I am still a Yullian just as you are a wolf."

"But you are no longer welcome in your tribe."

"This is true, yes. I've been exiled."

"Why?"

Lina sighed and looked away. She opened her mouth, but Cezomir knew what her response would be and cut her off, "You've told me that you killed someone. I've killed and I've seen you kill. There are more details to that story, and I think today is the day you tell me the details."

Lina crossed her arms over her chest and made a noise that made all the nearest horses bray and trot in circles. "I murdered the queen."

"Murdered the queen? I know very little about the machinations of government, but it seems to me that exile is a weak punishment for killing a queen."

"She was my mother."

Cezomir laughed. "Your tale has become more compelling than most I hear from bards, filled with intrigue. Please continue and spare no detail."

"Very well. Our tradition dictated that no family shall have more than two children. If that does happen, then the youngest of the children are exiled on their twelfth birthday, unless one of the other children dies before that day. This was based on tradition when our tribe was a nomadic one, but hundreds of years ago we settled in the Yullia Mountains, so we no longer needed such antiquated ways. My older sister agreed with me, our mother did not, even though our youngest sister was small, frail, incapable of surviving more than a week away from the tribe. My sister and I made an agreement. I . . . upheld my end and she upheld hers. As soon as my sister became queen, she changed laws, allowing all families to remain whole. The tribe wanted me dead but found the changes in the laws from the new queen favorable, so they accepted her judgment of exiling me to be suitable."

Cezomir chuckled as he rooted through the satchel, sounds of metal clanking against metal until he found what he was looking for. A wide bracelet with two small holes on either side of a larger one. He tossed it to Lina.

Her nostrils flared and her eyes went wide. "This . . . this is a Yullian marriage bracelet. Where did you find this?"

"I made it. Remember the king's tax collector caravan we hit a year ago? The one with all the soldiers? I re-purposed a couple of strips of armor."

"But . . . but why?"

Cezomir's lips rippled along his teeth as he lifted his hand enough to show Lina the bracelet on his wrist, identical to hers. "Why do you think?"

"I . . . why now?"

"I needed to know if you still considered yourself a Yullian. I needed to know the one thing about you that I didn't."

"But—"

Cezomir placed his hands on her face, his thumbs gently grazing over her lips. "I know there is supposed to be a ceremony to go with this, but I can't imagine you giving a rat's dick about ceremonies. But promises? I can do promises. I promise to never hunt without you. I promise to honor your name every time I tear someone's heart from their chest. I promise to give that freshly plucked heart to you to feast upon. Until the day I die."

Lina studied the bracelet, turning it with her other hand, and then attacked his face with hers, shoving her tongue into his mouth. After she finished the kiss, she went back to admiring her bracelet. "You made this?"

"I did. And mine, too."

"I accept this marriage. But I forbid you from dying."

"Very well. For you, I shall not die."

Lina's smile faded as she looked back to the others still debating about the fate of the wizard. "What shall we do about Perciless? Do we separate ourselves from him now, or continue to make his journey our journey?"

When Cezomir decided to pledge his allegiance a decade ago, it was because he had been duped into helping Daedalus reunite with Oremethus, while also giving them the means to imbue twelve dragons with unimaginable power. No sense of guilt, but he wanted to explore the idea of honor that started to appeal to him. Plus the heavy dose of vengeance against those who tricked him. Dreams about killing Daedalus visited him some nights, the same dreams he once had about Bale.

Cezomir had blamed Bale for the years he spent in a dungeon. When he suddenly found himself joining Bale as a traveling partner, he realized that if it had not been for his time in the dungeon, he would not have met Lina. He since thanked Bale, which only led to a confusing and awkward conversation that he never wished to revisit. Now Lina presented him an opportunity to once again give up his quest for vengeance. He opened his mouth to give his answer, but the air above Perciless ripped open. "If we leave Perciless now, then I'm afraid we would never learn about the dragon that just appeared."

* * *

A fire ignited within Landyr as Chenessa flew through the portal. Silver followed behind her, his loose entrails flopping as he glided along the wind. Landyr had no care for the wizard and barely noticed that he was there. He watched only Chenessa. She was a demon who flew like an angel.

Gasps and murmurs came from those who had never seen her before. Much smaller than the other dragons, no bigger than one third the size of any of her other clutch-mates, she was still a dragon, one worthy of such open-mouth awe. If not for the tips of subtle red along her wings and claws, her scales were so black that she would have created a dragon-shaped hole in the sky.

"No need for worry, my friends," Perciless said, his tone joyful, excited. "They are our allies."

The Yullians still hissed and spat, gathering together as the dragon landed. She was close enough for Landyr to hear her breathing. Silver floated closer to Hemmer and Perciless. "I see you needed to reveal who you are."

"The Elite Troop is no more. All that remains is this." He pointed to the skeleton of Methel, standing patiently. "We have yet to determine what to do with him."

Perciless scowled. "The choice is obvious. He's now a minion of my brother's. We must destroy it."

Dearborn stepped forward and said, "But he saved my life and no longer seems to be under Daedalus' command."

An argument broke out, every voice expressing an opinion, not a single one could be heard above any of the others. Landyr used the distraction of the arguing to start toward Chenessa, hoping no one would notice, but stopped when Woe ended the argument. He dropped from the sky and landed on Methel with both feet, reducing the general's remains to splinters. Frowning, he said, "Bones are not meant to move outside the body." He spread his wings and took flight again.

* * *

Of all the siblings, Woe was the one Nevin was least familiar with. He certainly bore no ill will toward the winged ogre; however, moments when they would share conversation were few and far between. Had he the proclivity, the only conversation Nevin would have been able to muster was concerning Woe's affinity to fried rat tails, the different ways to prepare them and the accompanying spices to make the dish perfect. It was a topic to which Nevin could offer little contribution. Woe had neither the mind nor the fingers for larceny, never joining any of his brothers or sisters in concocting or participating in a scheme designed to lighten the gold pouches of those who had an abundance. Despite having minimal interaction with the young ogre, Nevin never knew him to use violence as a solution to any predicament. Judging from the slack jaws of Rue and Hope, they were just as surprised by Woe's outburst.

"By the gods," Rue whispered, neck craned back as his brother flew higher and higher.

"Has he done anything like that before?" Ideria asked, eyes to the heavens.

"No," Hope said. She too had watched him fly away, but then turned to Nevin and grabbed his hand. "I've never seen him so angry."

Hope wore minimal furs to keep her wings from becoming too encumbered, but her hand was warm. Nevin said, "He's probably never been in a situation like this. In fact, I doubt anyone here has been in a situation like this. The only reason why we're not reacting the same way is because of our closeness with each other."

Hope's grip tightened. "We're close?"

Nevin reached to her face with his other hand and wiped away her tears. "Yes. We're close."

Nevin's mind usually burned like a fire, ever-changing, always consuming, but now standing so close to Hope with his hand in hers, his mind cooled, slowed. He liked it.

"Hope!" boomed from behind Nevin. He jumped and spun, releasing Hope's hand.

Bale. "Hope. Go see if you can find your brother. Rue, help with consultating the supplies. We're leaving."

Hope's cheeks darkened, blushing as she gave Nevin one last glance before taking to the sky. Rue followed his father toward the carts and horses.

Nevin's mother accompanied Bale to the children but stayed after he and Rue left. It was as if the gods themselves carved the frown upon her face. Nevin wondered if what she saw upset her. "Mother?"

Dearborn's expression softened as she reached out for her children. Her hands on their cheeks, she said, "I'm afraid Bale is correct. We're leaving. And it seems Ideria will be getting her wish."

"What . . . what wish?" Ideria asked.

"The Yullians. They gave us information about who sent them and why. An old 'friend,' one I wish was dead, found something important he wishes to give to us. Thankfully Hemmer contacted Silver because we will have to travel to the other end of the continent. Silver is quite powerful and can open a door large enough for all of us to pass through. This has given Perciless the hope that we can finally attack Oremethus and bring an end to his reign. He's sending Hemmer through a portal to Tsinel to pass the information on to the wizards residing there. He's taking Thorna with him. She was badly injured and the wizards will be able to help her."

Ideria bowed her head in shame, desiring war when their mother wanted to live out the rest of her years in peace. She whispered, "But wouldn't ending the war be a good thing?"

"Yes, but not if we end up owing any favors to the man we're going to visit."

"Who?"

Dearborn opened her mouth but closed it to let a shiver pass through her body. Looking away did not hide that her deep frown had returned. After one last cleansing breath, preparing herself to utter this name, she finally spat it out as if it were soured wine.

"Praeker Trieste."

CWENCY~NINE

DAEDALUS DROPPED FROM the sky, the dragon's claws shattering a dozen of the cobblestones paving the market plaza outside of the castle's gate. The force of the landing should have hurt, but anger numbed his bones and joints. His face almost hit the saddle.

His appearance was so sudden that the crowd doing their shopping had no time to react. People froze mid-conversation or transaction, eyes wide from trying to comprehend what they were seeing. The panicked screaming started when the dragon sprayed its mist over the fruit stand patrons.

People slammed into each other, tripping and clawing to escape the instant madness. Daedalus held no regard for the fleeing masses. The living did not concern him, only the dead. Nine people were sprayed by the dragon's breath, and all nine tore their flesh from their bones, exposing the slave beneath. If there was one bit of comfort to be had since retreating from Kallistah Pass, it was that his dragon's breath still changed regular people to something better. Then why had Methel been able to resist Daedalus' commands? Why did the breath not affect those infernal cat people in the slightest? Speekore would know. The damnable goblin had better know or he would become a snack for one of the dragons.

Satisfied with his experiment's results, Daedalus commanded the skeletons to enter the castle through the opened gates. They would spend the next hour or so marching to his

chambers to await further orders, a sight probably discon-
certing to the staff and guards. Damn them as well, let the
ambulating bones serve as a constant reminder of what the
future held for them.

He guided his dragon over the walls and into the courtyard. Dismounting and dropping the reins, he spared no time
to wait for the handlers. There were many pressing issues to
attend to. As he strode into the building, he let everyone he
passed know to find and fetch every member of his advisory
council. He was calling an impromptu meeting.

Within the confines of the stone walls, Daedalus became
aware that his last bath was well more than a week ago. The
stench rolling off him was nauseating. He had no time for
such frivolities, but he could stand his own smell no longer.
He stripped as he walked to the council room, leaving his
filthy clothes to lie where he dropped them. If the servants
lacked the intelligence to pick them up, then he would simply send them all to Speekore and find new ones. There was
plenty of chattel within his kingdom.

Naked and angry, Daedalus turned the corner and almost ran into Oremethus. "Brother? I am surprised to see
you here."

"Why? You called a meeting. Wouldn't it be prudent for
the king to attend?"

Clearly, General Perrator was able to convince the king
he had been on a fool's errand and to return to the castle.
Did Oremethus come home because he understood the logic
of being too close to the war front? Or did he return home
because there were no demons to find? If standing naked
before him garnered no questions, then Daedalus would
simply forget that his brother had ever left the castle. "You
are absolutely correct."

"You look hungry."

"Nonsense. I have too much to discuss to pause for food."

"No one said anything about pausing." Oremethus
snapped his fingers to a guard walking patrol. "You! Come
here."

The man did as commanded, jogging to cover the distance between them. "Yes, Sire?"

"The prince is famished. I believe I heard talk that the kitchen just finished a roast pig. Have them bring it to the meeting chambers in ten minutes. Remind them that the prince has created more . . . assistants. If the kitchen staff needs help fulfilling my request, we can always send Daedalus' new assistants to hasten their pace."

Eyes widening with every word, the guard audibly gulped once the king finished his request. Oremethus' tone was conversational, but there was an underlying insidiousness that gave Daedalus pause. The guard saluted, offered a, "Yes, Sire," and ran down the hallway.

Upon mention of the word "pig," noises emanated from Daedalus' gurgling stomach. "Well, it appears that you and my belly are in agreeance."

Oremethus put his arm around his brother's shoulders and kept it there for the rest of the trip to the meeting chamber. "My dear Daedalus, it's my responsibility and honor as your older brother to make sure that all your needs are met, even if you are unaware of them."

Daedalus found it interesting that his brother knew he was lacking food but seemed to have no idea that he was lacking clothes. He pushed the thought from his mind as he followed his brother into the meeting chambers.

The table was originally created to comfortably accommodate banquet guests. During the entirety of Oremethus' reign, exactly zero banquets were held. The room was designed to allow musicians to play, nobility to dance, jesters to entertain, and all to feast. Now, it was a meeting room. Instead of delicate members of society flitting to and fro, the room was populated by grizzled men. General Perrator. Speekore. The Seneschal. Two dozen sergeants, little more than messengers to the generals on the front lines. Everyone was milling about when Daedalus and Oremethus entered the room. Half started toward the table, taking the closest seats available. One sergeant, with an eye-patch, whom Daedalus had never seen before, looked down at the prince's crotch. "Didya' forget somethin' this morning, Sire?"

The closest man to the sergeant grabbed his arm. "Are you daft? Apologize immediately."

Yanking his arm from the other's grasp, the sergeant offered a wide smile to Daedalus. "Apologize? Surely our fine prince knows my words were meant as a jest, not a slight."

Keeping his fingers tightly together, Daedalus rammed his skeletal hand through the sergeant's face, the tips poking out from the back of his head. Daedalus withdrew his hand, the sergeant's brain slopping onto the floor. *A much better place for it*, Daedalus thought as he took his seat. Gasps came from the two servants carrying a small cooked pig on a tray. They hurried from the doorway, dropped it off on the table before Daedalus, and scurried from the room with their heads down in an effort to hide their faces.

Eyelids heavy as if boredom weighed upon them, Oremethus took his seat at the head of the table, paying no mind to the dead body on the floor nor his brother using his bloodied fingers to dig a hunk of meat from the pig's rump.

Sloppy bits of ham sprayed from Daedalus' mouth as he said, "Well, dear brother, it seems as though the kitchen servants are the only ones in this room who have succeeded with their duties."

Those who had yet to take a seat did so with haste; the men who were already sitting straightened their posture, casting furtive glances to their fallen peer.

"Our kingdom is in a terrible state of disarray and there is really no one else to blame except for all of you," Oremethus started.

Daedalus was surprised by his brother's opening statement. Usually, he sat back and let Daedalus handle these situations and never stated any form of disappointment. Was this how he wanted to help? Oremethus studied the pig, within his reach, and grabbed a loose piece of meat dangling from the hole that Daedalus had created. "The war effort has been atrocious. My grandfather won wars in a matter of minutes and my father never once went to war with Tsinel, because of their perception of our army. Now we must continue our struggle with them because they refuse to see that I am the one who should truly rule them. Yet we still have not won. It has been years and our borders with them have not changed one iota."

General Perrator cleared his throat. "The town of Green-gate was lost after your demon hunt."

Oremethus picked another small chunk of meat from behind the front shoulder of the pig. "We'll host a festival for them."

"I apologize for the lack of clarity in my statement. I meant that after you burned half of the town down in your quest for demons, Tsinel's troops advanced into it and now occupy it."

Meat pinched between his fingers, mere inches from his mouth, Oremethus paused and scowled at the general. "Then let Tsinel host the festival. Obviously, Greengate is no longer our concern, so why are we still going on about it like a group of clucking hens?"

"Were we to use your dragons and any of your wizards, we may find an advantage."

Now Oremethus showed emotion, one of contempt. "Were you to prove you could use them properly, I would allow you to use them. Time and time again the battlefield generals have shown that they shouldn't be there, and we must relieve them of their duties. In fact, their incompetence has been spreading."

Daedalus stopped chewing, curious, and a little concerned, as to what his brother might say next. He certainly agreed with Perrator about using the dragons and wizards for battlefield purposes, but he was surprised by the general's bluntness. The sergeants were uneasy as well, shifting around in their seats. Oremethus continued, "The recruits residing at the castle allowed a dungeon escape. A woman and a buffoon of an ogre. Incompetence. Then we sent the Elite Troop after my brother. They found him. After ten years and a ton of gold in effort and nothing until recently. They found him and then failed to capture him. Incompetence. A washed-up bureaucratic fop teams up with a woman and an ogre to defeat the greatest warriors in the land and the most advanced creations science has to offer. Incompetence."

Daedalus almost smiled at the way Oremethus snapped his gaze to Speekore for the last word of his speech. The hobgoblin's head was more metal and glass than flesh, but there was fear upon his face. Daedalus tore the hock from the pig and took a full bite, oily juices streamed over his chin. "Now, brother, he may prove useful as long as he has knowledge."

"What would you like to know, m'lord?" the hobgoblin asked, his voice more subdued and less shrill.

"My dragon's breath seemed to have failed during my battle with my brother and his band of miscreants. I had them cornered and a group of Yullians came to their rescue. My dragon engulfed them with its mist and there was no effect. Then, everyone disappeared, vanishing as if they were never there."

"Yullians you say? Well, they are a mystical race, one more created from magic than breeding. Strong magic, indeed."

"They are magical you say? Very well. Then explain why Elite Troop General Methel was immune to my orders? The mist turned him into a skeleton, but he was not under my command."

"Oh, that's because his hatred for you ran deep, too deep for you to assume control of him."

Daedalus scowled at those words but continued to eat. "Be that as it may, we need to pull troops from the war effort to chase them through Kallistah Pass."

General Perrator cleared his throat again. "I do not think that would be such a wise idea."

Daedalus' rage was a beast that needed constant feedings. Now was a rare time when actual food sated it for a moment, keeping it quiet long enough for a few rational thoughts to appeal to his mind. The general had given good advice in the past and even if Daedalus ordered every man in this room to attack the general, he doubted that general would be defeated. "How so?"

"Because it's no longer likely they will be going through the pass."

Daedalus slammed the hock against the table, meat exploding from the cracking bone. "Damnation! You told me they were going to Kallistah Pass to flee Albathia and that is exactly where I found them and what they were doing. Now you're telling me they're not?"

"I believed that you would find either the escaped prisoners or your brother. I did not expect that they would have found each other. Were there citizens attempting to flee via the pass?"

"Yes. A few dozen, but I turned most of them into skeletons."

"And there were Yullians?"

"Yes. Also, a couple dozen of them as well."

"This will change the plans of your brother and Dearborn, therefore we need to change our plans. Our sources and spies have been telling us that over the years Perciless has been going from town to town building and fortifying a secret army."

"That is not news to anyone at this table."

"What is news is that no one at this table thought now would be the time for them to strike."

"Why do you think it would the perfect time?"

"They just bested you."

Pulped meat oozed from between bone fingers as Daedalus squeezed his skeletal hand in a fist. "I told you they just blinked out of existence."

"Magic. That means they have at least one wizard. And that won't be the story your brother tells his secret army as he assembles it. He will tell them it's time to gather. He'll tell them that he and a small band of brave souls bested Prince Daedalus and his bone dragon. He'll tell that story, again and again, all the while parading around Ideria Stillheart, the girl who single-handedly killed the king's metal dragon. Yullians have joined him. Greengate is lost to Tsinel. Crime is on the rise. What more push do the people need to secure a weapon and gather to storm the castle?"

Daedalus wanted to crush the half-giant's skull, but it would little good. The general spoke the truth, no matter how much Daedalus wanted to deny it. "What do you propose?"

"We wait. We have been chasing your brother for years and those efforts yielded nothing more than giving the citizens confidence as Perciless continued to evade your capture. We sought the dungeon escapees and lost our entire Elite Troop. We've been fighting a war that the soldiers don't want to win. We wait. We stop giving our enemies the fuel that burns in the furnace of their war machine. Every household in the city will host one soldier until the attack. If a household refuses, then living skeletons equal to the number of those who live there shall inhabit the dwelling until the day of the attack. This will save us gold to use for different resources and stymie the flow of secret information. We wait for our enemies to come to us."

Perrator was right. Every effort that Oremethus and Daedalus made this past decade had been thwarted. But Daedalus could not form the words. Instead, he stood and stormed from the room.

He aimed for his chambers, the one place he could clear his mind. He should have a few moving skeletons shambling around in there, mindlessly awaiting his commands. There was no greater Hell than being without one's mind, and there was no greater power than putting someone in Hell. There was no one better at putting individuals in Hell than Daedalus and he enjoyed it. Only one person ever escaped from one of his Hells—Dearborn. And she took her pet ogre with her.

As he walked along, his thoughts became muddled and jumbled, flowing through his mind thick like cold molasses. His vision blurred, starting at edges. An attack was coming on. Daedalus slumped against the wall and slid to the floor before . . .

. . . being transported back to his chambers. The stones were cleaner, and the decorations were not befitting an adult. He was younger, a child now. Luck graced him with an opportunity, a turn of his head and a mirror passed by his field of vision. Nine years old, he guessed. He was sitting on the bed and there were toys in front of him. Toys? He never owned any toys and rarely played with the ones that belonged to either of his brothers. His father, King Theomann, used toys and other gifts as markers to keep track of subordination. Follow his orders and get a reward. Perciless had the most toys, of course, never once disobeying Father. Oremethus had plenty, but not as many as Perciless, a sycophant even at such an early age. No, Daedalus owned no toys, and this was certainly his room, but there he was with toys on his bed.

Painted knights made of wood, gray armor on stiff legs, swords secured in unmoving arms. A music box that played an ominous tone and hid a dragon under its lid. Bejeweled tops that created rainbows when spun. Mechanized carts that rolled under their own power whenever there was enough twisted tension upon the strings hidden within the carriage. And more.

Daedalus remembered these toys and coveted them. He did not remember this moment, though, and jumped up with a start when his father burst into his room, Perciless in tow. Red-faced with anger, Theomann scolded Daedalus for stealing his brother's toys. He tried to think of a lie, but his mind remained empty. His mouth simply hung open, while the king repeated his demand for an answer.

"It was my idea," Oremethus, age eleven, said as he strolled past his father and climbed onto the bed next to his youngest brother. "I was the one who took the toys from Perciless' room."

"'Twas not!" Perciless yelled. Even though anger weighed upon his words, his voice sounded no different than any average girls at the same age. Had Daedalus spoken, he would have sounded no different, just another whelp waiting his turn for adolescence. Oremethus' voice had started to deepen, hinting that manhood would be soon.

"Oh, it was, brother. You have all of the toys and Daedalus none. I figured it to be time to atone for such inequities."

The king wore a twisted expression of surprise and disgust, looking at his son as if he had dropped his trousers and defecated in the middle of the room. "If you clamor for a reduction of inequality, then I shall grant it—your possessions shall equal that of Daedalus."

As calmly as if he had expected that exact sentence, Oremethus said, "Very well. A good solution indeed. I shall help Daedalus return these toys to Perciless' room and then I will gather my toys and donate them to the orphanage."

King Theomann's face hid no emotions. He was taken aback by the Oremethus' words and confused as to why he said them. He turned on his heel and muttered, "Come, Perciless, let us get you to horse riding lessons."

After they left, Oremethus pulled at the bottom of his shirt and used it to help him collect the toys. Daedalus slid from the bed and mimicked his brother's actions. "Why? I took the toys. Why are you willing to sacrifice your toys by telling father that you were the one who took them? Why pay for my crime?"

Even as a child, Oremethus had the presence of royalty. Tall and lean, never once gangly or awkward, his voice resonated with confidence. "Because you are my youngest brother. You have the least, so I strive to make sure you have the most. Just because what's important to you isn't important to Father doesn't mean I should ignore it. I will support you when no one else will."

Daedalus added another toy to the pile forming in his arms and . . .

. . . awoke on the floor in his brother's arms. Oremethus ran his hand over Daedalus' sweat-soaked hair and whispered, "I will support you when no one else will."

"You speak the truth, don't you?"

"I do."

"Why have I gone my whole life without that memory?"

"You didn't need it until now."

They both got to their feet, Oremethus taking time to brush the dust from his youngest brother. Daedalus found it difficult to believe that once upon a time he hated the man before him. Oremethus had spent ten years living in caves, the damage to his skin still evident in the formation of early wrinkles, tiny spots of discoloration, and looseness when he turned certain ways. He was still tall and had a regal bearing, but no one would sense he was the king unless bequeathed with that information beforehand. "These attacks always seem to come when we least expect them, don't they?"

Never once had Daedalus suspected that his oldest brother suffered from the same affliction. Because of the attacks within the past few months, Daedalus began recalling memories that proved he and Oremethus used to be closer in spirit than he knew. Now this information? "You suffer from the same attacks that I do? Ones that take you into the past not just to remember a moment, but to relive it?"

Oremethus smiled, and the bottom dropped out from Daedalus' belly. This was not a smile of happiness, mirth, or glee, but one of madness. Yet his eyes held such a lucidity that Daedalus felt unbridled zeal with every word. Oremethus placed his hands on Daedalus' cheeks and moved close enough that they breathed the same air. "Yes, brother, I do. Sometimes they leave me feeling as if I'm without my mind. In fact, it's tomorrow and next week and next year and I'm having an attack at this very moment to bring me back to *this* very moment. This is nothing but a memory, one I've lived already and will live again. A moment that binds us as brothers, a moment that reminds us that we are of the same blood and bodies, a moment where we must remember that we're willing to do anything for each other, no matter how distasteful. Now, if you'll excuse me."

Gone.

Oremethus vanished from the hallway so quickly, Daedalus wondered if he were but a specter. He replayed moments within his mind, recalling other interactions with Oremethus. He wondered if Oremethus would see those same moments, or were they gone from his mind as his brother implied they might be. Daedalus now understood his brother's ramblings. They were more than just an incoherent jumble of syllables. They were a cry for help, a plea for his brother to set him free.

Yes, Daedalus thought, *Yes, dear brother, after I kill Perciless, I shall set you free.*

After all, there was no greater Hell than being without one's mind, and no greater mercy than releasing someone from Hell.

ThIRTY

DEARBORN WAS HOT. Thanks to Silver's ability to create portals to anywhere imaginable, one moment she was standing at the snow-covered mouth of the Kallistah Pass, now she was in the deep jungles of the Dark Corner, the least detailed part of any map of the continent. Albathia laid claim to it because it was nowhere near Tsinel, but no king ever made an effort to explore the land, let alone attempt to tame it.

Wild. Sweltering. Dangerous. All descriptions Dearborn had heard used to describe the area. She agreed with them all and more. Both suns were sharing the sky and would continue to do so for a few more hours, but the canopy of wide leaves blocked their existence, the rays struggling to get through. It was so humid, that condensation formed on the lowest layer of leaves and immediately fell as if the trees themselves were perspiring. Every drop of water that dripped on her did nothing to cool her skin. Adding to her misery was the fire raging inside of her.

Of all the people who could have saved them, who they might have solicited help from, she would have been satisfied with anyone, just not the one man they were here to see.

Praeker Trieste.

The mad man had trod the world for centuries and sought the accursed stones. Gems, that when combined with dragon's blood, gave the user the ability to control the demons of hell. Praeker desired that power. He assembled the Horde, a collection of humans and non-humans alike all cast out from society. There was no discrimination in membership, the only requisite for following Praeker was the desire to destroy Albathia and everything in it.

Praeker sought the stones through brute force. The only strategy he employed was razing a town, questioning the survivors, and then moving on to the next target. It was this destruction that spurred others on to seek the stones. Dearborn's Elite Troop was one of those parties seeking them out, as was the trio of thieves that included her future husband, Diminutia.

In Dearborn's mind, Praeker was the impetus of the Demon War two decades ago. She knew very well that if not for the failed quests she never would have met Diminutia, nor have had the notion of happiness personified in the form of her two children. Ten years ago Praeker found a city of scorpion creatures that worshiped him as a god-king, yet he opted to back down as Daedalus and Oremethus assembled their power in the form of twelve enchanted dragons. Thanks to the encouragement of Draymon, Praeker changed his mind and his army disrupted the insurrection long enough to allow Perciless escape. But during the period of his inaction, Diminutia died. When Praeker stepped away from the struggle, she lost her freedom, and her children lost their parents. This monster stole those same things from thousands of other people and their families. Praeker needed to die. But now they were here to beg for his help.

They waited outside a stone archway completely ensconced in leafy vines. Praeker had built his new home, new country, in the remains of an ancient city, lost to time and forgotten by historians and scholars. Dearborn found this offensive and yet typical of Praeker. Why not share a find such as this? A city no other king of Albathia or Tsinel knew about and Praeker kept it a secret. He did what he had always done—conquer.

"Mother? What are your thoughts?"

Ideria and Nevin had been whispering next to her, not to hide their words, rather due to the oppressive feeling the jungle exuded. It made one feel the need to whisper. Even

Dearborn succumbed to the environment as well and whispered back, "My thoughts are too grim to share, I'm afraid. Endless loops of me killing Praeker."

"I'm . . . I'm sorry."

Ideria dropped her gaze, her inference mistaken. Dearborn faced her children and put a hand on each of their shoulders. "No. It is I who need to apologize. More than once I let my blind hatred for him jeopardize what matters most to me in my life. I have the most important things in my life in my hands right now and I must never let *anything* come between me and you."

The leaves rustled around the archway and Dearborn wondered if she had to prove her words already. Phyl hid behind Bale and Lapin stood ready alongside the rest of the children. Draymon and Landyr had their weapons ready but kept looking around for any other potential threat. Emerging were half a dozen of Praeker's followers, scorpion hybrids, led by his general, Lyrus—a creature with a muscled torso of a human male sprouting from the shelled body of a scorpion. Instead of a human face atop its neck, a unicorn's head sprouted between the shoulders, pale green skin and opalescent horn. All of the creatures were armed but did not wield their weapons aggressively. "King Praeker welcomes you all," Lyrus said. Dearborn found the way his horse lips rippled as he spoke unnerving. Though he was some form of centaur, Dearborn could tell by his posture that he was little more than a sycophant, proud to be serving his monster. She did not like this creature at all. "He has granted you an audience. Please, follow me," Lyrus said waving them onward.

Through the archway was the skeleton of the city. Long deceased and reclaimed by the greens and browns of the jungle, its bones showed through in the form of columns and more archways, some tilted or broken, many still standing as straight as the day they were created. But all of them covered in moss and vines and bushes. Tall trees grew through a few of the buildings, the crumbled walls bowing before them as if they were new gods.

The road they walked upon was covered by leafy brush and a layer of dirt, but every few steps Dearborn could feel the stones that once paved the road poking through like discontented ghosts.

Lyrus led them to a grand building, just as consumed by nature as every other shell of a structure. For the entire journey, the denizens of the lost city watched from the shadows. Ten years ago Praeker declared his mission to unite the hidden societies of myth, ones consisting of unique creatures that followed no government other than what the tradition of their tribes dictated. It appeared as though he had succeeded in that mission.

All kinds of scorpion hybrid creatures skittered about, ranging in size from a human's finger to a horse's body. These were not the only hybrid creatures to scamper from one shadow to the next to get a better view of the city's guests. All kinds of other animal heads grew from snake bodies. Torsos and other parts sprouted from spider bodies. Things with feathered wings and bird beaks rustled amongst the leaves.

Small pockets of other creatures huddled together, uncertain. A group of rodent faced beasts that walked on two legs, standing taller than any man, congregated among the dilapidated pillars of a building, their tails twitching from concern. Another edifice offered cover for bat-like creatures. The Yullians that accompanied Dearborn and her companions broke away from the group and joined other feline creatures.

The building had many wide steps. Made from stone cracked by roots, a few pieces moved underfoot, but no one fell. After walking past two rows of columns, they entered what was left of a grand hall. Trees had destroyed the whole wall to the right, while more grew freely in the middle space, no roof encumbering any of them. At the far end was a dais that held a seated figure. No back wall was visible, just crumbled stone fading into darkness.

Just as everything else in the city, the throne was veiled with green growth, the occasional twig or branch poking free. The man on the throne was covered in viridian as well, but not by any kind of plant. Hundreds of emerald-hued scorpions formed a suit of armor. He held a scepter topped with a glowing red stone the size of a fist. Praeker Trieste arose from his throne and extended his arms. "Welcome, King Perciless. From one monarch to another, I, King Praeker, welcome you to New Vierennia."

Had Dearborn a spear in her hands, she would have thrown it through his chest. Alas, she had no access to such a weapon, just the short sword at her side. Though thoughts of throwing it tickled her mind, she remembered that Praeker had promised an army to Perciless. For now, she would see if this monster followed through with his deal or not.

Praeker returned to his seat as Perciless approached, climbing the steps of the dais. "Greetings to you as well and a lifetime of thanks for sending your Yullian friends to our rescue. My heart warms at the sight of your success. Judging from what I saw after being invited into your city, you have found many different societies ready to partake in the benefits of liberating Albathia."

Praeker chuckled. "Your platitudes are brief and heartfelt; your words are true yet concise. I admire that. You compliment me while referencing our deal. Well, I have altered our deal."

"Mother," Ideria whispered into Dearborn's ear to capture her attention. Dearborn followed her daughter's hands running down her arm to her hand. Her palm was moist. She unclenched her fist and a sense of relief tingled throughout her arm. She had been squeezing her fists so tightly that she drew blood.

"It breaks my heart to hear that," Perciless said. "How has it been altered?"

Praeker leaned back and smiled, indicating the conversation was proceeding as he planned. He held up the scepter. "The stone in this staff is The Dragon's Soul."

"The Dragon's Soul? I thought that was mere myth?"

Something moved in the darkness behind Praeker. Everyone in the room gasped as the snout of a green scaled dragon emerged. The air in front of the dragon's nostrils rippled as it delivered a low growl, rumbling through the passages of the great hall. Praeker leaned forward and tossed the scepter to Perciless. "Whoever possesses this stone can control the actions of any dragon. This one stone can take control of your brothers' most powerful weapons. I bequeath it to you."

Perciless came across as a person who could never lose the delicate game of discourse, yet staring at the staff in his hands, he stammered, "This . . . this is amazing . . . a . . . gift of immeasurable value. My many, many thanks."

"You and your people may stay in New Vierennia as my personal guests as long as you wish. What travel supplies you require, I will provide, but judging from how you arrived, I assume your journey will a brief one."

Perciless did not take his eyes off the scepter in his hands, almost caressing it. "You truly will not lend an army to aid us in dethroning the king?"

"I have to think of my people. In war, it is the king's people who die, very rarely the king."

"Unfortunately true, but this is not a war I began. It is one fought for the freedom of all. The kings involved are oppressor and liberator, not the typical kings of ego and ignorance. I assure you, this war will end with the death of a king."

"You talk of human kings, human freedoms and egos. My subjects and I have no interest in human politics."

"Tyranny is not a political notion that is bandied about in a council room. Both Albathia and Tsinel have non-human citizens who enjoy the same freedoms when a benevolent king is upon the throne and share the same sufferings under the rule of my brothers. As long as Oremethus sits upon the throne and Daedalus has access to his ear, you and your people are not safe."

Praeker slouched back in his throne and extended his arms as an invitation for all to observe their surroundings. "We reside in a city so ancient that history itself has forgotten it. No matter who rules Albathia, they take no interest in this land."

"That's because my family took no interest in conquest until now. My brothers have designs for the entire world, not just the continent divided by Albathia and Tsinel. They will find you. They will come for you."

"It will be years before the likes of any king sends an army here. If they do, then we will fight, and win, by using our strengths and not merely charge forth and hope that attrition ends in our favor. My subjects are insects and birds, scorpions, bats, rats, snakes, and cats. Should they need to turn soldier, they can infiltrate everywhere before the enemy knows they've lost. So, no, good Perciless, I shall not offer the deaths of those whom I rule for an outcome that will not affect us."

Perciless bowed gracefully, extending the scepter with both hands. "You have spoken Your Highness, and I have heard. I respect your decision and thank you again for this gift."

Praeker placed his palms together and nodded his head. Perciless turned and descended the stairs of the dais. Those who had been following him continued to do so as he aimed for the exit. Except for Dearborn. Statue stiff, she glared at Praeker.

"Mother?" Ideria called for her.

Dearborn heard her daughter and debated following Perciless out of the great hall, leaving Praeker behind. But her feet would not move. She could not leave, pass up this opportunity. This monster orchestrated nightmares. Even if she could live a life without him in it, she would not be content, always wondering when he would return. How many other lives he might be destroying. Every death that came from his hand would be no different than as if she made the kill herself. Her children might have to watch her die, but they would eventually understand.

"Mother?" Ideria asked again.

Dearborn ignored her daughter's words, lest she soften her resolve and convince her to pass up this opportunity. She walked up the stairs of the dais. "You will not aid us?"

"No."

"Fine. Then I'm going to kill you."

Praeker laughed. "I don't doubt that you want to."

Dearborn was tired of her present melting into her past because of this tyrant. He had devoured it, consumed her hope because of his actions. He sat on a throne made from futures stolen from innocents. Dearborn strode up to the throne and spat at the feet of the man occupying it. "I've beaten you before but kept you alive at the behest of others. There is no one to stop me from killing you now."

Praeker stood and Dearborn had to crane her neck back lest her part of the conversation be aimed at his sternum. His scorpion armor shifted, the hard shells of the many living pieces pulling tightly together. His face remained free from encumbrances as he looked down upon her and said, "You had the help of two other warriors and a machination that spewed fire."

The tone of her voice calm and even, Dearborn spoke only truth. "If you've failed to realize this, then I will let you take a moment to notice that those same two warriors are with us now, among others who would be more than happy to join me in killing you. It is true that I do not have any machine to spew fire, but my hatred for you runs so deeply I have no doubt that should I need to, I could call upon that vitriol within me to spew flames from my own mouth. But I do not require the assistance of other warriors or war machines. If you do not join us, then you will die. I will kill you."

Praeker puffed out his chest and a wave of scorpions flowed over his head, forming a helmet. "I believe you may want to rethink your words. This is your last warning."

Dearborn found nothing about his action intimidating. "Then those will be your last words. I will kill you. There is no truer fact in this world other than the suns will set and rise again. Except, when they rise tomorrow, you will not be here to witness them."

Praeker's helmet split in half and then the pieces skittered away. His scowl faded, his expression shifted into confusion. Dearborn assumed that over the centuries Praeker faced down foe after foe, each undoubtedly attempting to intimidate him through red-faced anger. Every one of them attempting to show him the possibility of a future if things went their way. Dearborn displayed no anger, no rage burning her face red, no spittle spraying from her mouth. Her eyes held the truth, one that Praeker saw with perfect clarity.

After a moment, he whispered, "I believe you. I am looking upon death, inescapable, unavoidable."

"You can simply prolong your execution for the length of time it takes to get the rightful king Perciless back into his throne."

"Death has never been a concern of mine, but now that I've seen its face, I prefer to stave it off."

Praeker's words had been for Dearborn only. He walked past her and down the steps to address his to his guests and his followers. "I have changed my mind. King Perciless surrounds himself with those who display great levels of bravery, dedication, and loyalty. He promises a bright future for all. Judging those who follow him, I believe him. We will lend our numbers and desire to build a better world for our true king of Albathia."

Everyone cheered.

CHIRTY~ONE

DAEDALUS WATCHED THE raging battle from the turret, men scurrying about like insects on a once green field, now brown from mud and blood. Armored soldiers in matching colors carrying swords and shields clashed with waves of men in plain clothes carrying pitchforks and clubs. Just as the two forces met, the air behind the organized soldiers rippled and a flood of more men in plain clothing rushed through the newly formed portal. With the element of surprise, pitchforks and clubs were deadlier than swords and shields.

Every rib in his chest rattled to the beat of his angry heart and Daedalus slammed his skeletal fist against the top of the turret's stone wall reducing a span to rubble. "Damnation!"

The wizard showing the watery images of a battle happening miles away jerked at the outburst, just as he did every time Daedalus watched his soldiers fail. Oremethus considered the same view while leaning against the castle wall, arms crossed over his chest.

Daedalus ran his other hand through his hair as he paced around the ballista. The open-air turret was the tallest point in Phenomere and often a place of solace for him, the best vantage point to see the city and the streets below. The greatest view of his minions below.

The streets were no more or less busy than any other day, people moving about their lives, blissfully unaware of the war on the other side of the forest. The war should be here. The buildings should be burning, and the streets should be flooded with blood. Each house had two or more soldiers awaiting the king's command to attack the invading forces. Instead, the soldiers sat idly at tables, eating the owner's food, while leering at his wife or daughter. Daedalus cursed Perciless for not behaving the way his council thought he would.

Yes, Perciless gathered his secret army, but the rebels were far greater numbers than Daedalus or any other advisor imagined. Nor did these insurgents make their way to Phenomere, instead marching for Greengate to join forces with the Tsinel invasion. They marched west toward Phenomere, "liberating" every town along the way. General Perrator had left the city to take a more hands-on approach and sent the fastest riders to advise the troops to pull back to lure Perciless and his armies into the trap within Phenomere. Yet again, Perciless did not follow their plan. He stopped short of invading the city and moved northward to "free" more towns. The bastard was going to conquer the entire country one town at a time!

The advisors on the council did not believe this was Perciless' plan. Too many logistical issues, they had said. They encouraged Oremethus to wait, and wait he did, no matter how loudly Daedalus voiced his opinion otherwise.

With too much frustration pent up within his chest, Daedalus released it the only way he knew how—by smashing his fist into more stone. As the last rattle of gravel came to a stop on the floor, he blurted, "What more needs to happen before we act?"

Oremethus sighed. "I understand your frustration, brother, but I believe in this plan."

Oremethus appeared focused and lucid. Daedalus hated that. Whenever his brother went on about demons, Daedalus could manipulate that conversation, sway the king to his wishes. But when his jaw was set, his gaze firm, Oremethus looked every bit the monarch he portrayed. That did not keep Daedalus from expressing his opinion, though. "We have dragons and wizards that are at our disposal in this very castle. They have one dragon unchecked and two dozen wizards. We have seven dragons and twice as many wizards who are doing nothing."

"They are lying in wait. Once Perciless's armies descend upon Phenomere, it will be the last thing they do. We wait and end the war with one final battle."

"We can end the war *now* with one final battle."

"We don't know that. Right now, it is their entire force against a fraction of ours fighting their way into our trap. If we send everything we have, then we lose the advantage."

"It's only taken them weeks to lay claim to the towns around Phenomere."

"Exactly. They will be marching into the city very soon."

"Our advantage lies in the number of our dragons and wizards we have, not in swords and shields."

"They have been surprising us at every turn, so we have to assume that they have a gambit waiting for our dragons and wizards on that battlefield."

"On the battlefield, or right in front of you, dear brother!" Both Oremethus and Daedalus turned to the voice of Perciless yet found themselves looking into the face of a dragon.

The beast needed only one flap of his wings to remain hovering in front of the turret. As large as any of the seven still in their cages under the castle, its scales were green, fading to yellow along its underside. Upon its back were Perciless and Dearborn, both smirking as Daedalus stood gaping at the two people he hated the most. The dragon flapped once more and opened its mouth.

Too surprised to move, Daedalus remained frozen. Oremethus leaped into motion thrusting them both through the open door, just as the beast released a torrent of flame, setting the ballista ablaze and reducing the wizard to ash.

The brothers tumbled down the stairs, each scrape against the wall, each slap against the stone feeding the conflagration of anger blazing within Daedalus' heart. At the bottom, they disentangled from each other and Oremethus said, "You ready the dragons, I will gather the wizards."

Daedalus sprinted to the dragon pens, the beasts on their feet when he arrived, their tails twitching. The handlers fussed about nervously and one addressed Daedalus, "Your Highness! The dragons suddenly seemed discontent. They had all been resting and then for no reason became restless."

"I know," Daedalus replied walking to the cage that held the bone dragon. When Oremethus received his ability to control the dragons with mere thought at their birth, an unintended benefit was Daedalus now possessed the same ability. He awakened the dragons on his way to them. "Open all of the cages."

"Sire? It's unwise to release them all at once. Wouldn't you prefer we open the cages one at a—?"

"Open them now!"

The handlers moved with alacrity, their lives depending on the speed with which they carried out their orders. They had barely finished the final buckles of his riding leathers when he spewed a few final curses at them and mounted the bone dragon. All seven dragons funneled up the ramp and took to the air as soon as they saw sunlight. Daedalus was greeted with madness on the streets.

Not a spot of cobblestone could be seen under the mass of people. Citizens fought with soldiers. How could the army of Perciless or Tsinel have made it into Phenomere so quickly? But it was neither of those armies, rather the citizens of Phenomere rising to aid Perciless.

A dozen rippling images of Perciless taller than a three-story building hovered over the rooftops like benevolent specters, announcing to the citizens his intentions, letting them know that his armies were fighting for them, *he* was fighting for them. This was the only encouragement the people needed to rebel.

Entire families dragged the soldiers from their homes and killed them in the streets with farming tools and kitchen utensils. On other streets, the soldiers gained the upper hand and running through any citizen in their path, whether they participated in the insurrection or not. Daedalus had no time to bother with this or what wizardry was projecting the multiple images of his brother. He had one single desire—catch Perciless and Dearborn.

Filling the sky were the wizards of Albathia, almost fifty in number. They propelled themselves through the air, some using arcane magic to fly, others mystical tools. A small herd of horses, both winged and not, galloped through the air, each carrying at least one rider. One wizard rode a snake made from bright white light, while another sat upon a griffon engulfed in orange and red flame.

Daedalus considered having his brother command them to end the riots in the streets, but thought better against it. He needed the wizards for the larger battle beyond the forest. Once he crushed the armies of Perciless and Tsinel, then the rebellions would end. His immediate need was the death of the dragon carrying Perciless and Dearborn. A wizard levitated Oremethus high into the sky, allowing the gem dragon to take its rightful place as the King's steed.

Perciless' green dragon was slower than the Phenomere dragons. Daedalus gained on it from the right side, while Oremethus closed in from the left. Both of their dragons opened their mouths to release their horrible breaths, but the green dragon dove toward the ground.

It banked and shot back upward, stream of fire leading the way. Daedalus had started to follow, but adjusted just in time, able to feel the heat passing by. Oremethus altered his attack as well and escaped unharmed.

Daedalus recovered quickly and wasted no time continuing his pursuit. Oremethus continued as well, but stationed his beast below the other dragons in case the green one decided to try the same maneuver. Daedalus called upon the other five dragons, having them close in on their target from different directions. It was working, the dragons cutting off escape routes, corralling the green one. Now was the moment for Daedalus's dragon to unleash its deadly breath— had the green dragon remained in front of him.

A portal opened in front of the green dragon and closed immediately, the bone dragon's breath dissipating harmlessly. The green dragon was now farther ahead of all the other ones. It disappeared again only to fly from a newly opened portal right in front of Daedalus. Cursing, he commanded his winged steed to drop, avoiding the bloom of fire. Another portal and the green dragon vanished once more.

Daedalus tried another tactic. He knew it was that wizard, Silver, creating the portals, so he must be near, high in the sky above the fracas. Daedalus found the wizard, entrails flopping from his torso. Daedalus commanded the dragons to fly at him.

There was no hope in catching the wizard, capable of creating a portal to escape through, but Daedalus was happy to keep him off balance, never allowing him more than a few seconds peace after flying out of a new portal. The other five dragons chased Silver, while Daedalus and Oremethus tailed the green dragon. The cohort of wizards behind them asserted themselves with a rogue fireball or random lightning strike. A taller building at the edge of town burst into flinders. The resulting rubble formed into a hand cobbled together of brick and mortar reaching for the green dragon but missed.

Neither the green dragon nor Silver made any further attacks, content to stay just out of range of their pursuers, while they fled the city. Buildings gave way to farms and fields and then to the forest, so thick that Daedalus was not able to see the fighting until he flew halfway over it. The battlefield was an amazing sight.

Tens of thousands of his soldiers covered the land. Some marched along in tight formations, regiments splitting into battalions. Many were engaged in combat, cutting down those who opposed the king. They all looked glorious, their armor gleaming, the colors of their king bright. The enemy had double the numbers, though, as well as wizards.

Fire moved in unnatural ways, burning specific soldiers while avoiding others. Arcs of lightning flashed without the necessity of storm clouds, striking many soldiers at once. Trees reached down to soldiers who got too close and tore them apart. Suddenly the trees exploded into tinder, the lightning was engulfed in darkness, and the fire turned on its masters. Daedalus' wizards had arrived.

Colorful explosions filled the air as the sorcerers battled. Creatures made from flame grappled with monsters formed from the earth. Blinding light stabbed at cold darkness. The air crackled and the ground shook. Then it all stopped.

The clanging metal and screams of the dying continued with traditional battle, but the magic stopped. The wizards no longer manipulated the elements. This had to be Silver's doing.

Daedalus flew higher to gain a better view of the battlefield. He could find no sign of the meddling wizard, just that damn void dragon. It was odd that it remained on the ground, wings twitching and flapping as it agitated. No matter. Daedalus had one concern—killing his brother and Dearborn. He found them where he expected them to be, on Castle Hill.

An ancient king built his castle atop this hill and forbade anyone from building on the lands around it. The king wished for solitude and legends said he died alone. The dilapidated stones were left behind to serve a reminder that no king should not isolate himself from his people. The reminder hardly mattered now as that king was long gone as was the semblance of a castle. Whatever wooden boards and supports might have been a part of the castle had rotted away a long time ago. A carpet of soft grass was kept short by roaming herd animals. Some of the outside walls remained straight, while most of the interior walls lay in jumbled masses of rubble, resting wherever they collapsed from when the floors above gave way. No matter the condition of the stone, emerald coats of moss covered them, while thick vines laced over them all.

Dearborn and Perciless stood in front of the ruins; her sword drawn and ever ready, he held a scepter in his hands, but undoubtedly hid a dagger or two under his robes. The green dragon prowled among the interior stones, hissing at the sky. Daedalus and Oremethus circled over their targets, striving to imbue them with a sense of dread. When their actions did not yield the desired effect, Daedalus tried a different approach to elicit a response. He decided to bring the other five dragons into the conflict, specifically along the tree line.

Trained in combat, the soldiers of the Albathian army were familiar with the disciplines of hand-to-hand and weaponry. The rebelling citizens knew this, so at the western end of the battlefield, they used the tree line to aid them, launching what projectiles they had from cover and taking advantage of the terrain to ambush the soldiers anytime they entered the forest. This was the area Daedalus deemed his army needed the most help.

The fire dragon spewed lava, setting the trees ablaze in an instant. Jagged bolts of electricity crackled from the lightning dragon's open mouth, the strikes hot enough to start fires. Anyone trying to flee the forest was either pushed back in by the winds of the air dragon or melted by the spraying vomit of the acid dragon or shredded by the rock particulate from the stone dragon's breath.

This was what Oremethus should have done since the beginning, used the dragons as weapons of war, not as servants for his demon hunts. They were pure power and Daedalus vowed never to use them for anything less than destroying his enemies. The wizards had stopped their little tricks for reasons unknown, but Daedalus and his dragons would single-handedly win this war. Then he could rule the continent and consider his designs to seize the entire world. His fantasies were cut short as his dragon lurched to the side.

Tugging the reins was more of a ceremonial act since he nary controlled his steed by such means, but his connection with the dragon felt weaker, as if moving from a full embrace to a mere handshake. His dragon descended, despite his commands to stay sky-bound and landed upon the top of Castle Hill. It shook Daedalus from its back and took flight once more. Oremethus stood next to him, the gem dragon circling overhead.

"What manner of madness is this?" Daedalus cried skyward after his traitorous pet.

"I do not know," Oremethus replied. "But I fear our brother will tell us soon enough."

Perciless stood by a stone archway, Dearborn by his side. "Greetings my beloved siblings. I believe it is time to put an end to this war and find a more peaceful solution to our problems."

"What have you done to my dragon?" Daedalus shouted, spittle streaming from his erubescent face.

Perciless raised the scepter over his head and pointed toward the forest. "This staff is crowned with the Dragon

Soul, a mystical stone, which allows the possessor to control the actions of all dragons. Indulge me a moment to demonstrate, if you will."

The other five dragons stopped their attacks and then flew in harmless circles above the battlefield. The air dragon's wings stiffened as it broke from formation and dropped from the sky. Staying low to the ground, it flew along the edge of the forest and used its breath to blow the flames away.

"Well done, Your Highness," came from behind another wall. Applauding, Praeker Trieste walked out from behind the wall and stood next to Dearborn.

Growling at Praeker, Dearborn said, "You have no other place to be?"

"There are three kings on this hill, awaiting the fate of the country, if not the world, so where else should I be?"

"Far away from me, or do I need to remind you that no matter which of these other kings remain standing, you will surely die."

Smile broad and bright, Praeker replied, "I do not doubt your intentions."

"No!" Daedalus shouted. This was not how he was going to lose this war. He was not going to be outwitted by his brother, this most loathsome man. Every advantage Perciless had as a child, every rule he had ever followed, flashed through his mind. "No!"

Daedalus used his anger to fuel his muscle, the rage rushing through his blood. He charged at Perciless. Dearborn and Praeker rushed to intercept but were too late. Daedalus threw himself at Perciless.

The brothers rolled along the ground until they slammed into one of the walls. Perciless extended his arm with the scepter as far from the conflict as he could, while punching Daedalus. Completely focused on the Dragon Soul, Daedalus took the blows, fighting through the pain and blood streaming from his nose and mouth. Only the damnable stone mattered. Daedalus stretched and kicked, getting closer to it. One lunge and he had the Dragon Soul with his skeletal hand.

And squeezed.

The stone shattered.

Daedalus felt his connection with the dragons return.

Thirty-two

IDERIA'S EXPERIENCE WITH war could be measured in weeks, almost as long as she had been exposed to fatal violence. She did not care for it.

For more than half her life she had been trained for combat, so she bested even the most seasoned veterans of the king's army. The look of utter surprise was the same on their faces as she ran them through. *How could a young farm girl be skilled enough to kill me?* must have been their last conscious thought. She understood how others could come to crave the rush of battle, the excitement of victory, the euphoria of beating death by meting it out. This was not the discipline she wished to dedicate her life to. But battle was the only way to end the war. She fought and killed now, so she would never have to do it again.

She hated the way the tides of war ebbed and flowed. Advantage and disadvantage danced with each other, taking turns leading the footsteps of the participants. She was with her brother, uncle, and lifelong friends in the forest now, accompanied by over a thousand rebellious citizens. A wizard was with them, giving them an advantage over the two thousand soldiers loyal to the king trying to storm their position. Those skilled with the sword stayed at the front, while those who lacked the fighting prowess remained farther back using bows and slingshots to create a fusillade of arrows and pebbles. Should the soldiers advance too far into the forest, the wizard ended their crusade with a pernicious spell or two. Their advantage ended when the king's wizards arrived.

The trees of the forest turned on those who sought solace from them, their branches drawing blood from her allies. Small fires burst forth from random points on the ground. Men and woman ran in disorganized circles, a few right into the paths of the advancing wizards. Their efforts were rewarded by their lungs exploding or their flesh melting from their bones.

Ideria's magician ally fought valiantly but was outnumbered by four dark mages. He floated into the air and judging by the way his arms flailed and legs kicked, this was not by his own volition. His struggles were short-lived, coming to an end as he convulsed, followed by all his internal organs flying out of his body from his mouth.

This was more than Phyl could handle. The satyr screamed, somehow standing out from among the other shouts and screams echoing among the trees and ran.

"Uncle Phyl!" Rue called out.

"Don't worry, boy, I'll get him," Lapin said hopped away.

"Me, too," Bale yelled as he gave chase.

"Ideria!" Draymon called out. Standing next to Bale's children, he waved for her to follow. She wished to help the citizen-built army of Perciless, but so many were too far gone, engulfed in flame, skin melting, limbs being wrenched from their bodies. The only thing she could do was survive. She grabbed Nevin's arm and they ran to their uncle, but their path was blocked by one of the king's wizards descending before them.

Horns sprouting upward from the top of his head made him look like a denizen of the underworld as did the jagged teeth within his nefarious smile. Filaments of yellow energy swirled around his arms as if he was strangling one of the suns and it fought to escape. Floating before them like a god, the yellow light in his hands became brighter. Then as suddenly as he appeared, the energy winked out and he fell. With a sickening crunch, his breaking bones tore through his flesh as he hit the ground. Woe wasted no time in taking flight only to allow gravity dominion over his body, landing on the wizard's back with both feet.

No, Ideria did not like the way war twisted and turned before settling on an outcome. Too much relied on the fortunes of the enemy. When running a scam, she and her trusted comrades planned and strategized. If something started to go wrong, then all they had to do was abandon the scam and simply try again after more thought. War was not like planning for a caper at all.

Many of the rebels cheered and whooped at the good fortune of the king's wizards losing their ability to use magic. Ideria and her companions continued to follow the path that Bale and Lapin took to chase Phyl, but as soon as they broke from the tree line, Draymon yelled, "Turn around! Back into the forest!"

Dragons.

Five of the king's dragons flew directly toward the edge of the forest. Ideria had more than enough experience with the lightning dragon and wondered if it would remember her. Not wanting to find out, she sprinted back into the trees.

Other men and women were running about as well with no set destination, desperately trying to escape the winged beasts that breathed death. The fire dragon made the first pass, vomiting its lava. Molten rain poured from the sky, setting everything it touched ablaze. The lightning dragon followed, releasing its bolts.

It was difficult to run through a forest on a good day let alone with the need to look up. Ideria pressed onward through the chaos, avoiding droplets and puddles of liquid fire as it splashed against branches on its way down. Some of the lightning strikes were strong enough to sheer through the trunks of a few trees, the tops falling in different directions and into other trees, spreading the fires. Cries of pain sounded over the crackle of burning wood but were drowned as another tree fell.

The ogres were clumsy, unable to effectively run without looking down at their feet. Ideria heard a loud crack from overhead and saw the falling branch separate from the tree. Rue focused on his steps, unaware of what was happening above him. About the same size as she, it took a considerable tackle to move him out of the way. They landed next to the base of an untouched sturdy tree.

More branches fell as did a nearby tree. Maneuverability was difficult for any creature trying to fly, but Woe impressed Ideria with his deftness as he grabbed Draymon and flew away from the madness. Hope and Nevin needed much more luck.

Nevin grabbed Hope and pulled her from the path of a burning branch just before it hit the ground. She yelped, but from where she landed, she could see the top of a falling tree coming for them. Wrapping her arms around Nevin, she flapped her wings and guided them both between the moving branches. Not as strong as her brother, she had to touch down once that danger passed, but it was in the way of more branches. Nevin spun as soon as his feet hit the ground.

Away from any immediate danger, Hope tightened her embrace. "You saved me."

Nevin tucked a lock of it behind her ear and let his hand rest on her cheek. "We saved each other."

Backlit by the burning forest, they kissed.

"Maybe this is something you and I should discuss also."

Ideria had forgotten that she was still on top of Rue until he spoke. She was not sure how to take his comment. Did he wish to discuss the romance between his sister and her brother? Or was he suggesting that he and she start one of their own? Neither choice was one she wished to explore any further. She jumped to her feet and scanned the forest for any possible escape from the inferno. "Not now. We have to get out of here."

Again, the tide of war shifted without notice or reason. The air dragon flew along the tree line and extinguished the flames with its breath. The gusts were enough to knock everyone off their feet, but not strong enough to cause any harm more than a few bruises and scrapes. This was an acceptable sacrifice to Ideria, who was merely thankful for a chance to get free of the forest.

The battlefield continued to be a tumultuous sea of flesh and metal. There were no wizards to be seen and five of the dragons flew in a lazy circle overhead. She could not see Bale, but there in the distance was her mother on Castle Hill. She and Perciless were joined by Praeker to stand against Oremethus and Daedalus. Perciless used the Dragon Soul, which explained the change in the behavior of the dragons.

Then Daedalus rushed toward Perciless and drove him to the ground.

In the resulting struggle, Daedalus destroyed the Dragon Soul.

No, Ideria did not like the way the winds of fate shifted during war. She did not like it at all.

* * *

Cezomir never knew love. He knew of it and always assumed he knew the concept, but he never understood the need for it. Love meant weakness; weakness led to death. His parents demonstrated this.

Over a hundred years ago—a specific number, Cezomir could not conjure—when he was a child and still human, his father joined a militia in the name of the king to fight for freedom. His father said he fought for the love of his family. That love led to him getting disemboweled, according to the stories the surviving militia members passed along. The same love forced his mother to take those same soldiers, and later their friends, into her bed for a coin or two over the next three years. Love killed her as it was destined to do when the beast attacked. After it scratched Cezomir, his mother sacrificed herself, sating the creature's appetite with her own innards giving her son the opportunity to run.

Love was the reason why a child had to live alone in the forest as he tried to master his new curse of lycanthropy. Love was weakness; weakness led to death. Cezomir fed on weaker animals and had no intention of becoming one of them. He dedicated the rest of his life to be strong. Then he met Lina.

For the past decade, they spent every day together. And he enjoyed that. At first, he thought it was simply a lack of other options—she was exiled from her kind and he was forever trapped in werewolf form. Very few women could live through his passions and he had no interest in nonhumans. Even if he did, there would be none available, Landyr finding their beds as soon as they entered a new town. Lina offered a place to put his dick. At first, he thought that was the extent of their relationship, but little by little, he found her to be interesting. The way she thought, the things that made her laugh, the way she hunted. During skirmishes, he always kept sight of her in his peripheral. She was an adept warrior with a blend of confidence and skill very few possessed. But sometimes luck was a factor during battle, so he wanted to be there to shift her fortune in the opposite direction, should at any time it turn bad. Just as it suddenly did now.

Praeker's army of lost civilizations started as one cohesive unit, but as with most war situations, the soldiers stuck to what they trusted. Cezomir and Lina found themselves between a battalion of a hundred Yullian and a thousand spider creatures. They had been winning this battle, a few wizards of Tsinel floating above them and raining down pernicious spells to give their unit a definitive advantage. Then Daedalus and Oremethus arrived bringing with them a contingent of wizards and dragons.

The dragons spent little time with this area of the battlefield; only the acid dragon made one pass, bathing a portion of the mass of spider creatures and dissolving them within seconds. Cezomir would never forget the screams. The dragons instead focused on the army of citizens driving the king's forces into the forest, burning the trees from above and killing the ersatz soldiers from below. The wizards were a different story.

The king's mages worked their magics to alter the terrain; hills and valleys spontaneously forming to keep the army of Yullians and spider-creatures confused. A few pits opened and swallowed a dozen Yullians and then closed again. A roll of ground folded over on a dozen more spider creatures. Cezomir hated wizards for this very reason, they never fought with honor, always hiding behind deception. Then suddenly their magic ceased and as one, the king's wizards fell from the sky.

No one paused to question why. They simply adjusted to the new situation and continued the battle. This did not bode well for Cezomir and Lina, who now found themselves in a valley that funneled two hundred enemy soldiers their way.

They had speed and instinct and a special lust for blood, but the king's army had weapons and numbers.

As with everything else in their lives, Cezomir and Lina met the troops head-on. The first few fell quickly because they were not prepared for such a brazen attack. Then their shields came up and their swords came out. Lina cried out in pain.

Cezomir knew love was weakness. He knew love was death and he accepted that would be his fate. He did not see who wounded her or how, just that one of the soldiers harmed his love. Claws slashed and teeth bit. He unleashed every bit of animal within him. But there were just so many to kill. One, two, three fell and twice as many took their place. Four, six, eight. A sword slashed the back of his right thigh. He adjusted, tried to use the pain as fuel. Ten, fifteen, twenty. A stab to his left arm. His momentum lost.

Armored fists punched his snout, face, and neck. He felt another cut across his back. He hit the ground and cringed. All he could do was look up and marvel how the many, many soldiers blotted out the suns. He forewent any prayers to gods, who were nothing but fictitious stories at best, and spent his last thoughts on Lina. A prayer of sorts to her, a prayer to love.

Then he heard her.

He heard love.

He had been wrong about his original assessment regarding love. It was no weakness, rather a strength. Love was the strength to tear apart the enemies of love. Love was anger and claws and teeth. Love was death; not accepting death but giving it.

Cezomir had no strength to move, but he did not need to. He was loved and that meant the fury behind the blood-curdling howls were for him, that every slit throat and opened belly was in his name. This beautiful goddess of death and love answered his prayers. Even when the last of the soldiers tried to flee, Love chased them down and sliced them to pieces.

Love rushed over to him and dropped to her knees beside him. "Cezomir? Are you still alive?"

Chunks of meat slid along with the blood flowing over her matted fur. Cezomir reached up and placed his hand on her cheek, using his thumb to wipe away a gobbet of flesh. "I am. Thanks to you."

Lina smiled. "You are my husband after all. I need to preserve my possession."

This was enough to encourage Cezomir to sit up. "Your possession?"

"Yes. Since we married under a Yullian ceremony, we should follow Yullian marriage customs. Therefore, I own you."

Cezomir frowned despite the pain rampaging through his head to do so. "Let's not forget the actual ceremony was—"

Lina laughed and placed her hand over his mouth. "You own me, too. We own each other."

She stood and grabbed his arm to help him to his feet. He looked over his wounds, impressive but he would survive. When he saw the piles of dismembered bodies all his pain disappeared. With Lina as his wife, he could do anything. "What next?"

"We leave."

Yellow eyes glowed against the flowing backdrop of deep crimson, haunting islands in an ocean of blood. Cezomir could see that she said her statement with earnestness. "Leave? What about King Perciless?"

"We've given all we can give to him. Look upon Castle Hill." Perciless struggled with Oremethus while Praeker and Dearborn focused on Daedalus. "We can do nothing more for him now. If he does not take back the throne, then our last ten years will become a crime and Daedalus will want our hides. If Perciless takes his rightful place, then there will be no place for us."

"I'm sure he would be thankful enough to allow us to reside within the castle."

"Then what? We while away our days staring longingly into each other's eyes? We join aged soldiers telling our tales of battlefield glory over and over and over? Or worse, Perciless asks us to be members of his court, or advisors, or ambassadors. We would have respect only within the castle walls." Lina pointed to the Yullians at the top of the one hill that formed the valley. "They will not accept me back into the tribe, even though I fought to save the world." She then pointed to the top of the other hill, to the spider creatures. "And they are how the rest of the world would view us. Just creatures. Ugly. Frightening. Unwelcomed."

Placing her hands on his shoulders, Lina looked into Cezomir's eyes. "No matter who is king there is no benefit to us, so why should we wait around to see whose ass ends up on the throne?"

Cezomir had been wrong about love. It was not weakness. It was strength. It was the courage to walk headfirst into the unknown, away from what was known. Without another word to the contrary, he took her hand in his and they walked away without ever looking back.

* * *

Bale ran to keep pace with Phyl, his cloven hooves leaving tracks easy to follow in the battlefield ground. He cursed his friend for running through the thickest part of the battle. Bale had to dodge sword swings from just as many allies as he did from enemies. Sprays of blood painted him. A freshly severed head bounced off his shoulder. Men locked in hand-to-hand combat caromed off Bale. Screams of both victory and pain were so loud that Bale never once bothered to call out to Phyl, knowing the Satyr would never hear him. Where was Phyl running to?

There were stones at the base of Castle Hill, toppled walls that had fallen down the slope. Phyl hopped behind the broken walls. After fighting his way through a small contingent of soldiers, Bale made it to the stones to find his friend crying. "Hey, little buddy. What's wrong?"

"All of it, Bale. All of this is wrong. We're always some-how in the middle of world-altering events."

Bale shrugged his shoulders. "So?"

"So? It's too much! There's constant war. Constant death. Constant fear. Fear of getting caught, getting tortured, get-ting killed. I'm so afraid, Bale. I'm afraid that my fear will get me caught or tortured or killed. I killed a man recently. Me! I'm a poet and a lover, Bale. Now I must live with that. My mind won't allow me to think of anything other than that. Usually, I'm trying to find ways to hide the fact that I like the affections of men from everyone, but now I have to reconcile myself with killing a man."

Phyl stopped crying and went wide-eyed, suddenly aware of what he had just said. He followed with, "So . . . what do you think of that?"

"Killing someone is difficult. I've done it, too. I've done it a lot. This is a world where sometimes to stay alive or protect your friends and family, you need to kill someone else."

"No, not that. I mean . . . the part where I said I like men."

Bale shrugged his shoulders again. "So?"

"So? I was worried that it would change how you view me, that it would change our friendship."

"Why? You didn't change. You're still Phyl. You're still annoying and somehow smell like vanilla and wet dog fur. I don't care what you want to put your dick into, as long as it's not me. I'm far more concerned that you referred to yourself as a poet."

Phyl's eyes glistened with the onset of new tears. "Oh, Bale. Your heart is so sweet it must be made of candy."

"Are you sure you want to call yourself a poet?"

"What? Why not? That was a perfectly used metaphor."

Bale rolled his eyes. "I have no idea what a meta even is let alone what one is used for."

Phyl laughed. "You're the best thing that has ever hap-pened to me. Now let's find your children and figure out what to do next."

"I agree with both of those things you said."

As they exited from their hiding spot, Bale was expecting to step once more into the horrors of battle. He could not have imagined that, instead, a half-giant was waiting for him.

"My name is General Perrator." Even though men hacked at each other with swords and shields and the sounds of battle roared, Bale could hear the general as if he stood next to him. The half giant approached, swatting away would be attackers like flies until it was just he and Bale. "I have heard a great deal about you, ogre."

Bale clenched his fists and rolled his neck, each crack a small relief of pressure. He had no idea who this person was or what he had heard, nor did he know how to reply, so he responded with a simple, "You're welcome."

General Perrator laughed and curled his fingers, knuckles cracking from the effort. "Your hubris will be your downfall."

This statement confused Bale. He stood straighter and sucked in his bulbous gut as best he could to look over it as he pulled away the top of his pants. "I know it's big, but it's never caused me to fall down before."

"Enough!" Perrator barked. "No more mind games. It's time I end you."

Bale was tired. He had been fighting for so long that he no longer knew when an old day ended and a new one began. His memories of his children were those of tiny green creatures toddling around on unsteady legs. Now they were all grown, and he had missed all the moments in between then and now because of fighting, because of war, because of people who wanted to kill him. Before him stood yet another person he did not know who wished to kill him. So be it. Bale had no taste for killing but had feasted more times than he could count at the buffet of war. This time would be no different, but afterward he wanted to take his children and go home.

Just one more time, he thought to himself as he raised his fists in front of him, trying to predict how the half-giant would attack. Before either of them could make a move, Lapin hopped in front of Bale and said, "It's okay. I got this."

Bale was happy to have someone else fight for him and wanted to support his friend. "Okay. Did you have enough to drink?"

The rabbit hiccupped in affirmation and turned to face the half-giant.

Bale was satisfied that Lapin was inebriated enough to handle Perrator. Tiny gauntlets covered the tops of all four of the rabbit's feet, silver and glinting in the sunlight as he hopped toward the half-giant. Bale almost mentioned how cute he thought they were but remembered the last time he had called Lapin cute. The rabbit shit in his ale. Well more than a decade separated Bale from that incident, but he could still taste it. "Go get 'em, Lapin!"

"I will! This shit stain doesn't stand a chance against me and my—!"

Perrator ended Lapin's battle call by stepping on him.

Bale had seen this before and knew what to expect. Perrator continued to stride toward Bale, unaware that the rabbit was still alive until Lapin shook off the hit and yelled, "Hey, shit stain! I'm not finished with you yet."

Perrator stopped and turned around. Before him was a rabbit still very much alive after being stepped on. The half-giant brought his foot down hard enough to leave an indent in the ground. But Lapin had leaped out of the way. "Oh yeah, shit stain? Is that how it's gonna be? Well, I got a little somethin' for you."

Lapin arose to his haunches and did a shimmy, twitching all four of his legs. Three crescent-shaped claws popped from each gauntlet. A tiny primal roar escaped from deep within his tiny chest. Lapin charged.

At first, Perrator remained frozen, stunned that a creature small enough to fit in his mouth suddenly attacked him, but that changed when the rabbit drew blood. He had half a dozen cuts along his shins. He reached down to swat at Lapin, but his efforts yielded sliced wrists and forearms.

Roaring, Perrator jumped from one foot to the next trying to stomp his opponent. He kept missing and Lapin kept cutting. The claws were minuscule, but were sharp and durable, strong enough to sever the tendons at Perrator's heels and calves, dropping the half-giant to his knees.

No longer able to stand, Perrator knelt and pounded on the ground anytime he saw the rabbit, his fists no faster than his feet. Even when the rabbit climbed upon him, digging his knives into flesh.

Lapin left a trail of bloodied tracks along Perrator's torso. He climbed up the half-giant's chest and dragged his claws down his back. Perrator kept swatting, his hands moving faster in panic, but each strike was too late.

Over shoulders and head, the rabbit continued to race along. Slices. Cuts. Gouges. If not for the claws, Lapin would have slipped in the flow of blood. Face. Head. Neck. Lapin did not let up.

The swats diminished in power and frequency.

General Perrator's eyes rolled up into his head and he collapsed.

Standing on top of the newly made carcass, Lapin licked the blood from his front paws. "Okay, *now* let's find your children and figure out what to do next."

CHIRCY-CHREE

LANDYR HAD SEEN horror before. The gore of battle. The insidiousness of demons. Some would even say his sexual exploits with the likes of goblins, orcs, and boggarts would be considered a horror. But he had never seen the likes of Speekore's experiments.

He had battled against his chimeras before, and there were plenty of them now. Well over a dozen were tearing into the pitchfork-wielding militia. These other creatures that wriggled and crawled their way out of his laboratory and onto the battlefield would find new homes in his future nightmares. Men with six arms, made possible by three torsos stacked upon each other, wielded a sword in each hand. Human heads on the bodies of spiders and snakes scurried and slithered about. One monstrosity had the upper half of human faces attached to its shoulders, back, thighs, and chest, all sets of eyes functioning, looking around for the dangers of battle. Landyr personally killed this one, an act of mercy if there ever was one, but it still took a high level of swordsmanship to finish him off.

Speekore's battalion did not exclusively consist of humans; the vile hobgoblin was more than happy to experiment on any race. What confounded Landyr now were the giants. Specifically, their heads.

Years ago, while hunting for wizards, Daedalus' Elite Troop stumbled upon a village of giants. It took a regiment of soldiers, but the entire population was captured. Landyr never heard what happened to the giants after that. Now, he knew; Speekore removed their heads from their bodies and attached their arms to the sides. Their vital innards were relocated to the backs of their heads, contained in a pouch of skin that flopped about as they ran around on their hands. Eight of these abominations were wreaking havoc on the battlefield.

With a mouth the size of a doorway, they used their teeth as their main form of weapon. They also crushed people by landing on them. While at rest, the abominations used their hands either to strike soldiers or tear them apart. They were far nimbler than they appeared.

Landyr ran from one only to have it race after him on its hands and then drop. Landyr timed his jump well enough not to get crushed. He leaped to his feet and slashed at fingers larger than he with his sword leaving mere scratches. The giant's hands were too large, too fast for Landyr to get close enough to its face, so he ran away again.

The chase was shorter this time and the giant landed much closer. Landyr fell to the ground again but had no opportunity to get back to his feet, scrabbling around to avoid the grabbing fingers of the giant. This was a part of the plan, however. Then Chenessa dropped from the sky to squash the head like an over-ripened tomato.

Landyr stood and went to his love. He pressed his cheek to her muzzle and stroked her snout between her nostrils. "That was close."

"Apologies, but some of Speekore's creatures are more monstrous than I."

To add validity to her statement, one such creature landed next to her. Speekore did not discard the bottom half of the giants, he added dragon heads and wings to them. Dragons were elusive, hard to find creatures, but Landyr assumed that with the backing of the king's resources nothing could remain hidden from Speekore's motivations.

The dragon head snapped its jaws at Chenessa's tail, but she flicked it out of the way. This distracted her enough for one of the feet to kick her shoulder. She roared and pushed away from the ground. The creature flapped its own wings and quickly rose to a higher elevation, forcing Chenessa to fly too close to the ground into the massive hands of two of the giant heads. One grabbed her tail and the other one held her claws, dragging her back to the ground.

As soon as she touched down, she bent around and bit into the fleshy sack at the back of one of the heads and pulled. Innards exploded from the sack and splashed against her other two attackers. It was not enough to distract them.

The giant head rushed to Chenessa, hands slapping the ground. Then it winked out of existence only to reappear above in the sky. It was far enough above the ground that when it struck, its skull shattered like an egg, splattering the yolk of its brains. Silver. The dragon creature was faster and could fly, so Silver used the more traditional fireballs and lightning bolts to turn the thing into a ball of melted flesh.

Landyr had grown tired of this game. The only way to stop these things was to kill the master. Speekore controlled them and if he died, they died. Like a cowardly general, Speekore remained hidden in a small tent on a cart driven by more abominations. Each steed was the head of a man on four legs, two sets of hips connected back to back. Ten of these things pulled his carriage, usually away from any skirmish that grew too close to him. Now was the time to end this.

"Silver!" Landyr shouted. When he garnered the wizard's attention, he pointed to the carriage. "Time to do your trick."

Landyr ran to the carriage, careful not to let anything slow him down. He dodged the swinging swords of multi-armed soldiers and slashed the throat of a chimera who ran into his path. Nothing would stop him from this.

The carriage never stayed still, the beasts' feet in a constant state of movement. The directional changes were sudden and random. When Silver created a portal under the carriage, only a third of the steeds fell in but were quickly yanked back out by the others. He created another portal and once again missed. Another portal, then another. Finally, he made a portal so large that more than half of the hideous steeds fell through. As the carriage toppled into the hole, Speekore scrambled free onto solid ground. Landyr anticipated as much and drove his sword through the hobgoblin's chest to the hilt.

No cry of pain. No blood.

The hobgoblin grabbed Landyr by the throat.

Landyr lost his grip on the sword and hit the hobgoblin's arms as hard as he could, but bent elbows were the only result. Squirming, he decided to return the embrace reaching for his attacker's neck but withdrew his hands as metal jaws snapped shut just short of his fingers. Darkness crept into his vision from the sides. Soon all he would be able to see nothing else other than Speekore's glass shielded eyes. His eyes. Something was irregular about his eyes.

They were fake.

The bulbous eyes did not look natural, more like boiled eggs after they had been shelled. Landyr dug his fingers under the glass lenses to pop them free, then shoved his thumbs into the sockets. They slid in with ease and thin yellow worms wriggled out of the opening around his thumbs.

Speekore screamed and stopped his attack on Landyr, now struggling to push him away. Landyr extracted his thumbs to grab the hobgoblin's head with both hands and shake it. The worms cascaded from the orbits of Speekore's skull and Landyr stepped on them, bursting them open with purulent gushes. The hobgoblin flailed his arms and strained to escape, but Landyr refused to let go, shaking more worms free and crushing them.

Eventually, Speekore's body went limp. Landyr tossed it to the ground. It burst into flame as Silver floated closer. Chenessa joined them as well while Landyr watched Speekore's abominations collapse. Those who were fighting them cheered, some running their swords through the bodies for good measure.

As much as it pained him, Landyr said to Silver, "Nicely done. This could prove to be a turning point in this war."

"Unfortunately, as with all wars, there is rarely only one turning point."

Landyr frowned and tried to think of a sarcastic comment but noticed that the wizard was not looking at him, rather the forest. Dearborn and King Perciless returned on their green dragon, flying over the battlefield to Castle Hill. Right behind them were Oremethus and Daedalus on their bone dragon and gemstone dragon. Following them was madness.

Half a hundred of the king's wizards and five dragons. They wasted no time throwing themselves into the war. This was another turning point. A bad one.

"Can you two handle that?" Landyr asked.

"I'm grossly outnumbered," Chenessa said.

"As am I," Silver muttered. There was a tone in his words that implied his statement was incomplete as if he could handle the situation, but there might be a steep price for someone to pay. Landyr waited a heartbeat. Two. Three. Four. When Silver spoke again, his voice was but a whisper. "However, there is something I can do."

"And that is?"

As Silver straightened his back and extended his arms, palm up, the putrid organs hanging from his torso jiggled. He slowly ascended into the air. "When I possessed this body a decade ago, I was gifted with its immense power. This wizard is an ancient one. In fact, one of the first ones involved with acquiring the magic of this world. If you can understand something, then you can destroy it."

"You're saying that you're going to destroy magic?"

Silver closed his eyes. "Not destroy it, but strip away everyone's knowledge of how to use it. Magic will still exist, but no one will remember how to access it. Spells will be forgotten, written instructions will be incomprehensible languages, words will be nothing more than common sounds."

"No!" Chenessa yelled. Tail twitching, she clawed at the ground while pacing in circles. "No, you can't!"

Landyr ran both hands over her neck hoping to calm her down. "I don't know, Chenessa. A world where no one can use magic might not be a bad thing. It actually might be a very, very good thing."

"You don't understand! Without magic, I will forever be trapped in this form."

Landyr stroked her neck, his fingers gliding over her shoulder. "Actually, it is you who don't understand. I love you, no matter what form you're in."

"Don't be ridiculous! A human and a dragon cannot know love."

Landyr looked into her right eye and said, "Too late. We know love."

A tear rolled from her eye, slicking her black scales. "I don't want to be around people in this form."

"Then we won't. I've come to find I have a healthy distaste for human company. We can make a home in one of Praeker's tribes. We can live in the forest or inhabit a cave or find an island no one knows about."

"Truly?"

"Truly."

Silver floated higher, arms extended. From Landyr's perspective, it looked as if Silver held the suns, one in each hand. Then their brightness intensified and Landyr understood true power. Too much. Landyr looked away, his eyes burning from the suns' brightness, and swore he heard the entire world die. When he looked back, everything was how it was moments ago. The suns bathed the land with their rays. The sky, cloudless. The sounds of war and death raged on. But the wizards that had been floating far above the ground all fell from the sky.

Silver did it. He removed everyone's ability to use magic.

Landyr looked up to thank the wizard but he was not there. He looked to the ground to see if he had fallen like all the others. "Where'd he go?"

"He's gone," Chenessa answered. "The body was an ancient being made of magic, but Silver was born and raised a human. With no knowledge of how to use magic . . ."

". . . he could not remember how to maintain the body. He sacrificed himself."

"And now no one can remember how to use magic."

Landyr turned back to Chenessa and went back to stroking her face. "I would disagree with that."

"Why is that?"

"I can access magic."

Her scaled brow furrowed. "I'm in no mood to jest."

Landyr shrugged his shoulders. "No jest. I love you. What greater form of magic is there than that?"

The corner of her mouth curved upward. "Oh, so this is how you plan to spend your days after the war, by being a poet."

Landyr smiled. "Well, it is a profession that pays well."

"It pays in nothing but adoration."

"As long as it's yours then I'm the richest man in the world."

Chenessa sighed. "Thank all the gods you're still a soldier until the war is over."

Landyr laughed and looked at the top of Castle Hill.

His laughter faded.

The war was over.

★ ★ ★

A sword. That was all Dearborn had to defend herself with against two madmen and seven dragons. Her allies were a sibling of the two madmen and a despot of abnormalities. She had a dragon of her own, however, it flew away after Daedalus destroyed the Dragon Soul and Perciless lost control of it.

Daedalus tossed aside the broken bits of the shattered gemstone and howled in triumph. Perciless took advantage of the distraction and struck his younger brother, knocking him away. Before he could gain any form of tactical advantage, Oremethus charged and shouldered Perciless, allowing Daedalus to regain his senses.

Both Dearborn and Praeker ran to Daedalus, their swords raised high. They swung downward in unison, aiming for his head. Their weapons ricocheted off his up thrust skeletal arm. Daedalus got to his feet and blocked another strike from Praeker by catching the sword and yanking it away. He squeezed, bending the sword into a useless shape, and then tossed it aside. In one fluid motion, he blocked a strike from Dearborn and followed through to backhand Praeker with enough force to take him off his feet.

Dearborn had clashed swords more times than she could remember and was proficient with a multitude of other weapons. None of those experiences helped with steel against bone. Her sword did not react the way she expected after every block. She tried slicing his legs and stabbing his torso, but Daedalus deflected each attack until she put every bit of her strength into a strike at his neck. He caught the sword and the blade crumpled in his grasp. Daedalus's next move was a blow to her face with his human hand. She blocked that with ease, but in doing so left herself vulnerable to the punch from his skeletal hand.

Bursts of starlight exploded throughout her vision and her world tilted. Backing away, she held her hands in front of her for balance and defense. Retreat was short lived as she backed into a stone wall. Her world righted and her vision cleared enough to see him running toward her with the fingers of his skeletal hand pulled together, a spear tip made of unbreakable bone. That hand reduced stone to dust, so she knew there was nothing she could do to stop his charge.

Praeker launched himself in front of her, Daedalus' hand exploding out from his back. The momentum pulled Daedalus away from Dearborn as he and Praeker tumbled along the ground. Before they came to a stop, Daedalus yanked his hand from Praeker's chest and backed away.

Blood pouring from his mouth and chest, Praeker got to his knees and coughed. "Well, Dearborn, you did promise to be my death."

The ground shook as the bone dragon landed next to him. Praeker had been many things over the centuries: warrior, warlord, king, god. His life ended as a snack for a dragon. Dearborn had little time to even recognize that he was gone let alone muse the cruel joke of fate bestowing such an inglorious death upon one of its longest living creatures. Instead, she ran.

No plan in mind, although one could hardly devise a viable plan against dragons, she ran into the ruins. She, a great warrior, now reduced to vermin like the rats she would chase and corral during her time in the dungeon. Learning from her experience, she did what they had done—run to any space where she could hide.

Her tactic did not work as well for her as it did for the rats in her cell. There were plenty of toppled walls resting at odd angles for her to hide under, but she could spend little time there as the acid dragon belched a flow of liquid death toward her or the air dragon breathed a tornado to knock away the loose stones. A flow of lava seeped its way through the cracks of the next hiding space she found, forcing her to run again. No matter what ancient doorway she ran through or rock pile she ran around, the dragons would simply climb along the castle ruins to chase her or cut off her path. It was time to try a different approach.

As she ran up a slope of broken stones, she recalled her daughter's story about slaying the metal dragon. It was not she who delivered the killing blow, rather the lightning dragon tricked into doing it for her.

Dearborn slid on her hip down the other side of the slope narrowly avoiding the nebulous breath of the bone dragon and as soon as her feet touched the ground, she ran toward the stone dragon, the closest to her. It opened its mouth but held its breath as she ran past its front claw, toward its tail. It growled a huff of frustration as it shifted about and slammed into the lightning dragon's blind side.

The two dragons snapped at each other, wings and tails twitching. The stone dragon swiped a claw at the other and that was enough provocation for the lightning dragon to release bright arcs of electricity. The strikes did no harm to the stone dragon, but the outburst did cause the bone dragon and the air dragon to take flight.

Dearborn pushed through the pain, actively reminding herself that if she gave into her body's burning requests for rest, she would die. Her knees felt as if they were made of broken glass, summoning tears with every step, but she refused to give in. She stifled her tears as crying would blur her vision. While she hated the idea, she ran between the acid dragon and the fire dragon. During the confusion of the final battle of the insurrection ten years ago, the fire dragon scarred the water dragon. Dearborn hoped that she could get one of these two to do the same to the other and studied their movements, looking for a primal signal as to which would attack first. The fire dragon exposed its teeth and lowered its head. Perfect! She would change direction and run to the acid dragon. But before she could turn, the stone dragon dropped from the sky in between the other two.

Dearborn turned to run, but the other three dragons skulked over the ruins behind her. None of them attacked, though, saving that reward for their master.

Daedalus strode between two piles of rubble, hands behind his back. "This is it, Dearborn. This is it. You will finally get what you deserve. I will finally get my revenge."

"Revenge? You speak as if I had destroyed your life or harmed your family."

"You embarrassed me in public! You harmed my standing with the nobles and weakened me in the eyes of my father."

"We were teens. What I did to you was no different than an awkward kiss. It was a situation that no one else cared about. No one but you."

"Because it *happened to me*! No one else. Me! My humiliation! My shame!"

Dearborn laughed and spat on the ground. "That is what I think of your humiliation, shame, and revenge."

Dearborn had no plan, just the simple knowledge that people never thought properly when they succumbed to anger. And it was so easy to get Daedalus angry. She had no idea what his anger would lead to. Would it pass into the dragons and make them fight each other out of blind rage? Would it make him myopic to the point of forgetting he even had dragons? Daedalus clenched his fists and released a roar to rival any that his dragons could offer, and Dearborn readied herself. She could never have guessed what came next.

The dragons flew away.

"No!" Daedalus screamed to the sky. "Nooooooo!"

Dearborn cared not as to what happened or why. She was merely grateful for the opportunity to dictate her fate. While Daedalus was distracted, she threw her arms about a stone about one-third of her weight and then launched it at Daedalus.

The screaming prince saw it just in time to strike it with his skeletal hand. The stone exploded into pebbles the force pushing him back several paces. Dearborn put every amount of energy she could muster into rushing to him. He swung at her on the backswing. She caught his arm with her left hand and his wrist with her right. She pushed with her left and squeezed with her right, forcing his fingers to extend.

Daedalus sprayed obscenities and spittle, but Dearborn had one opportunity, her last. If she failed now there would no second chance. She kept pushing, guiding his bone fingertips. The timbre of his screams changed, shifting from anger to fear. He grabbed her left shoulder and dug in his fingers.

The pain radiated through her whole chest. She flexed harder to fight against his grip, moving the bones of his skeletal fingers closer to him, to his jaw. Daedalus fought, but could not stop her progress. He stopped screaming as the tips of his phalanges made their way up under his chin.

His eyes still held rage, but he had descended into whimpers. Dearborn's heart was devoid of any pity. The tips of his fingers drew blood.

Daedalus tilted his chin back as far as he could. Dearborn wanted to end this, to rid this world of the worst thing to ever happened to it. She wanted to tell him that she was doing this to save her children, but she would say nothing. No words could ever convey what was in her heart. Words would simply waste time. She had already wasted too much time with him.

Dearborn released his wrist to grab the back of his head and shoved it downward. The noise of his bones grinding around inside his own skull would forever be heard in her dreams. It would bring a smile to her face every time.

* * *

Perciless stood, the shattered remains of the Dragon Soul by his feet. The best way to end the war with the least loss of life, gone. Now thousands upon thousands would sacrifice their lives following one king or another, and that was even if they knew what they were even fighting for. Some were fighting because they simply knew no other way to live. "Oremethus, please stop."

"Is this your surrender?"

Perciless considered those words. He had thought about those words again and again over the years. People would no longer have to die in his name. But they would still die, nonetheless. Either Oremethus would kill them thinking they were demons or Daedalus would turn them into those horrid skeletons of his to fight in the war with Tsinel and wherever else his lust for conquest might take him. No. He could not surrender. "It was my offer for you to surrender."

Oremethus laughed. "Even though Daedalus was the dourest of us, it was always you who had the least amount of humor. You should try it since your joke is rather amusing."

"It is no joke, brother. You are not well. Neither is Daedalus, in much more sinister ways, I'm afraid. Neither of you should be on the throne."

Oremethus' face went taut, skin pulling tight from his scowl. "This is what you've always done, brother. You belittle. You never rise above anyone, you simply push them down lower than where you are standing."

"Not true. You allow Daedalus to kill without reason because you see demons where there are none."

Sweat beaded along his hairline as he ground his teeth. "Do not tell me that demons don't exist simply because you can't see them. I have visions, brother. So, does Daedalus. We travel to the past to see where fate went awry within the confines of certain events so that we might change our future."

The sting of tears played about behind his eyes. Perciless hated to see his brother like this and wanted to help him. "I have those visions, too, Oremethus, as did father. But that's all they are—just visions. Intense memories that sometimes take over our senses."

"No!" Oremethus stormed and strode nearer stopping close enough for Perciless to feel the anger on his hot breath. "Your mind is too small to understand what they are. Right now, this is nothing more than a trip to the past from a future you can't comprehend. A future where I sit upon the world throne and Daedalus is by my side."

Waves of heat from Oremethus washed over Perciless as beads of sweat turned into streams. "Oremethus, there is no world throne. No king has ever conquered more than his fair share."

"My fair share is the whole world and I shall be the first king to take it. I have the dragons. Daedalus and I control the beasts and we shall ride them far and wide, conquering everything we fly over!"

The dragons. The one weapon Perciless could no longer stop now that the Dragon Soul has been destroyed. Or . . . could he? He heard the stories from Landyr and Silver. An ancient wizard used Oremethus' blood to bind him to the dragons. Daedalus was not a part of the ceremony, yet he could control them as well. If Daedalus could control them, then that meant . . .

Perciless looked behind Oremethus to the gemstone dragon, crouched down and ready to strike.

Then the command was given.

The dragon turned and whipped its tail around, the tip connecting with Oremethus. His body flew through the air and struck a stone wall, coming to rest in a shattered heap.

Perciless wiped away tears as he walked to where his brother lay. Broken bones created odd shapes within his limbs. Perciless knelt and pulled his brother to his lap. He wiped away the blood from his face. Oremethus had always had the face of a king, even when they were children. Oremethus was born to be king, his looks, his demeanor, the very air he breathed lent itself to the inevitability of him ascending to the throne. The broken man in Perciless' arms, however, was no king.

Oremethus' whole body shook with every hitch in his breathing. Perciless smoothed his brother's hair. "I'm so sorry, brother. I let you down. I know Daedalus resented me for abiding by father's rules to a fault, but as a child, what better way was there to garner a parent's love? My fault was not in following father's rules, but in wishing for the wrong person's graces. I always treated you as a colleague when I should have treated you as a brother. I should have done more to garner your love."

Bloody foam frothed from the corners of Oremethus's mouth and slid down his chin. His tremors intensified and he grabbed Perciless' forearm with his right hand, his left bent in such impossible ways that it had been rendered useless. "Do . . . do not fear . . . Perciless . . . for this . . . this is merely a . . . vision. I shall . . . shall have another one . . . and come back from the . . . the future to correct this."

Oremethus' death was a mercy, a turbulent mind now allowed calmness.

Perciless closed his brother's eyes and gently slid him from his lap.

The gem dragon approached and sniffed the air around the king and his deceased brother. It then curled up on the ground near Oremethus. Perciless let it mourn.

The other six dragons stalked through the remains of the ancient castle. Releasing a roar or flapping their wings or breathing their deadly breaths. Dearborn was still alive. Perciless commanded them to fly away.

Daedalus screamed, angered at their sudden betrayal. As Perciless approached the castle, his brother's screams intensified, changed and then ended. Perciless stopped in front of what remained of the castle's entrance, knowing very well that he needed to go no farther.

The war was over. He and his kingdom would finally know peace.

ThIRTY~FOUR

IDERIA CRIED. SHE hated crying. It made her feel young and weak. But she was saying goodbye to her mother, so there was nothing she could do to stave off the tears. However, her mother was sobbing, too. And right in Ideria's ear as she felt the life being squeezed out of her from Dearborn's hug. "Mother, for being the world's greatest warrior, you cry a lot."

Dearborn loosened her embrace and laughed, still gripping her daughter's shoulders. "When you turn me into a grandmother, you will understand."

"I'm not leaving forever. I will return."

Dearborn cupped Ideria's face in her hands. Ideria wanted to tell her to stop because it felt too nice, too comforting. If her mother's hands stayed on her cheeks any longer, she might change her mind.

No. Staying was not an option. There was nothing here for her.

Ideria knew just about any citizen of Albathia would run a knife through her belly to have the opportunity to live in Castle Phenomere with the king as she had for these past two years. But castle life was not for her, nor was the fame.

A hero's welcome awaited Ideria after her mother and Perciless liberated Albathia from Oremethus and Daedalus. Within one week, everyone in the city knew Ideria's name. It felt that way to her, at least. Strangers kept coming up to her on the streets thanking her and singing her praises, telling her stories she had no desire to hear. It took almost a year before she could sneak to a pastry shop without being accosted. Then Perciless announced "Dearborn Day," the new annual festival celebrating the return of Albathia to its people.

Prosperity created smiles and happiness. The festival was spectacular, bringing in people from all over the country, even many from Tsinel. What surprised everyone was when the seven dragons, once controlled by Oremethus and Daedalus, returned. People assumed Perciless commanded them to do so, but he insisted that all he did was ask. The citizens greeted them with trepidation at first, but little by little a trust was formed. They simply flew over the city in lazy circles until Hope and Woe took the opportunity to fly with them. Other flying races took a chance as well and opted to join them on air. Perciless kept his promise to Praeker and assured the lost tribes of unique creatures that they were citizens of Albathia with the same rights as everyone else.

After the celebration, Ideria became popular again, the stories of her bravery refreshed in everyone's minds. The irritation of needing to greet strangers while walking along the street paled in comparison to the boredom that had taken root in her heart and bloomed into restlessness. Everyone else fell easily into this new way of life except for Ideria.

Lapin became a Sergeant in the king's new army, but specifically for individuals less than two feet in height. He still enjoyed winning bar bets by drinking competitors under the table.

Phyl enjoyed living his life as his true self, savoring the company of many different men from many different races.

Bale dedicated himself to being nothing more than a father. He even attended school teachings with his youngest. He did poorly with his studies but enjoyed the effort.

And her mother . . . she surprised Ideria the most. Finally releasing Ideria, Dearborn said, "I know you will return, and then you will leave again. And return again. And leave again."

"I vow I will return as many times as I leave."

Ideria's heart melted at making a promise that might be difficult to keep. Her mother knew better, knew it was a questionable oath but did not push the issue. She simply smiled. "I know."

"You could always leave after Dearborn Day," Uncle Draymon said. "The children are very excited for it and they love having you around."

The children. Dearborn and Draymon had dedicated their time to rehabilitating all one hundred of Daedalus' bastard children. At first, it was difficult, especially for the older ones, to undo the teachings of a madman. But Daedalus's influence was unnatural and hateful. After a few months of giving them unconditional love, while showing them all that the world had to offer, the children came around. The younger ones even took to calling them Mother Dearborn and Father Draymon.

"It does warm my heart when the children have fun," Ideria started, "But Dearborn Day is tomorrow. I feel I must depart before the celebrations start."

Draymon nodded, contemplating her words. "You are a wise woman. Please be wise enough to know when to use my quarterstaff."

Ideria had the weapon in her right hand. She tapped it against the stone floor of the hallway. "I will. I promise."

"And please don't be too proud to ask for help. I still have resources out there."

Ideria wanted a purpose in her life. Being a thief like her father no longer seemed noble enough. A member of the king's army hardly seemed satisfying. A member of the king's court made her soul sad. Sitting around all day was unacceptable. It was Draymon who inspired her. One day while training, he told a story that he had repeated a thousand times, one of finding a lost girl and returning her to her family. That was it. That was what Ideria needed to do—help others with no form of reward other than the balm for her soul. "I will, Uncle Draymon."

Dearborn brought her left hand to her mouth as silent tears rolled from both eyes. She interlocked the fingers of her right hand with Draymon's left hand.

"Mother, I'm going to leave now before we start this hugging, crying process all over again."

Dearborn nodded and Ideria left the hallway.

As Ideria made her way to the exit, she cursed Nevin. She was not fond of farewells, but at least she did not hide from them. She felt bad for thinking ill of him when she turned the final corner to see him standing in front of the exit with Rue, Woe, and Hope. All four of them had full traveling sacks by their feet. Her mouth drew down into a frown.

"What is this?" Ideria asked as she approached.

"What does it look like?" Nevin replied. "We're coming with you."

"No."

"Don't be coy. We've been a team for so long I don't remember a time before."

"No."

"We can't simply let you walk—"

Ideria slammed the end of her quarterstaff against the ground. "No!"

"But . . . why?"

"Because you have a life here. All of you. Nevin, you are the treasurer to the king. Rue, you are the premier scientist in the land. Woe is an aerial guard and Hope helps mother and Draymon with the children."

"These are certainly fun jobs, Ideria, but nothing that we can't walk away from."

"You can walk away from them today, but what about tomorrow? Next week? Next year? Regret will set in after the first argument any us of has with another. Regret turns into resentment. I love you all, which is why I cannot have any of you set aside your lives for me. You've all found answers in this castle. All I've found here are more questions."

They stood in silence for moments, but the tears made it feel like hours. Finally, Hope stepped forward and hugged Ideria. She whispered, "You've always been a sister to me."

"You, too."

Hope stepped away and Rue approached. He, too, gave her a hug and whispered, "This is the last chance to discuss us."

Ideria squeezed tightly and replied the same way she always had for the past two years any time he brought up romantic possibilities. "Now is not the time."

Rue looked at her, the hurt heavy in his eyes, but nodded and walked away.

Woe approached and handed his travel sack to her. It was heavy. "Thank you, Woe, but I have plenty of supplies in my own bags."

"Take it. It's filled with turkey legs." Woe walked away.

Nevin's turn. His shimmering blue eyes said everything. She replied in kind. He smirked and whispered, "You look like Mother."

Again, she replied in kind, "You look like father."

"Hope and I are to wed in two years. Her father insisted that it not happen an instant sooner, stating we need the time for the euphoria to wear off and to allow us to be certain."

"Two years? I will return in two years for your wedding."

Nevin stepped aside, allowing Ideria to leave . . .